Jan Lloyd

War Torn
BOOK 1

The Mermen
The Doctor

Disclaimer

This is a work of fiction. All characters, places,
and incidents in this book, even those based on real people, real places,
or real events, are the product of the author's imagination or are used
fictitiously.

Book interior design by fiverr.com/weformat
Book Cover design by Nabinkarna

ISBN (paperback): 978-1-7393556-3-0
ISBN (e book): 978-1-7393556-2-3

I dedicate War Torn to the memory of my brother
Brian Richard Owen, who gave me my love of history.
I am forever grateful.

I would like to thank Barbara, Kit, and Fiona
who carried out sterling work on the editing
of War Torn.

Last but not least I would like to thank Dawn
and my lovely friend Lorraine for reading War Torn
in its early stages and giving me such
thoughtful encouragement.

I thank my family. My husband, and my children
Meghan and Owen, for putting up with me, and offering
their views and advice, not always when I have asked for it.

Jan Lloyd is a retired teacher of mathematics and science. She lives with her husband and pets in a hamlet in the Welsh Marches. War Torn is her debut novel.

Chapter 1

Frances Meyer gazed into the wash of the fishing vessel, glancing up now and again, the white cliffs of Normandy slowly disappearing. She shivered, though she was warmly dressed against the chilly October weather in a pair of men's brown trousers, a heavy overcoat, and a thick scarf around her slender neck. Her hair was piled inside a blue woollen hat pulled low on her brow. Clinging to the rail of the fishing vessel, her heart felt heavy and dark in her chest. She was leaving France behind, her home of the last eight years, the place where she had found friends, fame, family, and love, but more recently, fear.

The boat, the *Etoile*, had left the relative safety of the fishing fleet behind more than an hour ago. The captain, Gerard, had worked his way to the far side of the local fishing fleet and then doused their lantern, making them virtually invisible in the still dark sky. Now an arm slipped around her shoulders and she leant into Steven's warmth.

"We're almost halfway, so Jacques just told me. I think we are going to make it, my dear," he said, his lips against her temple.

She sighed, and lifting her chin, met the gaze of her husband. His face had become ravaged by his illness; his eyes were dark-ringed and sunken, his cheeks hollow, but still she refused to admit to herself that his end was near, that even if they made it to safety, for him, it would be too late. It was all madness. What had made any of them believe escape was possible? Although fear and guilt knotted her throat, she smiled.

"Thank God, Steven, thank God. As soon as we make shore, we must find you a doctor and then you'll soon be good as new."

He let his arm slide from around her shoulder and grasped her hand. Lifting it to his lips, he kissed it gently.

"We've had this conversation. You know that's not right," he said, "but I will find comfort knowing you're safe. I want you to make me a promise, though."

She looked down at the deck.

"Frances, look at me. One promise, that's all I want."

Raising her eyes, she fought back the tears, wanting desperately to be strong for him. "What?"

"When I'm gone, promise me you'll find love. Real love."

"I have that already, don't I?"

He tried again. "I want you to find real love, nothing less. Not the love of a father figure who adores the child that you were, or the love of an obsessive fool like Otto, but the love of a man. A man who will love you for the woman you've become. That is—"

"Listen, both of you."

Startled, Steven broke off as a second older man joined them.

"Jacques? What is it?" Frances asked Jacques Cuvier, her elderly onetime tutor.

"Can you hear it?"

Steven dismissed the noise with a shrug. "Just the engine."

"No," Jacques disagreed. "Listen again, there's another engine, higher pitched, faster than ours further out. Yes?"

They concentrated, but Frances's pulse tapped so loudly in her ears she couldn't have said for sure what she was hearing.

"Gerard is hoping it's the British, and not the Germans. The E-boats shouldn't be this far out. He's not taking a chance, though. We're going to make a run for it." Jacques raised his voice as the *Etoile's* engine suddenly roared.

Frances grabbed the rail, steadying herself, as the small fishing boat ploughed through the water, gaining speed. They all heard the other engine speed up almost simultaneously.

"Christ!" Jacques shouted the word. Curse or prayer, Frances heard fear in his voice. "Get back to the bridge, both of you, now!" he ordered. "The bastard's coming in."

Following Jacques, Steven and Frances quickly made for the bridge as a searchlight from the approaching craft scanned the surrounding sea. It came to rest on the *Etoile,* lighting her up against the dark sky.

"Get in the hold, Frances, stay put and keep quiet," ordered Jacques. "Where's your violin case?"

"I left it on the bridge." Her glance dropped to the gun he held in his hands. "Where did you get that? Why—why do you have it?" Her mouth was dry. The sight of the pistol—her shock left her lightheaded. What had happened to her friend, the dear old man she'd known and loved for the last seven years? Her tutor Jacques, who should hold a violin, not a gun.

"Never mind," he told her. "Gerard, pass me that black case."

Looking over Jacques' shoulder, she saw the captain of the shipping vessel was also armed.

"Get into the hold," Jacques repeated his order.

"But I want to stay up here—"

"Girl, get in that bloody hold now!" Jacques lifted the hatch.

It was the panic in his voice that got Frances moving. She scrambled onto the ladder, her own heart booming in her chest. She lowered herself into the darkness.

Steven's ashen face peered briefly down at her. "Remember my wish for you, Frances," he spoke softly, keeping her gaze. He disappeared, and Jacques filled her view.

Wordlessly, he passed down the black case that held her precious violin and replaced the hatch, leaving her blind in the total darkness, and gagging on the sickening stench of fish. But there was no shutting out the throb of the approaching craft. No way of knowing if they were friend or foe.

Blood cold in her veins, she bumped around, hands outstretched, taking tiny steps for fear of falling. At the far side of the hold, she felt wooden crates and tarpaulin, but now a searchlight, that she assumed was from the approaching boat, lit the crack around the hold's hatch, giving the space she was in an eerie glow. As her eyes adjusted, she discovered a place in the far corner behind some boxes, and wedging herself into it, she covered herself with a tarpaulin. A wave of panic rose, causing her breath to stick in her throat. Concentrating hard, she forced air into her lungs, telling herself that it would be all right. The craft was British. They'd be escorted to England. But the fear that twisted in her gut told her otherwise.

"Turn off your engine now and come onto the deck where we can see you." The command came in accented French from the vessel drawn up beside them.

A scream shot into her mouth and she clenched her teeth against it.

The *Etoile's* engine sputtered to a stop, and in the silence Frances heard the slap of the waves against the hull of the craft, and footsteps moving across the deck that had to belong to Steven, Jacques, and Captain Gerard.

The same voice gave the order. "You men line up." Then in his mother tongue, "Hoess, check the hold."

There was no need to guess their nationality or what language they spoke. Frances knew they were German; she was fluent in their language. Booted feet trod the deck above her. One of them, Hoess, was on the *Etoile,* coming to check, coming for her. Sticking her fingers in her mouth, she bit them, hoping to stop herself from crying out. The hatch was lifted and the floodlight from the German vessel lit up the hold. She crouched low under the tarpaulin.

There was the clanking of boots on the metal rungs of the ladder as Hoess lowered himself down, and she felt the sweat run down her back as his footsteps took him across the small area. Boxes and crates were kicked aside and her heart rammed against her chest wall as the man got ever nearer to her hiding place. So great was her fear that she had an overwhelming urge to show herself, to give herself up so that it would all be over and she could breathe again. She could talk her way out, couldn't she? She had friends in high places, German friends.

"Why aren't you showing any lights?"

The question from the German officer above drew her attention away from that thought, and as she listened for the answer, boxes were pushed aside and smashed into her body. He was so close now she could hear his breathing and wondered if he could hear hers. Now the only thing separating them was the tarpaulin. She clasped her hand across her mouth, hoping to prevent the whimper that was rising in her throat from escaping, and then had the odd thought that this man was a smoker. She could smell the tobacco on him, just as she could on Steven. A crazy thought.

From above, the questioning continued. "I will ask you again, where are your lights?"

Frances's senses were on fire as the adrenaline rushed into her body, urging her to run, but to where? There was nowhere to go. And then she heard it.

"I'm sorry, my friends. Free France! Vive la France!"

Jacques! It was Jacques. Frances recognised his voice. His cry of daring and jubilation was that of the Free French Army, but it was cut short by a series of loud bangs.

Frances jolted. Gunshots? Now more shouting came, a mix of French and German. Someone cried out. More than one. Who? She didn't know. Hoess's booted feet moved quickly away from her hiding place, back towards the hatch and clanked up the rungs of the ladder. Open-mouthed, Frances gasped at the air, feeling her diaphragm rise and lungs inflate with relief. The feeling of relief didn't last long. Machine gunfire tore through the wooden decking above her, ripping into the boxes that surrounded her. Sparks flew as bullets bounced off the metal walls of the hold. She curled into a ball, knees tight to her chest, and prayed, "*Our Father....*" The gunfire continued for what seemed an eternity and when it stopped, the silence was unearthly and somehow more terrifying.

"Nothing in the hatch." At last, the report was given.

"Get back here then." The officer issued the order.

The booted feet moved over the hold of the *Etoile* to the waiting E-boat. "Shall I grenade her, sir?"

"She's already ablaze. No need to waste a grenade. She'll blow on her own," came the reply.

Fresh panic jolted up Frances's spine. She gripped her knees to keep from springing to her feet. She had to wait. Had to! Thoughts jostled through her head. Where were the others? Maybe they were being taken back to France. Yes, that was it. That must be it. What of her then? Had they left her behind — stuck on the *Etoile* — on her own? She had to know, but she'd not move yet. She would take no chance they'd see her. To calm herself, she took a deep breath, and when she did, she was certain she smelled it, the fire they'd spoken of. *Please, please, please.* The word chanted through her brain. It seemed an aeon passed before she heard the engine of the German vessel start up. But she remained frozen, listening as the sound faded into the distance. Only when she could no longer hear it did she struggle to her feet, coaxing her cramped limbs to support her, searching her brain for a plan.

The rowing boat. There was a rowing boat strapped to the side of the Etoile. She was sure of it. *We rowed out from the beach in it. So, it has to be here.*

She made her way towards the hatch. All light had been extinguished, there was just a dull glimmer to help her navigate around the debris strewn across the floor. Finding the ladder, she held onto it for a moment as you would an old friend. And as she placed her foot on the first rung, she remembered her violin.

"Fuck, Fuck, Fuck!" The expletive in her mother tongue was said with fervour, something she could thank her private schooling for. She was thankful that neither Steven nor Jacques had heard her use it.

Making her way back to her hiding place, she berated herself for not having lifted the hatch first to let in more light. Throwing back the tarpaulin, she thrust her hand amongst the boxes and felt for the case. Having hold of it, she then stumbled back through the debris to the ladder, climbing several rungs until she could reach to push a hand against the wooden hatch. As it slowly lifted, she was bathed in the watery light that was heralding the start of a new day. Breathing in the chilly October air, she was struck by the smell of gun smoke and burning wood, mixed with an odour she didn't recognise—something metallic—hanging in the air.

She pushed herself from the hold, noticing a plume of telltale smoke, and walked forwards to investigate. Horror! She caught sight of Jacques slumped. The gut-wrenching howl that came felt ripped from her throat. A spray of bullets had turned his dear old face to a pulpy mass that was virtually unrecognisable. Pieces of blood-soaked bone and hair were stuck to the bridge behind his fallen body in some grotesque collage. Collapsed nearby, the old skipper, Gerard, had fared nearly as bad, with a gaping wound between his eyes. But now her horrified gaze found Steven, her darling Steven. He lay face up in a widening pool of his own blood, which seeped from wounds in his chest. The breast of his coat was stained red, reminiscent of that time in Berlin when it had been red wine and not blood that had caused the damage. Bile rose in her throat and going to the boat rail, she vomited into the water. It hit her then, the source of the metallic smell—it was their blood.

Gripping the rail, she steeled herself, working to build up the courage she needed to approach the bodies of the men she had loved. Jacques' eyes, in what was left of his face, were wide and staring. Gently, she closed them.

Going to her knees beside Steven, she stroked her hand through his hair and caressed his bearded chin. Then leaning forward, she gently kissed his cooling brow. Sitting back, she waited, hoping that her kiss would bring him to life. The dream darkened as realisation stepped in that this was no fairy tale. It was, in actuality, pure horror. Running her palm down the side of his face, she murmured, "I'm so sorry, Steven, my love. This is my fault. All my fault." Her tears slipped from her eyes and ran down the edge of her chin, mixing with the blood oozing from his chest. But in a moment, her head jerked up.

Fire!

The threat of it penetrated her mind and, looking around, she saw a low row of flames skittering across the wooden decking. She knew she had to get off the *Etoile* before it reached the fuel line, but how could she leave these men, two whom she loved, here? Glancing back at Steven, she thought of lying down beside him. She could go with him into the next world. If there was one. For sure, this world was nothing but evil now, its own hell, which they had tried and so miserably failed to escape. Why should she live on if Steven was dead?

She would never know what impulse it was that jolted her out of her daze and onto her feet. But suddenly she was upright and running to the location of the rowing boat that was tied to the side of the *Etoile*.

* * *

Bay of Brest

October 20, 1942

Like a thick fog, steam hung in the air. Everywhere the hollow clang of metal on metal and the bright, incandescent showers of sparks from the welder's torches busy refitting vessels round the clock. The U-boat pens where the boats were moored and refitted were the usual hive of activity—all except the sentries, dotted around at intervals, sub-machine guns carelessly slung across their shoulders, guarding the impenetrable concrete bunkers.

Mueller detoured on his way to the pens. Stopping at the top of the concrete steps, he ran his gaze over the various boats below, laid out like bodies in a morgue. Only by some German miracle would they be raised again. But now a half-smile tugged at the corner of his mouth as he spied his boat waiting in all her glory in her shadowy berth, her new silver-grey gown scarcely visible against the murky water of the flooded pen. Length: 67.1 metres. Width: 6.2 metres. Wider where she ballooned, mid-hull, to accommodate the ballast tanks. Like huge hips on some grossly misshapen woman, they were beautiful all the same—and she was his. *UBA*. Together with her contents, she was lighter than the water she displaced, allowing her to bob around on the surface, decks about a metre above the surface of the water. The class VII C U underwater boat such as UBA was a mammoth feat of German engineering, perfect for the Atlantic, easily manoeuvrable. Surface range: 7,900 miles at a speed of ten knots. Dive range: 80 miles at four knots. Maximum speed: 17.3 knots, 7.6 submerged. He knew virtually all there was to know about her, although, like an old lover, she could still spring one or two surprises.

Chapter 2

Please, God, I don't want to die.

What an end! What an end to such a promising beginning. Everything had been going her way. Why her? Why this way? Why did things have to change? Everyone had left her. Gone! No one should have to face this alone. It was unfair. None of the people she loved were there when she needed them. Oh, she could feel them beckoning, calling in her mind. *"Come on, Frances, it's easy! Slip over the side, deliver yourself to the depths ... to the sea ... the fishes ... make it easy, deliver yourself."*

She heard their voices, their low, muttered instructions, but they were not the voices of the people she loved. They were the wrong people, speaking the wrong language. Her eyes fluttered open to see rough, hard-eyed faces peering at her, and she recognised none of them. Not one. She felt them pulling her now, lifting her up from the rowing boat. Had she died? Were they bearing away her soul? There must be some mistake. She tried to focus her thoughts, but it was all so murky. The sense of being borne aloft ended, and she felt herself being lowered. Perhaps her next stop would be the pits of the underworld. That was her last thought before total darkness enveloped her.

* * *

October 22, 0600 hours

It had been strangely quiet since they'd left port two days ago. So quiet that the atmosphere on the U-boat was relaxed. Those not on duty slept on like children. Even the sea remained calm. Cloudy skies soon cleared, streaks of purple and red retreating as the sun rose in the eastern sky.

On the morning of October 22, the day Second Officer Schumacher had reported the sighting of a small craft, Mueller had managed to grab four hours' sleep, albeit uneasily. The continued quiet haunted him through the night. It felt surreal. Where was Tommy? He reckoned they must be a good hundred miles out of port, and still there had been no sign, though he and the rest of the crew searched the water, the endless horizon, continuously. Usually, the Channel was swarming with Brits. It was a veritable and constant battleground since they had recently fitted their planes with radar.

Airborne radar had been a major setback for Vice Admiral Donitz and his boys in the U-boat arm of the Kriegsmarine. Radar made it easy to pinpoint a U-boat. Planes dropped out of the sky without warning, leaving little time to dive, like poor old Kissler last time out, he scarcely got out of the pens. Other boats, too, had been forced below water, some twenty-odd times in as little as a couple of hours because of these flying menaces. Some Kapitans skulked away through the Bay submerged, but this was slow, as the diesels could only produce a speed of 4 knots. The Brits were gaining strength, though where they were at present, the devil only knew.

Following Schumacher's report of the sighting of a craft, Mueller was on the bridge within seconds. "What's the problem, Second Officer?"

"There seems to be a small craft, Kapitanleutnant, about fifty degrees to starboard, a mile or so out." Mueller lifted his heavy Zeiss glasses and immediately spotted the object in question.

"Hmmm... could be a lifeboat. We'll go in for a look, though God knows what we'll find."

Orders were given and the U-boat changed course, making for the craft, which turned out to be a rowing boat.

"Someone's on board, sir," said Volk, the lookout, as they drew alongside the craft.

Peering down, Mueller recognised the small, huddled shape of a body. "Tiny," he murmured to himself. "Must be a kid. Both engines half power, Chief. Take her in gently."

"Permission to come up, sir?"

Mueller's voice echoed down the hatch, "Permission granted, Exec."

First Officer Werner climbed through the hatch onto the bridge.

"What do you make of it?" Mueller asked when Werner joined him.

"Might be from a capsized fishing vessel, huh? Someone got into trouble?"

"Maybe. Get a boat hook."

Half the crew were assembled under the chestnut tree, the name given to the space under the conning tower hatch, eager to find out what was going on. A boat hook was found and passed up to those on top, on the bridge.

"Cut both engines," Mueller ordered. He issued further instructions for the fore'ard hatch to be opened as the U-boat drifted the last few yards, closing the gap between the U-boat and the small craft. Once they were in position, he and several of the crew made their way along the casing. It was Werner who, at Mueller's command, hooked the rowing boat's side and pulled it against the starboard side of the U-boat. The body was seated on the floor, slumped face forward. Only the collar of a brown woollen jacket was visible, and a blue woollen hat drawn so low it covered the entire head.

"Has to be that a fishing vessel went down and this young lad must have survived for a time at least," Werner said.

"I reckon so," said Mueller. "Poor little sod. I wonder how long he's been stuck out here. Take-over, Leutnant Schumacher. Get him aboard. Let's hope the seagulls haven't had him for breakfast."

Mueller lowered himself through the hatch and made his way to the wardroom. The thought of breakfasting had made him hungry.

* * *

"Excuse me, sir."

Mueller had barely had time to settle at the table with his coffee when Simon spoke. He was a new member of the crew on his first patrol and the youngest on board at seventeen-years old. He took a ribbing for it, too. The crew mercilessly called him Toddler.

"What is it, Simon?"

"Leutnant Schumacher sent me, sir. He thinks there's something you should see."

"I just sat down. Can't Leutnant Werner deal with it?"

"He wants you to see it too, Kapitanleutnant."

"Does he now?" With a sigh, Mueller put down his mug. "Where are they?"

"Up in the fore-end, sir."

"Lead on then, Macduff."

"Sorry, Kapitanleutnant?"

"Never mind, Simon. Come on."

The petty officers' mess was deserted. Half the crew, it seemed, had crammed into the fore-end torpedo room, which doubled as accommodation for the ordinary seamen. Pushing his way through the throng, Mueller noted several faces lit with silly grins.

"What the hell's got into you lot?" he demanded. He caught Werner's gaze, and his smirk, and followed his nod toward Hengst, the medic, who knelt beside the prostrate form that had been dragged from the sea a bare five minutes earlier.

It was when Hengst moved aside that Mueller saw the source of everyone's hilarity, possibly even their chagrin. The form, the body Mueller had thought was that of a young boy, wasn't a boy at all. With the blue woolly hat now removed, there was no mistaking that the tumbling mass of rich brown waves framed the face of a young woman.

"My God," muttered Mueller. "Now what?"

There were one or two stifled chuckles, and a couple of lewd comments from odd members of the crew, but Mueller could sense most were waiting to see how he—the old man—would react.

"Well, we can hardly throw her back," he said, looking slowly from man to man, rubbing his whiskered jaw. "Or can we?" More chuckles. "How bad is she, Hengst?"

"No injuries as such, Kapitanleutnant, but she's suffering from cold pretty badly, and she's dehydrated. We need to get her out of these wet clothes."

"There's a job for Tiny," cracked Beckmann, one of the engine crew, "The only women he scores with are unconscious. They'd have to be!"

"Shut your gob!" returned Tiny Gotz, who, given his immense six-foot four frame, was anything but. He always bragged that no woman could resist him.

"That's enough!" Mueller cut in before things between Gotz and

Beckmann could get out of hand. He knew his men well. In a tight spot, they could all be relied upon, but he also knew there was little love lost between these two. Each saw himself as top dick. He turned to Hengst the medic. "Get her to my berth, Hengst. The rest of you, back to work." There were a few vulgar comments from the men, which Mueller ignored.

The medic swept the small woman easily into his arms and headed to Mueller's quarters. Mueller followed with Werner, but at a distance. Schumacher, as officer of the watch, returned to his duties.

Mueller turned to his First Officer. "Christ, Paul, what have we done to deserve this?" In his consternation he forgot for once the 'no first names on board' rule.

"Well, like you said, we can hardly throw her back."

"I don't like it," said Mueller. "It's going to cause problems."

"Problems? Like what?"

Mueller wagged his head. "Innocent! For God's sake, you can't put bread before a hungry man and tell him not to eat. There will be trouble, sooner or later, for certain. A young woman and a load of cocky little bastards?" He blew out his cheeks.

The two men entered Mueller's quarters. Hengst had laid the woman on the bunk.

"Carry on, Hengst," Mueller ordered. "You said she must be relieved of her wet clothing."

"Sorry, sir, I don't think I can."

"You're a medic, aren't you?"

"Yes, Kapitanleutnant. But this sort of thing—removing ladies' clothing, sir—well, it's not part of the training."

"Christ, you need training for that?" He turned to Werner. "There you are, you see, it's started already. Half the crew are behaving like lechers, the other half like damn saints."

Werner looked from Mueller to Hengst, humour dancing in his eyes. "May I suggest it would spare blushes all round if the lady's outer attire were taken off first, and then her undergarments, assuming she has some, are removed under cover of the blanket?"

Despite the situation, Mueller grinned. "Good idea, Exec. You've obviously had practice. The two of you carry on." He turned on his heel, not waiting for a response, and feeling relieved, returned to the

Wardroom. He'd been there less than five minutes, sitting with his cup of now-cold coffee, when Werner joined him.

"Done?" asked Mueller.

"Done." Werner sat down. "Where do you think the lady came from? And I emphasise 'lady.' Her underwear is silk."

Mueller raised his eyebrows. "Is it now? Not what you'd expect from a fisherman's wife, then?"

"Hardly. I don't think we'll be able to question her for a while, though, that's for sure. Hengst wondered whether you could open the medicine cupboard."

Mueller nodded. "Sure." Returning to his quarters, he drew back the curtain, unlocked the medicine cabinet and took out the medicinal cognac. He tipped a little into a small beaker, which he passed to Hengst, who then gently lifted the woman's head. But when he brought the tot to her swollen lips, she turned her head away, coughing, eyes flickering, and a moment later, she fell back against him.

"Dead to the world," mused Hengst.

"Maybe she's the lucky one," muttered Mueller.

"I think some soup or broth might be more palatable, Kapitanleutnant," Hengst suggested.

"Carry on then. See Hayman, see what he's got."

Hengst left for the galley, drawing the curtains behind him. Feeling curious, Mueller moved to his bunk for a closer look at the woman. She was most definitely young. In her early twenties, possibly. He noted the delicacy of her features, her small frame, the smattering of freckles that bridged her little turned-up nose, the fine line of her arched brows. He wondered what colour eyes she had beneath the closed lids. Her hair was somewhere between brown and red. Picking up her jacket, he checked the maker's name and address: Lafayette, Rue de Rivoli.

"Well, my little froggy girl," he murmured, "I wonder what your story is. Where were you going to? Or from? And why?" He pushed back a stray curl that had found its way into her mouth. "You're just another casualty of this damn war, poor kid." It was all too pathetically moving.

Turning sharply from her, he stuck his head out of the curtaining and called out to Heinemann, the telegraphist. "Message HQ. Tell them what's happened and that we're carrying on as normal. Any information they find on the woman or the boat she may have been on—let me know." Mueller then made an announcement over the microphone to his crew to assemble in the control room.

Five minutes later, Kapitanleutnant Mueller addressed his men on the do's and don'ts of having a female guest on board, for all the good it did, if the numbers of lewd comments and gestures going on in the background were any indication. Following his speech on how a lady should be addressed if you were to meet her on a U-boat, he went up top for some air, muttering to himself, "My God, my God, help us!"

Chapter 3

In a state of utter exhaustion, Frances sighed. She was becoming aware of her body, it ached furiously, reminding her of its existence. She wasn't dead. The thought shot through her mind again. I am not dead; I am in pain. I have feeling in my muscles and bones, pain. I am not dead. She tried to open her eyes, the lids fluttered under the effort and gave in, remaining shut, closing her off from reality. Her mind took her back to better times.

* * *

The Theatre Champs-Élysées, Paris.

March 12, 1938

Excitement! Elation! Her first solo performance, arranged by Phillip Gaubert of the Conservatoire. There had been worries that afternoon following the rehearsal that perhaps she wasn't quite ready, but she had shown them she was, by playing the Tchaikovsky *Concerto in D Major* like a seasoned professional and gaining a standing ovation. She had encored with a favourite piece, *Massenet's Meditation*.

Steven had suffered that night. Waiting in the wings, his nerves at breaking point, he had chain-smoked for the entire performance. She could pick out the glow of his cigarette, and just knowing he was there had bolstered her confidence.

Backstage, Aunt Edie, her father's sister, was waiting for her, large and effervescent, so unlike her father. She was with Jacques Cuvier, her old teacher. Wonderful Dickensian Jacques, of the beaky nose and wispy hair, and as she recalled from their first lesson, red fez, and carpet slippers. The two were often together, and she had never worked out exactly what the relationship was, even though she had lived under Edie's roof for the last four years. They both jumped up and down when they saw her, unable to contain their excitement, taking it in turns to embrace her and then embrace her again.

"Oh! Frances, I just wish your mother and father could have been here to share this night with you," Edie enthused with a tear in her eye. "They would have loved it. We are so proud of you, aren't we, Jacques?"

Jacques kissed her on the cheek and said, "Well done! I knew the minute I heard you play all of those years ago that you were something special."

And then there was her good friend Otto. Otto the traitor. A fellow student with yet another girl on his arm. He had begun his studies at the Conservatoire at the same time as she, but whereas she had worked and practised, he had treated his time there as a holiday.

He grabbed her hands as she left the stage, dragging her further back into the wings, towards the dust and the smell of greasepaint which hung heavy in the air. He hardly gave her time to put her violin into its case, leaving his date to stand alone. Then he swung her round in circles, making her dizzy, and his blond curls to bob, until she cried out with laughter, "Stop!"

He did stop. Taking her in his arms, he planted a kiss on both cheeks. "You were brilliant. Bravo, bravo!" he said in his heavily German-accented French, and then he kissed her again, this time on the lips, the first time anyone had done that. She pulled away, blinking her eyes at him in surprise, and wondered if she should have felt more, should she have liked it? Otto smiled his cheeky smile, from his round cherubic face, which many girls struggled to resist and found charming.

"For goodness' sake, Frances, it was just a kiss. We're friends, aren't we?" He laughed at her, and her reaction embarrassed her, to cover that embarrassment, she smiled back.

"Of course, we're friends—the best of friends," she said and gave him a quick peck on the lips in return.

Steven looked on from a distance, watching the antics of Von Liechtenstein, who, in private, he referred to as a waste of space. Steven, her professor, or more truthfully, he had made himself such. He had told her he had recognised in her a rare talent.

She sighed and fought back the tears which were threatening, conjuring up the image of Steven as he was then. A small dark man of Jewish descent, always bursting with energy as he puffed away at the inevitable cigarette. A little Bohemian. An eccentric. His clothes were ill-fitting and his hair worn a little longer than was fashionable. Outward appearance was of little importance to him. He was an academic through and through. All that mattered to him was the music, and more lately, herself, a young girl who was approaching womanhood. He had nurtured her, taking on the role of the father she had lost several years earlier to a respiratory disease. For four years, he had fed her appetite for the music, making her realise that being a musician wasn't just standing up in front of people and playing. Making her recognise the importance of her studies—those seemingly endless studies in listening, writing, keyboard harmony, music reading and analysis and creative writing, some of which bored her rigid.

He would often quote Franz Joseph Haydn. She could hear him, he was with her now, there in her head. "The educated ear, Frances, is the sole authority. This simple fact is the basis of teaching music, and all of your studies are of equal importance if you are to gain a high degree of musicianship."

He took care of her interests and her person, and introduced her into Parisian society, where, because of his eccentricity, they made him welcome, and because of her talent, so was she. There were two gay years, immune to the looming economic crisis, where none seemed to recognise, or maybe they chose to ignore, the imminent dangers brewing all around Europe.

And so, following that performance, he let her enjoy her moment of euphoria before pulling her to one side.

"You played with your head," he said, "not your heart, Frances. I've told you this many times. It's not enough. The aim of the Conservatoire is not just to produce excellent performers, but excellent musicians. It's clear that you still have a great deal to learn."

His remarks instantly flattened her.

"I want to go home," she said to Edie.

The following morning though, the headlines declared: 'Frances Lamont, France's Musical find of the Century.' She flicked through all the dailies and noticed that she had not been the only person to be enjoying a success that morning. They gave the dominant story of that day over to one Adolf Hitler, the Chancellor of Germany, who had somehow marched his army into Austria unopposed. She gazed hard at the photograph of this man, who looked out from between the pages until a chill ran through her.

* * *

On the bridge, Mueller turned to his First Officer. "Werner, what do you think? Does Tommy know we're out?"

"There was no special message on Radio Calais for us," Werner replied. "You'd think we could find out where the hell they get their information from."

Mueller nodded in agreement. "We can't be too careful. Plenty of people are always ready to inform, you see."

Several moments passed, and then Mueller spoke again, his hollow voice ringing out in the control room through the voice tube.

"Prepare to dive! Chief, sort out her trim."

Mueller wanted the boat perfectly balanced, and for that, the Chief had to adjust the amount of water in the ballast tanks. Werner and the first watch dropped through the conning tower in front of Mueller. By now, the sun had disappeared into the inky blue of the sea, and night had come. Mueller made the hatches fast before lowering himself down the ladder. "Well, men. So far, so good. Let's hope it continues."

* * *

October 22nd, 2000, hours

The watch had just begun. Mueller ordered supper from Hayman the cook and made his way to the wardroom, satisfied that the U-boat was on course, pushing her way towards her designated grid position through what, for now, was the relative calm of the Atlantic Ocean. The diesels hummed, muttering their old familiar song as they sped her on her way, and Mueller took pleasure in the sound. The engine noise: less when the exhausts were awash, then, when lifted on the crest of a wave, reaching a crescendo as the fumes found a means of escape.

They were now a couple of days out of Brest, and he was beginning to believe Tommy must not have been aware of their sailing time after all. Or maybe those keen-eyed pilots were the worse for wear. Maybe they were out on the town. He smiled to himself. As time went on, the chances of being spotted lessened. The U-boat's low silhouette would scarcely be distinguishable, little more than a shadow against the ocean once the sun had gone down.

* * *

In the boat's hull, men jostled with each other and the packed provisions, trying to find enough space to settle down and enjoy their meal. At the start of a patrol, meals were good, though they reckoned their old man's sense of humour was warped, the way he kept ordering soup. Still, the little cook, Hayman, was excellent, the soup was exceptional and there was fresh bread to go along with it, and as long as the sea stayed calm — "Alaaaaarm!" Mueller heard Werner's shout come down the hatch from the bridge.

The men of the watch tumbled through the conning tower. Werner made the inner hatch fast, and water that had collected on it from above spewed down on the men below.

Mueller made his way to the control room, crying out, "Dive, dive, dive!" The main vents were opened, and the hydroplanes were set, but the U-boat seemed stuck to the surface.

"Forward all hands!" Zeitler, the Chief, shouted, and a mad stampede ensued as men rushed through the control room, the wardroom, and into the bow torpedo room, the additional weight causing the bow to tip slowly forward, sinking it into the depths. Mugs of hot soup went flying, while off-duty crew members grasped desperately for something to hang onto, lurching and ducking to avoid the assorted debris which crashed across the deck plates.

In the control room, Mueller kept his eye on the depth gauge and, along with most of the other seamen present, fell silent, ears keenly attuned to any tell-tale sounds of impending attack.

Shifting his eyes to the depth gauge, he said, "Take her down further, Chief." A great groan rose from the hull as the U-boat complained at this indignity. She had been tested at 90 metres and levelled off now at 120 metres. Mueller checked his watch, then turned to Werner. "Not bad, Exec, not bad."

Second Officer Schumacher wiped the sweat from his face and breathed again. He glanced over at his commanding officer, who was wearing a broad smile on his face. God, he thought, it was just a practice dive.

An eerie silence fell as the rest of the crew registered relief, and then the chuckles began. Mueller's voice rang out through the boat. "Got to keep you on your toes, lads!" he shouted. "Periscope depth, Chief."

The crew of the U-boat relaxed. Some muttered oaths, but most just laughed at the old man's sense of timing.

* * *

Later, while taking time out in the petty officer's quarters, Mueller was joined by Paul Werner, his friend and First Officer. Werner pushed a coffee in front of Mueller and slumped down beside him.

"So, what do you make of our Second Officer?" he asked Mueller.

"What do you?" Mueller replied.

Werner made a Pffft noise. "Hitler Youth—all puff and party politics."

Mueller nodded. "We could do without a bloody propagandist on board. But I dare say he'll know his stuff."

"We'll soon put him right. By the way, I haven't congratulated you yet."

Mueller cocked his head and gave him a lopsided look. "Huh?"

"Sophie Heyne. Congratulations are due, I think. Tell me about it."

Congratulations—are they in order? I suppose they are, Mueller thought, but tell Paul about it? No, he'd never do that. He'd never tell Werner about that night in Berlin, and the party he'd been dragged to by his old friend Bertie Teichmann. The party attended by all those top ranking naval and military personnel, alongside tarts and showgirls, where champagne had flowed and camaraderie had spurted like shit from a donkey.

That party, where, as the evening had progressed, rank and officialdom were cast aside along with various articles of clothing, and they'd all been whores together. No, he wouldn't tell Paul about the party where he'd met Sophie Heyne—the elegant Sophie Heyne who had smelled so divine and looked so good, with her golden hair and the face of a saint. He'd not tell how, when they'd found somewhere to be alone, she had dropped the saintly mantle, along with the rest of her apparel, unleashing the body, appetites, and expertise of a woman one normally associated with a brothel. They'd enjoyed one another, and that should have been the end. But it wasn't.

He'd still had a few days to kill, and she'd invited him to spend them at her family retreat, just outside the city. Once there, he'd met her father, Secretary Heyne, and mixed with top ranking members of the Party. Their talk of German supremacy, their remarks regarding the Jews, had sickened him, but he'd not tell Paul that.

Neither would he tell of his embarrassment when Frau Heyne and her friend, the gossiping wife of the good doctor, had found him and Sophie in the gazebo with their pants around their ankles, moaning and grunting like a couple of rutting pigs. And that should certainly have been the end of it, but still it wasn't.

Heyne later summoned him to the library. He'd knocked on the door and been made to wait outside it like some pitiable schoolboy, a man near thirty, with a small harbour-load of shipping under his belt, made to wait and ponder his crime. Then Heyne had said, "Come," and he'd entered the room with his pulse racing and his palms sweating, waiting for the depth charge to be dropped. He could think of nothing to say, so he kept quiet, with his tongue thick in his mouth, waiting for Heyne to mete out the punishment. Secretary Heyne, standing behind his desk with a drink in his hand which he knew was not for him.

No, he'd never tell that Heyne had made the punishment fit the crime. Take the blame or be shamed, had been the order of the day. Heyne had suggested that perhaps an engagement should be announced, and because a man in his position does not argue with a man in Heyne's position, he had agreed to it. Poor bloody fool. Heyne had seen a way for the whole mess to work to the advantage of the Party, and he, Mueller, had become a news item, a morale booster for the people. Stability in these times of instability. The great German family unit could, and would, survive.

Hail it as the marriage of the year. 'Society girl to marry U-Boat Ace.' A marriage made in Heaven, true love conquers, and all that crap;

and he, the fatted calf. No, he most certainly wouldn't tell Werner all that, he wouldn't tell a soul. All that was between him and himself.

So, he just smiled and said, "Congratulations? Yes, thanks, Paul."

Werner was in a state of confusion when he left Mueller. He knew him well. They'd been through university together and were close friends. Things were not right. He had been excited about his own wedding a few years earlier, but Mueller had almost dismissed his own. He thought it an odd coupling anyway, Mueller and Sophie Heyne. Well, not the coupling exactly. That would have been inevitable, but marriage to Sophie Heyne? No, he just didn't understand it at all. The woman had quite a reputation, and the entire Heyne family was entrenched in the damn Party, and he was worried that his friend was going to be dragged into it without realising what was happening. Once in, he thought, there's only one way out: feet first with a hole in your head. *Ah, well,* he thought, *the old dog has a lot on his mind at present. No doubt he'll tell me more about it at some point.*

* * *

Frances was shaking as the blood coursed back through her veins. She felt hands gently lifting her head and supporting her as they put water to her lips. She tried to greedily quench her thirst, but the cup was removed, and she heard a man's voice speaking to her.

"A little at a time, Fraulein, a little at a time." Hengst removed his arm and laid her head back down on the pillow. "Rest now. Perhaps a little soup later?"

Chapter 4

Following breakfast and the daily trimming of the U-boat, Mueller made for the bridge and gave the men on watch a nod, noticing the look he received from his young second officer. It was still quiet, and the Atlantic was calm, so they were making good headway toward their grid position. He'd looked in on his passenger before breakfast, but the woman still seemed dead to the world. Hengst had assured him she would make a full recovery and that the woman had taken a little soup along with water.

Looking out onto the expanse of ocean, he thought about Sophie. Christ, what a mess. He'd gone to find her immediately following the interview with Heyne. Dreading an emotional outburst, he was somewhat surprised to find her coolly reading the latest society news in the drawing room.

"Darling," she'd said, "what fun! Just imagine—you and I an item!" She'd patted the sofa beside her. "Sit here with me a while—we've so much to talk about."

That was some understatement. They hardly knew a damn thing about each other. He wasn't sure it was wise to know too much. As far as Sophie Heyne was concerned, maybe ignorance was bliss. He remembered reading, or hearing, her name linked with a flyer, and she'd told him of her last amour, an army man. *My God*, he thought, *she's working her way through the armed forces.* He smiled to himself wryly, wondering whether she'd worked her way through the ranks first.

She was some woman, though. Oh, he was under no misapprehension. Sophie was not in love with him any more than he was with her. Love! No, love wasn't for the likes of them. He had built a wall around himself to keep it out, enjoying the physical side of a relationship but never getting involved. He didn't believe love really existed anyway, and even if it did, he'd found from a young age that someone special could give it to you one minute and then remove it in a second with scarcely a thought.

He and Sophie Heyne probably deserved one another, and as long as they understood each other and expected little from each other, then life, for as long as it lasted, would at least be tolerable.

* * *

In her weakened state, Frances did not know what the time was, not that it mattered. Time could stand still for all the difference it made to her now. She had lost everyone and everything. Her tongue was thick in her mouth, and her face was sore and chapped from the constant battering of the winter sea breeze. She'd lost everything, everyone she loved. She wished she'd had the courage to speed up her end and slip into the embrace of the water. Courage! Was courage what one needed? She had always thought that suicide was the coward's way out—it was for the weak, the people who couldn't cope. But perhaps it was a brave thing to do. To take one's own life, to deny one's inborn optimism. That would definitely take courage, and she didn't seem to have it.

She didn't have it in 1940 either, when France had fallen and they could have left Paris. Those with courage, she thought, had got out and gone, like Windsor, the onetime monarch of England. Edward the Eighth, who had chosen the love of a divorced woman, Wallis Simpson, over the love for his country and had abdicated. That was some love. That thought reawakened more memories.

* * *

As Paris returned to some sort of normality, most, like themselves, accepted the Occupation with a lack of distress. Paris, full of German soldiers who seemed to view the city as sightseers might. They behaved very correctly, which made their acceptance less of a burden for the Parisians. There were changes, of course. Because of the lack of petrol, those in the city became adept cyclists, and there was the curfew too, which, by July, was extended to eleven o'clock and soon after extended to midnight. Two weeks after the Armistice, nightclubs and cabarets were in full swing, and it was easy for German and French alike to stay in a club until five in the morning when the curfew was lifted.

"I think it's time we socialised again," she told Steven at the beginning of that September. "Maxim's, I think."

"Maxim's?" His brows rose. "Doesn't it bother you that all those German uniforms will be there?"

"Oh, I think it's time we faced up to them," she said. "I saw Georges van Parys today. He said it doesn't make him uneasy at all to be in the city."

If only she hadn't pushed, if only she had listened to Steven's concerns, perhaps they wouldn't have gone, and he would be beside her now. But she had bullied him, and he'd sighed, "Very well, my dear."

They had taken the Metro into the city as far as they could, some stations being closed off for fear of bombing. Then they had walked the short distance to Maxim's, arriving at about seven o'clock. The restaurant was brimming with uniforms, amongst which were dotted various members of Parisian society. One or two heads nodded in their direction as they waited in the vestibule, but mostly, Frances had the feeling that they, the Meyers, were 'definitely not in.' They had received the cold shoulder. She felt hurt and disappointed, like a child not allowed to join in a game.

"I don't know what we've done to deserve this," she said.

Steven patted her hand. "It's nothing you've done at all, my dear. I'm afraid it's all my fault."

"What do you mean? How have you offended so many people?"

He took her arm and squeezed it. "It's not that I have offended them. Rather, they just find me offensive."

"I don't understand."

"Are you still so naïve, Frances?" Her eyes widened. He seldom snapped at her. "Have you forgotten our treatment in Germany so soon?" he asked, softening his tone.

"Of course not. How could I?"

"Well, it's like a cancer. It has spread."

"But these people are our friends," she argued.

"Were our friends," he corrected.

Georges, the waiter, appeared and steered them—apologetically, Frances thought — across the room to a table well out of the way of the crowd. They sat in silence for some minutes, contemplating the contents of the menu and their treatment. Frances looked up to find Steven smiling over the top of his menu. Not at her, but at whoever was being seated at the table behind her. Glancing back, she saw it was a young German officer.

Looking back at Steven, she was angry. "Why are you smiling at him, for goodness' sake?" she asked. "Maybe it's you who's forgotten our treatment in Germany, Steven."

"Can't I even smile at people anymore? Maybe being pleasant is the way forward. Perhaps we can win them over. What do you think, Frances, a smile could win the war?"

"I think sometimes you are too nice."

Georges was talking to the officer. Frances could hear their muttered conversation. Within a few minutes, he came to take her and Steven's order. Before leaving, he placed a folded note before her. "From the gentleman behind you," he said, and with a slight bow, he left.

Opening it, she read, 'Madame, please join me.' She felt herself go red as she passed the note to Steven.

"Well, at least the man has taste," Steven quipped.

"Why don't you join him, Steven, since you appear to like him so much? I never thought I would see the day when you found a German so amusing."

Their meal arrived, along with a bottle of champagne.

"Compliments of the gentleman at the next table, Madame, Monsieur."

"See, I told you he had good taste," Steven said and threw another smile in the man's direction.

"Well, send it back; we don't want it," she whispered.

"Now, truthfully, aren't you a little flattered?"

"No, I'm not. Just who does he think he is, anyway?" she fumed. "Steven, what on earth are you grinning at?"

"Relax, enjoy the champagne. After all, it's free," he replied, passing her the glass.

Towards the end of the meal, a second letter was put before her. She passed it straight away to Steven, who unfolded it and read it, eyebrows raised.

"Well?" she asked.

"Oh, most definitely for you," he teased.

"Come on, Steven, what does it say?"

He read, "Please put me out of my misery. Run away with me tonight to Rouen."

"The cheeky sod! That's it. What the devil is going on?" she spluttered.

Steven laughed. "Calm down, Frances," he said.

"Well, I'm glad you think it's so funny. Most men would be offended!"

"Good evening, Frances, Professor." The voice spoke passable French.

Startled, she whipped her gaze to the German officer who had appeared at her shoulder and leapt to her feet, squealing, "Otto!" Suddenly, she laughed, realising the joke that Steven had played on her. "You? Here? What on Earth?"

He took her into a warm embrace, and setting her out of it, swept a hand down his front, showing his uniform. "Serving, I'm afraid."

She shook her head, still laughing. "Still up to mischief, I see. You could never resist a trick, could you?" She glanced at Steven. "And you were in on it all the time."

All three of them had enjoyed the joke. But that joke had turned sour, hadn't it?

Steven invited Count Otto von Liechtenstein to join them, and after kissing Frances on both cheeks, he drew up a chair and sat down at their table.

"So, did you enjoy the champagne?" he asked. "An excellent vintage, don't you think?"

"I'd have enjoyed it much more if I'd known where it came from," she admitted.

"Then just so that you can enjoy it, we had better have another one," he said, waving the waiter over and putting in his order.

"But why are you in Paris, Otto? Are you playing?"

"Only for my amusement these days."

"Just as well!" Steven smiled, but his disregard was clear.

It irked Frances. "Really, Steven, that's not fair. Otto is a talented player."

Otto laughed. "It's all right, Frances. It's no secret that I haven't a tenth of your talent nor any of your genius."

"You see, my dear," Steven said smoothly. "Otto is more than aware of his own shortcomings."

"Steven, please, why be so cutting?" His comments truly embarrassed her.

Otto bent his elbows on the table. "I think that Professor Meyer probably knows that when it comes to being accepted in a famous school of study such as the Conservatoire, a well-respected name such as Liechtenstein and the bulging bank balance of my family more than make up for any lack of talent. Now that's enough of me. Tell me about yourself. Where is your next engagement—and when?"

"Oh, Otto, I haven't played, you know, since all of this war happened."

"You? Not play? That's like living a death for you. Why ever not?"

"Well, it seems I'm not too much in demand these days."

"My fault, I should think," Steven said, rising and setting his napkin alongside his plate. He excused himself, making for the gentleman's room.

Frances turned to Otto. "You know why he's blaming himself? Because he's Jewish. He says I'm naïve for not taking the German attitude toward the Jews seriously. But it isn't serious, is it, Otto? You don't dislike Steven because of his heritage, do you?" She peered anxiously at him.

Otto's smile was brief and never reached his eyes. "I always thought you were a fool to get mixed up with him. I could get you back into society ... easily." He went on after a pause. "But with him in tow?" He shrugged.

Frances locked his gaze. "Steven is my husband. I shouldn't have to remind you of that. And just for the record? I wouldn't have it any other way."

He lifted his hands. "Very well. I'm sorry. I should have known better. Loyalty has always been one of your weaknesses."

"Unlike you, Casanova." She tried to be angry, but then smiled, remembering the good times when they were both young. When there was no war and they were just a couple of students. "Just how many hearts did you break? None of them could resist those curly golden locks, and now look at them." She ruffled his hair. "Haricot Vertes!" He frowned. "It's French for bean. Your haircut makes your head look like a bean."

"Thank you. You were always good at compliments. Anyway, you resisted very well."

Otto's tone, his grin, seemed forced, somehow ironic. But that was Otto, wasn't it? Ever having his tongue parked in his cheek. Frances shrugged off a feeling of unease. They were friends, after all. "I always had more sense—and there was Steven to warn me. Besides, the only interest you had in me was as a language tutor."

"Do you realise how much you helped me win over those poor, defenceless girls? Without the language, things would not have been so simple."

She laughed. "Come now, Otto, I will accept no responsibility for your amours—you don't need French for that. People already say that come this summer there will be lots of little Germans in Paris."

"The language of love is universal." Otto's look, while inscrutable, seemed to Frances somehow disturbing. But then he smiled, and with a wave of his hand, said, "Which reminds me, I have to tell you I am a married man now, with a two-year-old son and another on the way."

"Oh, Otto, how wonderful! What a lovely surprise. I know we lost contact when you went back to Germany and my career took off, but I thought of you often, you know." Leaning over, she kissed him on the cheek. "Congratulations, you must be a happy man."

He regarded her steadily for a long moment. "And you, Frances, are you happy with the good professor?"

"Yes, of course. He's a good man; of course, I'm happy."

"He doesn't look so well," Otto said. "The years haven't been kind to him."

"No, you're right, he's not well. Too much smoking, and his cough is getting worse now that winter is coming." Steven re-joined them. "You will never guess," she said as he sat down. "Otto's a married man now."

Surprised, Steven raised his eyebrows. "Really? Congratulations."

"Thank you."

A silence lingered. Otto broke it.

"I'm truly surprised to hear Frances isn't playing. She should be, you know. It's not fair to her, or to anyone who appreciates music, that she should be holed up like this. I'm sure I could help. If I have your permission, that is."

"Certainly. If that's what Frances wants," Steven said. "I'm afraid I don't have much standing these days, but I agree. Her talent should be out there, not hidden under a bushel."

* * *

The voices were back. Still foreign. Still not the voices of those she loved, but not threatening either. More, considering. They were no longer goading her to slip over the boat's side. She attempted to lift her head, wanting badly to sort it out—where she was, whether she was actually alive. But it was useless.

Chapter 5

October 24, 1942

Hovering somewhere between wakefulness and sleep, Frances knew she was no longer in the rowing boat, but how long since her rescue from it. An hour? A day? Weeks, months, years? What difference did it make? The outcome was the same, wasn't it? Everyone she cared for was gone! She'd been conscious enough to receive food, she thought. Her limbs still ached as her blood warmed and freely coursed through her veins again. She should be joyful, glad—relieved, at least—but for what? Everything was ruined. Those Germans, the bastards, had seen to that!

That noise, the constant humming, the hot and muggy air that smelled of oil and other unpleasant things, lulled her senses. She fought the curtain of darkness that approached, forcing her eyes to open, to focus and make sense of her circumstances, her surroundings. She tried to sit up and found straps around her waist and legs tied her to the bed. A tiny drum of panic jittered at her temples. Where was she? Who had rescued her and lashed her to this bed? The cover slipped, and she realised now she was naked. She fell back, clutching the blanket's edge to her chin.

Turning her head to the side, she studied the room. It was tiny, maybe 2.5 metres by two metres or so, including the width of the bunk. By rotating her head, a little, she could see there was also a desk with a chair and several small cupboards up to the ceiling against one wall. There was a green full-length curtain drawn across the space, separating the room, separating her—from what?

She lay flat, eyes wide, breathing shallow, listening hard. She could make out voices around the engine noise. A tangle of male voices. Guttural. *German?* Oh, God, no! Her pulse kicked up, hammering a jagged beat. So, these murdering pigs had picked her up? The E-boat must have come back for her, but why? Why couldn't they have left her to die like the others? She could have gone with them when the boat caught fire. They had been so close to making it. Their panicked escape from Paris ... had it been the right thing to do? She heard the clatter of footsteps. Boots on metal. They were coming her way. How many? Two, at least.

They stopped just outside, and she heard a low authoritative voice ask, "Still nothing on the girl?"

And the reply: "No, Kapitanleutnant."

So, the great Nazi powers of detection hadn't discovered who she was. Or had Otto reconsidered? Was it possible he hadn't tracked them after all? That would mean the sinking of the *Etoile* had been pure chance. Steven and Jacques, the old fisherman—their deaths had been a tragic accident. Her racing thoughts were cut short as the green curtain was drawn aside and two men appeared.

"So, how are you today?" the taller, scruffier of the two asked.

Rather than answer, she noted the details of his appearance. He wore a dirty white cap pushed back on his head, and beneath it his dark blue eyes were piercing. His high cheekbones and firm jaw were covered by a few days' growth of beard, and he had a Slavic look about him. She recognised his voice as the one she'd heard moments before, the authoritative one. But he'd addressed her in faltering French, which she chose to ignore. She shifted her glance from him.

He tried again, nodding encouragement at her. "I'm Kapitanleutnant Kristian Mueller. This is my First Officer, Leutnant Werner."

The second man, Werner, was smaller and very fair. He also had several days' worth of facial hair shading his chin. But despite that, she thought he had a gentle look about him. She clenched her teeth, damned if she would volunteer anything to them, these swine, who had murdered her family and friends. She was angry and afraid, so couldn't trust what might come out of her mouth, anyway.

"We need you to answer a few questions if you are up to it. You're quite safe now, believe me." Mueller seemed to recognise her fear.

His recognition of that, his reassurance about it—it only infuriated her more. She snapped her gaze to his. "I'm safe?" she spat the query in flawless French. "You kill old men and women for sport, and you dare to tell me I'm safe?"

Werner and Mueller exchanged questioning glances, and then Mueller shrugged, and his mouth worked as if he struggled to find the right way to respond in an alien tongue.

Possibly, Frances thought, the Kapitanleutnant had misunderstood her.

Unsure from the issuing venom that he and this woman completely understood one another, Mueller tried again. "Calm down, please, mademoiselle. Maybe if you just tell us who you are for a start, that could help us all, you see?"

Frances turned on him. For a moment, amber eyes held blue. She searched her brain for the worst insult she could think of, resorting to her mother tongue. "Fuck off, Kapitan!" she answered in English, and noted with pleasure the way he drew in his breath and tightened his mouth.

He spoke to Werner in German, and from what they said, Frances realised they had no idea she was fluent in their language as well. She fought a smile that she had got one over on them.

"Pleasant little thing, isn't she?" Mueller was asking Werner. "Now, I ask you, is that any way to say thank you? Given the obscenities, maybe she is a fisherman's wife, after all."

Werner shook his head, but he smiled at his commander's obvious offence and wondered what punishment he would have dished out to any of the men if they had addressed him in such a way.

Frances felt the return of Mueller's gaze and refused to meet it.

"Well then, Froggy," he said, once again in stilted French, "we'll talk when you're feeling a little better." And with that, the two men left.

Frances took a perverted pleasure in the way he laboured to make himself understood. She felt it somehow demeaned him. Calling her Froggy, however, was demeaning, too. How did he know she was French? Possibly the law of averages made it a good guess. For the present, at least, she decided not to let on how well she understood him.

* * *

"What do you think, then?" Werner asked Mueller. "English spy?"

"Hmm, why on her own in the middle of the Atlantic? Not even they would do that to a girl, would they?" Mueller followed Werner into the wardroom. "Ah, I have it," he said as Werner poured coffee into each of two mugs. "She's Churchill's new secret weapon. Tommy has scattered a few of these around to undermine our crews."

"Yep, of course, that would be it." Werner chuckled as he took the steaming mug to Mueller and handed it to him.

"To borrow an expression from our friend back there," Mueller said as he sat down, "it could cause fucking mayhem!"

"Kapitanleutnant?"

Mueller turned to find Simon standing in the wardroom hatchway. "What is it?" he asked.

"The lady, Kapitanleutnant, I think I know who she is."

"I think it's highly unlikely, Simon, that we've picked up someone you know in the middle of the Atlantic."

"She's a musician, a famous one. Frances Lamont. I went to a concert she gave at the Gewandhaus in Leipzig in '39. She was a soloist, performing with the Leipzig Symphony Orchestra. I'm fairly certain it's her."

"How fairly certain, Simon?" asked Werner.

"I'm sure, Leutnant."

Mueller gave Simon a knowing nod. "So, she's a favourite performer of yours, Simon, eh?" He couldn't help teasing the kid a bit, his admiration for the violinist was so obvious.

Simon blushed, ducking his gaze, clearly disconcerted. "She's very talented."

"Well, I'll have to take your word on that, Simon." Dismissing the boy, he turned back to his coffee, contemplating it, searching his mind ... but no, he didn't think he'd ever heard of Frances Lamont. But then he had little fondness for classical music.

Chapter 6

Feeling stronger and more awake, Frances's painful thoughts turned to Steven, remembering the evening after the party given by von Schaumburg. They'd almost had an argument, and then the arrests had begun and they took Steven from her. He told her how alone and desperate he felt at that time. It was how she felt now. Utterly alone and completely helpless. *Oh, Steven...* Tears for him, for herself, the life they'd shared, burned beneath her eyelids, and she fell back into an endless sea of memory.

* * *

After dining with them at Maxim's, Otto had been as good as his word. It was only days later when Frances heard from him. She'd been invited to play at a party that a senior member of the Wehrmacht had arranged. It was at Neuilly, virtually on her own doorstep. Neuilly, along with the grander, more central apartments, had become a favourite spot for senior German personnel to take up residence.

Von Schaumburg, an old-school Prussian officer called old Shatterhand by some, had been delighted by her and had asked her to play at his own home at 24 Avenue Raphael, a villa which had belonged to Coty, the perfume manufacturer, a few years earlier.

"You know, Madame Meyer," he had said upon their first meeting at the wonderful stone mansion, "music means friendship."

"Indeed, it does," she replied, giving him one of her most winning smiles and believing that she had been right all along in accepting Otto's help. This is where she belonged: in society, being entertained and entertaining—to go here or there, or to do this or that.

Along with von Schaumburg's acceptance came the acceptance of what was left of Parisian society. The Meyers were once again a part of the in-crowd. Parties, recitals, and concerts had followed her performance at Neuilly. She and Steven attended virtually all the important Franco-German social occasions. She played with the likes of Alfred Cortot—in fact, they had accompanied Germaine Lubin, a singer who, at the Bayreuth Festival in '38, had been singled out by Hitler for particular praise. Paris, as civilised as ever, had become the showpiece of the Reich, hadn't it? There were those who accepted and even liked it that way. Frances would not be drawn either way, as long as she was playing and being admired, she was happy to look the other way.

Because of her newfound popularity and her friendship with Otto, Steven's Jewish ancestry was overlooked. They had known of situations where Jews had been harassed in the streets or refused admittance to public places. Madame Courteline, widow of the playwright, who because of her Jewish blood was refused entry into one of her husband's plays, had been discussed frequently. Sometimes it had to be said with hilarity rather than outrage.

Oh, there were rumours of roundups, but not of anyone important. They both enjoyed their newfound popularity for a while. The relief of being well received and recognised was a blessing, and they felt safe again. There were shortages, but most things could be had at a price. Then, during the severe winter of '40 -'41, Steven's health deteriorated badly, and he suffered repeated respiratory infections. Come the early summer of '42, following an embassy 'do,' his mood had changed.

Otto had arranged for his driver to taxi them home as usual. Steven was quiet until the door of their home was closed tightly behind them.

"That's it. I've had it."

"What?" Her back was to him. She was unscrewing her earrings, heading into the bedroom.

"I said that's it. That's the last of these bloody 'do's' you'll get me to attend. It goes against the grain. I want nothing more to do with these people."

Biting back her annoyance, she came to the bedroom doorway, a childish pout on her lips. "Well, I thought it was a good evening, Steven. I enjoyed myself. So, what happened to you?"

"A good evening! A pretence! We're all playing the game of being something we're not. Of being friends and being nice to each other. Don't you think I know what people are saying? Let me tell you, I'm proud of my ancestry, and I'm not so proud now of being French. And it took a bloody Nazi to make me realise that."

She left the doorway, kicking off her heels, not knowing what to say. She'd heard things, disturbing accounts of German atrocities against the Jews, but she'd as often heard that what they said against them were lies, propaganda. Honestly, she didn't know what to believe. Sometimes the only time she felt truly herself and truly at peace was on stage, playing her beloved violin, losing herself in her music. Steven stood on the threshold.

"I'm sorry, my dear," he said, holding her gaze. "I shouldn't be taking it out on you."

Crossing the room, he turned her back to him and unhooked her gown. His touch was cool and didn't linger.

"Do you know what I heard tonight?" he asked. Going to the dresser, he removed his cufflinks. "I heard Abetz, the good German Ambassador, telling one of his cronies that he'd received all sorts of pleas from parliamentarians, municipal councillors, and prefects to magistrates. And out of fifty of these so-called dignitaries, forty-nine asked for special permissions of some sort or another for themselves or family members to worm their way around and bend the rules. It was only the fiftieth who spoke of France. These are the sort of people we are mixing with. The sort of people we are becoming. Because of Otto's protection."

"Things aren't so bad." Dressed in her nightgown now, she turned down the bedcovers. "We have money in the bank. We've not gone without, have we?" She said this to him, but there were times when even she had doubts about some of the company they were keeping.

He hung his suit in the closet. "This business so far with the Germans is the honeymoon period. Eventually, something has to give." He turned from the dresser, buttoning the shirt of his pyjamas, meeting her gaze. "Why do you think they're calling for the census to be taken?"

"But you said that the French police were organising that." Frances climbed into bed.

"Oh, Frances, please!" Glaring at her, Steven brought his right fist down on his left palm. "How can you remain so blinkered?"

"I'm not. I just think it's being blown up out of all proportion, that's all—"

"Who do you think they're doing it for? What about the sick exhibition at the Palais Berlitz?"

"It's propaganda. Granted, it's sick, but our friends don't take part. Von Schaumburg doesn't. Otto hasn't been. I don't know of anyone who has—"

"Friends—bah!" Steven spat the words, raking his hands over his hair, pacing. "You don't know what they do all day, what they say behind our backs, and don't think that Otto can be trusted, everything he does is because he's smitten with you."

"No, you're wrong. For goodness' sake, Steven, Otto is like a brother to me," she began, but she soon dropped her argument and her gaze. Hadn't she sensed it herself, that Otto's attentions to her were more than as a friend? Something in his eyes when he looked at her—as if he were mentally undressing her, as if they were alone in a room. It bothered her, but she'd dismissed her concern as ridiculous, her imagination, right along with her apprehension that Otto wasn't as tolerant of Steven's Jewish heritage as he would have her believe.

"What of the Jews they've already rounded up and deported to God knows where?" Steven spoke over her misgiving. "There'll be reprisals against those who have shown resistance, too. Mark my words."

It was only a matter of weeks later, in early December, when his prophecy came chillingly true. There was shouting in the street outside. This was not usual in Neuilly, and they both went to the window that looked out onto the avenue. There were several gendarmes and some of their neighbours arguing with them. Across the street was a police transport vehicle with a couple of people they didn't recognise being loaded inside.

"What on earth is going on, Steven?" she asked.

"Open your eyes, Frances. What do these people outside have in common, do you think?" He coughed, and she slapped him on the back to help ease it.

Shaking her head, she looked out of the window again. She couldn't see any common factor, she refused to see one.

"Look, for God's sake. They're all our Jewish neighbours, aren't they? See—there's Doctor Hoffman, Steinberg the writer and his wife, and isn't that Professor Samuels?"

"But he lectures at the Sorbonne, Steven."

There was a hammering on the door too heavy to be from a man's hand.

"And I, my dear, lecture at the Conservatoire occasionally." He took a deep breath and made his way to the front entrance, turning back in the doorway from the room. "I think, my dear, this is it," he said.

She raced across the room, grabbing hold of his arm as he made for the door. The knocking became more insistent. As he reached the door, he turned to her, cupping her chin in his hand. "Be strong, Frances, please be strong."

The door opened on a heavily built gendarme. "Steven Meyer?" he asked.

"Yes, I'm Steven Meyer."

"And this is Madame Meyer?"

"Yes, this is my wife, though she has no Jewish blood. I assume that's why I am being arrested—because I'm Jewish?"

"It is," replied the man.

"But you can't arrest a person because of their religion or heritage!" shrieked Frances, hanging on tightly to Steven's arm.

"I'm afraid I can, Madame. Step away from your husband, please. I really don't want to use any force."

Frances felt her heartbeat banging in her head. She never thought this would ever happen; she thought they were safe inside their little bubble. What now? The man had taken Steven's arm and was helping him to cross the threshold out into the street.

"Wait, please wait!" she shouted. "He needs a coat, he is sick. Please wait while I get his overcoat." Suddenly, there were floods of tears that had risen from somewhere deep inside her. The gendarme, moved by this young woman's plea, stopped, nodded, and waited while she went in search of an overcoat upstairs. By the time she returned, a small crowd had gathered in the avenue. Most out of sympathy, some out of malice, muttering anti-Semitic filth. Frances had loaded all the pockets of the coat with as much food as she could cram into it. She held it open for Steven to walk into, hardly able to see. She was crying so much.

"Can I kiss my wife?" he asked.

"You can."

Steven Meyer held his wife in his arms for a few seconds and then kissed her gently on her brow. "Remember, my love, be strong for me," he said as they led him away to the waiting truck.

She stood rooted to the spot as they loaded others into the transport vehicle. At that moment, she thought her heart would break in two.

* * *

Steven had been arrested along with other notable Jews and taken to the edge of the city and confined in the holding camp known as Drancy in the north-eastern suburb of Paris. While the Germans had set it up as a holding camp for Jews, the French police operated it.

Although Frances wanted no more reason to be indebted to Otto, she'd had no choice but to go to him for help. It took days for him to arrange Steven's release, and afterward, he told her he'd never have managed had it not been for the fact that he knew many of the French officers there in charge. "Even I can pull no strings as far as the S.S. and Gestapo are concerned," he said.

* * *

She woke with a start. Someone was near her bunk. She wanted to keep her eyes closed and feign sleep, but her bladder was crying out for relief. Pushing against the straps that restrained her, she managed to turn over. Through the aluminium bed railing, she could see Mueller stretched out on a pallet on the floor. What the hell was he doing there? She could hardly escape. He opened his eyes lazily, as if he'd felt her regard, aware of her movement.

"Madame Meyer, how are you?" Again, he spoke in the stilted French that was so offensive to her ears. She didn't answer. She watched as he pulled himself into a sitting position, massaging his bearded jaw and stretching his shoulders to ease the pain of sleeping in such cramped quarters.

She shifted her glance. So, they knew who she was. Knew who they'd blasted from the water. Otto must have tracked them to Fecamp after all. He must know too that she was still alive, and that Steven was dead, along with Jacques. And Aunt Edie, what had become of her? She took a deep breath to steady her voice, not wishing to give Mueller a glimpse of her fear, then she answered in perfect German.

"Kapitanleutnant, congratulations on blasting my husband, myself, and a dear old man out of the ocean. I'm sure it has helped your war effort considerably."

Mueller's eyebrows lifted in surprise. "You speak excellent German, Froggy."

"Better than your French, anyway," she snapped. "How long do you intend to keep me strapped to this bed?"

"That's up to you. If you feel strong enough to stand—fine."

"You'll untie me?"

Mueller smiled and got to his feet. She pulled back nervously as he approached her. He was quite tall, she noticed, but lean, and his ruggedness and beard gave him a rough appearance, which she found unnerving.

"Is that what you think? That we tied you up?" he asked, working the buckles. "We strapped you to the bunk, Froggy, so that you wouldn't fall off. The ride can be rough at times. It's what we do if people are injured, you see."

"And my clothes?" she asked, her tone sharply sarcastic. "I suppose they fell off when things got rough, did they? And don't call me Froggy."

It irked her when the bastard smiled at her, showing a small gap between his front teeth, which, despite herself, and the situation she was in, she found attractive.

"Removing your clothing was necessary if you weren't to catch pneumonia. It was all done decently; I can assure you."

"And can you assure me, Kapitanleutnant, that I am not your prisoner?" she asked.

He leant on the side of the bunk, causing her to shuffle towards the wall. "We'll take you back to port after our patrol, then it will be up to the authorities," he replied. He wanted to escape. He didn't like women who snapped and snarled at him, spitting venom. Women were supposed to be soft and gentle—vulnerable. They should at least pretend to be like Sophie. Even if they weren't. This woman, though, Frances Meyer, had been through some ordeal. Her husband lost, too. He'd checked back to base and learnt a little of the woman's history. It seemed Simon was correct. She was a quite famous violinist.

Mueller went to the exit of his nook. She called him back. "I suppose there is a bathroom on this ship, Kapitanleutnant?"

He turned, unable to keep the amusement from his face. "Come on, Froggy, I'll show you." He beckoned her to follow him.

"Am I expected to go like this?"

"Sorry. No, of course not." He opened a cupboard, revealing her clothes neatly folded on a shelf. "There's a towel, toothpaste, brush, and some soap. I make sure there's extra; there's always some idiot that forgets to bring their own. I'll wait outside for you." Drawing the curtain across the opening, he left.

Frances swung her legs over the side of the bunk, desperately hoping they would bear her weight and grateful for it when they did. Her thinking was much clearer, too, and questions flooded her brain. How long had she been in the water? Days, she thought. But how long here? Surely not that long. She dressed herself, noting her surroundings. There were a few books on a shelf: *Les Misérables*, *War and Peace* and *The Complete Works of Shakespeare*, all translated into German, along with several books on German law. What an odd collection.

She thought back to what Mueller had said minutes ago, that he would take her to port after their patrol. That might mean a matter of hours or days for all she knew. A patrol round the coastal waters would probably be a couple of days or so. So, she could be on dry land in a few hours. But then what? She would rather die than be returned to Otto.

Once dressed, she took a couple of unsteady steps and drew back the green curtain. Mueller was talking to a handsome, dark-haired young man seated at a wireless and wearing headphones. She noted he also had the start of a beard.

"Ah, Heinemann," Mueller said, "this is our passenger, Frau Meyer."

Heinemann gave her a huge smile, which she determined not to return. To keep from it, she looked around at the narrow passageway where she found herself. It was tiny, little more than a metre wide. To her right, there was a hatch leading into what appeared to be a larger compartment or room. Men were seated or standing amongst dials, wheels, pipes—and sausages. Sausages! The place was hung with all types of German sausage.

"That's the control room," Mueller said. "The heart of my old lady. We're going this way, though." He gestured left.

"Kapitanleutnant Mueller, can you tell me where my case is?"

He turned and shook his head. "Case, Froggy?"

"My black violin case. It was in the life raft with me."

"Then I'm afraid it's still there."

"But it can't be! It's my Stradivarius. Please don't tell me you left it behind."

Mueller gave a shrug. "Well, it's not here."

Frances felt sick. The heat of oncoming anger and disbelief knotted her brow. "You left my bloody Stradivarius. Have you any idea what an instrument like that is worth?"

"No, Froggy, I haven't a clue," said Mueller, "but if I had, I would have made sure we saved the violin and left you on the rowing boat. Come on."

He left her, and she had no choice but to follow him, ducking through a hatch into a smaller compartment where a couple of men were seated. She struggled to navigate the hatches, mind reeling with the shock of learning that they had left her violin to the mercy of the sea.

"The officer's wardroom," Mueller explained.

She recognised the fair head of Leutnant Werner seated at a table.

Werner jumped to his feet and gave a little bow, struggling to speak in broken French. "Frau Meyer, welcome aboard. This is our Second Officer, Leutnant Schumacher." Werner's nod indicated a younger man, also sitting at the table, who appeared engrossed in some reading material.

"She's fluent in German!" Mueller called back across his shoulder as Frances followed him into the next compartment that was full of bunk beds and men eating and drinking. She and Mueller had to continually dodge hammocks pulled tight into the ceiling or flat against any conceivable wall space. Every nook and cranny bulged with tinned supplies and fresh produce. Young men grinned foolishly at her as they passed.

"Petty Officers," Mueller muttered. Evidently, he felt the need to give her some kind of explanation, a running commentary, as she hurried to keep up with him. At last, he paused before a door, thrusting it open to reveal a small foul-smelling cubicle housing a lavatory, small washbasin, and mirror, and announced, "Here you go."

Frances took a step back. "I can't use that!"

"It's the only one."

Frances glared at him. Was the bastard laughing at her?

"One between us all, and there are almost fifty of us," continued Mueller. "We have another, but that's full of provisions, you see."

"That's disgusting," said Frances, but ultimately, need overcame her repulsion, and she stepped into the cubicle, slamming the door behind her.

Mueller was in a dilemma as to what she found so disgusting. Was it the state of the head, or that food was stored in the second one? He rapped on the cubicle door. "By the way, take note of the flushing system, Froggy. I'd hate you to jettison yourself."

Not expecting a reply, he returned to the wardroom for breakfast. He always made a point of keeping the U-boat submerged for a couple of hours at this time, giving his men a chance to relax and enjoy what his grandmother had always insisted was the most important meal of the day. The respite also allowed the U-boat to be trimmed at the same time.

Frances could hear male whisperings and low laughter outside the cubicle and suspected she was the butt of their joking. She finished her ablutions and washed her hands, wondering where the hell she was. On some sort of supply ship, perhaps? She eyed her reflection in the mirror. As much as she might wish to hide herself in here, given the circumstances, the filth, and the stench, she couldn't take it, and summoning her courage, she opened the cubicle door. A group of young men scarcely out of boyhood, children almost, had gathered outside. She scowled at them, and, head held high, made her way quickly past them, bristling at the sound when a low whistle followed her.

"Coffee, food?" asked Mueller as she entered the wardroom.

While her mouth watered at both suggestions, Frances shot him a withering look. "I make a point of not eating with swine, Kapitanleutnant."

"Ouch!" said a dark man with curly hair across the table from Mueller. Werner introduced him as Klaus Zeitler, the Chief.

"Well, you're stuck in the pigsty with us, Froggy, my girl," said Mueller, relishing his own joke. "So, you might as well feed at the trough, I'd say."

"I'm not interested in what you'd say, Kapitan, and just for the record, I'm not your girl." Frances felt under scrutiny from the other men present. There were four in all; she felt their amusement, and it galled her.

"Well, thank heaven for that. Look," continued Mueller, "let's try to at least be polite, shall we, Froggy? Like it or not, you are stuck here, and things can get unpleasant enough."

"Just how long am I stuck with you? Can you at least tell me that?"

"Maybe six weeks, possibly longer," Werner said, smiling sympathetically.

She jerked her glance to his. "You're joking!" she exclaimed but knew from his sombre expression he was not. She felt the prick of tears, and a burning need to retreat to the seclusion of the bunk and her dreams of the past before this stupid war.

Werner, seeming to recognise her hopelessness, made room for her on the bench.

Swallowing, trying to compose herself, she sat next to him. "What about clothes and washing and things?" she asked.

The men around the table exchanged uncomfortable glances, leaving it to Mueller to answer. "I'm afraid you're stuck with the clothes you're wearing, Froggy, as are the rest of us. We must remain permanently ready to take action, so we stay dressed day and night. Maybe on a calm day we risk a change of underpants, but that's it."

"You're serious."

He smirked a bit, as if he were enjoying her discomfort. She wanted to slap him. "Gets quite unpleasant, I'm afraid," he continued. "We have to resort to deodorant."

"You're joking now, aren't you?" She looked to Werner for confirmation that they were not just having a laugh at her expense. He ruefully shook his head whilst Mueller carried on.

"By the way, for the record, Froggy, it wasn't us who sunk you."

"Well, someone else can claim the credit for that then!" she snapped.

Mueller rubbed his beard. "There is no credit to claim for that, Frau Meyer. We don't believe in making war on civilians. I'm sorry about what happened, sorry about your husband, and sorry about the way things are for you now."

"Sorry even though my husband was a Jew, Kapitanleutnant? I'm sure your Führer wouldn't like to hear you say that." Frances got up and left, too quickly for Mueller or any of the other men to reply. Returning to Mueller's quarters, she threw herself onto the bunk, fighting the continued threat of tears. She'd be damned if she would let them flow and damned if she'd be polite. So, what if this wasn't the boat that had sunk the *Etoile*? That hardly venerated this lot. They were just as guilty. Bloody pirates, that's what they were. Oh, they might pretend to be pleasant, but she could see through all that. Like all Nazis, like Otto, they were rotten to the core.

Chapter 7

Her thoughts flashed back to Otto. Damn Otto! Otto took so long getting Steven out of Drancy that she wondered if he was dragging out the procedure on purpose in the hope of further weakening him. He spent hours at the apartment with her, reassuring her. He sat too close. He took her hand—his attention, the nearness of him—she didn't like it. But what could she do other than trust him? Steven had said Otto wasn't trustworthy, that he was as anti-Semitic as any member of the Nazi Party. Frances knew Otto was a personal friend of the charming—and she had to admit after meeting the man—dashing Theo Dannecker, who had come to Paris to oversee what Otto termed the Jewish question. She'd tried pushing him for more information on that, but he had given her no more, other than saying, "Trust me, Frances, everything will be fine." Prior to his arrest, though, Steven had said Dannecker was in Paris only to round up Jews and deport them, that he was operating under orders from Adolf Eichmann. She didn't want to believe Otto would lie to her. She had no proof with which to confront him, and he was her only hope of having Steven home with her again.

When it finally happened, when Otto brought Steven home, it horrified her. His appearance was as grey as ash. He'd lost weight. His hands trembled, and he had a terrible cough that wracked his whole body. Not long after his release, he spat blood, and when he finally consented to seeing a doctor, they diagnosed him with tuberculosis. If the illness weakened his body, the rumour going around—that a thousand or so people with whom he'd been interned at Drancy—had been taken by rail on March 27 to some place called Auschwitz had an even worse effect. The deportation was for re-education purposes, it was said.

She questioned Otto later, while Steven was resting, hoping that he could give her some sort of reassurance. "I don't understand what's going on, Otto. What's the damn purpose of these roundups? Many of these people are academics, and yet you're telling us they have taken these people away for re-education. It makes no sense at all."

Otto took her by the arm and led her into the lounge, out of Steven's hearing.

"Sometimes, Frances, it's best to keep quiet and not ask questions. You don't want to know the details."

"But I do," she argued.

"You want to keep Steven safe, don't you?"

"Yes, of course."

"Then keep him off the streets and out of the public eye," Otto advised.

It wasn't hard advice to follow. Steven was too weak to go anywhere, and there were few invitations circulating in any case. They stayed in except for Frances's treks to the grocery where food was scarce, or to visit her Aunt Edie. It was Edie who told her of the new order. It was May 30, the day after the order was issued. Frances was seated on the sofa in Edie's living room, having tea.

"How's Steven?" asked Edie, bringing in the tray and setting it down on a low table.

Frances's face said it all. She shrugged and said, "No better. Oh, sometimes he has days that are not quite as bad as others, when the cough is not so bad, but overall..." She shook her head. "He's using his time to write music. He's such a talent, you know."

Edie sat beside her on the sofa and took her niece's hand and gave it a pat. "I do know, of course, I do. Jacques asks after him continually; he is anxious about him. About you both, Frances. You know what they are doing now, don't you?" Edie asked, pouring the tea.

"No, what are you talking about? Who?" Frances took the cup and saucer her aunt handed her.

"You didn't hear? Everyone of Jewish ancestry is to wear a yellow star, embroidered 'Juif,' on their clothing. I've heard they're even making them trade their textile coupons in exchange for the stars."

"Those pigs! God, Edie, when will it all end?" Frances set her cup down hard enough that tea sloshed over into the saucer.

In the days to come, it amazed her at how most of the Jewish population seemed to accept it. When she questioned Steven about their compliance, he shrugged.

"As far as they know, they've done no wrong, so they don't feel there's anything to be afraid of. You've seen the newspapers. They fully approve."

She nodded. Only recently, the 'Paris Midi' had written, "The abundance of Jews on the streets of Paris has opened the eyes of the most blind."

"I pity them—all of them," Steven said, and his air of irony was tinged with bitterness. Frances couldn't blame him. When she thought it couldn't possibly get worse, it did.

On a further visit to her aunt, in mid-July, after they had forbidden all Jews to enter public places, Frances raised her latest fears.

"People are going to use it against each other, Edie; you can see it coming, can't you? Old petty hatreds are going to raise their ugly heads, and neighbours are going to turn on one another."

"I don't understand why they are letting it happen, why there is no protest. What does Steven say?" asked Edie.

"Oh, that they'll comply because, as far as they are aware, they haven't done anything wrong. Where the hell is their fight, Edie, their pride, their bloody backbone?"

"Maybe, my sweet, they are just very frightened."

* * *

Steven was showing her the manuscript that he'd written for her to play when Otto came to the house one evening at the end of July. He refused Frances's offer to have a drink and also Steven's invitation to sit. Something in his demeanour made Frances's heart pound.

"You know Eichmann's in Paris."

Frances winced inwardly at the mention of the name that was becoming synonymous with evil, with ruthlessness. She glanced at Steven and saw that while he was pale, his jaw was rigid.

Keeping Otto's gaze, he said, "Yes, rumour has it he's in discussions with your friend"—Steven's emphasis on the word friend was bitter— "Dannecker, and the aim of their talks is to lie out the means of transporting all the French Jews as soon as possible for re-education." There was no mistaking Steven's derision, his utter contempt.

"Yes, well..." Otto looked pointedly at Frances. It was as if they were alone in the room. "I can't promise constant protection in the current state of play. It looks as though Dannecker may well be leaving us. He is to be replaced by his deputy, Heinz Rothke. He's not long been in Paris, so he's still a bit of an unknown. I wanted you to know. I'm concerned for you." His gaze burned into hers. Because of him, his gaze seemed to say. Being married to a Jew in these times—it could become complicated.

Later, after Otto left, Steven sat her down beside him, and taking her hands in his, he said as little as he trusted Otto; he agreed with him. "There could well be trouble ahead for you because of me. I've felt it for a while, that it would be wise for us to make some sort of break for your own safety."

"No, Steven, surely it's not so serious. Otto is only making more of it, possibly because he thinks somehow he can scare me into leaving you. Is that so crazy?" She was asking truly; she didn't know. It dismayed her when Steven shook his head.

He said, "No, not at all. It's obvious the man has feelings for you, which tells me the situation is even more precarious, you see? If he can't protect a woman for whom he has such deep affection—ah!" Steven broke off. He ran his hands roughly over his hair. Turning back to her, locking her gaze, he said, "You do know, Frances, that I love you, don't you? That I've always loved you." He stood up and paced the room, continuing. "Not as I should have, perhaps. I know that, but I've always had your best interests at heart, even though I think I made some wrong decisions." He paused.

"What wrong decisions? When Steven? I've never known—"

He went on as if she hadn't spoken. "Sometimes, Frances, I think I was cruel in marrying you—to shackle you to an older man, to not give you the chance to be young."

"But I've never thought, or felt, any such thing," she protested.

"Maybe not, my dear," he resumed, sitting beside her, and taking her hand, he brought it to his mouth, brushing a kiss across her knuckles. "I'm not judging you, rather myself," he told her with a rueful smile. "I'm trying to explain my feelings. I never have, have I?"

Setting her hand aside, he ran his hands down his thighs to his knees and sighed, looking to the floor. "I've always envied you your talent, you know. I wanted to keep it for myself. I didn't want it over-used and spoiled, didn't want you spoiled, and even though at times it infuriates me, you're still the child that you were. Let us be honest, Frances, it is time for honesty now. I think I have played the part of a father rather than a husband." He looked at her.

"But I love you, Steven," she answered automatically, even truthfully, and yet somehow she saw in the moment that Steven was right. They had rarely shared the love of a man and woman, and the realisation shocked her.

Patting her arm, he said, "I don't doubt it. Nevertheless, Otto has made me see—I must leave you."

"Leave me?" She jumped up. "But you can't. I need you here!" She sounded like a child, even to her own ears. And yet, how could he go if he loved her? How could he just abandon her?

"I don't want you around if I'm arrested again."

"They won't—"

"You heard Otto. They are rounding up Jews, and there's a new man in charge—I'm moving into Jacques' house, so you'll know where to find me. It's not far for you to come."

"You've been planning this for some time, haven't you?" She stared at him accusingly, and he recognised the mounting anger in her face, in her eyes.

He continued. "You must go back into the city to live with your Aunt Edie in her apartment. You'll be better off and safer there without me. We'll lease our place here for the time being."

"What of my career? Our plans?" She sat again beside him, looking at the floor, fighting tears.

His arm came around her shoulders. He kissed her temple. "Nothing lasts forever, sweetheart. Not even war."

Though she tried over the next several days, nothing she said, no argument she put forth, changed Steven's mind. Worn down, finally, she agreed. Boxes were packed and her belongings moved. They stood in the hallway of the house they'd shared since they'd married. He looked at her with tenderness and tucked a tendril of her hair behind her ear.

"I'll see you every day," she told him. "It will be all right. Possibly, there is still something Otto can do, some dispensation—"

"Like what? To make me an honorary Aryan, you mean. No, Frances, leave me a little dignity, please."

Otto thought Steven had made a sensible decision, and Frances accepted his reassurance. He loaned Steven his car and driver to help transport him and his possessions to Jacques' home. He saw to it they were given extra rations. She began to feel foolish for having assumed Otto acted out of anything but kindness. Hadn't they been friends, all three of them?

When Otto adamantly objected to her decision to give up the house in Neuilly for rental and move back in with Aunt Edie, Frances dismissed a fresh outbreak of unease at his motive—that with Steven gone, had she chosen to stay in the house, she would have been alone. Otto could have taken advantage, she thought. Then it didn't matter. The point was moot. Frances pushed away her unease.

Watching Otto's driver assist Steven into the front seat, she decided they'd both been wrong about him. Otto was the soul of kindness. How often had he come to their aid throughout this ordeal? The car pulled away from the curb, and she waved, thinking when she saw Steven again, she would remind him that Otto was married with children. Remembering that was a comfort it would be for Steven too. So, Steven had moved out. She had moved in with Edie. Then Otto had made his move.

Chapter 8

If only she had heeded Steven's and Jacques' warnings, but she'd been bored, longing to go out. Otto had insisted she should join him. *Otto, charming, respectable Otto, her friend Otto.*

* * *

The invitation to play at the party came at the end of August. Otto had arranged for her to be included by Madame Abetz, the hostess. The gala, the highlight of a dismal social season, was being held at the Château de Chantilly about thirty kilometres out of Paris. The French government had put it at the disposal of Madame and Monsieur Abetz. Frances was to play and stay over the weekend with all the other guests, a glittering cast of dignitaries and celebrities. Nearly in the next moment after receiving the invitation, she went to her closet, and pulling out a dusky pink silk evening dress, she held it to her body, twirling before her image in the Cheval mirror. A party in Chantilly! The prospect thrilled her. Other than to perform, she had not attended a single social occasion since Steven had become ill.

Through the end of the hot summer, she made visits to Jacques Cuvier's, spending time with Steven, caring for him, at least once a day, every day growing more frightened as his illness progressed. He had never been a big man, and he'd become wasted very quickly; his sunken eyes had lost their spark of life. She knew, they all knew—Edie and Jacques, even Otto knew—but no one said it: that Steven was dying. What he needed was good medical attention, but getting good medical attention for the likes of him was difficult. He had refused her every offer to ask Otto for help, saying he wanted nothing further from the man other than that Otto take care of her safety.

"Listen, my love," he had said only yesterday, "I'm ready to go as long as I know you will be looked after. Now, please, don't waste too many tears on me. You have so many good years ahead of you. This war will be over by the New Year."

Frances thought that was an overly optimistic view. She perched now on the end of her bed, absently smoothing the silk of the dress. She had continued to play for audiences when invited, but only sporadically. The Paris social scene was almost silent nowadays since she and Steven had moved from Neuilly. People were frightened since the Vel d'Hiv roundup back in July when 15,000 Jewish men, women, and children were taken from the city to the Velodrome sports arena. And according to the rumours that continued to persist, there had not been a single German in evidence!

"It's all contrived," Aunt Edie had said, with more than a little offence. "The Germans put the French police up to it to make it appear as if France's own countrymen were to blame."

She was so worried. Worried sick that they would come once again for Steven, but Otto, dearest Otto, had made certain that Steven's name was not one of the 27,000 names that had reportedly been on the original list. Despite Otto's reassurances, she was still frightened.

She thought back to those horrifying reports of the atrocities that had come out of the Velodrome. Children were torn, screaming, from their parents. Sanitation had been non-existent. People had died for lack of food and water. Many had taken their own lives. The tragedy, the terrible loss—it was all so unbelievable. She closed her eyes against the hot sting of tears. She'd wept then too, wondering what would become of them all—Steven, herself, Aunt Edie—any of them? But what use was it, sitting, weeping and afraid? Rising, she returned to her closet, and flinging open the door, she brought out many evening gowns, laying them across her bed, trying to decide which to wear. This afternoon, when she visited Steven, she would tell him of the party. He would be happy for her. Twirling before the mirror again, this time holding an oyster-coloured gown, she thought he would agree with her that she needed— possibly even deserved—a break.

But that wasn't his reaction at all. He asked her not to go.

"But why not, Steven?" She perched on the ottoman, next to his slippered feet. "It will do me good." Steven had asked her not to go.

Jacques was concerned too—she knew all that, but she'd made her mind up.

"But my friends will be there," she argued.

"I don't disagree, my dear, and if the circumstances were different, I'd encourage you to get out, but surely you realise the precariousness of these relationships. After all that's happened—the Velodrome—" He broke off.

But I'm not Jewish. Frances wanted to say it. She bit her lip instead.

"You may not be Jewish," Jacques said, entering the room with a tray laden with the makings of tea, "but you are married to one who is." He seemed to have read Frances's mind.

"One day, my dear," Jacques said, handing her an ersatz coffee, "you may be called to account for those friendships you claim. Just take care, should you choose to attend."

She hardened her jaw, refusing to look at either man, thinking how foolish they were, more like a pair of old mother hens. They worried too much. Otto would watch out for her. Even Steven trusted him to do that much.

"We are concerned for you, that's all," Steven said.

Red rag to a bull, she thought, sipping her drink. The two should have known that once they suggested she shouldn't do a thing, she was duty bound to prove them wrong. It wouldn't be until later that she would look back and think all she proved by acting with such wilful stubbornness was her own stupidity, her own blind selfishness. And she hadn't had an inkling of the consequences of her actions, the nightmare that was only deepening.

* * *

Arriving at the party in Chantilly, she lost herself in the gaiety. Everyone did. Once inside the chateau gates, surrounded by all the wonderful opulence, no one thought of the war. The uniformed men were not enemy soldiers but military gentlemen, some handsome and charming, all so very self-assured. They and the beautifully gowned women, including herself in her dusky pink silk, were there to enjoy themselves, and enjoy themselves they did.

She performed an array of classical pieces as soloist with an ensemble. She had wanted to play the piece that Steven had composed for her, but he had refused to let her, saying it was just for her. Later, she dined, danced, talked, and drank champagne—though only a little. She laughed more than she had in weeks, enjoying the company of young men.

Did she flirt? Well, a bit. It hadn't meant anything.

It was closing in on one a.m., and she was pleasantly tired. The party had been a great success. Madame Abetz was pleased with the way it had gone. She couldn't wait to tell Edie, Steven, and Jacques all about it. They would be glad, after all, that she'd come, she thought, flopping onto the bed. She admired her surroundings. Even though she had been given one of the smaller rooms, it was nonetheless beautifully furnished. Silk brocade drapes puddled the floor of the long, many-paned window. A matching canopy arched above the graceful four-poster bed, and the oak floor was laid with several silk Persian rugs. The walls were papered in a quietly understated floral pattern. Sitting up, she slipped off her heels, letting go with a grateful sigh as she pushed her stockinged feet into the thick pile of the carpet.

A soft knock came, startling her from her reverie. *Who on earth could be at her door at this hour?* She wondered. Still, as she crossed the room, she had no sense of threat, no portent of the calamity that lay in wait, one she would realise later she had unleashed herself. She had even less concern when, at her request, to know who was there, Otto announced himself.

"What is it?" she asked, without opening the door, so perhaps she'd had some prescience after all. If only she'd held to it, kept the door between them closed. Instead, she asked, "What's wrong, Otto?"

"I need to talk to you, Frances," he answered in a voice thick and slurred with all he'd had to drink. "Can I come in? Please?"

He sounded so pathetic. She opened the door, and when he stumbled, crossing the threshold, and grabbed her, crushing her to him, she still didn't understand his motive. It was only when he kicked the door closed and pushed his face, red with drink, against her neck, when she felt the wetness of his mouth there, that her heart paused.

"Otto! Otto, what are you doing?" She squirmed hard, but his embrace only tightened.

"Oh, Frances, at last! My darling! Tell me, tell me you feel the same way as I do! Oh, it shouldn't have taken us all this time, all this wasted time. Frances—"

"Let go, Otto! What has got into you?" She got her hands against his chest. She felt no actual fear. Foolishly, she believed she was the one in control, a belief that was confirmed when he took a step back, immediately releasing her. She thought he had recovered himself, his good sense. "You've had a great deal to drink—" she began, straightening her gown, her hair.

He regarded her through widened eyes, as if her response surprised him. "But, Frances, it's time. You must feel it—that we're meant to be together. Now. Here." He gestured broadly with his arm, taking in the room. "This place. It's perfect."

"Perfect for what, Otto?" she asked, although she knew, and it dismayed her. He was drunker than she thought. Sober, he'd never have—but intuition told her otherwise, didn't it?

She kept his gaze. "If what's on your mind is what I think it is, then go now, and we'll say no more about it."

He laughed. "You don't mean that, Frances. I know you don't."

"Don't be silly, Otto. We're both married, for goodness' sake. You've had too much to drink, that's all. Tomorrow I'll be able to tease you about all of this." She went to the door. "Go now, please."

"Nothing!" Behind her, his voice broke on a stifled sob that caught in his throat.

Frances turned to look at him in some astonishment.

"All these years, feeling this way about you, and it's meant nothing to you."

"Oh, Otto, I'm sorry. I had no idea, truly I didn't. I have always thought of you as a friend. Nothing more. If I had known of your feelings—" Again, the lie.

"But you must have known." His eyes glittered with accusation, and something else. Was it malice? It was as if he could see through her.

Frances crossed her arms, blood cooling in her veins.

He pointed a finger at her. "You should have known. It was always you. But you set yourself on a pedestal, didn't you, in those early days as a student? You were perfect and untouchable. Why do you think I asked you to help me woo all those pathetic girls? If I were near you, then there was always a chance that you would see me as someone other than good, old, dependable Otto. And Meyer was there to keep other men at bay. He knew my feelings for you. He always knew."

"No, Otto, you're wrong," she said, although she knew he wasn't. After all, it had been Steven who first pointed it out—that Otto was in love with her. She dropped her gaze and spoke to her stockinged feet. "Steven will be as surprised as I am by all of this."

"Then he's as unfeeling as you." Otto regarded her and the moment lingered. Frances's pulse tapped lightly in her ears, every nerve ending on alert with the sense he might once again come at her. Instead, he clicked his heels together in salute, and going to the door, he rested his hand on the doorknob as if to steady himself. A moment later, after stepping into the hallway, he drew a deep breath and turned back to her. "My mistake, Frau Meyer, and I am sorry for it." He then clicked his heels together a second time and walked away.

She left early the next morning, making excuses to her hostess to the effect that Steven's illness was the cause for cutting short the visit. She didn't see Otto before she left, though she sent him a note advising him of her intention to leave and apologising for her apparent lack of feeling. He sent back a curt note, putting his driver at her disposal.

She didn't tell Steven about Otto's overtures, his protestations of love. Why go into it—the actions of a drunken man? For that was all it had amounted to. Otto had been drunk; much more drunk than even he was aware. She imagined his regret, and in the following days, the memory receded from her mind. Compared to Steven's illness, the incident seemed unimportant.

Chapter 9

October 25, 1942

She received two visitors that day. First Hengst, the medic, who she learnt also doubled as the radio operator, brought her another towel, a flannel, and some wound pads.

"I thought you may need something at some point, Frau Meyer, since you'll be here for the long haul, I thought possibly..." he trailed off, reddening slightly.

Thanking him for his thoughtfulness, she realised she hadn't had a show for some time, due to all the stress, she thought. It was impossible for her to be pregnant; she was certain of that.

"Do keep as clean as you can, Frau Meyer." She glanced at Hengst. "Not saying you wouldn't, of course, but it gets really damp and warm in here. It can be a regular breeding ground for all sorts of germs, and while there's plenty of water to wash in, I'm afraid it is sea water."

She thanked him and made herself smile, but her thought as he left, pulling the curtain carefully across the opening as he did so, was bitter. What he'd advised meant she would have to stay even longer in their damned toilet or bloody head, as they called it.

"Frau Meyer?"

Looking at the curtain, she spotted the toes of another pair of boots.

"Frau Meyer, may I come in, please?"

The voice was one she hadn't heard before and sounded youthful. "Come in, yes," she replied.

The curtains parted, revealing a fair youth, juggling a mug of coffee with a plate of bread and cheese. "Ordinary Seaman, Simon," he said by way of introduction.

"My God, you're just a child," Frances said, noting his smooth brow and cheeks, his beardless jaw.

He stiffened, manfully. "I'm eighteen!" he informed her, lowering his voice by almost an octave.

She couldn't hide her smile. "I don't believe you."

He coloured under her gaze and averted his eyes, clearly hurt by her disbelief. "Well, I nearly am," he admitted. He bobbed his head, showing the tray. "The old man told me to bring you some coffee and food, if you're up to it."

"Thank you, Simon. Leave it there, would you?" She pointed at the desk. "Who's the old man?"

"Kapitanleutnant Mueller." He grinned briefly. "Look, I'd down the coffee quickly if I were you. We'll be surfacing in a bit."

"Surfacing?"

"Going up top." Simon jerked a thumb toward the ceiling. "It's not too choppy up there, but you might find it easier to drink down here until you're used to the movement."

"Exactly where is 'up there'?"

"Oh, somewhere in the North Atlantic. We are making for our grid position wherever that may be. That's as much as I know." He saw she was still confused. "We're a U-boat—a submarine."

So that was it, she thought, and smiled. "That explains a great deal, Simon. Thank you."

"I'll be back later, Frau Meyer. If you need anything, just say. The old man told me to see to it." Simon hovered, looking expectant.

From his expression, she had the feeling he would do his best to accommodate her regardless of his old man. It could be useful, she decided, to nurture this boy's friendship. Giving him one of her most charming smiles, she thanked him again. "You are most kind," she said.

A blush peeped over the top of his vest and quickly consumed his entire face. He nodded shortly and left, drawing the curtain behind him.

Frances went to the desk, and retrieving the mug of coffee, she drank, savouring the taste. It was the real thing, rarely to be had these days. The rye bread and cheese were good too, though she ate little, anxiety having eroded her appetite. She still had little idea of how long it was since they had picked her up. How long since Steven and Jacques had... she couldn't bear to even think the words. And Edie? Please God, let her have got back to Paris safely. The more she thought, the more consumed with guilt she became. She'd courted Otto's attention at that damn party in Chantilly, and not just his either, she thought.

They'd asked her not to go, Steven, Jacques, and Edie, but like a spoilt child she told herself and them she deserved some fun in such dark times. She'd thought herself so clever, mixing with what was left of Parisian society and all those uniformed men that night, and because of her so-called cleverness, the people she loved had paid the ultimate price. If she had not got into that situation with Otto, then they would not have rushed things and left that night for Fecamp. They would have arrived at a different time on a different day, and maybe there would have been no E-boat, and Steven and Jacques would have made it safely to England. She hated herself.

She had become morose and didn't know what to do with herself. Now used to the tiny space of Mueller's quarters, it felt smaller than ever. She felt awake for the first time in however many days though. Her eyes scanned the cabin—not a thing out of place, everything in order, even his bloody bookshelf, everything arranged in size. She walked over to it, taking in the books again, and removed *Les Misérables* from the shelf. How fitting a title was that? She thought. At least she hadn't read it. Out of pure peevishness, she then mixed the rest of the shelf up, laying some books flat and some on top of others, mixing up the sizes, gaining a childish satisfaction from it. Then she settled herself on the bunk and read. '*An hour before sunset, on the evening of a day in the beginning of October, 1815...*'

* * *

October 26, 1942

She woke after a fitful sleep, unsure of how much time had passed. The pitching of the boat told her they had certainly surfaced. Shifting only her gaze, she saw Mueller at his desk. The tray Simon had brought the evening before was gone, and the Kapitanleutnant was scratching away in some sort of book. His war diary? Beyond him, Heinemann was visible through the open curtain, still seated, still wearing his headphones. Frances wondered if he slept in them.

It was warm in the cabin. She felt sweaty and dirty, and tossing aside the blanket, she set her feet on the floor. Her stomach rolled. "Just what are you writing in your damn book about me, Kapitanleutnant?" She shoved her hair off her face, suddenly irritable, angry even.

Mueller didn't even give her the pleasure of looking up from his writing; he just carried on scratching away. "Now why would you think I am writing about you at all, Froggy? You're hardly of any importance to our war effort now, are you?"

"Pig!"

"Hmm, carry on then, swine will be the next insult, I think. Well, I'm a pure-bred German swine and not some scratty little, half-bred mongrel." He sat back in his chair and looked at her, brows raised.

She looked back at him through narrowed eyes. "My God, you're hateful!"

"Look, let's just agree that we don't like each other, shall we? I really haven't got time for your temper tantrums, Froggy. I'm busy." He gestured towards the copy of Les Misérables lying on the side of the bunk. "Just get on with your—sorry—my book." Mueller went back to his writing, seemingly unperturbed, which only added to her fury.

She hurled the copy of Les Misérables at his head, aiming too low, but still catching him on the shoulder.

"Jesus!" He laughed, rubbing the spot. "Good shot."

"Not good enough," she snarled, just as Simon appeared.

"Excuse me, sir, I was just checking Frau Meyer—"

"Come on in then, Toddler. But watch out—she's dangerous."

Frances felt the boy's embarrassment and felt her own a little too. The boy must have seen or at least heard her exchange with Mueller.

"Toddler?" she questioned.

"It's my nickname." Simon flushed once again.

"Really? And do you like it?" she asked.

He thought for a moment. "Well, it could be worse, I suppose." His smile now was wry.

"So, what would you prefer I called you?" Frances asked.

"Dieter, Frau Meyer," the boy replied immediately.

"Very well, Dieter, you may call me Frances."

"How very pally!" Mueller rose from his desk. "Ah well, I hate to interrupt, Froggy, but don't forget you have other duties, Dieter dear!"

"Obnoxious man!" Frances spoke to Mueller's retreating back. "My God, he should rot in hell." Hot stare fixed on the curtained opening, she thought how she'd like to send the whole bloody boatload there. Some revenge that would be. Maybe for that, it would be worth going herself.

Simon dragged her from her thoughts. "He's the best."

"Pardon?"

"The old man—he's the best there is. You couldn't wish for a better skipper. They reckon he's got out of some awful scrapes."

"You like him?" she asked in disbelief.

"Wouldn't want to serve with anyone else. He's thoughtful, too. Some blokes have sailed with some right bastards in the past, I can tell you. They'd all agree the old man is the best there is."

Hero worship, she thought. The boy was as smitten with his Kapitan as he was with her. She turned to him. "How long have I been on board, Dieter? Sit down, why don't you?"

"Four days, Frau—I mean Frances." Dieter sat down in the desk chair Mueller had vacated moments ago.

Four days, she mused. That meant Steven and Jacques had been dead for over a week then. "My husband was killed on the same boat, the *Etoile*. I managed to escape. Did you know that Dieter? I also lost my very good friend, Jacques."

"I think I heard it mentioned," he mumbled.

They sat for a while in silence. Simon broke it. "Why were you at sea, anyway?"

Frances shot him a look. "Have you been asked to question me?"

"No," Simon answered, clearly hurt. "I... I wouldn't do that without telling you. I just wanted to know," he said defensively. "You don't have to tell me anything."

Immediately contrite, she said, "Oh, I'm sorry, Dieter. Look, suffice it to say for now that I had to get out of France. My husband's life depended on it. Maybe mine, too." She crossed her arms, staring at the floor, speaking to it. "And now he's dead, anyway." She paused and looked up at Dieter. "Maybe I will tell you sometime." What harm could it do? But at that moment, it was still too painful to talk about.

Dieter rose. "Are you hungry? I will get you a mug of soup and some stollen. You must eat to build up your strength."

"Very well, Sir Knight," she said, wishing to lighten the atmosphere. "Though how I shall manage to eat..."

"Do you feel ill, Frau Meyer? The movement of the boat, perhaps? Sometimes it takes a little getting used to."

"No, I'm fine," she lied. "Cast iron guts. What happened to Frances?"

"I should be respectful, Kapitanleutnant said."

Well, what a hypocritical sod Mueller is, she thought when Dieter disappeared. *Froggy indeed.*

The boy returned moments later with a mug of hot soup, more of the rye bread, and an ample slice of stollen. "The skipper will probably take us down later so that we can enjoy dinner."

"Dinner?" queried Frances.

"Food's always good at the start. Things can go off a bit later, mind you."

"You sound like an old sea dog, Dieter. How many voyages have you made?" She spooned soup into her mouth and was surprised to find she relished it.

"This is my second patrol—my first on this boat. But if you get back from one, that makes you an expert!" He smiled and turned to go, but then, as quickly, he turned back. "I heard you play in Leipzig in '39."

"Really?" She set the soup onto the desk. "That was what—over three years ago, right?" He nodded.

"It feels like much longer, a lifetime." Her mind went back to that tour that started so well and ended so badly. Was that the start of the change in her fortune?

"It was one of the most exciting moments of my life," said Dieter, and his enthusiasm disarmed her. "I play a little myself. My fiddle is on board. I wondered—would you like to see it sometime?"

"Oh yes, Dieter, I would like that very much."

He nodded again and smiled, and obviously feeling encouraged, he went on. "Do you know, my parents and I followed you to Berlin, but you took ill or something — and cancelled? I can remember that. We were all so disappointed."

The memory of the occasion, the way she and Steven had been treated, still burned in her head. She averted her gaze. So, that's what they'd said, was it? She had often wondered what excuse they had given for her non-appearance. They wouldn't have wanted people finding out that they'd invited the wife of a Jew into their country, would they? No, that wouldn't have done at all. They could make no mistakes, could they? Damn it, this boy should know the truth. She glanced at Dieter and away, then bringing her gaze back, she said, "You want to know, I will tell you exactly why there was no concert in Berlin. It wasn't sickness that caused the cancellation, or if it was, it was theirs, not mine—the sickness of a whole damn country."

Dieter fed on her face with puppy dog eyes, and she went on telling him of her and Steven's trip to his country. She remembered every despicable detail and spared him none of them. He visibly flinched when she mentioned Steven's Jewish heritage. "Were there no Jews in your town?"

"There were many—a while ago, anyway," he replied. "In fact, when I was small, my best pal was a Jewish boy, but when we all realised what they were really like, my parents forbade me to play with him. Sammy was his name. Do you know I even cried for a while when Mother stopped me from seeing him?"

"Really, Dieter, fancy that!" she said, unable to keep the disappointment from her voice. "And what became of Sammy, do you think?"

Dieter shrugged. "Who can say? I sort of remember families moving out some years back, even before Kristallnacht. The Kristallnacht was a good thing, I think. At least that is what I have been told."

"And do you think it was right of the authorities to force my husband and me out of Germany the way they did?"

Dieter thought for just a little too long, leaving her in no doubt as to his true feelings.

"I think you shouldn't be blamed," he said. "You were young and mesmerised by that evil man."

By "evil man" he meant Steven. The boy had obviously been brainwashed. By himself, Frances was certain he could never have been capable of buying into such lies and filth as they had taught him. "Dieter, what sort of woman do you think I am?" she asked him softly.

He smiled at her adoringly. "I think you are wonderful, Frau, and beautiful," he added, blushing even more.

"And reasonably intelligent, I hope?"

"Of course. To memorise a whole concerto—wow. You must be."

She smiled, disarmed by his sincerity. "Then let me tell you something, Dieter Simon. Steven Meyer was one of the most intelligent, kind, generous, and gentle, men ever to have lived. Not only that, but he was also honest. Honest to all and to himself. How could a man like that be a member of an inferior race? Think about it. Einstein, Mahler, Kafka, Mendelssohn even—why, compared to these men, your blessed Führer is an imbecile."

Dieter recoiled. "I only know what I have been taught," he said in some sort of defence.

"Then learn some more, Dieter. A good student should look further than his tutor." Frances repeated what Steven had told her.

Dieter stood up, looking desperate to leave.

Frances stood too, placing her hands on his shoulders. "You're a good boy, Dieter Simon. I know you are, and it's with young men like you that our future lies. Please don't accept all that they tell you. Think for yourself. Think and remember Sammy; remember Steven for me, too."

Chapter 10

Without a word or so much as a nod, Dieter left, pulling the curtain sharply across the opening, shutting himself from her view. She turned, folding her arm about her torso, pacing a bit, thinking. So, that is how they found out who she was, she thought. Dieter was a fan, or he had been then. Who knew now? He'd been at that concert in Leipzig in '39. Was that when things had started to go wrong?

* * *

The excitement had started one day late in the year of '38. Whilst resting between engagements at the house they had bought in Neuilly Súr Seine, Steven told her they had been contacted on behalf of Richard Strauss, the president of the German Reich Chamber of Music, with the offer of playing with three of Germany's greatest orchestras.

"We won't accept, of course," he said after telling her.

"Why wouldn't we? It's a wonderful opportunity, isn't it?" she replied.

"Frances, it's one we can do without."

"Well, I want to do it. My God, Steven, this is the best offer yet. To play in Dresden, Leipzig, and Berlin with some of the best orchestras in the world."

"Are you so totally blinkered, so wrapped up in yourself?" Steven shouted, shocking her. It was the first time that he had ever raised his voice and spoken to her in that way. "Don't you know what's going on there, for goodness' sake?" he continued. "Just look at the talent that's fled Germany, and I don't mean just we Jews. Academics, intellectuals, cultural leaders, actors, producers, wonderful composers, Paul Hindemith and Kurt Weill, and conductors, Bruno Walter, Otto Klemperer, and many, many more, Frances. These talented people have left a void. That's why they want you, to fill the bloody gap they've left."

She was cross. Cross that he couldn't see what a brilliant opportunity this gave her. He made her cry, and she saw that it clearly worried him, so she fought her corner.

"I want to do it. I want to go. Most of what we read is lies, you know it is. It's called journalism, Steven. They will do and say anything for a story, you know that!"

He shook his head at her with frustration. "Come on, Frances, open your damn eyes. Anti-Semitism is the order of the day, it's happening everywhere, particularly in Germany."

"Rubbish!" She fought back. "It's the communists who need watching. You know it is, you've said so yourself. And anyway, it's my choice, not yours. You are my agent, and I want you to accept."

"And if I refuse to go with you?"

"Then I'll go alone. I mean it. I won't miss this for anything."

Steven caved, and the New Year tour went well. At least, the start did. They both laughed together and wondered if the invitation would have been forthcoming if she had adopted her married name of Meyer as a performer instead of her maiden name of Lamont.

First stop, Dresden, one of the most beautiful cities in the world, it was said. There was little sign of Nazi terror in the streets, and she had to fight with herself to not say *I told you so* to Steven. The German people, it seemed, were just getting on with their lives, but then from the radio in their hotel room there were broadcasts every hour on the hour from the Führer's headquarters. The newspapers were full of news of parades and meetings. They soon found out that Germany was drowning in a sea of Nazi propaganda. There were anti-Jewish slogans everywhere within the city, and she was glad that she had kept quiet.

They were both relieved when the concert with the Dresdner Staatskapelle was over. It was a great success, but they couldn't wait to move the hundred or so kilometres to Leipzig.

Steven told her it would be the same story there, and he was right, it was, but she had played in the amazing Gewandhaus Concert Hall, which a year before would have been only a dream. She took Leipzig by storm.

To Berlin, last stop, home to the great Berlin philharmonic. They checked into the Adlon Hotel in WilhelmStrasse on January 14 at four pm. The service they received on arrival was excellent, and their rooms were first rate, clean and comfortable. Both were looking forward to a good rest before the rehearsal the next morning, and after unpacking, they asked for a light meal to be sent up to their room. She freshened up and left Steven relaxing with a glass of red wine in the lounge room, which overlooked the busy city streets. She was just about to step into the bath when there came a heavy hammering on their door, and a commotion outside, causing her to slip into a wrap and return to the lounge and Steven.

They looked at one another in astonishment, but before either of them could recover enough to speak, the door opened from the outside, admitting two men in overcoats, ugly in their assertiveness. Behind them stood a very flustered hotel manager, who was dismissed by the taller thin man who reminded her of a weasel. They had pushed past Steven as if he were of no account and stood before her, their arrogant faces assessing the state of her undress.

"Fraulein Frances Lamont?" the weasel questioned.

"Yes," she replied.

"Or are you Frau Frances Meyer?" spat the second man. "Which, Frau?"

Steven recovered himself and crossed the room to come to her help. "My wife uses her maiden name when performing," he explained in broken German.

The weasel swatted him aside with a brutality that was needless, automatic, and violent. She heard herself scream as Steven fell and hit the floor. The glass of wine spilled, staining his shirt blood red, causing her to shake uncontrollably for a second or two, seeing a premonition of his future mapped out before her eyes. Then the sudden fear was replaced by anger, and she turned her eyes on them.

"Get out!" she muttered. "How dare you come into these rooms and strike my husband?" Then, in a voice unrecognisable, she shrieked, "Get out!"

The weasel took control again. "It's you and your husband who will get out, Frau Meyer. You'll no longer be required to fulfil the terms of your contract by performing in Berlin."

"There'll be no remuneration since you sought to delude the Chamber of Music by performing under an assumed name," announced the other man.

She felt the heat of anger burning in her face as she slammed the door behind them.

* * *

She felt it now on a U-boat in the Atlantic as she re-lived it again. What fools they had been. No! Wasn't it she who had pushed, she who had been the fool? She had tried to convince Steven that all that they read and heard had been exaggerated. It was not likely she had told him that an entire nation would allow itself to be governed by the rantings of a madman. Steven, though, had known all along how it would be.

Chapter 11

October 29, 1942

The U-boat ploughed her way across the north-western approaches in the last light of day. A rough, mounting wind whipped the water into a flurry of spray against the ever-watchful eyes of the lookouts. On the bridge, Mueller drew the fresh sea air deep into his lungs, enjoying the lashing of the wind and water across his face. The lonely chanting chorus of the diesels broke the silence of the great desert of ocean which was the Atlantic.

"Lone ship on the horizon, sir!" called a lookout.

Mueller, instantly alerted, raised his binoculars, sweeping the horizon with his magnified glance. "Freighter heading towards the north coast of Ireland, I suspect. Can't see any escorts; it's a sitting duck. Keep your eyes open, watch."

He fled the bridge for the control room, missing most of the steps of the ladder in his haste and feeling the landing on his lower back, not for the first time. He needed to quickly set a course and speed that he calculated would bring them into a good attacking position by nightfall, ahead of their target. Their low silhouette made it unlikely that they would be spotted. He decided he would make the surface attack.

He had studied Otto Kretschmer's tactics at length, agreeing with his formula of a close surface attack and 'one torpedo-one ship' technique instead of the safer principles laid down in attack training of firing a fan of fish at periscope depth, usually during the day. A waste of torpedoes— no doubt about it. Precision firing—that was the way forward, making every fish count.

* * *

The British freighter zigzagged its way towards the U-boat, which was lying ready in wait in the darkness. On the bridge, Mueller turned to his First Officer, unable to keep the excitement from his voice. "Christ, look at her; she's big. Where the hell is her escort, do you think?" Werner shook his head. "She's a sitting duck."

"I almost feel guilty for attacking her." Mueller gave his First Officer a smile and, as the *Norseman* got to within 100 metres, he barked his order.

"Fire One, Exec!" A hiss of air. The submarine rocked as the lone torpedo found its depth and began its deadly journey.

* * *

Aboard the British freighter *Norseman*, Finbarr Looney whistled merrily as he prepared vegetables for the next day's meals. Life had been good to him. He had enjoyed his life at sea for the last thirty-five years and tomorrow would see him reach his half-century. He continued whistling, but the tune he whistled increased in melancholy as he thought briefly of the young kids serving in the British forces. Just how many lives would this bleeding war cut short, anyway? Abroad or at home—Jerry was not particular where he made his kill. Optimistic by nature, Finbarr preferred not to dwell upon such things. He was lucky; as part of a convoy or as a loner, *Norseman* had never crossed paths with old Jerry. He had his doubts whether the buggers were out there at all.

Three years on, and Finbarr remained reasonably untouched by the war. He made his voyage as usual. There were girls in ready supply in all the ports, and he had no problem, still, in rising to the occasion. He had no ties. No worries.

Back home, food was a little scarcer than he would have liked, but the booze and the tarts more than made up for it. He'd married once, years ago, but while he was away, she'd sodded off with another bloke. Ah well, such was life! He bore her no ill will, he bore no one ill will. Life was too short, Ma had always said.

Finbarr Looney didn't realise just how brief life was, and maybe it was for the best that he didn't see the grey spectre speeding its way under the waves, right on target, to hit *Norseman* amidships. Right beneath Finbarr Looney.

* * *

Excitement, elation, sorrow, confusion all ploughed through the sea of emotions that was Mueller. The excitement and the adrenaline when an enemy ship came into view pumped through his body, honing his senses, making him the precision part of one of the most awesome weapons so far known to man. So much depended on his skill, upon his judgement. Is that what he found so irresistible then? Is that why the adrenaline never failed him? And his crew? He had enough for them too; they all fed upon it. Each a cog in Hitler's perfect predator, the Kriegsmarine's U-boat.

There was silence on the bridge, and down below, since he had given that last command, 'Fire One.' This was the part Mueller dreaded: the wait. They all waited, counting time away. Over a minute before they'd know if his calculation had been correct, all wondering whether they'd have their first pennant of this patrol, and another few thousand tonnes of shipping to add to their running total.

Mueller lifted the binoculars to his eyes, aware of his shallow breathing and the pulse beating in his neck. About enough time had elapsed, he reckoned—over a minute. He turned his gaze upon the U-boat's latest prey in time to see a quick flash before the dull roar reached his ears, along with a loud cheer from his men. The torpedo had made a direct hit amidships. He leapt down the ladder from the hatch to the control room, eager to find out the name of his latest kill. Heinemann had already picked up a burst of activity on the wireless. Intercepting the name of the ship as *Norseman*, he glanced at a Lloyds register handed to him by his Chief, which gave *Norseman* a tonnage of eight and a half thousand. There was a crack as the ship broke in two, collapsing like a pair of scissors followed by one last bellowing explosion as *Norseman* yelled her fury and sank.

The men on the bridge and below were jubilant. Mueller stood in the wireless room, shoulders slumped, belly hollow with some kind of bleak sorrow, a snare of confusion. It happened more and more lately, that he'd feel this emptiness after a kill. He didn't know what was wrong. The sorrow was becoming a regular, a sorrow that gripped his guts now at this sinking. He'd stay below. It was sad to see a ship in her last throes, to watch men swarming like ants across the decks before leaping like lemmings into a sea of fire. It was sad to witness what, for many men, were their last moments. He now thought more and more of the men. At first, they were just the enemy, and, if they were human beings as well, it had scarcely bothered his conscience. It was kill or be killed. But now he was tiring of it all, and there was confusion as to why the bloody hell he carried on.

Vice Admiral Karl Donitz was more than just a little fond of him. He was one of his best boys and a godson, the son of a very dear comrade from the last war. He had plagued him with offers of a shore job back at Kiel, in the training schools. At first, Mueller hadn't been interested, but now, well, maybe. Perhaps when you started thinking in terms of men instead of tonnage, then it was time.

Out of the corner of his eye, he saw Heinemann in the radio room stiffen. "Propellers approaching, Kapitanleutnant."

Immediately, Mueller was back in the control room as Werner's shout came from the bridge. "Alaaaaaarm! Dive!"

There was barely time to get the U-boat underwater. His fault, he thought, for not being on the bridge. The lookouts were through the hatch. If he'd kept his mind on the business at hand...

Werner was making the hatch fast and leapt from the last few rungs of the ladder into the control room. Several of the crew were already rushing into the fore of the boat, trying to speed the dive. The sound of the approaching destroyer sounded ominously close by. Amongst the jubilant few on the bridge, Werner was telling him that someone had noticed, though almost too late, the destroyer bearing down on them, little over 700 metres away.

"Hold her at fifty metres, full speed, and maintain course, Chief," Mueller ordered.

* * *

Frances was thrown heavily against the metal cupboard as the U-boat submerged herself in the cloak of the Atlantic. She'd seen no one for the past few hours but was aware of the mounting excitement within the boat. First, the excitement, then the whispered voices, and finally the jubilation. Then Mueller's rush to the wireless room and Heinemann's report on the *Norseman*. So, the pirates had done it, had they?

As the boat settled, she found her footing, and plucked up enough courage to peep through and draw back the green curtain. Most of the men were assembling around the control room area. Beyond Heinemann, she could see Mueller, smiling at his crew, who looked on with adoring eyes. His own eyes, though, were cold, she thought. From the kill, she decided. Heartless bastard.

"Sound of propellers coming in fast, sir," she heard Heinemann say.

Frances watched as the men shifted around uneasily. Was it fear she saw on their faces? She gloated inwardly. She was glad if they were afraid. Served them right. She cast a nervous glance around the control room, amazed by the mass of wheels and levers.

"Easy, men," Mueller said. "The debt collector's coming to call."

Some men managed a low chuckle. They seemed to relax; Frances noticed. After all, if the old man wasn't too worried —

"Shush," he whispered, patting the air with his hands, forcing a half smile. He wasn't relaxed, far from it. The dull roar of the propeller was making straight for them, though the absence of the ASDIC was a bonus. Looking over Heinemann's head, he encountered Frances Meyer's gaze, looking at him with her hate-filled wolf's eyes. Christ, he had completely forgotten about her existence over the last few hours.

The propellers ground the water right overhead. The men braced themselves, knowing that the first batch of depth charges was already falling their way. Mueller caught Werner's eye.

"Quick, Exec, make sure the girl's secure."

Werner moved a couple of steps towards Frances, where she stood just inside the control room. "Things are going to get rough," he warned her. "Grab hold of a pipe or dial, just something you can hold on to."

In the circumstances, she thought it wise to heed his warning just as the first batch of depth charges exploded, not as close as expected. The shock waves reached the boat a little after each explosion, causing it to pitch, nothing more.

"He's not sure of our position," said Mueller with a fatherly smile at his crew. His relaxed attitude kept the men calm as again Heinemann reported.

"Propeller noise approaching—fast."

"Shush now, nothing to give the game away. Easy... Easy." Mueller spoke softly to his men as the propellor sound became apparent to all, and the thought that she had nothing at all to lose apart from her miserable life crossed the mind of Frances Meyer. She decided the way to go would be French. Let the bastards hear it, she thought as she sang out *"La Marseillaise."*

"Allons enfants de la patrie, Le jour de gloire est arrivé!" loudly sang out the voice of Frances Meyer.

"Jesus Christ! You bloody madwoman!" cursed Mueller.

Frances delighted, momentarily, as dozens of fear-filled eyes turned upon her and in the look of anger mixed with utter disbelief on the face of Kristian Mueller. Her performance, though, was cut short as he crossed to her and dealt her a right uppercut to the jaw. Werner broke her fall as Mueller gave new instructions.

"Take her down to 100 metres, Chief. Alter course, port, full rudder, and keep your fingers crossed we have a bloody learner up there."

Chapter 12

October 30, 1942

S he surfaced slowly to a throbbing pain in her jaw. Moments passed while she tried to sort out where she was, what had happened, and when the memory returned, she groaned.

"If you ever put my men or my boat in danger again, I'll put a bullet through your head."

Mueller's voice, sounding like ground glass, came to her from somewhere nearby. Shifting a bit, she saw he was lying on a pallet on the floor next to her. She was strapped once again to the bunk, where he'd likely tossed her after punching her. Fury rose, heating her blood.

"You'd be doing me a favour, Kapitan." She spat the words through clenched teeth. "And you'd be doing me another if you'd spare me your company." Ignoring how it hurt to move, she pulled herself up, removing the straps from her body.

Getting to his feet, Mueller pushed his thick hair from his face. "In case you hadn't noticed, space is somewhat limited, but I suppose I could find somewhere for you with the boys up front. What do you say?"

"Why can't you bed down with the men up the front, Kapitanleutnant?" she asked, glaring at him.

"They're two to a bed as it is, and anyway, I need to be near the wireless room."

"Then I suppose I'm stuck with you. Just don't come near me, that's all." She averted her glance, suddenly weary. Her jaw—her entire face—ached from the blow he'd given her. She put her hand to her cheek, felt the swelling there. She fought a threat of tears; damned if she'd let him see her cry.

"Froggy, let me reassure you, you're not my type at all." Mueller paused. Frances felt his gaze, and when he stepped to the bunk's side, she flinched. He spread his hands, palms down, a placating gesture. "Look, I'm sorry for hurting you, but you left me with little alternative, you see. I've never hit a woman before, never had to."

"Well, Kapitanleutnant, you do surprise me, I had you down as a wife beater," Frances replied scornfully.

"I'm sure I would be if you were my girl." He nodded slowly, considering her. "Yes, I think I'd beat you regularly, daily, even."

"Thank goodness I'm not your girl," she told him, and the words came harder than they had to, burdened as they were by her fury and her scorn.

"Amen to that. Well, can't stay here chatting all day."

He rolled up his blanket, stowed it in one of his cupboards, found his cap and set it on his head. In a stride, he was at the cabin doorway. "I'll send Toddler in with some breakfast. It might improve your mood, but understand, Froggy, that I meant what I said about the bullet."

* * *

Dieter came as Mueller promised, setting the tray on the desk, and when he met Frances's gaze, when he registered the injury to her jaw, he brought his eyes to her face, darkened with anguish. "I'm so sorry," he mumbled. "I shouldn't have let him hit you like that. I should have seen it coming, prevented it. He shouldn't have struck you."

Frances half rose, protesting. "No, Dieter—"

"I was frightened," Dieter went on, stricken, as if she hadn't spoken. The glaze of tears shone in his eyes. "That's the first time I've ever been depth charged. I couldn't move. Then when you—" his breath caught on a sob "—when you sang, I wanted him to silence you. I'm sorry. Sorry and ashamed." He wiped his face, pinched the bridge of his nose, fighting for control.

"Don't be ashamed, Dieter. Everyone was frightened." It hurt to speak. She tried a smile, wishing to reassure him, but that hurt, too.

"Not the skipper, not you."

"Well, he is not natural, and speaking for myself, life has no meaning now. My country is defeated, my family is dead, I have no one. I've lost my faith in humanity. That's why I wasn't frightened. But you—you have everything to live for." Rising, she took his hands in hers and squeezed them. "Did things get terrible after—" She indicated her jaw.

"Bad enough, though the old man said they were nowhere near."

"Do you want to talk about it?"

"I'm not sure I should even be here."

"Why ever not?"

"You've confused me, Frau Meyer. You've made me question myself, the way they brought me up. You're so lovely, so marvellously talented, but it is hard for me—knowing you were married to a Jew. It goes against—against—" he faltered to a stop.

A painful silence grew. She glanced at the floor. He was only mouthing the brainwashing given him by his countrymen, his parents. He was little more than a child. She thought about how hate was passed from one generation to the next. She sighed, and finding his gaze, she said, "Let us speak of other things, hmm?" She went on when he didn't answer. "You can't go back into the company of your crewmates looking like that, right? With your eyes all red." She sat on the edge of the bunk, patted the space beside her. "Now tell me how it was for you, your first encounter with the enemy."

He scrubbed his hands down his face and then did as she asked. "Those couple of hours were the longest of my life." He leant forward with his elbows on his knees. After a few moments, he began.

"It was terrifying. One depth charge after another. We barely recovered from one before the next one came. As each one exploded, I thought my heart would leap out of my mouth. I found I was holding my breath, and then as I started breathing again, each breath came so loud I thought the enemy would hear it on the surface. Men not holding onto something stationary or not holding on tight enough were thrown across the control room, here, there, and everywhere, crying out. I don't think anyone got away without an injury of some kind or another. Some took refuge on the decks of their quarters, but that was just as bad. The Chief counted forty-one depth charges in all over those two hours."

"What of your Kapitan?" Frances asked, hoping that he may have sustained a significant injury.

"The old man? He quietly chatted throughout the whole attack. He even cracked a few jokes, though what they were now, I couldn't say.

A couple of explosions were really close, closer than the others, hurting everyone's eardrums. The old man, though, seemed to sense when they were coming—warning us, calming us. I cried aloud on one occasion, and he was there beside me. He rested a hand on my shoulder."

The boy broke down in tears again, and Frances lay a hand on his shoulder, giving it a gentle pat. It seemed to have the desired effect, as Dieter continued. "Do you want to know the worst bit? Dying to go but not being able to use the head for fear of giving away our position. We had to pee in cups or anywhere, probably everywhere. The skipper continually altered course—always a step ahead. Like a chess player, reading the enemy's next move, trying to confuse him, and eventually, we crept away like a thief in the night." She let him sit for a while, quiet. "You wouldn't tell anyone about me blubbering like this, would you?" he asked.

"No, of course not," she said. "It's our little secret."

"Thank you, Frau---Frances. I'd better go. They'll be wondering where I am."

As Dieter left, exhaustion and the pain throbbing through her jaw overcame her. She sank back on Mueller's bunk and tried to sleep but found instead that she couldn't shift the spectre of Steven from her mind.

* * *

Her Aunt Edie raised an eyebrow when she had mentioned their marriage. "Frances, reflect before you rush into things."

"There's nothing to reflect on. I love Steven. I thought you did too," she replied.

"You know I do," Edie said, "but he is so much older than you. I think perhaps you are confusing the love for a father, for the love that a younger man would give you."

She threw back her head and laughed. "You think I don't understand love? Of course, I do. And before you bring it up, I understand Steven's Jewish background, too."

Edie took her in her arms and hugged her. "Things are changing, sweetheart," she said. "Look at the rest of Europe; the Jews are being made to take the blame for all manner of things."

"That's the rest of Europe, isn't it? We will be fine. It won't happen in France. Anyway, we French are only interested in laying the blame at the door of the communists."

She married Steven on her birthday: August 3, 1937. She was just twenty, Steven was more than twice her age, at forty-one.

He loved her; she knew that. But as they settled into married life, she felt that the love he felt was built on an admiration of her talent, combined with a strong spiritual connection. A mutual desire for companionship and a sharing of the emotion that the music had brought to them. The physical side of the union, it seemed, was going to be a rarity, and she thought about all the books and novels that she had read. She was disappointed and wondered at times if the relationship they shared was quite normal. Putting it to the back of her mind, she decided that maybe a relationship of the spiritual kind was more likely to survive the rigours of time, and anyway, all that she had read or heard regarding sex was probably only true in romantic novels.

Her life became one of practice, practice, as for hours he made her play and replay phrases. He told her repeatedly that she needed to feel the emotion of the piece. And then, from nowhere, he felt she was ready and accepted various engagements on her behalf. He also made her a gift of a Stradivarius violin.

* * *

And married life, though not of her dreams, had been good because Steven Meyer, as she had told Dieter Simon, had been the most intelligent, kind, generous and gentle man ever to have lived, which is why she had married him and why she missed him so terribly.

Chapter 13

Tossed like a match on a whirlpool, the U-boat beat her way against waves of molten lead as she became swept up in a great Atlantic storm. The ocean had erupted, causing them alternatively to be lifted on high, riding piggyback on a wave, and then to plunge into a trough which rained down tonnes of water as the gargantuan waves descended.

For the men on watch, life for those four hours had become a hell—only hell was supposed to be hot, wasn't it? Well, they might even be tempted to sell their souls for just a little of its warmth. To them, straining their eyes against the onslaught, it seemed slightly paradoxical to be 'on watch' when the visibility was recorded as zero and you couldn't see a bloody thing.

They were slap in the middle of a vast mountainside of water, belted to the railings of the bridge, which quaked and rattled under each new barrage of wind and water. Facing the huge swell of man-eating waves, knowing that no belt was a guarantee in such conditions. Whole watches had disappeared, swept away like flotsam, not even missed until it was time for others to take their place. Red-eyed, red-faced, skin chafed raw by oilskins which gave them but limited protection against such raging weather. Weather which flooded the entire deck and bludgeoned them to their knees, forcing them to pray to Neptune to lull the waves, or to any other god that may be listening, to rain down, calming oil on to the great heaving vortex of the Atlantic.

Below deck, conditions were scarcely better. Men not on duty were finding it difficult to rest, difficult to live. It was almost impossible to balance on a bunk, which had become a roller coaster, pitching continuously this way and that in every direction. Those who had found their sea legs found their tempers beginning to fray as they became increasingly intolerant of those who hadn't, those crew members who stumbled around wearing permanently green faces and improvised puke tins round their necks. The smell of unwashed bodies mixed with the acid smell of partially digested food that had been thrown up was intolerable.

The upper lid was shut, though not secured so that the control room was continually awash, causing the bilge pumps to work noisily, almost nonstop. The innards of the U-boat had become host to a parasitic mildew. Mildew on bedding, mildew on clothing, mildew on food. Bread and cheese had to be whittled away now before it could be considered edible.

For the first few days of that storm, Frances had been forced, like many others, to keep to her bunk. The feeling of losing one's insides was bad enough, but worse still was the boredom. At least though, she thought, thankful for small mercies, her jaw had finally stopped aching. She helped herself to another one of Mueller's books, but again reading whilst the boat tumbled every which way only added to her nausea. There was one positive: on her trips to the head, there were no leering faces or lewd comments. The men, it seemed, felt as sick as she did. If she bumped into anyone on her visits, they would rush past her, eager to get back to their bunk.

Dieter appeared from time to time, but she had only to look at him to know that he was feeling at least as bad, if not worse, than herself. He'd brought her a couple of his books for her to read too, but mostly, it was simply too arduous a task, and she struggled to even mutter her thanks.

After the first few days, she felt slightly better and looked forward, like the hardened few, to the daily trim, when a meal could be eaten in peace, far beneath the tumult above. As for Mueller, she saw little of him and preferred it that way. He appeared to require hardly any sleep, although she suspected he did bed down somewhere else on occasions, maybe in the wardroom.

Sometimes she would be aware of his breathing or his movements, and she would feign sleep so that she needn't acknowledge his presence. A few times he'd walked in to fill in his War Diary or to talk to a crew member about a misdemeanour or give support or news when someone was worried or missing their home. She had resisted the temptation to even look up from her book. There was just that one occasion which she preferred not to think about, but which kept jumping into her head, and for the life of her, she couldn't understand why.

Returning from the head and almost back in the nook, Mueller had come in the opposite direction. The weather was atrocious, and she congratulated herself on being able to keep her footing. Then the boat had taken a nosedive and rolled, causing her to stumble. He put his arm out and steadied her, grasping her around the shoulders, and she felt his warmth and smelt the scent of his body mixed with oil, damp, and salt. She felt her hackles rise. She hated him near her.

"A bit on the choppy side, Froggy," he remarked.

She twisted in his grasp. "Don't you touch me! Take your hands off me!" She heard the intake of his breath and saw his lips tighten into the hard line that she'd noticed on other occasions, and which signalled his lack of amusement.

"Now, Froggy?" he asked. "You want me to take my hands off you now, right?"

"Yes, of course, now!"

He waited for a few seconds, and then he let her go. The movement of the boat threw her through the curtains and she hit the bunk hard, which threw her off her feet. He stood, staring through the curtain, eyebrows raised, not even having the decency to help her to her feet.

"Pig!" she exploded.

"Well, it seems that I can't win," he said. Then he shrugged and made off for the wardroom, no doubt to laugh with his comrades at her expense. The more she thought about that encounter, the more she realised he had sensed in advance how the boat would move and pitch. He'd waited until that happened, and then he let her go, knowing that she would fall against the bunk—the bastard.

A couple of days after that episode, the weather had deteriorated further so that even at forty-five metres below, there was still considerable movement. Ehrhart, the Navigation Officer, had been unable to plot a course for some days, there having been no sighting of stars, moon, or sun. Outside, the sky had remained throughout a flat grey.

Mueller decided that all would benefit by spending more time below. The headway they were making in such conditions would be negligible, and with the visibility the way it was, they might as well be the only vessel in the Atlantic, for all the chances they had of spotting a convoy. "Take her down, Chief," he ordered.

It was sixty metres down before they found repose. They stayed below for seven-hour stints, only returning to the surface to recharge the batteries. Everyone began to recover, with the decent periods of rest and calmer mealtimes, boredom became the only enemy to be conquered. And then, after ten days, just as suddenly as it came, the storm subsided, the sky cleared, and the Atlantic became like a millpond, and all relaxed.

It didn't last.

* * *

November 16, 1942

Gotz, third watch, first spotted the tell-tale smoke on the horizon.

Mueller was already on the bridge. "A damn great British convoy. Well done, Gotz. Keep your eyes open. We don't want these babies to get away."

They increased their speed and were now about a couple of miles off from the convoy, perfectly poised for an attack, confident that from this distance, their low silhouette would not be spotted. Following his usual pattern of attack, Mueller would wait a few more hours until nightfall, then he'd move through the protective screen of the destroyers and make a surface attack from inside the centre of the convoy. In the meantime, he'd send out radio messages so that any other wolves in the area could move in and form a pack. There would be plenty to go round, for sure.

Frances's limbs ached, they were taking no chances this time. They had taken her to the control room, and Schumacher made her sit on the floor, and then bound her. The bonds were cutting into her wrists and ankles. He pulled them as tight as he could, making her wince and taking delight in his minor task, smiling at her discomfort. For now, at least her mouth was not taped, but she had heard Mueller's instructions that, as they prepared for the attack, she should be silenced.

On the bridge, Mueller's sensitive hearing picked up the sound of the engines, giving them those few extra, all important seconds.

"Alaaaarm, dive!" he yelled out.

At his command, the men on the bridge leapt through the hatch.

Mueller brought up the rear, securing it behind him. "Shit, a Sunderland. It came out of the sun," Mueller complained. "Damn, planes are a nightmare! Recheck our position, Ehrhart, when you can. We must be closer to the coast than we thought. Damn the storm! Verdammt. Heinemann, make sure you don't lose that damn propeller noise."

Heinemann leant forward into the aisle, raising his thumb.

Mueller paced the control room floor for a full ten minutes before sweeping the horizon with the periscope and giving the order to resurface. Going into the conning tower, he turned the heavy wheel which secured the hatch, and opened it, soaking himself and those immediately below. Hauling himself out onto the bridge, he smiled to himself with relief; the convoy was still in sight. Less than a minute later, though, hearing the same tell-tale thundering of propellers, he was forced to shout the command to dive once again. They repeated the exercise twice more, resurfacing only to be forced underwater again as the Sunderland continued to circle.

"Looks like he's not giving up." Werner appeared at Mueller's elbow.

"Pesky great gnat!" Mueller muttered. He paced the control room, wishing he had the means to swat the damn thing from the sky. Every minute they stayed below, the convoy would steam further away, changing course to fully distance itself from the U-boat. Already Heinemann was finding it difficult to pick up the propeller noise on his headphones.

They waited another hour, then resurfaced, and Mueller once more pushed open the hatch, ready to take up his position on the bridge. "First watch ready below, sir," reported Werner. The only reply they got from above was a barrage of abuse.

"Shit! Not a damn stack in sight. We've shaken off the sodding Sunderland and lost the convoy in the bargain. Verdammt! Chief, sweep the area, give her a radius of a couple of miles. Heinemann keep those ears open. Let's hope we can pick them up again."

That was one of the worst feelings, thought Mueller, being psyched up for a kill, ready, and then losing the prey. That convoy must have been strung out over thirty odd miles. He stamped his feet in a pretence of keeping warm but really just giving vent to his frustration.

"Permission to come up, Kapitanleutnant?" asked Werner.

"Permission granted. Come on up, there's nothing to see."

* * *

Later, it was Werner who removed Frances's bonds. Throughout the last few hours, they had forced her into sitting quietly, finding that even the smallest movements caused the rope to chafe her skin. Her legs had gone dead, and her arms and shoulders ached intolerably. The smell of many unwashed bodies crammed into a small space had turned her stomach. Werner took hold of her arm and helped her to her feet.

"Stamp around a bit, get the blood flowing," he advised. She thought under different circumstances she would have liked Werner, with his fair complexion and gentle brown eyes. He, of all of them, was a gentleman, she decided.

Chapter 14

November 20, 1942

"Who the hell do you think you're kidding?" Koenig asked. Simon looked up from his book.

"I'm telling you," Said Gotz, "one kiss from these lips and—" He thrust his hips back and forth, leaving his audience in no doubt as to what he meant.

Simon sighed to himself. He'd heard it all before on his last patrol. That's all they ever talked about—sex—and this lot was just as bad. The next thing would be the post cards, they'd definitely be the next thing.

"Here, have a look at this," said Koenig only moments later, waving a postcard of a partially clad young woman. A group of men gathered round, making lewd comments, and then other cards were produced and the women compared.

Mueller wouldn't have girlie posters on board—they had caused too many arguments in the past when they had been stolen or defaced. So, the men had thought of a way around the problem. Postcard-sized photographs of stars of stage and screen had replaced the girlie posters. He could hardly ban photographs of loved ones, now, could he? Though he had commented to several of his boys that they all seemed to be dating the same girl.

The ritualistic pawing over each other's photographs had taken place, and Simon was hoping things would settle down, but the men didn't seem to be in the mood for resting, and Gotz had carried on keeping his captive audience enthralled by reliving some of his latest 'sexperiences.'

"'Course, they all find me irresistible," Gotz bragged.

"Not my old lady!" said Petersen. He was an older man; Simon knew he had been married since before the start of the war. The lads referred to him as Father.

"Ah, don't give me that, Father!" retorted Gotz.

"Well, I'll tell you what she'd give you, laddie. A kick in the balls is what she'd give you—which is just what you deserve, you randy little bleeder!"

The other men laughed and nodded their agreement while Simon turned a page and tried not to listen.

"You're a fine one to talk, Father," needled Gotz, "or aren't all those kiddies at home yours then?"

Petersen jumped to his feet, clearly offended.

"Come on!" Gotz taunted. "What do you think your old lady's doing at this moment? Ironing and changing nappies? Married women are the worst, they get used to having it, see, then when it comes to it, they can't do without it."

Simon's pulse tapped in his ears. He expected Father to react. Instead, he sat down and stared into the middle distance, brow furrowed as if he was considering what Gotz had said.

"I'll tell you what," chirped Beckmann. "Next time we're on shore, you can show me your technique, Gotz!"

"Fine by me," he agreed.

While Simon had found Gotz's lewd tales fascinating, like most of the men, he considered Gotz a foul-mouthed braggart and decided to throw in his Ffenigsworth worth.

"You get to choose the woman, Beckmann," he said, then grinned, thinking how he'd enjoy seeing Gotz make an ass of himself. "None of his usual tarts, either."

"Good thinking, Toddler," said Beckmann. Switching his glance to Gotz, he said, "And I'll bet a month's wages that gob of yours doesn't have her begging for it, like you say."

"Done!" Gotz shouted.

"Why wait until next shore leave, Beckmann?"

Simon looked at Petersen—the man they called Father—and there was something fishy in his eyes, something off-kilter and malicious. It was as if Father was challenging Gotz, egging him on. Maybe he was angry at Gotz for making slurs against his wife.

"What's that you say, eh?" Beckmann asked.

"What do you mean, Father?" Simon wanted to know.

"Put Gotz's gob to the test now." Petersen nodded his head in the control room's direction. "The woman."

"Oh, no," Simon began.

"Are you mad?" Koenig cut Simon off. "The old man would have us keelhauled."

"Not if he didn't know," Petersen said. "He's up top. Exec as well."

"He'd soon find out, though." Gotz sounded worried.

"What's up, Gotz? Got cold feet?" Father asked. "What about that irresistible cock of yours? If you get her begging for it like you reckon, then she's hardly going to let on to the old man, now is she?" Petersen sounded pleased with himself.

"OK, Father," Gotz answered, "but if the old man finds out, you're for it!"

Toddler flew to his feet. "Look, hang on, you lot. Frau Meyer's a lady."

"All the better, Toddler, old chap." Koenig grinned. "You get her here. It'll be easy for you, she trusts you."

"Not likely," Simon said, not bothering to hide his disgust. "I'm not in on this one."

"Aw, come on," whoever said this cajoled. "It's only a bit of fun. No one's going to get hurt."

"I said no, Koenig!" Gut in a heated knot, Simon made for the hatch, only to find it blocked by Gotz's immense frame.

"Sit down, son. Leave this to the men," said Beckmann.

Not seeing a way out, Simon returned to his bunk, feeling sick, wishing for once that he was up top, on watch. He listened while it was decided that Koenig and Beckmann should be the ones to get Frances Meyer to the fore end, raking his mind for a way to warn her and finding none.

* * *

"Hey, Heinemann, anything exciting?"

Frances lifted her attention from the book she was reading. She recognised the man addressing Heinemann. Beckmann, she thought his name was. She stretched her legs out the length of the bunk.

"Not much." Heinemann's answer drifted through the curtain. "Convoy picked up on the Northern Approaches."

"Nothing for us then." A pause, then Beckmann asked, "Old man up top, is he?"

"As far as I know, yes," Heinemann answered.

Frances was turning a page when the curtain to the cubicle was jerked aside and a man she knew as Koenig stepped into the recess. It frightened her. No one was ever to come in here other than Mueller or Dieter, Kapitan's orders. She jumped up, heart pounding. The book fell to the floor.

"What do you want?" she demanded in a steely voice.

"You've to come with me, Frau. Kapitanleutnant wants to see you."

"Kapitanleutnant Mueller knows where to find me if he wants me." Stooping, she retrieved her book. Something in the man's expression, his twitchy eyes, disturbed her.

"Please, Frau. He would like you to go to the fore end quarters. It's... er ... Simon."

Frances stared at him. He was off, something wasn't right. She heard it in his voice, the uncertainty, possibly panic.

"Is Dieter ill?" she asked.

That must be it, the reason for Koenig's anxiety, why Mueller had sent for her, something he'd never done before. They had an unspoken understanding. They gave each other a wide berth. When Koenig nodded, she said, "Very well."

He led the way through the wardroom towards the fore end, and it wasn't until Beckmann fell in behind them that her uneasiness returned. But then she never enjoyed making this journey, which was the same as going to the washroom. It was like running the gauntlet—she hated the men, their leering faces.

Schumacher glanced up from his paper as she passed by, and his look, while cold, seemed questioning somehow, as if he found her appearance here, in the company of two crew members, a surprise, but then he dropped his glance, quickly dismissing her. Later, she would think she should have known what was in store for her, the Jew's bitch. After all, hadn't she felt their contempt, their wish to see her get her just desserts?

Reaching the fore end quarters, Frances noticed Dieter first, sitting on a lower bunk. Relieved that he was at least upright, she said, "Dieter, what is it? Are you ill?"

He looked at her, wide-eyed, distressed. "Sorry, there was nothing I could do."

A tremor in his voice reignited her fear. She sensed the other men hovering around her, their tension. The very air was rife with their tension, the electricity of anticipation. A frisson of unease twisted through her stomach, eased up her spine. She turned to Koenig. "Where is your Kapitan?" she asked, fighting to keep her voice level.

He shrugged.

"I want to see him—" Frances spoke over the heated pounding of her heart.

Gotz moved in, rotating in a circle around her, whistling through his teeth. "Not bad," he commented, running his gaze from her ankles to her hips, letting it linger on her breasts. "In fact, very nice. Few years older than I like them, maybe, but all the same, very nice."

Frances turned, but Gotz seized her around her waist, crushing her to him. He smelled of sweat and oil, badly enough that she gagged on the stench and her fear.

He brought his lips to her ear. "Thought you might be lonely, Fraulein, missing a bit of company—if you get my meaning."

"Get away from me!" she shouted, writhing in his grasp.

"Aw, come on, darling." Gotz spun her around as if she were a doll. She felt his hands squeeze her buttocks hard. He ground his pelvis against her. She could feel his erection, and a wave of nausea choked her. She felt lightheaded. "Don't be shy," he told her. "We're all friends together here."

Frances planted her palms on his chest, and she shoved him, but to little avail.

"Leave her alone, Gotz!"

She heard Dieter's yell, and over Gotz's shoulder, she watched, helplessly, as Beckmann dealt him a crippling blow to the guts.

Someone else called for Gotz to stop, but instinct warned her he'd passed the point of reason. Letting go of her buttocks, he wrapped her in a bear hug and strong-armed her across the floor to one of the bunks.

"Come on then, Gotz!" Frances recognized Koenig's voice. "Let's see the famous technique!"

The men crowded around even as Frances twisted hard in his grasp, but Gotz held her fast, and working his hand between them, he ripped open the front of her shirt. She felt the coolness of the air on her bare breast and shoulder. She heard the men whistle.

"Relax, darling, enjoy it!" Gotz reared back to look at her, licking his fleshy lips.

He had her pinned against the bunk now, one hand holding her face tight. The foul heat of his breath bathed her face. She tightened her teeth and closed her eyes, not wanting to see those lips descending towards her mouth, not wanting to feel it when he pawed at her, twisting her nipple too hard for pleasure. She heard the other men, their hoots of encouragement as if from a far distance.

So, this was to be the last humiliation, she thought, to escape Otto's assault, only to be ravaged by these animals.

"Gotz!" Mueller shouted, catching sight of the man bent over Frau Meyer, mouth buried in her bosom. He'd known it would come to this. Hadn't he known? "Let go of her. Now, Gotz!"

The man froze and then stepped back, letting go of the Meyer woman. She sagged like a rag doll. "She came here looking for it, sir," Gotz said, and the whine in his voice grated on Mueller's nerves. "Ask the others." Gotz hunted for support and got none.

Mueller found Frau Meyer's gaze and knew from her reddened face she was seething, but he saw fear darting through her eyes, too.

"Well?" Mueller ran a questioning glance over the faces of the men who were present.

"It's not true, sir, what Gotz said." Father spoke to the floor. "The girl was tricked here. We made a stupid bet."

"I know about that already!" Mueller barked, glancing back at Simon huddled in the shadow behind him.

Following Mueller's glance, Gotz shouted, "You squealing little shit!"

"Stand to attention, Gotz! All of you, straighten up!" Mueller was tight-jawed, furious.

"Is this the well-ordered crew you command, Kapitanleutnant?"

The Meyer woman was on her feet as well, arms tightly crossed over her bare chest. Her amber glance locked on his, hotly accusing.

"Get her out of here." Mueller addressed no one in particular, grabbing a blanket from the nearest bunk and throwing it at her. "Here, cover yourself."

Thankfully, Werner had appeared, and it was he who stepped to her side as she drew the blanket tightly about her. "Get her back to my quarters," he told Werner, who nodded.

Moments later, joining them, he slung his cap onto his desk. "Verdammt! What did I tell you?" he demanded, staring hard at her. He glanced at Werner. "It was bound to happen sooner or later; didn't I tell you? Bored out of their tiny brains, poor sods. Can't blame them."

"Can't blame them?" Offence rode hotly through Frau Meyer's voice. "Then who do you blame?"

"You!" Mueller stabbed a forefinger at her. "I blame you!"

"How dare you!" she shouted.

"Oh... just shut your mouth, will you? You're not hurt. Stop whining."

"Not hurt? There's no blood, so I'm not hurt, is that it? What about pride, Kapitanleutnant?"

"Oh, Christ. Just listen to it. What do you French know of pride, Froggy?" Mueller opened his cupboard and grabbed a spare shirt. He threw it at her. "Here, you can wear this." Sitting heavily in his desk chair, he eyed Werner. "No skat for any of the men involved for a week, Exec, and extra watch duties for Gotz and Petersen, starting now. I'll deal with them better when we get back to port. And where in the hell was the quartermaster? Find out, will you? He's in for extra duties, too."

Werner snapped his heels together, saying, "I'll see to all of this now," and he disappeared, almost too quickly, clearly he was glad to be leaving.

"Extra duties and no cards. Is that to be the extent of their punishment?" The Meyer woman was incensed.

"What do you suggest? That I make them walk the damn plank?" Mueller retorted.

"Well, I'm surprised that you bothered stopping them at all, or perhaps you wanted to be first, is that it? Some sort of Right de Seignior?"

Mueller shot to his feet, a rare red mist of rage dancing behind his eyes. She'd crossed a line, and from the way she shrank from him, he knew she knew it. His gaze locked on hers. One long step and he closed the gap between them. Grabbing the back of her head with one hand, he encircled her waist with the other, drawing her towards him. Fingers tangled in her hair, he forced her chin up. Her glare was unwavering, and he felt a kind of fire leap between them. When a spasm shook through her, he sensed she felt it, too. A silence stretched, thin and icy hot, between them, as they held each other's eyes. He released her suddenly, all at once, and snatching his hat, he said, "Like I said before, Froggy, you're not my type."

He was aware as he left of her collapsing on the bunk, and the sound of her harsh sobs, although muffled, followed him. He fought an urge to plug his ears.

Chapter 15

The weather remaining clement, the U-boat neared her grid position, the part of the Atlantic that she had been sent out to patrol. She was far enough away now from the British coast to be in no danger from aerial attacks, and, whilst the lookouts remained on the alert for convoys, life on board had become relatively relaxed.

Frances confined herself to the nook and only ran the gauntlet when nature called. She saw little of anyone apart from Dieter, who brought her meals, and Mueller, who grabbed a couple of hours' sleep from time to time—she reckoned he tried to organise his own sleep whilst she slept. She thought back several times to the feelings that she had when he had dragged her from the seat. The feeling was one she had never experienced; it shot through her, and she didn't really understand it. She wondered if it was related to fear, fear of him and the anger he had following the assault on her. But it hadn't felt like fear.

On the few occasions that Mueller and she were consciously together, there remained an icy silence between them. She was becoming more and more depressed, Mueller thought, giving up on reading and spending most of her time in a semi-comatose state on the bunk. Life on board didn't seem to suit his guest at all.

"Wasting away to nothing," he remarked to the other officers in the wardroom. Less than twenty-four hours after that remark, Toddler rushed through to the wardroom where the officers were relaxing after the evening meal.

"Sir, it's Frau Meyer."

"What about her?"

"She's ill."

"Get the medic!" shouted Mueller, making his way to the cabin. Toddler was already on his way in front of him, and Mueller pushed him aside to find the prostrate form of Frances Meyer on the floor.

Werner was close on his heels. "What's happened?"

"How do I know?" snapped Mueller. "Can't rouse her. God, I prefer it when she's being insulting." He picked her up and laid her gently on the bunk.

Hengst arrived, and taking in her condition, noting the sunken eyes and the slack skin, said, "Looks like she hasn't eaten or had a drink for days."

Mueller turned on Dieter, who was standing, ashen faced. "Toddler, what do you know about this?"

He stuttered in an effort to find the right words. "I'm sorry, Kapitanleutnant. She...she made me promise, made me promise not to bother anyone, see? I didn't know what to do. A promise is a promise, isn't it? She told me her stomach was upset, women's problems, and she...she didn't feel like eating, and she'd be all right in a few days."

"How long?"

"Sir?"

"How long is it since she's eaten, Toddler?"

"Four days, I think, Kapitanleutnant, at least. It was following that other trouble. She said she felt ill after that." He paused. "I'd do anything for her, sir."

"Even let her die, it seems," muttered Mueller, rubbing his face in disbelief. "Simon, you're an idiot. Get out of here."

Turning to go, the boy's relief was palpable; he'd expected a lot worse.

Mueller eyed Hengst. "What now?"

"We've got to get her eating, Kapitanleutnant, that's for sure. She's so weak, she fainted."

Mueller thought for a moment. "Send Simon some food, sauerkraut, and sausages. Werner, you stay here. I might need your powers of persuasion."

"I hardly think sauerkraut and sausages are the best thing, Kapitanleutnant," said Hengst. "If you don't mind me saying, soup would be more appropriate."

"Sauerkraut and sausages, Hengst. That's an order."

Returning to Frances's side, Mueller took in her pallid skin and sunken cheeks. He bent and slapped her on the cheek, pulled her to a sitting position, and shook her. He watched with relief as her lashes fluttered over her eyes and then eventually opened.

She gazed up into the face of her tormentor and groaned. "Leave me alone, Mueller, please."

"Not likely, Froggy. Come on, up you get!" He dragged her from the bunk and unceremoniously dumped her into the chair.

Werner shifted uneasily; he had never seen Mueller behave this way with a woman. He was always a gentleman, always respectful. There was a hitherto unknown anger in him, and yet a few moments previous he had shown a deep concern for the girl. Or more than concern, was it?

"Find out what's happening to that food," Mueller told Werner, who was shaken from his reverie and, thankfully, left bumping straight into Toddler, returning with a plate of sauerkraut and sausages.

"Christ, Simon, you'd better get in there quick, before he blows a fuse," said Werner.

Simon drew back the curtains.

"Put the food on the table and get out," ordered Mueller. "Exec, stay here. I may need you."

Werner nodded and watched as Simon threw Frances a pitying glance before he left. Mueller pushed the plate towards her. "Right, Froggy, my girl, eat!"

Frances Meyer pointed her gaze forward, looking at neither the plate nor Mueller. The smell of the food and their presence were making her stomach churn, and the bile rise into her throat. It was obvious.

Mueller sighed and addressed the girl. He'd calmed down and was trying a gentler approach. "Look," he said, "I know the situation you're in is less than perfect, but it's the same for us all. You're getting three meals a day, and you have a roof over your head, so to speak."

She turned and stared at him. "Are you suggesting that I'm lucky to be here?" Werner watched as Mueller locked his eyes on hers.

"I think you've been lucky all your life. I bet you've never gone without anything. Think what it's like for people who have lost the lot."

"Haven't I lost the lot, as you put it? All I have left is my life, and I don't want that anymore. Just leave me alone." Werner saw the tears well up in her eyes. "If you have any pity at all, Kapitan Mueller, then leave me, please. I've had enough. There's no one left, nothing left inside me."

It was such a pitiful reply that Werner thought Mueller would leave her for a while to just give her time to think.

"Pity, my arse!" said Mueller. "As far as I'm concerned, you can do what you like with your worthless life once we get back to shore, but you will not end it on my boat." "While you're here, I'm responsible for you, and losing any member of the crew is bad for morale. Now eat! Have you forgotten there's a war on? Out there, people are dying through no fault of their own, and if you think I'm going to let some selfish little bitch starve herself to death and do nothing about it—" He broke off, gnawing on his lip. "Look, I don't want to get unpleasant."

"Oh, Kapitanleutnant, you're that already," Frances tiredly retorted. "There's no way you can make me eat, so just go away and play with your damn boat."

"Well, we'll see if I can make you eat. Exec, hold her down."

Werner hesitated; he disliked the idea of using force on a woman. "Kapitanleutnant, I—"

"That's an order, Exec."

Trained to obey his commanding officer, Werner held Frances firmly by the shoulders, whilst Mueller loaded a fork with food.

"Now open up like a good girl."

Angered, Frances found some strength and hissed like a cornered cat. "Go to hell, why don't you!"

By way of answering, Mueller pinched her nose hard, and as she opened her mouth to breathe, with his free hand, he pulled her head back against him, deftly depositing the contents of the loaded fork into her mouth. She struggled, but Mueller held his hand fast over her mouth as she gagged. He repeated the procedure several times until her eyes brimmed with fresh tears, and she gasped out, "Sick!"

Werner pleaded her case. "She's had enough, for God's sake."

Mueller shot his First Officer a filthy look, but he released her, only to leave and return moments later with a bucket, which he placed on the retching woman's lap.

"Look after her, Exec," he told Werner. "I'll have some soup sent.

Let's see if she prefers that." Then Mueller shook the girl's shoulder until she looked up from the bucket, gasping. "Sauerkraut or soup, Froggy, it's up to you. I'll be back to check to see what your preference is and will assume that if you don't eat the soup, then you want me to carry on administering the sauerkraut. Do you understand?" Mueller took her shoulder again and shook it roughly. "Do you understand, Froggy?"

She nodded, tears streaming, and muttered weakly, "Yes, yes, all right."

Mueller scowled at them both and left.

* * *

After he'd gone, Werner tried to apologise for Mueller's actions. "I'm so sorry he put you through that, Frau Meyer."

The soup had arrived, and Frances was slowly sipping away at spoonful's of it. He went on, trying to explain, trying to excuse Mueller, wondering himself what the hell his commanding officer and friend had been trying to achieve by force-feeding her.

"He couldn't just leave you, Frau Meyer. He's right, you know. If anything had happened to you, it would have been dreadful for morale." He smiled at her. "And if it leaked out that he couldn't control a woman, then it wouldn't have done his standing as a commander a lot of good either, eh? Come on, eat a little more, and then have a rest."

Frances looked up from the soup bowl and conjured up a weak smile. "Thank you, Leutnant Werner."

"Paul, my name is Paul. Hopefully, you will feel better when you have some food in your stomach."

* * *

Satisfied that he could do little else, Mueller retreated to the control room, letting his head fill with the worries of fighting a war with the Brits instead of dwelling on the problems of some pig-headed girl. Why some people needed others to live for was beyond his understanding. Surely just being alive was enough, especially these days with a war on. Or perhaps it was love that made them so weak? If that's what it did, he definitely wanted none of it.

He climbed the rungs of the conning tower ladder and sprung himself out onto the bridge, nodding to the lookouts. The weather was mild for the end of November, but the brisk wind was chilly; the air whipped across his face, making his skin glow. He took a few deep breaths. These were the times when his command was enjoyable. Briefly, he could forget the war. He was at one with nature. His soul soared, and his spirit lifted, as it had done when he'd boated with his father all those years ago. It was good to be alive, but he wished he could clear his mind of Frances Meyer.

A few minutes later, Werner asked for permission to come up and joined Mueller on the bridge.

"Well," asked Mueller, "any luck with the soup?"

Werner nodded and grinned. "How the hell did you come up with that one?"

"Liver!" Seeing the confusion on his executive officer's face, he smiled. "Do you remember Anna, our cook?"

Werner nodded. "Once seen, never forgotten."

Mueller chuckled. "Hmm. Well, when Karin died, she looked after me for a while. Mutti, you see, couldn't cope. I must have been difficult over my food, refusing to eat it, I suppose. Anna sat me down at the kitchen table and stuck a great load of liver in front of me. God, I hated the stuff, still do, and she knew that. She made me eat the lot, and I puked it all back. She told me if I refused her good food in the future, she would make sure I ate a plate of liver again. My God, just the thought. I figured if the treatment worked for a small wilful boy, it would work on a small wilful girl. Sauerkraut on an empty stomach, eh? Doesn't bear thinking about."

Werner smiled at his commanding officer. "Well, I'll leave you. I'd better go down and monitor what's going on below."

Mueller nodded at him thoughtfully.

After a couple of hours, he called down the voice tube. "Send Frau Meyer up to the bridge."

A few minutes later, he heard the hollow ring of feet striking the ladder and Werner's voice. "Mind how you go. I'll climb up behind you just in case. You're still weak."

Mueller crossed to the hatch as her head appeared and offered his hand to help with the last steps. The amber eyes burned into him as she ignored his gesture and, with difficulty, hauled herself out onto the bridge, the sudden freshness of the air making her light-headed and knocking her off balance.

"Christ, woman, relax. See, there isn't a plank after all," quipped Mueller.

"Relax? With you around, Kapitanleutnant? Not possible! Why am I here anyway? What detestable thing are you going to do now?"

So, he thought, she has already recovered her temper. She must be feeling better. "I thought the fresh air might do you good."

Frances audibly sniffed. "I can't smell anything fresh around here at all."

God, how she angered him. He was trying to be pleasant, trying to help her, yet she was venomous at every opportunity. He tried again. "Open your ears, Froggy. Listen for a while, what do you hear?"

"That's easy. I hear a Nazi pig, Kapitanleutnant."

He refused to rise to the unaccustomed anger inside him. Besides, he knew the lookouts would almost certainly be taking in the situation.

He asked again, "And your eyes, Frau, what do they see?"

"A whole shipload of Nazi pigs." She pointed towards the men on watch. "Now you've questioned my ears, my eyes, and my nose, and if you want to know what I'm feeling right now, I'm feeling cold, and nauseous, and I don't like your company. So, do you mind if I go?"

Mueller bit on his lip and decided she wasn't worth bothering with. He waved his arm at her. "Go! Go on, you're a waste of damn time."

Full of fury, Frances made her way through the control room and back to Mueller's nook. There she threw herself onto the berth. The fresh air on top of going without food for several days had exhausted her. Her last thoughts as she drifted into sleep were who she detested the most: Otto or Kapitanleutnant, Kristian bastard Mueller. She dreamt of the last time she had seen Otto.

* * *

It was some weeks later, after the party at Chantilly, that she had bumped into Otto again purely by chance, following a concert she attended with her Aunt Edie at Notre Dame. She spotted him standing among a group of young officers as she and Edie were leaving the cathedral. One of the officers was Heinz Roethke. He'd attended Madame Abetz's party too. He was a Doctor of Law, and she found him interesting to talk to, though she made sure that she steered their conversation away from his work. Noticing her, Roethke tugged on Otto's arm, pointing her out across the crowded transept. For a fleeting moment, she imagined Otto would approach her, offer an apology, but he merely made her a stiff little bow. Still sulking, she thought.

She told Edie what had happened that night in Chantilly on the way home. "Men can be such children," she said. The metro was packed, but two officers had given up their seats for the women.

"Leave well alone, my darling. It will pass." Edie said, patting her hand. "And don't tell Steven or Jacques," she added. "They have worries enough."

She agreed, believing she understood the extent of those worries, only to learn the following day, while visiting Steven with her aunt, that she'd been kept in blind ignorance.

"We've considered it carefully, Frances." Steven set his teacup down on its saucer.

"Thought what through?" she asked, looking from him to Edie and then to Jacques.

"We are taking Steven to England," Jacques said.

"Where he can get proper medical attention," Edie said.

Horrified, Frances exclaimed, "What about me?"

Steven said, "We think it's safer for you to stay put, for the time being at least, and Edie will be here for you."

At first, she had argued. It hurt that everything was arranged without her knowledge, and it hurt even more that they wouldn't share their plan with her.

"It's best that you don't know," Edie said.

She cried out, "You don't trust me, do you?"

"Frances, it's not a case of not trusting you," Steven said, taking her hand and sitting her down in a grand old armchair.

"The less anyone knows, the better," Jacques explained. "Of course, we know you wouldn't knowingly let on our plans, but you could unknowingly let something drop."

Jacques had contacts, and he organised new papers and identities, and help on the journey. They reassured her she would be fine.

"You have Otto for protection," Steven said. "He'll make sure that you're safe."

Frances flinched inwardly and looked at Edie, who gave her head a small warning shake, and she was right. It would only worry Steven needlessly to tell how Otto had accosted her. "Once Steven is safely on the boat for England, Jacques and I will return," Edie said. "You won't be alone for long." She wrapped her arms around her, meaning her to take comfort from it. And she did. She would be fine. How would Otto even know she was on her own? And even if he were to discover it, and come to see her, she'd always been able to handle him. He wouldn't hurt her. She was convinced of that.

"We've got last-minute details to see to," Edie said. "There's no need for you to wait while we take care of them."

"You want me to leave? Now?"

"The less you know, the better, my dear," Steven said.

"How will I know when you're going?" she asked, shrugging into her coat.

"We'll give you notice," Jacques said.

"We promise farewells will be properly said." Edie came to her, hugging her once more, recognising how hurt she was.

"And I promise that once in England, I'll find some way of letting you know I'm safe," Steven said.

She kissed his cheek. Walking back to Edie's apartment, her sense of injury over being left out faded. It was certain Steven needed good medical attention or he would surely die, though her inbred medical knowledge led her to doubt that very little could be done for his condition other than making him comfortable. But there was little chance of finding that as a Jew while living in France now, was there?

Five minutes from the flat, it rained, and she was, as usual, caught without an umbrella. The downpour increased, and she made a run for it, getting drenched to the skin and breaking the heel on her shoe into the bargain. She paused her step, looking down, muttering, "Oh, sod it! Talk about it never rains but pours."

Fed up and soaked, she limped the last metre or so to the flat. She was at the door, fishing in her bag for her keys, when he greeted her.

"Hello, Frances."

She wheeled. "Otto!"

"Pleased to see me?" He sounded strange; an odd light haunted his eyes.

"Of course," she replied. She got the lock to open, though her hand trembled. "Come in. I—I've missed you." They walked in, and he crossed the room, removing his cap and placing it on the back of a chair.

"Are you alone?"

"Edie will be back in a little while. Why do you ask?"

"We need to talk."

It was what he'd said before, breaking into her room after the party. She wondered if he meant to apologise for his behaviour. It was what she wanted to believe. She smiled. "Sit down, Otto, please," she said, showing the sofa as she seated herself in a gilt chair opposite it.

"No. Thank you. I prefer to stand."

"Look," she began with some exasperation, "if it's about what happened in Chantilly, then forget it. I have."

His lip curled. "You fool of a woman. You still don't see, do you? I can't forget, and it offends me deeply, Frances, that you can so easily brush me aside."

"But I haven't—"

"Shut up," he told her, and it shocked her badly enough that she obeyed. "I tried to forget what happened, for all the good it did me. I tried to forget about you and the way I feel about you. I had three weeks at home with my wife and boys, and for those three weeks I told myself I hated you for the way you have toyed with my feelings. And after those three weeks, I felt strong and determined again, a new man. I longed to get back to Paris and my job; that is what I thought until I saw you the other night after the concert, and then I realised it was not Paris at all, but you I longed to return to."

"Please, Otto—" Protesting, she jumped to her feet.

He pushed her back into the chair. His mouth was hard, and his eyes on her were cruel.

She realised she was afraid of him now, afraid of the physical force she knew he could use.

"I haven't finished," he told her. "As I said, I am strong now, and side by side with the other feelings I have for you, there is hate, too. I am a determined man. One way or another, I will have you."

"You'll have to force me then, Otto. Is that the way you want it?" She didn't know where she found the courage to challenge him, but she was glad for it. Glad for the bite it put in her voice.

He sighed. "If I had wanted that, I would never have left your bedroom in Chantilly until I had you. God knows I would give up my family for you. Give you all you ever wanted." Using two fingers, he lifted her chin, holding her gaze.

"But I don't want you, Otto," she whispered.

"Oh, but I think you will."

She took her chin from his hand. "Please go," she said.

Quickly, he stepped behind her, and putting his hands on her shoulders, he used his thumbs to caress the back of her neck, making her flinch, making her stomach roll. "You need time, Frances. I understand."

"No, never, I will never want you."

He leant against the chair back, and bending, lay his cheek alongside hers. "I think you'll come to me of your own free will after you've had a couple of days to think about it. Hmm?"

She felt the heat of his breath against her ear and forced herself not to swat at it, at him. Jerking upright, she spun around to face him.

"My God, Otto, haven't I made myself clear? Are you so thick-headed? There is nothing to think about." Her voice shook with the effort of withholding tears. She would not let them fall; refused to have him see her cry.

His smile mocked her and left her cold. He took his cap from the chair, walked to the mirror, and deliberately placed it on his head.

She started for the door. He blocked her path, and she winced as he drew his fingertips across her cheek.

"Perhaps you don't realise it, my dear, but I'm the one holding all the cards."

"I don't know what you mean."

He smiled, full of himself, gloating. "Well, it's a bit of a game, and here's how it's played—if I don't hear from you in the next forty-eight hours, guess which Jew will be on the next convoy out of here."

The blood drained from her face. "No, you wouldn't—."

"Oh, but I will, and you know I can get it done, too. By the way, I've requisitioned your Neuilly residence."

She couldn't speak, could scarcely breathe.

"You look ill, my dear," he said, stepping toward the door. "You need to get out of those wet things before you catch a chill."

She barely heard the click of the door when he closed it behind him. Her head was swimming. Her knees were weak, and she sat down in the nearest chair. Steven arrested, and probably Jacques, too. She couldn't have that on her conscience and yet the alternative... the alternative she couldn't think about. There had to be a way out, but she would need help to find it, she thought, and taking up her purse, she went back out into the rain.

Chapter 16

The mood on board was strange, a mixture of boredom and disappointment because of the lack of enemy vessels, relief that they had not been called into too much action, and the knowledge that the fuel could not last forever. Soon they would be homeward bound. The unnaturally fair weather of late had helped the crew unwind—as much as they could, given their circumstances. They were safe in the knowledge that nothing but an enemy sub could creep up on them unawares—and that was unlikely.

For a few days Mueller kept a close watch on all that Frances ate. He made sure that she understood that the threat of being force-fed was ever present, so she complied. Despite her own feelings, she began to feel strong again. It was getting towards midday on one such morning that Frances became aware of excitement on board. At first, she thought that a convoy had been sighted—but this was not the predatory excitement prior to a kill—it was too good-natured for that. Activity was great; men were coming and going, hatches were being opened, and there was the sound of shouting from many men on deck. She stuck her head out of the curtain just as Klaus Zeitler, the Chief, was passing, and asked, "What's going on?"

"Whales!" he answered, giving her a broad smile through his bushy beard. "You should come and look, Frau. It's a once-in-a-lifetime opportunity."

Whales, she thought. How big? How close? How many? Yes, a once-in-a-lifetime opportunity. She shouted after Zeitler as he disappeared into the control room. "Do you think he'd let me go up?"

Zeitler turned and shrugged. "Only one way to find out: ask him.

He's on the bridge. Go on," he encouraged. "Shout up. Ask the Old Dog!"

"Perhaps," she said. She wanted first to consider Mueller's actions from the previous few days. She feared him for sure. No one had ever been physical with her the way he had, not even Otto, and Gotz, of course. But had she given Mueller any alternative to punching her when she had sung out the Marsellaise? She had given that plenty of thought already and decided that under the circumstances of a full-on attack from an enemy vessel, he had acted to save his men. It had been a knee-jerk reaction. A brief smile crossed her face as she remembered his attempt at an apology; she hadn't made that easy for him.

But following that business with his men, he had shown no sympathy at all for the way they had manhandled her, having the audacity to blame her. For what? Just for being there, it seems. He had been angry. She had made him angry, not his men, and for that, he had dragged her from her seat and held her so she couldn't move. She had thought he was going to kiss her, she was sure he was, but something had happened. For a moment, he froze, and she thought she had read confusion in his eyes. She had felt it too, whatever it was. And then he had unceremoniously dumped her and left her sobbing. The bastard.

Paul Werner had said that it would have been bad for morale if she had died, and that he, Mueller, would have lost standing with his crew, which is why he had made her eat. Forced her to, for the morale of his crew, not out of concern for her. She gave a deep sigh. Was he the ogre she was painting him to be? Only one way to find out, she thought.

She stepped up a couple of ladder rungs and, as she'd heard the men do, called out, "Permission to come up?" There was no reply apart from a good deal of shouting, and she thought maybe she hadn't been heard. She tried again. "Kapitanleutnant Mueller, permission to come up?" She added for good measure, "Please."

There was the sound of boots grating on the metal of the bridge. Rays of watery winter sunlight were extinguished as a figure moved across the hatch, and then a voice she recognized as Mueller's called down. "You want to see the show, Froggy? Come on up then."

As her head reached the hatch, he offered his hand as he had before, and this time in her hurry, she took it without thinking, feeling his strength, and feeling her pulse race. He hauled her up onto the bridge, letting go of her hand the second he saw she was safe.

She was excited. "Where are they?" she asked.

The deck was crowded with men pointing and shouting. She saw the fair head of Werner amongst them.

Mueller was keeping a space between them and gestured. "Over there. Do you see? About half a kilometre out."

She narrowed her eyes against the sun's glare. "I can't see anything."

"Here." Mueller held out his binoculars, and she took them, surprised by their weight. Lifting them to her eyes, she peered into the distance. "I still can't see anything. It's too blurry."

"You need to alter the focus, perhaps. Twist the rings by the eyepiece."

She tried, but it was impossible to hold the binoculars and adjust them at the same time.

"Keep watching," encouraged Mueller as she lowered the glasses. "You'll see them spouting. There's a whole pod of them. There, did you see?"

She frowned, squinting, searching the choppy water. "No..."

"Come on," Mueller said. "Look to port now. Look! See over there? They're breaking the surface!"

Frances caught the motion then, as the huge grey backs of several whales broke the ocean's surface, and in her delight, she shouted, "I saw! I saw! Is there a way to get closer?" She looked up at Mueller.

"Try the glasses again now that you know where to look," he answered.

When she raised the glasses to her eyes once more, Mueller moved in behind her. "Here, let me help you," he said, reaching around her to steady her hands. She flinched from his touch, pulling away as if scalded. Mueller just grabbed the binoculars and prevented them from crashing onto the deck.

The moment hung on, clumsy and heated, with mutual embarrassment.

Mueller apologised first. "Forgive me. I should have known better. I thought I could help, you see." He rubbed a line between his eyes, glancing around. The bridge suddenly seemed crowded with lookouts.

"I'm sorry, too, Kapitanleutnant. I didn't mean…" She ran out of words. "I think I need your help if I'm to get a really good look at them."

"Really? You're asking for help, then?" Mueller kept her gaze.

"Yes, really." She surprised herself by smiling and thought how boyish he'd become in his uncertainty. He moved behind her again, and she fought to remain calm.

"All right then," he said. "If you'll lift the glasses, I'll take the weight of them for you."

She did as he instructed, and as she felt his arms come around her, she suddenly forgot all the excitement of seeing the whales as she experienced a warm trembling through her body that she'd never experienced before.

"Do you see them?" The sound of his voice close to her ear brought her back to her senses, and she swept the area, and spotting the whales she cried, "Yes! Yes! Oh my! Just look. How fantastic."

He laughed at her reaction, a light baritone. "Worth seeing, then?"

"Yes! How on earth can anyone kill them? They're so beautiful, so majestic."

"But they do kill them," said Mueller. "There aren't many Atlantic whales left now. Whaling was a thriving industry until the war broke out. That's why it's so good to see them out there, doing so well."

"Yes," she said. "Yes, it is." She realised he hadn't moved from behind her, and that she was enjoying the warmth of him and the feel of his hands on hers. She relaxed a little, causing him to move in closer behind her so that the back of her head rested on his shoulder.

"So, Froggy," he said, "tell me again, what do you see?" There was a pause while she considered her answer. "Come on, it's beautiful out here, isn't it?" he encouraged.

"The flat grey ocean, you find it beautiful?"

"You're not looking, Froggy. It's not flat, is it? Look at the movement of the waves. Some break even this far out, see? Look at the whole vastness of it. It's awe-inspiring."

"Yes. I hadn't noticed, I suppose. The sky as well, the movement of the clouds, the sun breaking through hitting the water, making it shimmer, and the whales, of course."

He'd taken his binoculars and moved away from her, leaning over the bridge slightly, smiling at his men still caught up in the show that the whales were putting on.

"What do you hear, Froggy?" he asked. She moved to join him, and he looked at her, the straight line of his mouth turning right up either side in a smile.

"I can certainly hear young men enjoying themselves and the waves hitting the sides of the boat, the engine, and you, of course."

"The sound of the wind sometimes too, and the occasional call of a bird," he added. "What can you smell, apart from me, of course?"

"The freshness of the air, the sea, oil."

"And how does all of this make you feel?"

She thought for a moment. "Small," she said. "Insignificant, but a part of it all too. At one with it." She caught his gaze and held it for a moment. "Uplifted."

"And this is just here, now. Think about the sky at night, the stars that go on forever, walking barefoot through a meadow, swimming naked in a lake on a summer's night. Remember all this too, Froggy."

"I can't," she said.

Mueller looked at her. "What do you mean you can't?" he asked.

"I've done none of those things. I've always been too busy."

"Too busy to look into the night sky?"

She gave a shrug. "There isn't much of a night sky in Paris; the lights, I suppose. I think I remember starry nights when I was in England as a child." She thought for a few moments and gave a sigh. "I'd love to see the night sky out here. No lights, other than moonlight, of course. It must be beautiful."

"It is," he said. "Will you let me show it to you? Do we have a date? Next starry night, as long as we are in safe water, we'll come onto the bridge and look at the sky. What do you say?"

She held his gaze for a second or two, noting the smile tugging at the corners of his mouth again. *He's teasing me,* she thought. "What I say is, it's getting cold out here, Kapitanleutnant. I'm going back inside."

* * *

Following that conversation, she took herself off to the nook and thought long on what had happened. Mueller had rekindled the will to live in her. He had reawakened her senses. He'd questioned her as he had before, but this time she listened to the responses of her body, which were heightened not just by the presence of the whales, she realised, but also by the presence and nearness of him. She listened to her senses and answered, surprised by the depth of feeling that was left inside, in what she thought was the shell of a woman.

"See, you have all this. No one can take this away from you," he'd said. "Froggy, never say again that you have nothing to live for."

Had that pathetic suicide attempt been serious? Would she have carried it through if Mueller had not prevented it? He must have taken her seriously, at least, to respond the way he had. She'd hated him at the time for it, but now she realised that he could have saved her life and her sanity. Not for her, he had stressed, but for the good of the crew and bloody morale. Was that the only reason, she wondered, thinking back to the feeling of his arms around her and his hands on hers? Did he feel any of it the way she had?

Chapter 17

Leutnant Werner was wondering on his way to the wardroom if Frances would take him up on his invitation to join the officers there for the evening meal. Was he interfering? Possibly, but he'd noticed that morning that there was definitely something going on between Mueller and Frances Meyer. During the time that the crew were out with the whales, he'd watched them on the bridge together and seen with his own eyes how Mueller had wrapped his arms around the girl to help her with the binoculars. He'd seen the way that she had melted into his body. There was most definitely something going on; whether they realised it, he wasn't sure, but he knew Mueller well, and the aggressive manner that he had shown towards this woman up until then was out of character. He had shown his true colours, hadn't he, when she had fainted a few days earlier? The man had been beside himself, and he thought it had little to do with the morale of the crew should something happen to her, and more to do with his own.

He took his seat at the table and nodded to the other men. Mueller, Second Officer Schumacher and Klaus Zeitler, the Chief, were already seated, and it was with some elation that he saw Frances ducking through the hatch from the other end of the boat.

Tired of her solitude, she had accepted Werner's invitation to join the officers for the evening meal. He jumped to his feet when he saw her and gave his customary little bow.

"I asked Frau Meyer to join us, Kapitanleutnant," he explained to Mueller, who was slumped on what was both the Chief's bunk and a bench.

"Better get the lady a chair then, Exec. I hope you explained, though, that we don't dress for dinner."

Werner grabbed another folding chair but was stopped by

Schumacher, who had turned an even paler colour than his normal puce. "I'll not share my meal with this woman," he said.

Werner saw Mueller straighten up. "Why's that then?" he snapped.

"She's a Jew's whore, Kapitanleutnant."

Werner felt disgust shoot through his body. "Watch your mouth, Schumacher!" he spat.

Frances turned to him. "Please," she said, "I'll take my meal alone. It doesn't matter." She turned and was about to leave the wardroom when Mueller spoke.

"Get the lady a chair, Exec," he said.

"Sir, I must protest." Schumacher shot to his feet.

"You can protest all you like, mister, somewhere else!" Mueller informed him, his tone icy.

Schumacher pulled himself up to his full height and did his best to leave with a show of pride for all he believed in.

"Pompous little shit!" Mueller muttered. "No need to find a chair, sit there." He pointed to Schumacher's vacant one with a nod of his head to Frances.

They all sat quietly for a while, each lost in their own thoughts. Werner was thinking about Mueller's reaction to Schumacher's unpleasant remarks. He'd fought Frances's corner for her, and on the bridge that morning had held her close. He noticed she was watching Mueller surreptitiously, and then the meal was brought in. A tinned fish and more sauerkraut. He saw something akin to horror in her eyes.

"I'm sorry. I can't eat the sauerkraut," she said.

The start of a smile tugged at Mueller's mouth as he thought back to the incident a few days before. "Why's that, then? Were you not taught to eat what they put in front of you, Froggy?" he asked. Werner watched Frances and saw her spine stiffen, saw her turn her icy gaze on Mueller.

"I had food put in front of me that I liked, Kapitanleutnant," she replied.

Mueller stood, his eyes bored into hers. "Well, now, I'll just go to the galley and see if we have any caviar, then, shall I?"

Werner heard her sigh. She loaded the fork with sauerkraut.

"Don't bother," she said and began to eat. He thought she must be willing the stuff to stay in her stomach. Mueller rubbed at his beard and stared at her over his plate. After a moment, he took up his fork and mashed everything to a pulp.

"Can't stand the way they just lie on the plate and look at you," he explained. "I wish Hayman would remove their heads."

Werner laughed with relief—the tension had been broken. He'd thought that maybe asking Frances to join them for dinner had been a mistake. And then he heard her laughter. She was laughing too, and it sounded good to his ears. He saw her catch Mueller's eye across the table, and he joined in with their laughter. Klaus Zeitler, who had been heavy in thought, looked from one to the other.

"Have I missed something?" he asked, which caused another outburst from the other three.

"Get back to dreaming about washers and wing nuts, Chief," said Mueller, loading his fork with food again, but instead of lifting it to his mouth, he sniffed loudly and said, "Christ, I wish we knew just how many ships were getting through." He glanced from Werner to Zeitler. "How are we really doing, do you think?" Not waiting for an answer, he took the mouthful of food, chewing thoughtfully, and swallowed. "Bloody propaganda. That's all they broadcast. Fat windbags. Are our troops really pushing forward on the Eastern Front, do you think? Are the RAF suffering heavy losses? Are food supplies really not getting through to Great Britain?"

A pause lengthened, punctuated only by the sound of cutlery and a restless shifting of feet. Frances sat back in her chair, digesting some of what Mueller had said, waiting for one of the other men to pull him up short for his anti-Nazi comments. She had the feeling this was normal and wondered where exactly his loyalties lay.

"And what about the planes Goering promised us, huh? Can't even be bothered to get off his fat arse and sort something out. Over two years into this war and still no cooperation between our forces. Jealous of the Kriegsmarine's success, they are. Jesus, it's pathetic." Leaning back, Mueller tossed his fork down onto his plate.

"You won't win, you know," said Frances, surprising herself with the comment that had just been a thought in her head.

All three men turned their eyes on her. Mueller's look was hard, and she wished she had kept her mouth shut and her thoughts to herself. She looked away, feeling hot around the neck.

"There are no winners in a war," Mueller bit back. "That's what they say, isn't it? In battle, we're all losers." He exhaled loudly. "Chief, go and ask Heinemann to put some music on."

Zeitler rose from his seat and ducked through the bulkhead hatch to the radio room. Soon the strains of Edith Piaf filled the boat.

"Not to your taste, Froggy, I suppose," said Mueller, sitting forward slightly and holding her eyes with his own. Resting her elbow on the table, she set her chin on her hand and stared back at him.

"I quite like popular music, actually," she replied, "particularly the American stuff. Jane Froman, Glenn Miller, and Cole Porter's wonderful songs. Do you play an instrument, Kapitanleutnant?"

"Ah, well, now, there's a thing we seem to agree on. And no, I don't play any instrument. I haven't a musical bone in my body."

By now, the meal was finished, and coffee brought through. Werner was thumbing his way through a handful of snapshots.

"Your family?" Frances asked.

He nodded and gave her the ghost of a smile.

"May I see?" She held out her hand.

Werner gave each photograph a lingering look before passing them over, one at a time. Frances noticed that, like him, his wife was fair-haired. "She's beautiful." Werner looked up and smiled, nodding his head. "What's her name?"

"Inga, and the boys are Johann and little Kristian, after our celebrated Kapitan here, who is his godfather," Werner replied.

"Really?" When Mueller stuck out his hand and asked to see them, she passed them over. "You knew each other before the war, then?" Frances looked from Mueller to Werner.

"Both at Bonn University, reading Law," Werner said.

Frances ruminated on the information. Law—so they had both been reading Law. That explained the German law books. She wasn't surprised that Werner should have been a law student, but Mueller? She rather thought he was a law unto himself.

"What of you, Frances?" asked Werner. "Did you grow up in Paris? Have you family there?"

"My aunt lives in Paris. I joined her there when my father died. I was fourteen."

"So, where were you before that?"

"England; that's where I grew up. My mother was English. Papa, of course, was French."

Mueller had been listening in on the conversation whilst he thumbed through Werner's photographs. He looked up. "I knew there was something odd about you, Froggy. Half-English—that explains it."

Frances gave him a filthy look and turned her attention back to Werner.

"My father was a doctor. We lived in the Midlands."

"Midlands?" Werner shrugged.

"Middle England; it's pretty there. We had a lovely house just outside the town, with a garden that backed down to the river."

"Isn't it mostly industry in the Midlands?" asked Zeitler.

"Parts of it, the cities, Birmingham, and Coventry. It was mostly farming around the town where we lived, though."

"So how come you are fluent in German?" Werner asked.

Frances shrugged. "Good schooling, I suppose. Papa sent me to the private girls' school in town. I already spoke French fluently, so had no need of lessons in that, so I learnt German and Latin too."

"A regular little scholar, eh?" said Mueller, passing the photographs back to Werner. "Didn't you ever have any fun, Froggy?"

"Of course, I had fun. A great deal of fun. The local bandstand on Sundays in the park. Train journeys to concerts. We even went as far as London." Frances caught the gaze of the three men who were looking at one another, eyebrows raised.

"What?" she asked.

"Concerts were your fun?" asked Klaus Zeitler.

She scowled. "Yes, is there something wrong with that? My life has always revolved around music. I told Papa at an early age that I wanted to be a virtuoso, and he bought me a violin."

"Of course, he did," Mueller chimed. She whipped her gaze to his.

"What do you mean by that?" she asked, glaring at him.

He gave a shrug. "Whatever you want it to mean."

"What of your mother? Did she go to Paris with you?" Werner cut in quickly. It was good to have a conversation around the table other than talk of the war, he thought, but he could see that there was a battle brewing. He could feel the electricity between his commander and Frances. Soon the sparks would fly. He got no reply and wondered if they had heard him, as Frances continued to hold Mueller's gaze.

"Then I'll take it as a compliment," she said.

"How the hell can you turn that comment into a compliment?" asked Mueller, leaning forward across the table, chin in hand. She mirrored his stance, leaning towards him.

"My Papa could not refuse me anything, Kapitanleutnant," she said, and then gave him a coquettish smile, which Paul Werner noted.

"You're a spoilt brat," said Mueller, unable to prevent a smile from crossing his face. Frances turned her attention away from him and back to Werner.

"My mother died when I was eight, Paul. I suppose that's when the fun stopped."

* * *

Following his dismissal from the dinner table for remarking on his reticence to dine with the Jew's whore, Second Officer Schumacher was in a fury. He walked the U-boat, searching for a corner to hide away from everyone; finding such a place on a U-boat was not easy. He was in no mood to socialise, and anyway, all the officers were in the wardroom with the woman. He eventually found a quiet space in the radio room where he could clear his head of the anger that filled it, making room for him to plot his revenge on Kapitanleutnant Mueller. There would be plenty of officials, he thought, at flotilla headquarters who he was certain would be very interested in Mueller's anti-party politics. He'd heard of others being arrested and interred for speaking out to a much lesser degree than Mueller, and on top of that, he was breaking bread with that woman. Then there was to be the payback for that night in the Casino Bar. That night was etched in his brain, as was the morning after.

* * *

If he made a determined effort, he could just about focus his eyes. He'd made it to the pens housing *U.B.A*, and his head had reverberated with every step. Still feeling ill, he'd excused himself from the farewell lunch with the Flotilla Kapitan and was now dreading the moment when he'd have to face his fellow officers.

Realising too late that night that he was the butt of their jokes, he had tried to get away. He'd told them he'd had enough, but that fat shit, Kissler, had kept him there, toasting various party members, and then he'd stood up to make a speech, or so he had thought. Instead, the man had let loose a tirade. "Fight for the Führer. Die for the Führer! Surely, our Führer won't mind at all if we get pissed first."

He had looked to his Kapitan to object, but Mueller had just sat in his chair with a sleepy grin on his face, nodding in agreement from time to time. Such behaviour from a man decorated for his valour—it had been a shock. Knight's Cross with oak leaves. He wondered if Mueller deserved such a decoration.

He knew he had disgraced himself and all he believed in by drinking and being unable to hold his liquor. He would show them what he was made of, though. He had always done well, and he believed in his own achievement, top in his class, at naval college. It wouldn't be long until he wore the white cap of a Kapitan; then he would show them and then they'd see.

That fat pig Kissler! Remembering seared through his brain. Well, he comforted himself, thankfully he was not sailing with him. But what of Mueller, nodding his approval of Kissler's lack of respect for party values? Mueller, so totally in control, had sat and listened all evening, watching what was going on, throwing in the occasional jibe, but mostly quietly taking it all in. The iceman! And then he had sprung the last insult, the bastard! Whilst Kissler had been relating tales of his brothel creeping, Mueller had asked if he, Schumacher, enjoyed the ladies.

"Certainly," he'd replied, and then had foolishly added, "Often, sir."

Overhearing, Merkel, an officer of Kissler's, had asked, "How often, you smutty little sod? When was the last time?"

Red-faced, he had stammered, "I—I can't quite remember the last time."

"Can't remember your last poke? Something wrong with you, lad."

They'd all laughed, and then Mueller had said, "Leave the lad alone. He's still a virgin, I'd say. We've all been there, haven't we?"

His face had warmed, but not content with his embarrassment, Kissler had announced it over the P.A. to full musical accompaniment, that he, Schumacher, couldn't recall his last poke.

God! He jammed his hand over his head. The thought still made his face burn.

Madame and a couple of her tarts had heard the commotion and come in flaunting themselves, and he had become a sideshow for the entire bar. He had been plied with still more cognac, and those filthy bitches had fondled him in places they had no right to touch. They had thrust their wares in his face, and throughout it all, they had laughed.

"Leave it to us; we'll show him what it's for."

"Not just for pissing with."

"Not for stirring your coffee, darling."

It had been Mueller who'd finally had the decency to suggest that maybe he had better be taken back to his quarters, but his help hadn't come fast enough. There had been one last humiliation.

As Werner and Mueller had helped him to his feet, his head had spun and his legs had gone from under him. He thought they had tried to hold him, but he wasn't sure, and as he pitched forward, he'd put his hands out to stop himself from falling, grasping madly at anything to prevent his collision with the ground. Unfortunately, it had been Madame that he'd grasped, and his superior weight had sent them both crashing to the floor. The sudden jolt freed him from his last meal, which mixed with the cognac and a little lemonade, he noisily deposited on to Madame's décolleté.

He couldn't remember getting back to his room and assumed Mueller and Werner had escorted him. The next morning, he'd woken with a splitting headache and had barely made it to the toilet in time to heave his stomach lining into the pan.

* * *

How they had laughed, those tarts! But why should he be ashamed of keeping his body pure for the right girl? And when he found her, and at the right time, they would join and produce perfect offspring for his Führer.

His thoughts turned back to revenging himself on Mueller. The man was a complete disappointment both to himself and the Party. The trouble was that by not being welcome in the wardroom, he'd miss Mueller deriding his leaders. The only way he was going to be able to get back to mealtimes in the wardroom was by making some sort of apology. And then he would write down all of Mueller's anti-party comments and wait for the right time to use them against him.

* * *

Following the meal, alone in the nook, Frances's thoughts conjured up a pretty, beamed house…she recognized that house, and the garden that led down to the river. A memory shimmered of carefree and long English summers, and times when, if there had not been plenty, then there had been enough. She concentrated on trying to remain in the recollection of those heady, safe times. She had a privileged childhood; having been educated at the local private school, she knew that she could have done anything, gone anywhere. Her papa had wanted her to follow him into medicine, but it was the music that had captured her imagination, her very soul.

It had carried her on wings of majesty and delight, whether it came from the bandstand in the park or from the sumptuous confines of the concert halls in London. She had been given all of this by her parents, and she had rewarded them, hadn't she? How Mummy and Papa had teased and laughed after she'd proclaimed her goal of becoming a virtuoso. Papa had come home with a half-size violin and news of lessons with a local teacher, who she had amazed with her capacity for learning the instrument. She smiled to herself, remembering how they had to prise that violin from her fingers at night to get her to bed.

Her mother—she worked at it, trying to conjure an image, but her mind only succeeded in producing the spectral form of a woman seriously ill. The beautiful golden goddess had withered before her eyes, dying in 1927. So many happy years together had ended in a horrible, despicable death. Her English grandparents had travelled from Salisbury for the funeral, where they suggested she return to Salisbury and live with them, but she had refused. How could they expect her to leave her dear papa?

She would stay with him to support him in any way she could, and he was not about to let her go.

Though still young, she began helping him occasionally with his medical practice, assisting him with examinations and even minor operations. She had shown herself able to keep a clear head, and while her father had hoped she would follow him into the medical profession, he realised that her love of music governed her destiny. He encouraged her talent and her dream that someday she would study at the Conservatoire de Musique in Paris. She had never had any doubts on the subject.

She was thirteen years old when her dear papa had died after contracting a respiratory disorder; his lungs had been weakened during the Great War after inhaling mustard gas. "The war to end all wars," she muttered. That's what everyone had said about the Great War. How ironic. What would they say now if they were to see her here and know the circumstances? A harsh sound broke from her chest. Was she laughing? Crying? She brought her hands to her face, where they rested for a moment before falling away, unheeded by her.

She'd learnt then of his plan for her to return to France to live with his sister, Edie. So it was that at the beginning of 1932, she found herself in Paris, clasped to the loving and expansive bosom of her aunt, Edie, one step nearer to the Conservatoire de Musique and her goal. Papa had left her well provided for with instructions that she should continue her education, in particular her musical education, instructions with which her aunt was in full agreement. Yes, she had certainly been privileged. Many children her age were already in full-time employment.

An image hovered of dearest Jacques and her first lesson with him. How she cherished him. He had been a highly revered violinist in his day, having played with some of the finest orchestras in Europe. Over the two years she'd spent as his student, he had taught her everything he knew.

"Ah, now, look at that—you've improved upon my instruction tenfold," he told her when nearing the end of his tutorship. "That's the difference between us, Frances."

"What is?" she'd asked.

"I was damn good, but you, my girl, are exceptional. In my opinion, one of the finest string players France had ever produced."

Timing was everything, and Jacques had waited until he was sure she was ready before pulling a few strings of his own, making arrangements for her to attend an audition at the Conservatoire. He'd made her dream come to fruition. Dearest Jacques.

She imagined trailing her fingertips lovingly along the contours of the black case which housed her Stradivarius. Soon the music came, filling her ears, and she lost herself in the notes.

Chapter 18

The evening meal in the wardroom became a regular, and over one meal, Frances casually remarked upon her ignorance concerning the running of the U-boat. Klaus Zeitler's usually deadpan face leapt into life beneath the dark curls. The bushy brows lifted in anticipation and the dark eyes sparkled. A chance to talk at length about the love of his life—namely his U-boat. He'd studied engineering in Berlin, finding his consuming interest in all things mechanical so much more rewarding than the human relationships he'd known over his thirty or so years.

"I could give you a guided tour if you like," Zeitler suggested.

"I'd like that, thank you."

"I'll have to run it past the old man, of course, just to check."

Mueller okayed it after deciding that Frances offered a minor threat. He was almost certain that she wasn't an enemy spy, and anyway, the Brits had captured a couple of their U-boats, so they scarcely needed any further information on how they worked. It was the messaging they were interested in.

The next morning after breakfast, the trim Zeitler gave her a detailed account of every valve, duct, meter, pipe, switch and handwheel in the Control Room. He was in heaven as she asked, "What does this one do? How does that one work? What would happen if this failed, or that failed, and why is that here and not there?" Her genuine interest and intelligent questions encouraged him to continue. He took her to the engine room and introduced her to the two E.R.A.s, the engine room artificers, who fussed over each cog and piston as if it were an infant.

"Why are the men so pale? They look ill," she asked Zeitler.

He laughed at her question and then said, "They hardly ever go up top. They're much happier down here in the engine room with their diesels."

During the peace of a trim dive, just after breakfast on another morning, Zeitler left his second engineer in charge and took her to the fore'ard end. She hadn't been there since the incident with Gotz and felt uncomfortable about entering that place again..

"The torpedoes are being checked. Don't you want to see?" asked Zeitler.

The prospect of seeing these messengers of destruction, so-called fish, made her curious, and as she had Zeitler there to protect her, she carried on. The transformation was startling. No more the sleeping quarters of men. Gone were the bunks and hammocks, in their place now was block and tackle. The men were stripped to the waist and the smell of sweating bodies was overwhelming. All available hands had a task, and at the order from Smitt, the torpedo gunner's mate, all the men hauled together to remove the 'fish' from the tube, where it was then supported on hoisting rings. All parts were checked and rechecked, then it was topped up with compressed air, re-lubricated, and persuaded back into its tube. Each man had his own job to do, and she noted they didn't even know she was there. They were so totally wrapped up in their work. As the torpedo slid back into its tube, a voice that still sickened her drew a lewd comparison.

"Cor, look at that—slides in like a prick up a Parisian prostitute," said Tiny Gotz. His comment caused laughter amongst the men.

Frances wheeled round, making for the hatch to leave, but Zeitler put his hand on her arm and gave her a kindly smile. "Remember, you're a trespasser here," he said.

Gotz had moved round to the other side of the hoist and noticed the visitors for the first time. Visibly shaken and red-faced, he moved towards them. He addressed the floor. "I'm sorry, Chief. I didn't know the lady was here."

"That's all right, Gotz. The lady understands you meant no offence, right, Frau Meyer?" The man was too close for comfort. She could smell him, and it made her flesh creep. She couldn't look at him. Zeitler's hand was still on her arm, he gave it a friendly squeeze. He repeated, "Right, Frau Meyer?"

She gave a nod in acceptance of his apology. Gotz shuffled on his feet, for once lost for words.

"Is there something else, Gotz?" asked the Chief.

"Er, I'd like to apologise for that other business too, sir."

Frances lifted her eyes from the floor and turned them on Gotz. He coloured up under her scrutiny, and she enjoyed his discomfort for a while before she said simply, "Thank you, Gotz."

* * *

That evening during their meal, Mueller let them know he was pleased. "Good; can't afford to have ill feeling on board," he remarked when told of Gotz's apology. "So, did you find your tour interesting, Froggy?"

Even though Zeitler and Werner were on first-name terms now with Frances, Mueller, annoyingly still referred to her as Froggy. She shot him a disgruntled look, and he raised his eyebrows. Rather than explain the source of her irritation, she said, "I didn't realise how busy everyone was while I was stuck behind those curtains. I assumed there were a few people on watch and that was it."

"Thought the others were here just to enjoy the voyage, eh?" said Mueller. "Everyone has a job to do. No one is here just to enjoy the ride, apart from you, of course."

"How many of those torpedoes do you carry?" asked Frances.

"Fourteen," Zeitler replied. "Four in the bow tubes, one in the stern kept ready. The others are in stowage fore and aft."

"They have contact pistols, which detonate on impact. Kaput!" added Werner.

Frances shuddered. "They're evil!"

"I completely agree," said Mueller.

* * *

If a few meals were spent discussing the war or listening to Mueller deride his government, then most were spent in talking of trivial matters. This was what they all liked best, as it helped to ease the utter boredom they were all feeling. The relaxing talk of the past and their dreams of the future. Schumacher had made some sort of apology and Mueller had let him join them for meals in the wardroom again. At times, Ehrhart, the navigation officer, also joined them. Frances liked Ehrhart. He was quiet and thoughtful, a family man, she learnt, like Paul Werner.

During one meal, Paul Werner asked Frances about her past. She told them how her parents had met at the front during the Great War. Her father was a doctor and her mother a nurse. They had moved to England so full of optimism. She spoke of her childhood in England, preferring to dwell on the long past—the recent past being too painful. She talked of the loss of her mother and her close relationship with her father, of how on occasions she'd helped him on his rounds and with simple routine operations. The tears prickled behind her eyes as she remembered those wonderful times with her dear papa. And then an image of Steven, Jacques, and Edie flashed up, and memories of the good times in Paris came flooding back. For a moment, she thought she was going to embarrass herself by crying. Mueller's voice brought her back to the present.

"So, you helped your father, then." He sat back and looked at her across the table. "I didn't really think of you as a practical person at all."

"Really, Kapitanleutnant? Then how did you think of me?" she asked.

He sniffed. "Oh, overindulged and spoilt."

"Well, thanks so much," Frances said with all the venom she could muster.

"You're welcome." He regarded her from under his brows, a corner of his mouth twitching. "By the way, I still think of you that way."

Frances wanted to feel angry, but like Mueller, the other men had a teasing light in their eyes.

"God, you're hateful," she said, flicking him a glance.

"Thank you," returned Mueller.

"You're welcome," she said.

"Touché!" Klaus Zeitler said with a laugh, which they all joined in with.

Werner turned to her. "What will be the first thing you will do when you get back onto dry land?"

"Oh, that's easy," said Frances. "A bath, a hair wash, and a change of clothing. Oh, what I'd give for a tub of hot water. And you, Paul? What will you do?"

"Read my mail. Then if the C in C will allow it, I'll go home. I just want to hold my family, smell their hair. That's what I miss most, just holding them. In fact, I could count on the fingers of one hand the number of times that I've held little Kristian. God, I hope they're safe."

They all stayed quiet for a few moments, each lost in their own thoughts and worries.

Zeitler broke the silence. "No need to ask our commander what he'll be doing when he gets back."

"Eh?" Mueller looked up.

"Ah, come on," said Zeitler, "don't tell us you've forgotten you have a very important role to play in a very important society wedding?"

"Oh, that." He blew out his cheeks. "I haven't given it a thought since we left port."

Ehrhart chuckled. "Jesu, some bridegroom you'll make."

Mueller was engaged. The heat of surprise crawled out of Frances's shirt collar and spread over her face. He'd never said—but why should he? She squirmed, brought her hand to her face, making a show of rubbing her mouth. What did it matter to her, anyway? It was true she had wondered whether he was married, but he'd never mentioned a family, apart from his parents and their farm. He'd never spoken of anyone special, and yet he was to be married. Why should she find the information so disagreeable, even painful? She disliked him; he was horrid, a beast—and yet—and yet, she was perversely attracted to him. Physically, that was. He was tall and athletic, and she found his face fascinating—the high cheekbones, the jaw, strong but not heavy, the deep clefts which ran from the sides of his finely bridged nose to the corners of his straight, sardonic mouth. She'd noticed the way his eyes crinkled when he laughed and the small gap in his teeth, which at times made him look so very young. My God, she thought, had she really noticed all that about him? But Mueller was speaking, addressing her. She tried to concentrate.

"That's the colour for you, Froggy."

"Pardon?"

Paul Werner laughed. "Pfennig, for your thoughts, Frances. Where have you been? You missed our leader reminiscing over the colour and feel of satin gowns. Do you know he's had a thing about satin since I've known him?"

Mueller turned his eyes on her. "Next best thing to the feel of a woman's skin," he said. "I was just saying that bottle green is the colour for you, off the shoulder and fitted tight across the hips."

Frances felt herself going hot again and looked away. Was the man embarrassing her on purpose? She felt his gaze, the ghost of his smile. "Well, I'll remember that Kapitanleutnant," she said, rising. "Next week when I shop for an evening gown. Excuse me, gentlemen."

Paul Werner, as always, did her the courtesy of standing as she left. Mueller just sat, watching her. She could feel his eyes burning her back.

Chapter 19

That night Frances dreamed. She dreamed of the good times. Of expensive Balenciaga perfume and bottle-green satin gowns. Then her dream turned traitor, and she dreamed instead of having nowhere to wear it, of having been ostracised by the people she thought of as her friends. And Otto appeared, jeering, sniggering. Telling her there was nowhere to hide, that she belonged to him.

A clamour of voices rose abruptly in the way of dreams. "Come on, Frances. Run!" they shouted, and she saw Steven and Jacques, and she ran to them, but she couldn't catch them. Stumbling, falling, getting up again, she shouted for them to stop, but it was as if they couldn't hear her. But now she felt Steven's arms surround her, and she clung to him, sobbing, hungry for his caresses. His hand stroked her hair. His voice calmed her.

"Hush, sweetheart. It's all fine. You're safe now. You're all right."

And then she realised that the voice, though reassuring, belonged to Mueller, not Steven, and pushing away, she apologised, wiping the tears from her eyes. "I'm sorry. I was dreaming, and I disturbed you."

Mueller smiled. Not his usual sardonic smile, but one which was warmly sympathetic. "Why don't you just talk it over?"

Fully awake now, she was immediately on her guard. "I told you before, I don't know anything."

He held up his hands. "All right, I accept that. But look, I don't think bottling things up is doing you any good. You've obviously been through an ordeal. Maybe you need to get it off your chest." He paused, and Frances wondered whether she should point out that some of his behaviour had added to that ordeal. "Sometimes it's good to talk it through, you see." He lifted his eyebrows. "Huh?"

Frances cradled her head in her hands. "Maybe you're right. Strange, isn't it?" She lifted her gaze to his. "The way things change, I mean. Three years ago, I would say I had everything. A brilliant career, money, good friends, talent, a husband to take care of me—now look."

"Hey, things will sort out. Do you want to talk? I'm a good listener, and no questions, I promise." She considered and then nodded. "Then I'll get us a coffee, shall I?" asked Mueller, rising from the bunk to his feet.

She nodded a second time. "Please."

Over that coffee, Mueller learnt of the Meyers' flight from Paris. He learnt too, of Otto and the threats he had made, forcing them all to quit Paris, to try to escape to England.

"It nearly worked too; we got all the way to Fecamp," said Frances. "Gosh, it was some journey, though. It was surreal at times. Some kilometres out of Paris, we came across lots of deserted cars just left by the side of the road. Steven said that they were left over from when people made the exodus from Paris. That would have been two years previous, but they were still there, left to rot. The only moving motor vehicles we came across were German, apart from close to towns, but then only one or two."

"Run out of fuel, I guess," said Mueller. He was sitting beside her on the bunk, his long legs dangled over the side, like her, sipping at his coffee, watching her intently, listening to her tale.

"Yes, I suppose so. I had the worst of that journey because our leaving was rushed. There were no papers for me, so I had to hide in a false bottom of the cart that they fitted for most of the time."

"Where did the papers come from?" Mueller asked.

She looked up, her eyes flashing. "You said no questions, remember?"

He raised his hands. "Sorry."

She continued. "Truly, I can't tell you, anyway. Jacques arranged everything. I think. Papers for the others, somewhere to sleep at night, food. Real names were never used. It was extraordinary because I have known Jacques for years; he was my teacher, just an old man and yet..." She shook her head thoughtfully.

"Could he have been working for the Resistance army, do you think?" suggested Mueller.

Frances contemplated this for a few moments and then gave a satirical laugh.

"They didn't tell me any of the plan, you know. It seems that they didn't trust me enough. They thought me weak, and that hurt a little." Her eyes had filled up, and Mueller lay his hand on hers, stroking his thumb across the back of it.

"Hey, you're hardly weak, Froggy. What about the way you sang the damn Marsellaise?" She looked at him and gave a little laugh, removing her hand from beneath his to wipe her tears from her eyes. "I really am sorry I hit you, you know," he said. "I hope you understand why I did."

"Because I sang the 'Marseillaise'?"

Mueller laughed out loud at her answer. "Not because you sang it, Froggy, but when and where you sang it. I had to shut you up quick, you see. You were giving our position away. You really could have caused the death of us all." He leant towards her a little and looked into her eyes. "I'll tell you what, you can sing the 'Marsellaise' for me now if you like— all of it — and I promise I won't punch you in the jaw."

She gave the glimmer of a smile. "I don't think I'm in the mood for singing."

"No? Good. That's a relief."

They both sat in silence for a minute or two until Mueller broke it. "Come on, then, let's hear the rest of it."

She nodded. "I'm accumulating my thoughts," she said, and then after a few moments, she continued.

"It took about four days to get to Fecamp—a small village near Fecamp, not the town itself," she explained. "It's heavily occupied by your lot. I thought my aunt was coming with us to England, but she only made the coast and went back to Paris. Nothing would drag her from Paris for long. Jacques, too, was just going to make the journey to England, and then he intended to return to face the music, and Otto, of course."

"Bastard Otto," growled Mueller, and then he frowned. "He didn't hurt you, did he, Froggy?"

Despite the situation, she couldn't prevent a broad smile from lighting her face. "Not as much as you did," she said, turning her eyes on him. He laughed, realising what he'd said. They caught each other's gaze, and Frances felt the same warm shudder run through her body and glanced down to cover her confusion. He leant towards her, knocking her shoulder with his own.

"Hey, you can't stop now."

She chewed on her lip for a moment before continuing.

"There seemed to be a highly developed network of help across the countryside. We got to the coast, to the village, and hid in an area of woodland until evening. An elderly fisherman met us. He introduced himself as Gerard, but I don't think that was his name. He took us to a cottage just outside the village. I don't think it was his home. We were given food and somewhere to sleep for a few hours, and I think he got rid of the horse and cart, and I have no idea where to, so please don't ask," she said, turning her eyes on him once more. Mueller shook his head, eyes wide and innocent. "The plan was that come dusk, Steven and Jacques, heavily muffled, would pose as Gerard's sons. Your coastal patrols know who's who and expect the old fisherman and his boys nightly. Of course, I got the short straw again."

"How so?"

"I was an extra—no one had expected me when the plan was laid— so after a couple of hours' sleep and a somewhat emotional farewell to Aunt Edie, I was smuggled down to the beach and hidden in their rowing boat under the tarpaulin. I had to wait until it was time to fish. If found, I was to say I was the old man's grandson and was sneaking aboard. I was there on my own for hours. All I could think about was wondering if Edie had gotten safely away. The second part of the plan worked too, and we got out to the *Etoile* without a hitch. All we had to do then was mingle with the fishing fleet and at an opportune moment extinguish the lights, drift away and make for the English coast."

Mueller bent his leg up onto the bunk so that he could turn to her and see her better. "So near and yet so far, Froggy, eh? What happened?"

"I was with Steven when Jacques told us to listen. We heard another engine, a patrol boat. I'm not sure, but I think we were about twelve miles out of Fecamp. Jacques made me get down the hold. It stank of fish, and before they closed it on me, I saw... I saw they had guns." She struggled to continue as the memories came flooding back. "What chance did they have, two old men and one disabled by sickness, to fight their way out? But that's what they did." She paused. "I could only listen to the rest."

She cried again, and Mueller gently lay his hand on hers, watching her, concerned as she fought to regain control of her emotions.

"I heard the patrol boat approach, and then a voice asked why there were no lights. No one answered, and they asked again. I heard Jacques shout out to the others, 'Vive La France!'"

"I don't know who fired first, but it seemed to go on for an age. I thought my heart or my head was going to explode. The bullets ripped into the decking, and some made their way into the hold. There were sparks as they hit and bounced off the metal. I'd managed to get behind some wooden pallets and cover myself in a tarpaulin. The fear. And then the shooting stopped, and somehow that was worse. I heard boots above me on the deck..." She paused again, looking down at her knees, taking deep breaths, reliving it.

"Hey, you're doing really well," he encouraged. She took some deep breaths and swallowed back her tears before continuing once more.

"They shone a light down the hold. I crammed a fist in my mouth to stop myself from screaming. A grenade was mentioned, and I thought that was it. Then I heard them say fire, and I knew I had to get out. Had to get off the boat. I waited until the engine noise disappeared, and then I climbed the ladder and got out of the hold. There was a plume of smoke. And a strange metallic smell." She wrapped her arms around herself, giving an involuntary shiver. "I can't...I can't..." She paused, breathing deeply. "I vomited."

He placed his hands on her shoulders, and she lifted her eyes, and he saw that all the fire in them had been extinguished. She fell against his chest. "All dead," she said through her tears, and she shuddered uncontrollably. He held her close until she recovered enough to carry on.

"I saw Jacques slumped. His dear old face was gone. Just blood and bone. Gerard had a gaping wound between his eyes. And then I saw Steven. My darling Steven. He lay face up in a widening pool of his own blood. There was blood seeping from wounds in his chest. That's when I rushed to the boat rail and vomited into the water. I realised then, you see, the source of the metallic smell—it was their blood."

"I steeled myself to approach the bodies of these men who I had loved. Jacques' eyes, in what was left of his face, were wide open and staring. I took a deep breath and closed them."

"I knelt beside Steven and stroked my hand through his hair, and I kissed his brow, it was cold already. Stupidly, I waited, hoping that kiss would breathe life into him like in a dream. But it was no fairy tale. I sat with him for a while. I should have stayed with him. It was my fault, all my fault that they were dead."

"Hey," said Mueller, "of course, it wasn't your fault."

"Oh, it was. If we hadn't had to leave in a hurry. If I hadn't been so stupid, trusting Otto. Then I remembered the fire. The threat must have penetrated my mind. There was a row of flames skittering across the wooden deck. I knew I had to get off the *Etoile*, but how could I leave these men? Lying down next to Steven was something I thought of. I thought of going with them into the next world. If there is one. I remember thinking for sure this world is nothing but evil now, its own hell, which we had tried and so miserably failed to escape. Why should I live on if Steven was dead?"

"Some impulse jolted me out of a daze. *No need for a grenade; she'll blow.* That's what the German commander had said. His words banged through my brain. I ran to the rowing boat tied to the side of the *Etoile*. There was some sort of mechanism for lowering it which I didn't understand. I knew I needed a knife."

"I thought maybe Gerard. I crossed to his body, trying not to look at his face, feeling in his pockets, round his belt. As I moved his body, there was a hiss of air that made me jump back, and for a split second, I thought he was still alive. I felt an almost sickening sense of relief when I found a penknife tucked in his belt."

"I sawed at those damn ropes until my hands ached. They were so thick. After what felt like hours, I cut through one, and the boat dropped the couple of metres into the water, but it was still secured by a second rope to the *Etoile*. I knew I'd have to cut that too once I was in the boat."

"Then I remembered my violin. I'd left it in the hold. There was no way I could leave without it."

She shook again, and Mueller pulled her to him, stroking the back of her head, wondering if his suggestion that she should talk about the horrors of that night and unburden herself had been the right thing to do. It had all been so much worse than he could ever have imagined, and he felt guilty for reawakening those memories. After a while, Frances pushed herself gently out of his embrace and raised her eyes to his.

"I knew I had to get off the *Etoile*; the fire was taking hold. I felt guilty about leaving them there—I still feel guilty—but I didn't want to die. I cut the ropes tying the rowing boat. I don't know how long it was until you found me."

Mueller rubbed at his beard thoughtfully, his gaze on her steady. "I'm so sorry, Froggy, that you went through all of that. It must have been dreadful for you. This is the horror of modern warfare, you see. Civilians get caught up in it."

"What of the patrol boat?" she asked. "I've been thinking. God knows I've had plenty of time to. Do you think Otto—"

"What? Had something to do with it? Doubtful. You could have been heading anywhere, and if he were having you followed, he would have had you picked up way before." He shook his head. "Just bad luck, I'd say."

"And Aunt Edie. Kapitanleutnant, do you think she got back to Paris?" Frances knew that the question was unanswerable, and she wasn't surprised when Mueller didn't even try.

"Is that where you'll go then?" he asked instead.

"I suppose so. I've nowhere else to go, and Edie and all my clothes and money are there. My home is Paris." She looked at him, and his eyes locked onto hers. And for that moment, for them both, there was no war, nothing, not even another soul—just the two of them. She tore her eyes away from him and sighed.

"Everything is in Paris," she said.

Recovering himself, Mueller puffed out his cheeks, exhaled, and said, "Come on, it's late. I hope talking about it has helped, a little, at least. Now you should try to get some sleep for a couple of hours, huh?"

Chapter 20

December 10, 1942

Several days later whilst surfaced, Heinemann picked up a message, which was passed onto Schumacher as second officer to decode. Mueller was busy with Ehrhart at the chart table, and Frances was chatting to the Chief nearby in the control room when Schumacher reported.

"Sir, we've just picked up this report."

Zeitler and Frances looked up in time to see Mueller's face drain of all colours. He stood for a few seconds, taking deep breaths, steadying himself. Then, without a backward glance, he made towards his quarters.

Zeitler looked questioningly at Schumacher.

"Bad news, I'm afraid," he said.

Picking up the message, Zeitler read it aloud. "Regret to report the loss of UBG 03:00 hrs December 9th. Grid position A L. Ten members of crew lost, including Kapitanleutnant, Hermann Kissler."

"Who is Hermann Kissler?" asked Frances.

"A friend ... a very close friend of the old man's," said Zeitler.

Frances followed Mueller and found him in the wireless room, trying to find out if there was further information from any of the crew members that had been picked up by other U-boats in the pack. She waited for him in the nook, and then as he turned to leave the wireless room, she called out to him. "Kapitanleutnant!" He stopped but didn't turn.

"Not now, Froggy," he said and carried on into the control room and up onto the bridge. He kept his own company for a few hours and made it clear that he was in no mood for sharing the news or socialising. He chose not to take the evening meal in the wardroom, sitting alone in his nook, and then as the U-boat resurfaced under the blanket of night, he took again to the bridge, his only company the watch and the endless swirling mass of the Atlantic.

Just six weeks ago, he was with his good friend Hermann Kissler at the Casino Bar club. The memory was still so fresh in his head.

* * *

Tasks completed, he found himself with the last remains of a sunny October day and was determined to enjoy what was left of it. Who knew what might happen during the patrol? He had been down to the bunkers and checked out his command, Underwater Boat A, his submarine, finding her totally refitted and with a fresh coat of grey paint covering the red scars of the last mission. The Chief had declared her good as new, and that was good enough for him. As for the new boy, Schumacher? He didn't like him; he was clearly one of those damn Hitler Youth boys. All the same, it made him feel mean. After all, he was only a kid. He was determined to give the chap a chance.

Leaving Schumacher to oversee the loading of provisions, he went into town for the remainder of the afternoon, patting his belt for the reassuring presence of his pistol, though doubting the need to use it in a city that was bustling with German uniforms. Brest, a thriving city with bistros, picturesque bookstores, and cafes, was also a hotbed of espionage. It was wise to be careful in Brest; there had been abductions and even murders by the Maquis.

After choosing one of the many excellent restaurants, he ordered a meal of seafood in a rich cream sauce and settled back, sipping champagne. He returned the smile of a pretty girl sitting across the aisle and toyed with the idea of asking her to join him, deciding against it. He left the restaurant just in time for a leisurely stroll to the Casino Bar to work off his meal.

The Casino Bar, favourite haunt of all the Flotilla officers. Madame and her lovelies always made them welcome. Madame herself was very understanding if one of the boys lost his temper, along with his loot, or was somewhat too drunk to hold his liquor. He had frequently wondered how much they paid the poor sod that cleaned up the puke in the washroom.

Arriving at the C.B. at around eight-thirty, he glanced around not for the first time at the décor and grimaced—too much pink and gold going on for his taste, or for anyone else who had taste, he thought. Loud music was coming from the direction of the bar, along with raucous singing. He looked in on the casino that appeared to be doing a roaring trade too. He remembered then that they were only one of three U-boats due out the next morning—this could turn into some night.

Leaving his overcoat in the cloakroom, he made his way to the bar, easily picking out the familiar, blond-topped figure of Paul Werner across the room. Cecile, the barmaid, gave him her usual seductive smile when she saw him.

"What can I give you tonight, Kapitan?" she asked, leaning over the bar, giving him a better view of her cleavage, and licking her lips with the tip of her tongue.

"Just a beer, Cecile, thank you." He nodded at her and smiled.

She walked along the bar to the beer tap furthest away to give him the best view of her swaying hips and bobbing breasts. In an obvious, cheap way, he found her attractive, but he stayed away from her kind for two reasons. The first was mercenary. Why should he pay for a pleasure enjoyed by two? The second was clinical. There were plenty of harbours to slip into, where women were much less likely to carry the curse. Nurses or local girls, like the one at the restaurant—all it took was an enjoyable meal, perhaps a bottle of champagne, and a few well-chosen compliments.

Cecile returned with his beer. She let her hand slip from the cool moistness of the glass and caressed his fingers.

"Are you sure there is nothing else I can do for you, Kapitanleutnant?" she asked.

He shook his head, dispatching his most disarming smile. "Thank you, Cecile. I'm sure."

"Shame." She smiled back.

Beer in hand, he joined Paul and some other lads who he recognised as officers from Hermann Kissler's boat. They'd seen him coming and were busy dragging a comfortable chair to the table for his benefit. Merkel, a strapping great lad in his twenties and a hardened submariner, took his arm and steered him round the table.

"Come on, old man, you'll be thankful for somewhere to park your arse after a couple more beers!"

He took a swipe at his head. "Hey! Less of the old man, if you please!"

* * *

It was true, though. By U-boat standards, at twenty-nine, he was indeed an old man. One of the last surviving aces. Schepke and Prien, two of the best submarine commanders, had bought it—*not many of us old timers left,* he thought.

After reading law at Bonn, he had practised for a couple of years locally. As the German Navy rebuilt itself, he had applied to Naval College, following in the footsteps of his father, along with his friend from University, Paul Werner. Then, in 1939, they both had applied to the German Navy's submarine branch. There, the waves had parted, and they had both gone off in different directions to serve as executive officers. He'd served a year in that capacity before being promoted to Kapitanleutnant early in 1940, and against all odds, they had assigned Paul as his executive officer on the U-boat.

That had been when the training was good. Mostly now, the navy was populated by young kids who were thrown into the thick of action by the Naval colleges. All narrow mouths, narrow hips, and narrow minds. Poor sods had had all their own thoughts removed, brainwashed by the Party into thinking it was a glorious thing to fight and die for the Fatherland and the honour of the Führer. He supposed that was the way of things; as the older commanders bought it, their replacements would get younger and younger.

There had been a group of new boys in the corner that night. A couple of Oberleutnants were comparing notes on their first commands. Well, at least they'd survived them. How many, he wondered, would crack when the pressure was really on when the lives of forty or so men depended on their judgement.

* * *

Crohn, Kissler's Number One, was relating a tale about one of their missions. Evidently, a couple of their torpedoes had let them down at a crucial moment.

"Seems to happen more and more. You'd think they'd be improving the damn fish, wouldn't you?" Werner said to him.

"Sabotage, I'd say."

"Could be," returned Crohn, "but in the factories or over here?"

He blew out his cheeks. "Who knows?"

A commotion at the bar entrance drew his glance—Kapitanleutnant Hermann Kissler had appeared, shouting greetings. He was wearing his customary long black leather coat, a black cigar poking at a rakish angle from between his fat lips. Herman Kissler, big, bold, blonde, and brash.

"Stand to attention, you ugly bastards!" shouted Kissler. A cheer went up.

"Kissler!"

Kissler staggered briefly, nine sheets to the wind as usual, and, grabbing the bar edge, propped himself up.

He was glad to see Kissler; his antics always amused him. "Mad bastard," he muttered under his breath.

Raising his hands above his shoulders, Kissler called for quiet, and when he was certain that he had everyone's attention, he stumbled to the small stage set up for the evening's cabaret act and climbed onto it. The room waited in silence as Kissler turned on the microphone, took it from the stand, and then, whilst giving a party salute, farted into the mic.

A collective cheer went up. "Kissler, Kissler!" The men in the crowded bar never tired of him. A beer was put into his hand as a reward, and he removed the cigar from his mouth to enjoy a large swig as he left the stage and lurched towards Werner, himself, and the other men at the table.

"Don't ask where he's been, for God's sake," begged Merkel.

"You know he's going to tell us anyway," Paul Werner said. "With all the gory details. Several times over."

Mueller shook his head as he thought of Kissler. Renowned for leading his men to the rating's brothels as soon as the boat docked. The dirtier the better was the way he said he liked his women. Just a good unemotional poke, and the chance to relive the experience in the C. B. by telling the lads every detail over and over. That was the way he made sure of getting his money's worth. Over-daring, overweight and oversexed—that was Kissler, with scarcely a decent thought in his head. He reckoned it was Kissler's way of dealing with the stress, a sort of overreaction.

* * *

Cecile had come from behind the relative safety of the bar to clear a few glasses and was now paying for her mistake by being openly mauled by Kissler. Her shrieking once more drew everyone's attention to Kissler's antics. She could speak enough German to leave Kissler in little doubt as to whether his attentions were out of line, but encouragement from the onlookers egged him on.

"Take your hands off me, you randy sod!" she squealed. And then, as if to underline her meaning, she brought her knee up into his groin with a dull thud that every man in the room felt. Kissler winced. Every man in the room did. "Christ, woman! It was only a bit of fun. Where's your sense of humour?"

"If it's fun you want," Cecile retorted, "you can pay for it like everyone else."

Kissler grunted. "I just have."

"In future, keep your hands off me unless you have the money. I know how to look after myself very well, and I will."

Mueller had looked on and was amused by the idea that Cecile objected to Kissler's unsolicited attention. He was also impressed that throughout the entire episode, the angle of the cigar Kissler kept clenched in his teeth had remained unaltered.

Kissler straightened, taking a bow. Another round of cheers rose.

He knew Kissler and his boys were leaving tomorrow, too. They'd spent the last couple of weeks on shore, living down the embarrassment of not even getting out of port before being hit by the Brits at the start of their last patrol.

"Bastards swooped straight down out of the sun," Kissler had told him. "Didn't even see them before it was too late." They'd managed to dive, Kissler had said, but had sustained enough damage that they had had to limp back to port, and that patrol was cancelled. Now he was raring to get back to sea and ram a few fishes up Churchill's fat arse.

He wondered who was the most dangerous, the new boys, with

their lack of experience, or Kissler, with his lack of self-control? He was exceedingly fond of Herman Kissler, but he recognised that the man was becoming a danger to his own men as well as the Brits.

* * *

Standing on the bridge of the U-boat, he wished now that he had found a way to tell Kissler that he was taking the war far too bloody personally, but how do you say that to a man who'd lost his entire family in an air raid? He thanked God that his own folks lived in the relative safety of the countryside. He also thanked God that he knew when to stop drinking on the night before a patrol.

* * *

"Saw your ugly mug in the papers, Kristian, my boy," shouted Kissler as he approached the table, wiping sweat from his bloated face. "Surprised you bother with the likes of us nowadays."

"What, miss a social in the C.B.? It's the highlight of my life," he said.

"Poor sod. If you want some fun, why don't you join me?"

"No thanks, Hermann. I've had my fill of women for a good while."

"Christ, you're easy to please." Kissler stubbed out the end of his black cigar and immediately lit another, glancing over to the staircase that led to the many chambers housing Madame's charms.

"Looks like the ladies are having a busy night. No end of traffic."

He looked over his shoulder and nodded. "You thinking of joining the queue, Hermann? One for the road, eh?"

"What? And let the girls round the corner down?"

Round the corner from the C.B. was the rating's brothel. He wondered how many of his own boys were getting a last one in before morning and hoped that they wouldn't be getting into too much trouble.

"My God, what's that with Klaus?" asked Merkel, who had just turned to head for the washroom and caught sight of Mueller's chief officer at the bar with a new boy. Schumacher, dressed impeccably in his blues, with creases in his trousers you could cut your hands on and badges buffed to perfection. As he caught sight of Schumacher, Kissler gave vent to a fart that had been a long-time brewing. "Bloody Hell, who does that belong to?" Kissler exclaimed, choking on his cigar.

"You! You filthy bastard! What the hell have you been eating?" Mueller waved his hand in front of his face. Kissler grinned.

"No, not that—that!" He pointed towards Schumacher.

"Ah, well, that would be mine, I'm afraid," he admitted with a nod. "Don't worry, Herman; he won't stay clean for long."

Schumacher and Klaus Zeitler made their way over to the group. Zeitler had been working like a Trojan for the past few days, and this was the first time he'd set foot near the C.B. for some time. Mueller took solace in the fact that if he was here, then the boat must be ready. Zeitler always dealt with the minutest detail himself, leaving nothing to a clumsy prat of a mechanic.

Schumacher drew himself to attention in front of him, his Kapitan. "May I get you a drink, Kapitanleutnant?"

"If you're buying, why not? Beer, then."

"Make that two." Kissler burped. "What's that you're drinking?"

"Lemonade, sir."

"Lemonade? Man, you're a disgrace to the uniform you're wearing. Have a proper drink!"

"I will decline, sir. If you don't mind, I want a clear head for tomorrow."

Kissler laughed. "You'll have a clear head for the next six weeks, at least," he said, "unless you get the bugger blown off! Have a real drink, I insist. Cecile, bring us some cognac."

Schumacher clearly didn't want to argue with a senior officer and downed the cognac, which soon loosened his tongue, and he admitted that even though he had been out on two patrols, he hadn't seen any active service. Setting his glass down, he addressed his Kapitan.

"What I want to know," he said, "is what are the various options regarding the most rational course of action if under attack by enemy depth charges?"

Mueller wondered if of late the Admiralty had become stupid enough to give any hard and fast ruling on that. He was about to answer that it would depend on each individual case when Klaus Zeitler, who'd been attempting to educate the lad in the art of U-boat warfare for most of the day, cut him off.

~ 146 ~

"Well, I suppose there are three courses of action. You can try to outmanoeuvre, which is often difficult once you're picked up by the ASDIC. You can sit pretty well down and hope they misjudge your depth, or you can try a combination of the two."

"Don't forget the fourth alternative," Kissler said, butting in. All eyes turned on him.

"And what might that be?" asked Klaus, miffed that he may have forgotten something.

Kissler took a couple of gulps of cognac and wiped the surplus from his thick lips. "If all else fails, shit yourself, of course!"

* * *

Mueller was lost in the echoing memory of Kissler's laughter when Frances shouted up to the officer of the watch for permission to come up onto the bridge. Second Officer Schumacher granted her permission, and she climbed the rungs of the ladder and stepped out. There was a bit of a swell, and she shivered against the northern Atlantic wind. Mueller was standing with his back to her, gazing out at the U-boat's wash, a lonely figure.

Approaching him, she spoke softly. "Kapitanleutnant?"

He wheeled when he heard her voice. "Come to gloat?" His mood was caustic.

She stepped back, hurt, shocked by his anger. "No! Of course not."

"One less pirate for you anyway, right?" He turned away again, gripping the rail of the bridge.

"I came to say I'm sorry."

Mueller turned back and, dipping his chin, looked down.

She waited, uncertain what to say next, wondering if she should just leave well alone. Finally, she said, "I've lost people, too, remember."

He met her gaze and sighed. "They rammed him," he said, looking away into the middle distance. "Poor sod didn't even have a chance to dive. Destroyer cut straight through, sliced both his legs off at the trunk."

Frances felt herself pale.

"Somehow he got off the bridge and tried to swim for it. Just like him, that. He'd never give up. Jesus!" Mueller slammed his fists down on the rail. "What are we all doing to each other?"

Frances touched his hand briefly with her fingertips. She was unable to give an answer; she was unsure that he really knew that she was even there, and so she merely repeated, "I'm so sorry." She didn't know what else to say.

"Were you planning to stay up here for a while?" he asked her.

"Yes, if it's all right. I could do with some air."

He nodded. "Safe enough for now, though you'll have to excuse me. I've got my men to see to. I've left them on their own for long enough."

"I think they understand, Kapitanleutnant."

"Hmm, maybe." He looked at her as if properly noticing her for the first time. "Goodness, Froggy, where's your coat? It's freezing out here. You realise it's December, not June." He took off his lambskin jacket and, passing it to her, said, "Here. We don't want you catching cold."

She thanked him. He left a moment later, and she watched him go, feeling his grief for the loss of a friend, something she shared with him. Wondering how he could seemingly put it to the back of his mind and return to his command. She'd poured her heart out to him, and he'd held her in her grief and comforted her. She wanted to comfort him, but he'd closed himself off, not just from her, but from everyone.

She listened to his footsteps descending the ladder and his voice rapping out sharp commands. So, she thought, that's it then. The time for mourning is over. She pulled on the jacket, enjoying the softness and warmth, savouring the smell of the lambskin and the strange mixture of oil, salt, and sea, and the comforting odour that was him.

Chapter 21

Comforting? Comfortable? Yes, that's how it had become. Floating in the middle of the Atlantic Ocean at the mercy of the elements and the enemy, and yet for the first time in an age, she felt comfortable. Mueller had decided that she offered little threat to his men and let her have more freedom to move around. She learnt to close her ears to the obscenities that she heard, understanding that the language was that of a load of men together, and that it wasn't directed at her. There was a positive too. As they used the food up, the second toilet was in use.

The crew accepted her. Ehrhart even referred to her as Ordinary Seaman Froggy one day when she walked into the control room. His remark had caused a deal of merriment between the men who heard it until Zeitler pointed out that she was far from ordinary. She even manipulated a revenge upon Leutnant Schumacher. Childish though it was, she gleaned a terrific satisfaction from it and suspected that she wasn't the only one to do so.

A couple of mornings after the loss of Mueller's friend, she entered the wardroom. Finding it vacant, she came across Schumacher's party paper lying around, and the temptation was just too great. She took it to her bunk and hid it while she went in search of Mueller. She found him in the control room.

"I need a pencil," she told him.

"Do you now?" He crossed to the chart table, found one, and handed it to her.

"What are you going to do? Write?"

"No, drawing."

"You'll want some paper then."

"No, it's all right. I've got some."

She returned to the nook and set to work defacing every photograph of every top-ranking Nazi in that paper. Finding a photograph of

Hermann Göring, she scribbled in a Hitler type moustache and a pointed beard, then Eichmann type spectacles, and to complete her work, drew on a few hairs hanging from his nose. She went through the paper, drawing on moustaches, beards, spectacles, so that all the top brass Nazis whose photographs were in the paper looked remarkably similar. Pleased with her handiwork, she rolled up the paper and returned it to the wardroom, knowing that it wouldn't be long until Schumacher returned to pore over his paper one more time.

Scarcely an hour later, she was delighted to see Schumacher seething, though strictly speaking, she heard him first as she was in the nook.

"It is imperative that I speak with the Kapitanleutnant," she heard him say, and then someone replied, "He's in the engine room."

He strode past the wireless room and nook without even looking in, going in the direction of the engine room. Then she heard him closer than expected, retracing his steps into the wardroom, she thought.

"Excuse me, Kapitanleutnant, I wish something to be done about this."

She heard Mueller then, disinterested. "What, Schumacher, what?"

"This, it's tantamount to treason."

"For goodness' sake, Leutnant, what is?" Mueller asked.

Frances felt frustration; it was all very well being able to listen in, but for optimum satisfaction she needed to see, too. When she got to the wardroom, Mueller had the paper laid out in front of him, turning the pages, savouring its contents with an ill-concealed smile. He looked up when she appeared.

"Ahh. See what someone's done to our Leutnant's paper, Froggy. 'Tantamount to treason,' he calls it. What do you think? Do we have a traitor on board?"

"You know your crew better than I do, Kapitanleutnant, but I wouldn't have said so." She clasped her hands, wide-eyed, playing the innocent.

"No, not treason, Second Officer, more like high spirits, I'd say." Mueller suppressed a chuckle.

"I'm sorry, Kapitanleutnant, but I don't think it's very funny." Schumacher was red-faced.

"No, you wouldn't. What's up? Don't they train you to have a sense of humour in the Hitler Youth?"

Schumacher realised he was not going to get anywhere and was forced once again to retreat, shoulders dropped in defeat, angry and disappointed one more time with his commander. This was not the way things should be dealt with; this was not the way he would run his command. A few home truths had to be told back at base regarding Kapitanleutnant Mueller, he thought. Mueller waited until Schumacher was out of earshot.

"Tut, you really are a naughty child," he chided.

"Kapitanleutnant," Frances said with mock offence. "I really don't know what you're talking about." She turned to leave, but he continued speaking.

"Of course, you don't, but you are going to find Schumacher and offer to rub out the graffiti from his Bible." She turned back to him, and he leant forward on the bench; eyes locked on hers. "You will sit down at this table with a rubber and remove all your artwork without tearing a page. Do I make myself clear?"

She gave Mueller a wide grin, and despite trying not to, he grinned back at her before he regained control.

"I'm serious," he said, the sparkle in his eyes belying the sternness of his tone. "They have shot men for less."

* * *

Lemon eating on board was mandatory, and for the majority, it was not a source of enjoyment. It didn't bother Frances at all, she could happily spoon one down, just like eating a grapefruit. Seated in the wardroom at breakfast with all the officers, she realised that the men were watching her eat a lemon with relish.

"What?" she asked.

"My God, I don't know how you can do that," remarked Zeitler. "Gives me the willies eating these damn things, I've tried eating them with cake, with sweetener, in coffee, in fruit juice—"

"Have you tried them on crepes?" she asked.

"Can't say I have," replied Zeitler.

"That's the way the English eat them on Shrove Tuesday. Pancake Day, they call it. Did you know?" Zeitler shook his head.

"I've heard of it. Filling themselves up before fasting; for Lent, isn't it?" said Paul Werner.

"What've lemons got to do with Lent?" asked Zeitler, still trying to think of some other way to make his lemon palatable.

"Well," continued Frances, "they squeeze lemon juice and sprinkle sugar on pancakes. They're what the French call crepes, more or less. I used to love them when I was a child in England."

Werner laughed. "So, let me get things right. While we have a magnificent Karneval before Lent, the Brits sit and eat a few pancakes. While we are singing and dancing and having fun, they stuff a few crepes down themselves."

"So, what do you need for these pancakes, then?" asked Mueller, who'd been sucking at a lemon and pulling faces throughout the conversation.

"Flour, milk, water, eggs, butter, sugar—"

"Is that it?"

Frances nodded.

"Right. Tell Hayman then that I've ordered pancakes for today."

Hayman hadn't heard of pancakes, but he had heard of crepes. He shook his head at Frances. "Don't know what they'll be like with dried milk, dried eggs and butter that's going rancid. Plus, we've got no sugar left." He made a face. "Still, if pancakes is what the old man wants, then pancakes is what he'll be getting."

It had been pure enjoyment helping Hayman for that hour. They had cooked pancakes non-stop. It had been fun, though they tasted so disgusting that no one complained about just sucking on lemons ever again.

* * *

During an evening meal, Frances announced with an audible sigh, "I am so bored. I've actually read *War and Peace* and *Les Misérables* cover to bloody cover."

"Are you bored with the practice dives, then?" asked Zeitler. "Fed up with wondering if you're going to get trampled already, are you?"

"You get to go up the top, don't you?" Mueller reminded her.

"Surprisingly, yes, I am fed up with the practice dives, and I rarely am allowed up the top," she said, eyeing Mueller.

"Looks like we need to organise a trip to the park, then," said Zeitler, breaking into a grin.

"Or you could take up knitting," Ehrhart, the navigation officer, suggested. Frances enjoyed his company as he would often talk to her about music, and his home and family in Berlin, but now he was being as bad as the others.

"Oh, you are all so funny, aren't you?" she remarked.

"You've still got the *Complete Works of Shakespeare* to read; that should keep you quiet," threw in Mueller.

"I've told you before, I'm just not into Shakespeare."

"Well, I recommend it, Froggy. You could learn a thing or two from his stories, you see."

"Oh, could I now, and is there a particular story that I could learn something from, Kapitanleutnant?"

"Page 1058. *The Taming of the Shrew*," Mueller announced.

The other men broke into laughter as Frances glared at Mueller, who looked back at her, eyebrows raised, doing his best to control the smile that was tugging at the sides of his mouth.

Undeterred, she continued, "I do actually have an idea."

Paul Werner joined in too. "You have an idea. Well done!"

She groaned. "What on earth did you all do before you had me to deride?"

The men looked from one to the other and shrugged. "I reckon our conversations were pretty boring before you came on board," said Zeitler. "I think now, though, we are all a little in love with you."

"Ha! a compliment at last." She beamed.

Mueller shook his head. "Not really a compliment, Froggy. What the Chief means is that we are all a little in love with your bosom and your cute arse." Before she could think of a suitable retort, Mueller rose to leave. "We surface in fifteen minutes, gentlemen."

"But I haven't told you my idea, Kapitan."

"The one to stop you from being bored. Perhaps it will work for us all, huh? Come on then, let's hear it. I haven't got all day." Mueller sat.

"Dieter has lent me his violin, and I would like some practice time, if you agree."

Mueller sighed. "And how long do you need to practise, Froggy?"

"Well, normally, I would practise for five or six hours each day."

"Well, it can't be done, as it will interfere with the men's sleep." Getting up again, he made to leave the wardroom.

"How about an hour in the morning during the trim?" Werner called after him. "While we all have breakfast."

Frances seized on Werner's suggestion. "An hour, please; that's better than nothing."

Mueller looked at her thoughtfully for a few seconds. "I'll make a deal with you, Froggy. I reckon you're mended now from all of your trials and tribulations, aren't you?"

"Well, yes," she replied. "But I hold you responsible for most of those trials and tribulations, Kapitanleutnant."

"Do you now?" Mueller gave a sniff and fixed her with his eyes. "So, where's your gratitude, Froggy? We saved your miserable arse from getting frozen off in the Atlantic, I seem to recall."

She held his gaze. "Is that the same miserable arse you very recently referred to as cute, Kapitanleutnant?"

The other men broke into laughter, and Mueller looked to the floor to hide his amusement.

"Please," she begged.

"Gratitude, Froggy. I gave you my bed, didn't I?"

"But it's killing me not being able to play. It's been my life for the last nine years. I'm asking for an hour a day, that's all. Please, Kapitanleutnant?" Mueller raised his eyebrows, and she murmured again, "Please."

He made a big thing of rubbing at his beard and looking thoughtful for a while before giving his reply. As the other men looked on, unable to fully conceal their amusement, he played to the gallery. "You don't get something for nothing, Froggy. You know that, right?" She nodded. "Then I'm glad we understand one another. You can have your hour, but I want my bed back. My damn back is killing me."

"But where do I go?"

Mueller raised his hand. "Shush. We each have two six-hour stints a day when the bed's ours."

"What happens if you don't make it back for your stint?" asked Frances, not altogether trusting him.

"If I'm not there, it's yours."

"Done, Kapitan!" She held out her hand to shake on it.

"Hold on, I haven't finished. The hour you practise comes out of your bunk time. And if I get any complaints, your practice stops, and if for any reason, I tell you to stop at any time, you do so immediately. Is that clear?"

She held out her hand a second time. "Done."

He took her hand briefly and left, shaking his head.

Frances rose early the following morning. Too excited to sleep when she took to the bunk at 2200 hours, she reckoned she had just nodded off around midnight when Mueller had relieved her of it. She had taken up an uncomfortable position on the floor with a blanket, and, unable to sleep, had given some thought to the deal she had made with Mueller. She reckoned he had tricked her. Her times on the bunk were from 1800 hours until midnight and 0600 hours until midday. Straight after evening meal, she thought, and first thing in the morning, when everyone is busy.

By 0800 hours she was holding a violin again, and she thought how wonderful it was. She lay her chin on the rest. Tipping her head slightly, feeling the smoothness of its body on her cheek, she breathed in the wonderful smell of the ageing wood. Then she raised the bow and drew it lightly across the strings, the mellow sound bringing tears to her eyes as her heart soared with joy.

For a good half hour, she practised scales, taking the instrument to its upper and lower limits, and then she played some movements from her favourite pieces. She was totally lost, and jumped when Mueller stuck his head through the curtains of the nook.

"Didn't think much of that first piece of music, Froggy. Who the hell composed that? They need shooting."

She lowered the instrument and turned to him. "Yes, hilarious. I haven't heard that before."

"Your hour's up," he said, lifting his eyebrows at the filthy look she was sending his way.

"Just a few more minutes, please. I've nearly finished."

Mueller stepped through the curtain. "One hour. I told you."

"Just three more minutes, that's all." She raised the bow, drew it over the strings.

"Time's up, Froggy." Mueller reached for the violin.

Frances turned from him, continuing to play. A beautiful tenor voice filled the hull of the U-boat. A voice singing the words to the melody she was playing.

Underneath the lantern, by the barrack gate.

She turned back to Mueller with a smile, seeing the emotion in his eyes, on his face, as several more voices rose in song. She couldn't very well stop now, could she?

Darling, I remember
The way you used to wait,
'Twas there that you whispered tenderly
That you loved me,
You'd always be
My Lili of the lamplight
My own Lili Marlene

Mueller gave his head a slight shake as if he read her mind. He laid a hand on her shoulder, and she felt it burning through to her skin as she continued to play. He bent his head down to hers.

"Good, Froggy," he said. "Very good. Carry on just to the end, huh, and make sure you finish your hour every day with this. It's good for morale, you see," he added as he left.

Time would come for roll call
Time for us to part,
Darling, I'd caress you
And press you to my heart,
And there neath that far off lantern light
I'd hold you tight,
We'd kiss goodnight
My Lili of the lamplight
My own Lili Marlene.

Orders came for sailing
Somewhere over there,
All confined to barracks
'Twas more than I could bear,
I knew you were waiting in the street

I heard your feet
But could not meet
My Lili of the lamplight
My own Lili Marlene.

Resting in our billet
Just behind the line,
Even though we're parted
Your lips are close to mine,
You wait where that lantern softly gleamed
Your sweet face seems
To haunt my dreams,
My Lili of the lamplight
My own Lili Marlene
My Lili of the lamplight
My own Lili Marlene.

Chapter 22

December 18, 1942

"**A** few more days patrol and then home," announced Mueller in the control room to anyone who may have been listening. No one answered. The old man was soliloquising again, mulling things over in his head. "Getting low on fuel, you see." He nodded to himself thoughtfully. "Another couple of days, then home. Should be back in port for some festivities at least. Not one of our best patrols, Ehrhart, huh?"

"No, Kapitanleutnant," replied Ehrhart, looking up from the chart table. Mueller looked around at his men. They appeared relaxed, each lost in his own private dream. Mueller thought of dry land, home, fires lit, warmth, and good food.

"Coded message, Kapitanleutnant."

Mueller looked up as Schumacher appeared; he was making for the wardroom, carrying the cipher machine. He placed it on the table, laying out the telegraphist's slip beside it. He checked and double-checked the settings, then tapped away at the keys as Mueller arrived from the control room, tearing the strip of paper from the machine almost before the message was completed.

He read it aloud. "C in C from UBR. Convoy sighted 0810 hours square BC, proceeding East." He made his way excitedly to the chart table in the control room, tracing his fingers over the map.

"Next grid position to ours." He smiled and nodded at Ehrhart. "We could be there within twenty-four hours. Let's try to intercept the convoy."

"Good chance we'd miss it, Kapitanleutnant, given we have only one chart reading."

"Sit tight for now then, huh?" Mueller returned to his corner of the wardroom, rewarding all that passed with one of his most amiable smiles, even Frances, who'd turned up in search of coffee.

"You look happy if I might say so, Kapitanleutnant," she remarked.

"Do I now? Well, looks like we might see some action and not before time, so perhaps that's why."

"Action?" She felt her spine stiffen and was instantly alert.

"Mnn, that's what we're here for, Froggy, not just for the cruise, delightful as it is. A convoy's been spotted."

"By us?"

Her use of the term 'us' amused him, enough that he ignored it. "No, by another U-boat. But my guess is it's heading straight for us."

"Oh! And I suppose your guesses are never wrong, Kapitan."

"Rarely, so we'll wait and see, shall we?"

Soon, they received a second message. "C in C from UBR convoy again sighted square BD uncertain of the exact course."

Well, they may not be certain, thought Mueller, as he pored over the charts a second time, *but I reckon I could hazard a damn good guess.* He turned from the table to find most of the off-duty crew had assembled, clearly aware that something was in the pipeline. Mueller smiled as his glance travelled amongst them, and then he issued his order. "Steer 170, full ahead both."

From her place at the table, Frances heard the words re-echoed. A shudder ran through the U-boat, then there was a slight lurch before the rhythmical sound of the engines at full power resounded through the boat. Wanting to be in the thick of all the excitement, Frances made her way to the control room.

"He's going for it without waiting for the OK from the C in C then." She overheard one crew member tell another, who nodded and answered.

"That's it, got the bit between his teeth. There'll be no stopping the old dog now."

The U-boat ploughed through the enormous waves and raced her way through troughs, leaving a foaming wake and the smell of diesel behind her. Several hours later, Mueller made his way to the bridge, pulling his cap low on his forehead and narrowing his eyes against the spray. He warned, "Keep your eyes open, boys."

It was afternoon before he left the bridge again. Making his way over to the chart table where Ehrhart had been plotting the convoy's latest positions, he found it was now possible to read its course and speed accurately. Whilst he was still digesting this latest information, Werner passed over the latest message.

Mueller's heart rose. "At last! Message from the C in C," he said to Ehrhart. "Intercept convoy reported by UBR. Utmost speed." He raised his voice in command. "Officer of the watch, steer 093."

The Helmsman's voice echoed the course back from the conning tower.

Mueller slapped his navigator on the back and grinned. "Well, Ehrhart, we should intercept by 0400 hours tomorrow, huh?"

Ehrhart nodded and smiled.

"Time to let them know what's going on, then." Mueller picked up the intercom. "My men," he announced to all compartments, "we're up against a convoy. Expect to intercept from 0400 hours. That's all."

Frances was in the wardroom when the message came over the intercom, and the excitement that followed hung in the air. At first, she fought the impulse to breathe it in. All men were on the alert now; each had his own job to do and when the time came, would carry it through with the utmost German efficiency. Try as she might, she could not help getting caught up in the mounting excitement. She spent most of her time squashed in a corner of the control room trying to keep out of the way, or else in the wardroom trying to trap someone in momentary conversation so that she might understand better what was going on.

0430 hours next day just as night drew back its curtains, allowing dawn to break in the East, the watch saw a destroyer clearly silhouetted on the horizon. Mueller gave the command. "Dive to periscope depth."

"Faint propeller noises bearing southwest," reported Heinemann.

They stayed below for an hour and then resurfaced into a fog up top. The watch reported a real pea-souper.

"Waste of bloody time," remarked Mueller after half an hour. "Take her down again, Chief. Heinemann, keep those ears of yours open. Shit!" Snatching off his cap, he slapped it against his leg. "If we've let this one go."

The U-boat made a graceful dive back into the depths of the Atlantic, and her crew prepared to sit it out once more, uncertain of the part they would play, if any, in this next episode of the Atlantic war.

It was midday when Heinemann's voice rang through to the control room, surprising everyone.

"Sweet bloody Mary!" Heinemann leapt in his seat. He was not a man who blasphemed without due cause. Mueller was beside him in an instant.

"What is it?"

"Propeller noises all round us, Kapitanleutnant."

Mueller raised his eyebrows and took the headphones. "Sweet Jesus, Mary, and Joseph, we're right in the middle of a convoy. Battle stations! Prepare to surface!" he shouted.

Schumacher made his way over to Frances, with the ropes to secure her in an out-of-the-way corner of the control room, which was now swarming with men, some of whom muttered doubtfully about the wisdom of surfacing. In such circumstances, there was a dangerous risk of collision. Frances tried to lose herself in the melee, but it was only seconds until Schumacher grabbed her by the arm and pulled her towards him.

"Hands behind your back, Frau," he instructed.

She tried to argue. "You really don't need to do this. Can you at least tie my hands in front?" Schumacher grabbed one of her arms and wrenched it behind her back and set to winding the rope around one of her wrists, enjoying the task. Even though the thought of being tied up and forgotten for several hours terrified her, she complied with Schumacher's demands, knowing that if she put up any kind of fight, he would tie the bonds even tighter.

Mueller was on his way. Deciding to take to the bridge alone in the first instance, he placed his cap firmly on his head and prepared to climb through the tower. Turning, he caught sight of Schumacher tying up Frances.

"Leutnant!" he called out. "No need to do that. Just keep an eye on her." Then, taking to the ladder, he said, "Stand by to equalise pressure."

Schumacher scowled as he loosened the bonds. It was enough that they had picked this woman up in the first place; now she was being treated as a member of the crew.

Mueller lifted the hatch, soaking all those immediately below as he hauled himself out into a thinning fog.

"First and second officers to the bridge. Standby to dive," came the muttered command via the hatch. Below, everyone held their breath. The metallic ring of boots on the ladder rungs sounded curiously intense, as did the whispered voices of their officers.

"We're inside their escort screen," they heard Mueller say. "Port side of convoy, two destroyers to starboard. Shit! And another coming straight for us. Alaaaarm Dive!"

Werner and Schumacher were below in seconds with Mueller right behind them, waiting only to secure the hatch. All eyes were on him, questioning, fearful as the propeller noise approached, reached a crescendo, and passed harmlessly overhead.

"Didn't spot us, I'm sure of that," he said, rubbing at his beard. "We'll drop back for a while."

The continuous beating of propellers was clearly heard below as the convoy made its way, oblivious on its course.

"That convoy is nicely packed together by the sounds of things," remarked Werner. He was standing close to Frances in the heaving control room. He turned and smiled at her. "Some sound that!"

Frances nodded.

"You pick up all sorts of sounds down here," he explained. "Listen! There's two speeds of propeller: the slow ones; they're the merchantmen. Then amongst them are the faster ones: the escorts, destroyers, and corvettes; hear them?"

She nodded a second time, thoughts flashing back to the *Etoile* and Jacques asking her and Steven if they could hear a second, faster engine. Paul was right. She clearly heard the sounds of the propellers rotating at different speeds, and she wondered just how many enemy craft there were on the surface. She berated herself—enemy craft? No, these men with whom she had spent the last few weeks, eating and drinking, laughing, and exchanging stories, these were the enemy, weren't they?

Mueller waited for the convoy to pass, keeping the U-boat submerged for some time after that. When they did surface, the fog had lifted, and he stayed astern of the convoy by about five miles.

"We'll wait until early evening," he said to Werner. "That way, the night will cloak us."

"Surface attack?" asked Werner, knowing what the answer would be before he'd even asked the question. A surface attack was always Mueller's preference.

"Surface attack," replied Mueller, nodding, and giving his First Officer a wide smile. "Heinemann, report our position. Let's see if there's anyone else around to join in the party, huh?" Leaving his Officer of the Watch in charge, he went to rest, taking to his bunk. Much of the night's success would depend upon his being alert.

* * *

A couple of hours later, drawing back the curtain to the nook quietly so as not to disturb him, Frances went in search of her book. It surprised her to find Mueller sitting upright on the bunk, eyes closed, taking deep breaths.

"Excuse me, Kapitanleutnant."

Mueller jumped visibly at the intrusion. "If you're coming in, get inside and shut the flaming curtains. No privacy anymore in this place." He sounded bitter.

"I'm sorry. I thought you were asleep. I wanted my book." When Mueller scowled, she pretended not to notice. "Have you slept?" she asked.

He sighed. "Off and on. You should get some rest now while you can. It could get rough later." He swung his legs off the bunk and stood up, and grabbing his cap, left.

She lay down, feeling his body heat, taking comfort from it. Thinking she wouldn't sleep; it surprised her when she woke later to find the boat in silence. She made her way quietly to the control room, which was in virtual darkness, lit only by a dim red lamp. The hatch was open, and starlight shone down on the men assembled below. Going up to Zeitler, she whispered, "What's going on?"

"We're going in. The old man's taking us into the middle of the convoy. We've got good light, a Hunter's Moon, bright. Conditions are good, though we could do with a bit more cloud cover. Escort's strong: four destroyers and several smaller warships."

Frances nodded as if she understood, but truthfully, Hunter's Moons and strong escorts meant little to her. What she did grasp was that they were poised for an attack, and every man was edgy. She felt a prickle run up her spine and realised that she was edgy, too.

"Where are the rest of the men?"

"The old man and the Exec are up top. So are the gun crew. Torpedo crew is on standby."

Frances looked at the clock. 2215 hours. She heard soft tuneless whistling from above.

"The old dog's getting ready," a disembodied voice said. There were low chuckles from some of the men.

"We're on the port side of the convoy." Mueller's hushed voice fell from above. "There's a gap between a couple of escorts. We're going in. Both engines at full power. Left rudder steer 160."

Breaking into their harmonious duet with their usual vigour, the diesels sounded dangerously loud to those below.

"Large tanker, middle of outside port column. Range just under a mile. Check her course and speed, Exec," came Mueller's quiet order. "Fire one when you're ready."

A silent pause, then Werner spoke through the voice tube. "Fire One!"

The U-boat shuddered slightly, indicative to those below that their attack had begun in earnest. A vast sheet of flame illuminated them as the first torpedo struck home. Having no time to enjoy the fireworks for fear of being discovered in the virtual daylight caused by the exploding tanker, Mueller cursed and manoeuvred them round to the stern of the convoy. The mood below was jubilant. "Shush, my men," the voice of Mueller from above quietened them.

From their position astern, they crept between the stern escorts and made their way up the centre columns, choosing their targets: the fattest, the biggest. A second large tanker chugged her way in the centre column about 500 yards away, and Mueller manoeuvred them into a perfect attacking position. "Fire Two!" came the command, and everyone below held their breath, counting the seconds and listening for the agonising death throes of the vessel. There was a dull boom.

"Hit!" a voice from above informed them. The tanker capsized immediately, hissing and sizzling its way to the bottom. Again, cheers from below as up above the remaining ships in the convoy began zigzagging and twisting independently, each in an effort to avoid attack. A large freighter was spotted in the port column. Range was quickly calculated and the U-boat fired on the turn. The torpedo streaked the 1500 yards towards the massive target, striking her amidships, causing her to bellow out clouds of smoke.

"My God, just look at that," muttered Mueller. "She's not even affected by that damn great hole in her side. Number Two, get over here. Right, get your gun crews in position and give her a helping hand."

"Gun crew at the ready. Fire!" Schumacher gave the order, and they blasted thirty shells into the hulk, which still refused to sink.

"Cheeky blighter!" Mueller exclaimed in English.

"Destroyer approaching target!" Werner yelled. Mueller stiffened as he watched the warship change her course towards them.

"Right, full rudder, full ahead both. Time to withdraw, give them time to lick their wounds."

Depth charges could be heard in the distance, and there was relief amongst the crew of the U-boat that this time, the target was another boat.

"Sounds like someone else made it to the party then," said Werner.

Mueller nodded. "Wonder which poor sods are taking the battering. Still one less escort for us to worry about, I suppose."

After a wait of an hour, confident that they had lost the destroyer, they set out once again in search of another target. The convoy was now strung out over several miles. Pockets of the ocean were lit with blazing star shell, and in places the sea itself was afire as huge tankers spewed their oily cargo. Looking at the carnage, Mueller reckoned there must be at least another three wolves in the pack.

"Shadows bearing 350!" called Werner.

The U-boat once more began her murderous course towards a small string of shipping that had remained together. They were strung out in a couple of short columns; incredibly, there appeared to be no escort.

"Escorts are off searching somewhere else," Mueller said with a nod. "Right, lads, we're going between them!" he shouted. "Both engines one third ahead. Exec, take one shot for each target. Make every one count. Shoot both sides dead centre."

The situation was unreal, thought Mueller. A surface attack where they could select and fire at their targets at leisure.

Werner repeated over and over all the target values, making certain that there was no misunderstanding. "Angle left 85 degrees. Distance 600, speed eleven knots."

"Fire!" shouted Mueller. "Let them have it."

Werner yelled, "Tube One! Ready. Fire! Tube Two. Ready. Fire!" Moments later, he gave the firing command to the other three tubes, unleashing five torpedoes at the sitting ducks.

Those on the bridge watched as savage detonations rocked the air as all hell appeared to be let loose. There came the hollow boom of collapsing bulkheads as the first victim raised her keel upwards and made a grotesque dive, wailing propellers cast upwards to the night sky. They hit the second amidship and split her straight in two. There were shooting fire columns and a dense curtain of black smoke and fumes enveloping two of the others. The fifth, a freighter, lost her bridge in the explosion. It was ripped clean off and rained down steel and debris, causing the U-boat to back off slightly. Those immediately below the tower were allowed up to view the holocaust whilst those remaining below gave an ear-splitting cheer. In less than five minutes, a few planks were all that remained of five of the allied merchant vessels.

Mueller left the bridge and was all smiles as he relayed the tonnages of the sunken vessels for the records. Only later, in privacy, would he dwell on the terrified crews of those ships who had played their part in the deadly devastation.

Chapter 23

There were slaps on the back all round in the belly of the U-boat. Seven more vessels to add to their tonnage, and still one more to finish on the surface, the one that refused to sink despite the battering it had received. Mueller was about to give the order to dive for tube reloading when the desperate cry came from the watch above. "Three destroyers bearing down astern!"

Closely followed by his officers, Mueller leapt onto the bridge, gut knotting as he took in the sight. Three huge predatory shadows were dipping and rising in the foaming sea, following in their wake. He took the decision to try to outrun them, but despite the hammering of the diesels and the prayers of the entire crew, the destroyers closed the gap, forcing the U-boat to dive.

The bridge cleared in seconds. Mueller secured the hatch and removed his lambskin, hanging it on the nearest hook, while seamen ran to the fore'ard-end of the boat to aid the dive with their weight.

"Take her to 150 metres, Chief," Mueller ordered. He caught sight of Frances and shouted to her, "Hold on to something tight, Froggy!"

He watched until she gripped a nearby valve wheel. Around him, the crew seized hold of whatever equipment was fixed to the boat's hull: ducts, pipes, wheels, to prepare for the onslaught of a certain attack. Mueller heard the muted but ominous swishing of the propellers overhead and sucked in his cheeks. "OK, lads, this is it."

Seconds later, the U-boat leapt in the deep like an absurdly bucking steer. Mueller watched as some of his men were thrown off their feet, hitting the deck plates or, more painfully, thrown against wheels or levers. There was a deafening roaring in his ears. Blast waves rocked the boat and every moveable object smashed under the onslaught of the depth charges. Then there were a few minutes of respite.

"Huh! Nowhere near!" Mueller nodded, forcing his clenched jaw to relax and allow his mouth to smile, wiping the sweat from his face with his sleeve. It was closer than he would have liked.

Heinemann reported, "Propellers approaching, Kapitanleutnant."

Mueller picked up the sound with the rest of his men, and alongside it heard the sound that every submariner feared. The *Ping! Ping!* that grabbed at a man's bowels and dragged them upwards into his mouth.

"What is it?" whispered Frances.

"ASDIC," a voice whispered back, close to her.

"What's ASDIC?" she whispered again and, getting no reply, remained   silent.

"Quiet, men. Shush now," Mueller softly cautioned.

The sound of the ASDIC ceased as the propellers passed overhead, followed by others quickly approaching. There was another barrage of ear-splitting explosions, which caused the boat to give a terrific leap, and immediately after a second, causing her to roll. Mueller watched, unable to do a thing to help his men as some of them were shaken loose and thrown once again across the deck. Many crashed into dials and instruments, the lights were extinguished and there was the tell-tale smell that someone's bowels had let him down.

A torch beam ran across the control room, lighting Mueller's face, beaded with sweat.

"Emergency lighting," his orders snapped out. "I want a damage report. Chief, take her down further. 150 metres, reverse course. Let's see who we've got up there. Maybe we can fool them." He could only hope and pray the strategy would work.

The lights came up dimly on the havoc caused by the last attack. Glass dials were smashed, chronometers broken, gauges sent haywire, and amongst the disorder lay Leutnant Schumacher, face down. Toddler was beside him.

"Kapitanleutnant, we need the medic."

"Who?"

"Leutnant Schumacher, sir." Hengst was beside the wounded man in seconds. It had been a freak accident, and as Hengst turned Schumacher onto his back, revealing a sharp piece of twisted metal embedded in his chest.

"How bad is it?" asked Mueller. Taking in Schumacher's clammy appearance, he knew it wasn't good.

"Hard to say, Kapitanleutnant. At this moment, we need to move him from here," reported Hengst.

"Right. Toddler, give Hengst a hand to move this man," Mueller ordered.

They moved Schumacher to a bunk in the petty officer's quarters reserved for the injured. He groaned as they lifted him, as ever nearer came the sound of the returning destroyers and the voice of Heinemann, "Propellers bearing…"

"No need; I can hear," snapped Mueller. "Change course, full rudder, sixty degrees left, take her down another fifty metres, Chief."

Frances felt the pressure bear down in her eardrums and the fear well up in her guts as the U-boat was taken still deeper, every rivet groaning for quarter. Terrified, she looked around at the faces of the men she had lived with for the past weeks, eyes wide with fear, hair plastered with sweat, bodies taut. Mueller was clinging tightly to a pipe running overhead, from which, at the beginning of the patrol, food had hung. She caught his eye, and he winked at her. The swish swishing of the propellers and the ping of the ASDIC was setting every nerve on edge, every fibre fit to break. A couple of men were whimpering somewhere as the swishing passed immediately overhead.

She felt the urge to cover the several feet to Mueller, to bury her face in him, but she was determined not to let him see her fear, and so she hung on, bracing herself for the next brutal attack. As explosion after explosion rocked them, she saw Mueller lose his footing and, with relief, heard his curse mingle with the cries of others. The shock waves subsided, giving them just enough time to recover to prepare themselves.

"All right?" asked a voice. She was standing, half dazed.

"All right?" the voice asked again.

She turned to the man. His eyes were bright in their sockets. He had a slight cut on his forehead. Did she know him? He put his hand on her shoulder, and then she recognised him. *Paul.* His name drifted like smoke through her mind. How different he looked. She wondered if she looked as bad as he did, and from somewhere, she conjured up a smile and replied. "Yes, all right. You? How are you, Paul? How long can this go on?"

Werner wiped his face across his sleeve. "Until they get fed up or run out of fireworks. They'll want revenge for the carnage we caused up there, but the old man has a trick or two up his sleeve."

"What trick?" she asked.

Werner wagged a finger at her. "Ah, just wait and see."

"Please tell me, Paul."

"A pillenwerfer."

"A what?"

"See, you're none the wiser." Werner tried to grin, but the tension of the last couple of hours had made the muscles in his face tighten, causing the grin he intended to become a grimace. "A pillenwerfer, my dear, is an SBT, a submarine bubble target. A metal cylinder about the size of a tin of fruit which we're going to release. It contains a chemical which produces a cloud of bubbles. The ASDIC will hopefully pick it up. To any but the most experienced operator, indistinguishable from a submarine."

"What is this ASDIC, Paul?"

"Sonar. They bounce sound waves from the hulls of the destroyers. If they hit something solid such as us, they get a ping, pinpointing where we are."

"I see."

Mueller joined them. "SBT away. Now we'll see." He cast his gaze over his men who had gathered round, working his mouth into one of his best fatherly smiles. "It's not over yet, lads. They're not going to give up easily, you see."

"Propellers approaching, Kapitanleutnant!" called Heinemann. Mueller nodded, rubbing at his beard. "They're changing course."

"Good, Heinemann." They all listened to the sound of exploding depth charges, not close enough to do them any damage. "Hah!" Relieved, Mueller shook his fist. "Put that in your pipe, Tommy!"

Unsure of how reliable their apparatus was after the damage caused by the depth charging, Mueller decided they should backtrack on what he thought was their original course. After forty-five minutes of propeller noise only being picked up at a distance, he thought it safe to surface.

"Equalise pressure," he ordered, grabbing his jacket. Lifting the lid of the hatch, he stepped out onto the bridge. The night was clear, and he briefly took in the night sky, lightening in the East. He called down the voice tube, "First Officer to bridge," and waited for Werner.

"Well, we could have done without that, I reckon," he said, giving a wry smile as Werner joined him. "The batteries need charging up, one of the diesels is crippled and apart from that, there's all the other apparatus that needs repairing."

"But at least our position is as you hoped. I reckon we are about a mile away from that stricken tanker, and the rest of the convoy must be far away by now. So, are you going to give her the last rites?" he asked Mueller, referring to the tanker.

"Can't claim her tonnage unless we do." He gave orders for the watch to join him and Werner on the bridge and waited while they swept in every direction with their glasses.

"Prepare Tubes One and Two ready for firing, Exec. Let's give her one right in the belly," he ordered.

"Destroyer bearing 050 starboard, Kapitanleutnant!" came the cry.

Mueller whipped his gaze in that direction. The destroyer was less than a half mile away and closing fast.

"Damn! Where did he come from?" Mueller exclaimed. "Clear the bridge. Alaaaarrm!"

Once again, men raced to the fore'ard-end to aid the dive.

"Take her down to 100 metres, Chief. Full ahead both."

"But that's going to take us right into that tanker, Kapitanleutnant," Zeitler warned.

"Hopefully not into it, Chief, but certainly under it. Right, you bastards, we'll sit it out and see how long it is 'til you get fed up, shall we?" said Mueller, trying to look more confident than he felt.

It was a good idea to take refuge beneath the groaning bulkheads of the tanker. After all, it just wasn't British to blow up one of your own vessels. They would sit it out the twelve hours or so until dusk, thought Mueller, by which time the destroyer should be fed up with the game. Twelve hours, that would give them time to make a few running repairs to the old tub, and themselves.

"Mother!" Schumacher's frightened voice echoed through the

boat, making ice run in every man's veins. "Mother, where are you? I'm hurting!"

Mueller went to check on the injured man. "How is he, Hengst?" he asked.

"Not good, Kapitanleutnant." Hengst mopped sweat from Schumacher's brow. "Trouble is, he's making it worse, upsetting himself this way."

Mueller looked down at his Second Officer's pasty face. His eyes were glazed and stared unseeingly as if he were searching for something or someone.

"Mother ... Mother," he continued to groan.

Mueller placed his hand on Hengst's shoulder. "Try to keep him quiet."

"There are others to see to, Kapitanleutnant. Quite a few. Fairly minor injuries, but they need seeing to, all the same."

"Can I help?" Frances joined them.

Mueller turned to her. "The best thing you can do is keep out of the way."

Ignoring him, she knelt beside Schumacher and took his hand. "Shush now, son, your mother is here," she cooed gently. The glazed eyes brightened slightly, and a weary smile came to the young man's face. He touched her hand to his lips.

"I knew you'd come, I knew you wouldn't let me down, Mother ... oh, but why do I hurt?"

"Shush. You're fine now. I'm here. Relax, sleep." Frances looked up at Mueller. "What is his first name?"

It was Hengst who answered. "Johann."

"Ah, Johann, it's good to have you home. Sleep now, my boy."

"It's good to be home." He squeezed her hand. "I will make you so proud of me when I get my command, Mother."

"I'm proud of you now, my Johann." Frances wiped his brow, hoping that she could keep him calm. He was just a boy, scarcely older than Toddler. Strange how she'd not noticed that before; he had hidden it behind all his aggression.

"Will you kiss me?" he murmured. "Our special way?" She looked at Hengst, who shrugged. Mueller had propped himself up at the foot of the bunk. He shook his head tiredly and walked away. Frances leant forward over the boy and kissed him gently, first on each eye and then gently on the lips.

"I love you," murmured the boy. "I'm so tired. I will sleep now." Frances's tears ran down her face, and she watched as they splashed onto the cover. Hengst took her hand and patted it.

"Well done," he whispered. "How did you know about the kiss?"

"I didn't, I just hoped. It's the way my mother used to kiss me," she added, in a ragged voice, and then, turning, she left, walking swiftly to the nook, afraid she wouldn't make it before she lost her self-control entirely. Her sorrow pushed at the walls of her throat. Her eyes burned with it and from lack of sleep, the hours of living under siege. If she were going to break down, she wouldn't do it in front of the men. They didn't need it, the burden of her grief. Yanking back the curtain, she drew in a sharp breath. Mueller was slumped against the bunk. His old blue sweater beside him on the floor was sodden with blood, as was his shirt. Her tears were left un-shed.

"What happened to you?" she asked.

"It's nothing. Only a scratch."

Holding up the sweater, she said, "You don't get that much blood from a scratch. I'll get Hengst."

"No!" Mueller recoiled. "He's busy seeing to others; this can wait."

"It most certainly cannot!"

"For goodness' sake, Froggy, can't you do as you're asked just for once?" Mueller grumbled.

"Very well, Kapitanleutnant, I'll fetch Leutnant Werner then. Maybe he can talk some sense into you." When she returned with Werner, Mueller was slumped in his chair at the desk.

"What's this? You're injured, then?" asked Werner.

"Nothing! Stop making a damn fuss, both of you."

"If it's nothing, it won't take long to patch up," said Werner. "Get your shirt off."

Too tired to argue, Mueller unbuttoned the front of his shirt and stood up to remove it. The material had stuck to the wound on his left shoulder, and he flinched as he pulled it loose.

"Sit down and lean forward." Frances took control. "Paul, I need something to clean this up, and it needs stitching. You'll have to get Hengst."

"No! And that's a bloody order. Not until the boys have been seen to," said Mueller.

Frances wiped some blood away with her hand. It had congealed round the sides of a deep, ugly wound running across Mueller's scapula. "It needs sorting now," she insisted.

Mueller's stiffened. "Then you do it," he said. "Go on, you do it. You said you helped your father with his operations. You stitch it up."

"Fine!" She felt her hackles rise. "Fine! Paul, I'll need water, lint, peroxide to cleanse it, gut, and a needle."

Werner looked from one to the other. "You're not serious, surely?" he asked, not sure which one he was addressing. Mueller had set his mouth and was staring unblinkingly in front of him.

"I am serious. If your Kapitan wants to risk an utter amateur stitching him up, that's fine by me; I'll enjoy it! And by the way, needlework was never one of my strong points." Werner went in search of Hengst.

Refusing to react, Mueller sat listening to the swishing overhead of the destroyer's propellers in silence, not glancing at Frances. *Awkward bastard,* she thought. It was only moments before Werner returned with her order.

"Right, Kapitanleutnant Mueller, I'm going to clean this up a bit for you," said Frances as she gently removed the old blood from around the wound, trying desperately not to notice the straight muscular back and the scatter of wiry hair across his chest. "I have to disinfect it now, and it might sting a bit."

"Just get on with it, Froggy, and forget the bloody commentary." Mueller was in a black mood.

Right, Kapitan Mueller, thought Frances. *Let's see how you like this.* She soaked a wad of lint in peroxide and slapped it onto the wound, gleefully noting the sharp intake of breath and the hands grabbing the table, knuckles turning white. She wished she could see his face but took solace in the fact that even Werner was wincing. Removing the lint, she saw the gash was bleeding profusely. "Damn!"

"What is it?" asked Werner.

"It's bleeding more now I've cleaned it. Look, Paul, I really do think that we need Hengst."

"No! I told you." Mueller exploded and tried to rise to his feet. Frances pushed him down as Werner left.

"Forget it. We need you fit, don't we? Sit still, or you'll make it bleed even more."

Werner returned with Hengst who bent to study the wound. He made himself immediately busy checking the injury.

"Pfff, nasty, Kapitanleutnant. How did you do it?"

"The bloody meat hooks." Mueller frowned. "Surprised it's never happened before. We need to take them down."

Hengst prepared the needle and gut. "Shame you hadn't got your jacket on. A good few stitches, and it will mend pretty well. Nice job of cleaning, Frau Meyer."

"Thank you." Frances gave Mueller an impertinent smile. "How's Leutnant Schumacher?" she asked.

"Tut, sleeping, still, but not good."

"Will he make it, do you think, Hengst?" asked Mueller.

"I wouldn't like to say, sir."

"The others, is everyone else all right?" Mueller asked after a few moments.

"Yes, Kapitanleutnant, all good as new."

Frances watched Hengst work quickly and deftly, and if the stitching wasn't quite as neat as her fathers, she had to admit that he made a pretty good job of it.

"Right, sir, that's it," said Hengst as he tied the last stitch. "Now I suggest you take a rest for a while. You've lost quite a lot of blood by the looks of things."

"I'll rest later when I know the Chief has things in hand. I'm hoping that I have a spare shirt and jumper somewhere." Werner ferreted around in the cupboard.

"Here, shirt and sweater. Do you need help?"

Mueller shook his head.

"It will take hours for the Chief to sort out the old girl," said Werner. "There's nothing to be done. We're stuck here till they get fed up." He jerked his thumb upwards. "Have a rest."

Mueller weakened. He was tired, and he yawned. "All right, damn the lot of you. Two hours, then wake me. It's ten-thirty, wake me in time for lunch. We could all do with a good meal."

They left him, and he stretched himself out on the bunk. How they expected him to sleep with that bloody destroyer circling round and the pain in his shoulder troubling him, the devil only knew.

* * *

He awoke to the swishing of that same destroyer as it relentlessly continued to circle overhead.

Paul Werner was shaking him gently. "It's twelve-thirty."

Mueller stretched himself and groaned. The stitches in his shoulder felt uncomfortably tight. "Bastards are still there then. What do you think, Paul? Is he just putting the frighteners on us, or does he mean business?"

Werner shrugged. "He'll be gone by nightfall."

"How's Schumacher?"

"Still hanging on," said Werner. "Weak, though."

"And our passenger?" asked Mueller, swinging his legs out of the bunk.

"Remarkably well."

Mueller nodded and smiled. "Some girl, our Froggy, isn't she?"

"Certainly is."

"Didn't get a squeak out of her when all of that shit was going on. Surprising really, I wouldn't have expected it. How do you think your Inga would have coped?"

Werner gave the question some thought before answering. "She would be fine as long as I was with her, I think. What about Sophie?"

Mueller grimaced. "She wouldn't cope if she laddered her stocking." He reckoned that was one of the first thoughts he had given Sophie Heyne on the entire patrol, other than wishing he could see some way out of the damn marriage. It looked as though it was going to happen unless, of course, they didn't make it back. His mind suddenly filled with thoughts of Frances Meyer.

"Very pretty too, isn't she?"

Werner smiled at his friend. "If you mean Frances, then yes, very."

"Some girl, eh?"

"You're taken with her." Werner watched as his friend coloured from the heat of his question.

"No, not my type," returned Mueller. He was thoughtful for a moment. "Shit, it's that obvious then, is it?"

"Are you asking me as your friend or your executive officer?" Mueller turned to Werner with a tired smile.

"As my friend, Paul."

"As your friend, then yes, it's obvious. I've played some part in many of your amours over the years. I think this one is different."

"The devil it is. I reckon a night in a hotel with her would get her out of my system."

"Then you're a fool, Kapitanleutnant, if you think that," said Werner as he rose and left Mueller alone, mulling over the attributes of Frances Meyer, and he found the more he thought of her, the more he wanted to know.

* * *

As nightfall came and the destroyer continued its monotonous routine of circling and lying-in wait, Mueller began to question his strategy. Was remaining under the ship's belly the right thing to do, or should they make a break for it? He'd ordered everyone, apart from Zeitler, the Second Engineer, and a couple of artificers, to don breathing apparatuses and keep to their bunks. By doing so, he hoped they could stretch out the estimated twelve hours of oxygen that they still had left. They were trapped and could do nothing; the batteries and the air were running dangerously low. They would have to surface to recharge them. He gave instructions to his men that the only movement allowed was to the heads, and that anything in the toilet pans was to stay put. There was to be no jettisoning of the contents which could give away their exact position. He ordered that biscuits and conserve should be dished out every four hours along with water. There was to be the minimum amount of noise.

Chapter 24

Frances could bear the solitude no longer; it had been hours. She'd slept for a while, exhausted from the fear and stress brought about by the attack. But a body only needed so much sleep, and now her need was for human contact. She removed the breathing apparatus, the obscene trunk of the potash cartridge dripping with saliva from her mouth. The nose clip pinched horribly, and she removed that too and sat for a moment, listening to the silence. She panicked and wondered if, by some strange quirk of fate, she was the only one left alive. No. If she concentrated, she could hear men breathing, the clicking of valves in the mouthpieces. She heard the low muttered conversation of Zeitler and Mueller from the control room.

Sick of the solitude, Frances quietly slipped through the green curtain and went fore'ard, into the wardroom. Hearing the all-too recognisable footsteps, she stood, frozen. He'd be cross. She'd disobeyed orders—so what? The footsteps faltered. He'd be checking the nook, wondering where she was. Then they continued, and Mueller ducked through the hatch into the poky space of the wardroom.

"What's this? You should be resting." He flopped onto the bench, exhausted, trying to decide where to put his legs. "Go and lie down, Froggy. Rest, sleep."

"I was wondering about your shoulder, how is it?" She slid onto the bench opposite him.

"Sore, thank you." He rested his head in his hands, elbows propped on the table, and she saw his suffering. The lines on his face appeared etched even deeper, and the blue eyes were streaked with red. He looked older than his years.

"Schumacher?" she ventured. "How's Schumacher?"

Mueller looked off, looked back, pulled his fingers through his tousled hair. "Leutnant Schumacher died about four hours ago, thankfully in his sleep."

Frances moved to sit beside him. "Oh, I'm so sorry," she murmured, blinking back the threat of tears. "He was just a kid, wasn't he? I only noticed that yesterday." She fell silent. "Can I stay here, just for a while?" she asked after a moment.

Mueller sighed, rubbing his eyes and beard. Finding her gaze, he said, "For a while." He returned to his original position, head in hands, fingers in hair, thoughtful, detached.

The silence lingered. She broke it.

"Are we going to get out of this, Kapitanleutnant?"

Mueller jumped, lost in his own thoughts and questions. For a moment, he had forgotten she was there. He pushed his head hard back against the wall and looked straight ahead, then he turned to her and gave her what he hoped was a comforting smile.

"We'll be fine, don't worry."

"Don't patronise me, please. I'm not a child, I'd rather know." She worked at keeping her voice level, wanting to sound braver than she felt.

His look seemed to consider her as if he might be gauging her strength. "All right then. I don't think we have much of a chance, Froggy. We can't surface for hours yet, not until it's dark again—otherwise, we'll get blasted. I don't think the air will last that long or long enough. I don't think there is an alternative. If things get desperate down here, then maybe we should risk running for it, but with a knackered engine, I don't know."

She swallowed hard. She had guessed what he would say, but it shook her just the same. They both sat staring straight ahead. "I'm sorry."

Frances glanced at him. "What for?"

"If we hadn't picked you up, you'd be safe in England by now instead of stuck in this damn tin sarcophagus."

"No, I'd most likely have been dead weeks ago, and at least I'm not alone, am I? That's what really frightens me, you know—being on my own. That rowing boat: the loneliness was terrifying. That's why I came out here, to find you ... or someone."

"I can understand that." His eyes on hers were tired, but gentle. It was killing him not being able to reassure her, but she had asked, and above all else, he wanted to be truthful with her.

"Then I can stay here with you?" she continued. Mueller hesitated as he gave the matter some thought.

"Yes, yes, all right, you can stay here." They sat in silence again for a while longer, then with a sigh, he stood up. "I'm going to check on the boys." Frances panicked.

"You are coming back, aren't you?"

Mueller forced a laugh. "Got nowhere else to go, Froggy. Wait here. I'll be back in a few minutes."

She heard his footsteps fade towards the front of the vessel.

After ten minutes or so, she heard the tell-tale footsteps once more, and he was back.

"It's getting colder, isn't it?" she said as he reappeared. "I'm cold anyhow, and clammy."

"Air's running out," Mueller explained. "It's like being at the top of a mountain."

Turning to leave again, he reassured her. "I'll be two minutes."

It was less than that when he returned with a couple of blankets, one of which he folded and placed around her shoulders; the other, he wrapped around himself.

"Better?" he asked.

She nodded, then sighed. "How did it happen, this war? You, your men, you are not Nazis. I don't understand, you fight and yet...?"

Mueller puffed out his cheeks and exhaled.

"No, few in the Kriegsmarine are in the Party. We have a certain political independence. That's the appeal of it, at least for me it was." He paused, thinking. He wanted her to know. "Patriotism ... Patriotism and young men's dreams."

"Then you are not fighting for the Nazi party?" He shook his head. "But I don't understand why, as a German, you would want to fight at all."

He looked at her, wanting her to understand. "It wasn't all our fault, you know. When you have nothing, you have nothing to lose. The Versailles Treaty would have been hard for any nation to swallow. Adolf came and gave us back our national pride. There were jobs, a thriving economy. You're carried away on the euphoria, and before you know it, things are out of hand—"

"Out of hand? That's an understatement. And what did you do about it, Kapitanleutnant?" interrupted Frances scornfully.

"Do you mean the Jewish question, Froggy? Because it's not just happening in Germany, is it?" She blinked. "What did you do about it?" he asked softly.

She looked down at her hands, twisted in her lap. "You're right, of course. The whole of Europe is to blame, I suppose." She thought about Steven and all the brilliant Jewish people she had known. "You don't believe what they say about the Jews, do you?" She looked anxiously at Mueller. Suddenly, it seemed very important for her to know, to hear his opinion from his own mouth.

"Of course, I don't!" he said with such force she was gratified. "I shouldn't think many of us on this U-boat do, but it's hard for people to make a stand, you see, much easier to pretend it's not happening. To turn your back on it and hope it goes away."

"But there must have been people you knew..."

Mueller bit on his lip. He disliked the recollections, and Frances thought of her own situation and realised that she had done little too.

"Of course, we felt; at first, we helped," said Mueller. "There were people even in our small town who were forced to leave Germany in the early days. I know my parents helped get people to the station with as much as they could carry. People we had known for years. But later, as the threats came, and the stories of people disappearing to God knows where–" He rubbed his beard and the side of his face as he thought back. "–Then we stopped helping." Frances opened her mouth to say something, but he cut her off. "Please, no preaching. I admit I'm not proud of the fact."

He was right—what had she actually done? True, she had married Steven, but that was in the good old days, and hadn't there been times later when their marriage had made things difficult for her? There had been times when she had wished that she hadn't been Madam Meyer, like in Berlin in '38 and pathetically later when they were placed in a corner at Maxim's. Never because she believed in all the filth people would have you believe, but merely because Steven was Jewish, and to be Jewish in

Europe in the 1930s just wasn't fashionable. Mueller was quite correct—she had no right to preach, and she felt ashamed.

Sitting there staring at her hands, she became guilt-ridden and questioned what her feelings for Steven had been over those last few months. When things had got bad in Paris, hadn't she been glad when he'd chosen to keep out of the limelight? There had been a certain amount of relief too when he had moved in with Jacques, and even more so when he had announced his intention of escaping to England. Had she convinced herself that she'd been concerned for his safety? She loved Steven, didn't she? A few well-chosen words from this man beside her now had made her doubt all of it. All the feelings she thought she had for him. If she was honest, wasn't the concern she had more for Frances Meyer? For the first time in her life, she hated herself.

"Pfennig for them, Froggy."

He brought her back to the present. She bit her lip and turned to him. "Listening to you has made me doubt everything about myself. I think I may even hate myself. The only person I think I have ever truly cared for is me."

"Hey, don't be so hard on yourself, Froggy."

She shook her head. "Kapitan Mueller, I'm so sorry."

He raised his eyebrows. "For what?"

"For all the problems I've caused you. I wish someone else had found me."

Mueller grinned briefly. "So, you are disappointed with the service, then?"

"No." She straightened. "What I meant was—"

"I know what you meant, Froggy. I can't pretend that there haven't been times when I've been tempted to throw you overboard."

"I suppose I would have deserved it."

"Yes, you would," he agreed.

He's right, of course, she thought. "I don't think I'm always a very nice person, am I?"

He looked at her quizzically. "Are you really interested in what I think?"

She held his gaze. "Yes, Kapitanleutnant. Yes, I think I am."

He gave a sniff and thought for a moment. "When we picked you up, you were scared, understandably. I think you have been spoiled and have always had your own way, which has made you difficult, selfish, and rude, and at times bloody confrontational. Yet over the weeks, you have shown yourself to be an extraordinary woman, Frances Meyer." She felt tears prickling behind her eyes, which he noticed. "Don't let tears quench the fire in your eyes, Froggy. I couldn't bear that." She turned away from him and gave an involuntary shudder. "Still cold?"

"A little."

He lifted his blanket, and she slid across the bench and tucked herself against him.

"How old are you?" he asked.

"Twenty-four, nearly—why?"

"I had a sister. I was thinking she would be about your age now."

"What happened?" She recognised the momentary grief on his face. "I'm sorry, you don't have to talk about it."

He smiled at her. "Measles; I had it too. I was eight, but she was only just four." He nodded. "Yes, she would have been about your age. I think she would have been like you, huh? Annoying." He cast Frances another weak smile. "My mother took it badly—it affected her for years. Still does, I think."

"I'm so sorry. What was her name?"

"Karin; her name was Karin."

They sat for a few moments, each lost in their own thoughts. "I was an only child," she suddenly announced.

"Really? Well, you do surprise me." He managed a chuckle. "They decided one of you was enough, then."

She smiled back at him and muttered, "Pig." And then she sighed. "I'm so tired."

"Do you want to go back to the bunk?"

"No! No, I don't. I want to stay here with you." She looked into his eyes, reddened from his lack of sleep, and she realised how tired he must be too. "Kapitanleutnant," she asked, "would you hold me, please? Then I think I might sleep."

He'd have given anything just then to be somewhere else with her. She was so unlike the other women he'd known, and God knows there had been so many of them he'd lost count. Was that the attraction, that she was just different, a challenge? He'd not lied on that occasion when he'd told her she wasn't his type. She wasn't! He liked his women tall, soft, and curvaceous, and yet over the weeks this small, snappy, troublesome female with her wolf's eyes had invaded his thoughts and actions until he had an ache in his balls the like of which he'd never experienced. It crossed his mind briefly that he could take her, and in the circumstances who would blame him? Who would even know? He was ashamed of that thought and dismissed it just as quickly as it had come. He turned towards her to check that he'd just heard her correctly,

"You just asked me to hold you, Froggy."

She nodded, and he thought how completely lost she looked at that moment. He put his arm around her shoulders, and she leant into him, putting her head on his chest so that he became a mass of chestnut curls. He groaned, and he wondered if she had any idea at all of what she was doing to him. She pulled away.

"I'm sorry, I've hurt your shoulder."

"No." He gave the ghost of a smile. "It's the other one."

"Oh, yes," she said, returning her head to his chest, nestling in against him. He let his arm slip from her shoulder, wrapping it around her, enjoying the pressure on it from her firm breast.

"Do you think we might have been friends if we'd met before the war?" she asked sleepily.

"Doubtful," he teased. "Do you?"

"Hmm, maybe, but probably not."

Frances Meyer sank into a deep oxygen-starved sleep. Mueller let his head sink onto hers. He was tired too. There was nothing else to be done. He may as well give in to this utter exhaustion which enveloped him. He drifted towards sleep, aware now and then of the sound of work coming from the engine room. Useless work. The sound of the destroyer reminded him of that. Forty-odd men and one woman. What a bastard time for his luck to run out.

Chapter 25

Werner was shaking him. "It's getting dark, Kapitanleutnant."

Mueller lifted his head; his eyes felt heavy, and his mouth was dry. He focused his eyes on Werner, who was smiling at him amiably.

"See you found each other then," he said, referring to the slight form of the woman who still lay sleeping curled against Mueller's chest.

"Nothing like it looks," Mueller rumbled. "How long since there was any propeller noise?"

"Six hours."

"Six hours? Looks like we've made it then. You should have woken me before this."

Werner took a seat opposite Mueller. "Why? There was nothing doing 'til now. Christ, I didn't think we'd make it this time. Forty hours we've been down, just about."

Mueller nodded, gently shifting Frances, and laying her down on the bench. Wiping his hands down his face, he said, "That was some bloody party, wasn't it?" He managed a smile. "We'll surface in twenty minutes. Wake up, sleepyhead," he said, shaking Frances by the arm. She wriggled and sighed. He tried again. "Wake up—we're alive. We're going up.

She lifted herself on an elbow, blinking. "We're alive?" she questioned sleepily. "We're going up?"

He stood up, nodding at her.

"We're alive!" she repeated fervently. Jumping up, she threw her arms round his neck and kissed him on both cheeks, French fashion. His eyes on hers widened with some combination of longing and surprise, and she clung to his neck, delighted, and kissed his cheeks once more.

They would neither one remember how she came to be in his arms, both of them standing, their mouths locked together.

Werner coughed. "I'll leave you to it, then."

Mueller recovered himself first, and pulling away, issued a brusque order. "Assemble the men, Exec!"

"Yes, sir!" Werner snorted.

Once he disappeared, Mueller took Frances by the wrist, pulling her behind him through the hatch and into his cabin. He closed the curtain behind him. "Now, where were we?" he asked, running his thumb over her lower lip.

She leant against the bunk for support, and he could see the beat of a pulse in her neck.

"We can't, it's not right."

Her voice, he thought, sounded breathless.

"Felt right to me, what's wrong?"

"We are. We are wrong. We're enemies, aren't we?"

He put his hands on her shoulders and drew her to him, and she tried to look away. Taking her chin gently, he turned her face to his. "We've never been enemies," he said, his voice thick with emotion. "And I can prove it." Lowering his head to hers, he kissed her once again. When her mouth opened beneath his, he knew he was right. Still, he was the one who put an end to it, telling her, "Don't move. Just be right here when I get back."

* * *

The periscope being jammed, Mueller gave the order to surface. He knew that at the back of every man's mind was the hope that they had sat it out long enough, and that the destroyer had assumed them dead and had given up and moved on. It could be getting on for maybe a hundred miles away by now. It was also possible that the destroyer was still sitting and waiting, making certain that they were condemned to their iron coffin.

The U-boat broke surface, the pressure was equalised, and Mueller resisted the temptation to force the hatch prematurely, he had heard of cases of commanders being popped out of the hatch like champagne corks, just through rushing and forcing the hatch before the pressure had levelled out. He didn't want to be another one of those; he thought it sounded painful. He looked at his assembled crew, admitting to himself that he had seen them all looking better. But at least they were alive, weren't they? Except for poor old Schumacher, of course. He'd been stowed away in an empty tube for safe keeping, and he, Kristian Mueller, despite his aches and pains, felt more alive than he had in an age, and for that he could thank Frances Meyer, who wasn't his type at all. He wiped the back of his hand across his nose and sniffed. He'd business to finish up top, and then content that all was well with his men, he'd make time to continue the business that had begun behind closed curtains. For now, though, that business had to be pigeonholed, put to the back of his mind.

He dragged himself up the rungs of the ladder, weary-legged, the injured shoulder giving him grief. The hatch felt twice its normal weight as he fought to push it open. Men gathered in the gap below, welcoming the soaking they received, greedily gasping for air. Mueller collapsed onto the bridge, open-mouthed, breathing in the freshness, choking on it, filling his starved lungs with it, willing them to work, desperate to clear his head. The men below were coughing and laughing as only condemned men who have earned a reprieve can laugh.

"Officers to the bridge!" came the strangled order from above.

Zeitler, Ehrhart and Werner joined Mueller. He let them savour the salt sea air for a few seconds. "Well, gentlemen, there she is. Seems a shame to sink her after all she's done for us.

The officers looked out to the stricken tanker about a half mile off, still bobbing about cheekily with her decks scarcely two metres out of the water, clearly standing out against the night sky.

"No sign of that destroyer," said Ehrhart scanning the starlit horizon, where already dawn was threatening, "Thank God!"

"Amen to that," said Mueller. "OK, Exec, finish her off. Stick one up her amidships."

* * *

One or two of the crew had pushed their way up top, out onto the crowded bridge to watch. Frances was amongst them. Her mind was still reeling. She'd let him kiss her! The recollection pounded through her brain. She touched her lips. They felt warm, bruised. And inside, she felt such heat, a deep visceral stirring—unfamiliar—and yet she was seduced by it, enchanted. She couldn't deny it—that she wanted more of him. Mueller. Wanted the strength of his arms about her, wanted to fill herself again with the scent of his body, wanted his mouth hotly demanding on hers. She watched him now in this place that was his. The boat, the sea, the war—they were all his, and she wanted to be part of them. She studied him for a while, how unlike Steven he was. Young, fit, and vigorous, lean but muscular, a body that emanated masculine power. She wondered how he'd look shorn of the beard and the locks of brown hair that fell in waves down his neck. What she could see of his face she loved. The crinkles around the deep blue eyes, the high prominent cheekbones, the finely bridged nose, and the straight-lipped sardonic mouth by which you could gauge his mood, and with which he could cut a man down to size and frequently did.

She had accused him of doing nothing to help his Jewish friends and neighbours, but what of her? She was Steven's wife, but over and above asking Otto to help them, she'd done little to help others. It was a case of self-preservation, wasn't it? Was that so very wrong? He'd said the same—politics and Party didn't come into it. He was fighting for his country, that's all.

Somewhere outside her thoughts, she was aware of an explosion. The men on the bridge were laughing. She watched him. The animated face and body, the hands with long sensitive square tipped fingers, a musician's hands. He was laughing now, a light baritone, and she remembered his declaration that he hadn't a musical bone in his body. But suddenly now, the mood changed...the laughter stopped. In place of the smiles, there were looks of horror and confusion. She searched the water for the destroyer, not finding it.

"Jerry, over here!" she heard a voice, definitely English, calling out. "Over here." Other voices to starboard, and then to port, shouted from close by.

"Hey, Jerry, we've injured men on board. Help us, will ya?"

"Help us, for pity's sake."

She pushed forward on the bridge, shouting at Mueller, "They're English. There are men in the water!" Then as her eyes became accustomed to the dark, she saw the bobbing lifeboats. "We're coming!" she called out in English. "Hang on."

A reply rang out. "Bloody hell, there's a bird on board."

"Hey, mate, are you Brits?"

Werner grabbed her as Mueller's words reached her ears. "Who the hell let her up here! Both engines quarter reverse, steady as you go." The U-boat backed off gently.

She struggled in Werner's arms, trying to get to Mueller, yelling, "You bastard! You're not going to pick them up, are you?"

Mueller turned on her. "Get that bloody woman below, for God's sake."

She was bundled below, confused, disappointed, and bitterly hurt. That same mouth that minutes ago had been kissing her now referred to her as that bloody woman. That bloody woman was all she was to him. How could she ever have thought otherwise? Well, he had shown his true colours. He loved what he was doing. He'd had the chance to pick men up, and he'd backed off. He was a bloody murderer after all.

Below, many of the men were in a state of shock, a few were in tears. They knew that it could so easily have been them on the life raft, not the Brits, and in their heads they were living every sailor's worst nightmare.

There was the sound of footsteps above, and Mueller dropped down through the hatch, his emotions in turmoil. He was beside her now, rubbing her shoulders, trying to placate her as though she were a child. She threw herself at him, beating his chest with her fists, and he let her because at that moment, he hated himself too.

She spat, "Don't you touch me! Who do you think you are? What the hell gives you the right to play God? You could have saved those men."

He threw back his head under her onslaught and she twisted the knife whilst she had the upper hand. "I hope the same thing happens to you, Kapitanleutnant Mueller. I hope you're left out there to think about your crimes before the elements finish you off. It's what you deserve."

He paled. The crew were listening, and she was glad. "Have you finished?" he asked softly, taking her hands and pushing her away.

"Yes, I've finished!"

"Then excuse me please, Frau," he said, retreating to his cabin.

* * *

Later in the wardroom, Werner approached her. "You were hard on him, Frances."

"Oh, I expected you to stick up for him," she snapped.

"It's not a case of sticking up for him; he really had no alternative."

"Rubbish!"

Werner grabbed her by the arm. "Look, just listen for a minute, will you? Quite apart from orders not to pick up enemy seamen, where did you expect him to put them all? There must have been getting on for a hundred fifty men out there."

"He could have—"

"He could have what? Taken some of them? You accused him earlier of playing God! How do you think he could choose? For goodness sake, don't you know him better than that? If there'd been one or two maybe, ten even, he would have ignored orders and taken them on board. He has done so in the past. He picked you up, didn't he? What he did out there was the only thing he could have done. He left food, water, and brandy."

"I know he did," Frances said weakly.

"And then, by the way, when we were clear, he got Heinemann to search for a wavelength and radio their position. He did all that he could, Frances, and more."

She was quiet for a few moments, trying to understand her outburst. "He radioed for help too?"

Werner nodded.

"I suppose I was angry more for what he said to me, Paul. You saw him kissing me, you were there. I stupidly thought he cared. That he felt something for me. But I'm just a bloody stupid woman to him, aren't I?"

"Frances, think about what we have all just been through. The stress of thinking that we were all likely to die. He not only had himself to think about, but the men too. They are his responsibility. On top of that, his own worst nightmare is played out in front of him. It could so easily have been us in the water. Do you think in the circumstances, he might have preferred that you weren't on the bridge at that time? Do you think he wanted you to see the suffering of those poor men?"

Frances was thoughtful, and then she took a deep breath and looked Paul Werner in the eye. "I think I should apologise, Paul."

"Yes, I think you should, but I'd keep away for a while. Let's have a pleasant Christmas, huh?" Frances looked at him, puzzled. "It's the 22nd of December," he said. "Had you forgotten? With our engines in the state they're in, we won't be back in time. Christmas at sea, I'm afraid. Perhaps we'll make it back for the New Year though, eh, with a bit of luck? We're on our way back to Brest. Frances, you're going home."

Chapter 26

Detestable brat! He hated everything about her. Everything she stood for. Spoilt—that's what she was. The thoughts burned through Mueller's brain as he paced the cabin. He hated her amber fire eyes. He hated her sensual mouth, her satin smooth skin. He flicked his glance toward the curtain. She was approaching him now; he didn't even need to see her. He could sense when she was near. The green curtain tentatively parted.

"Kapitan Mueller, could I speak to you?"

Her voice, trembling with appeal, drifted featherlike in the air. He shoved his hands over his head, turned his back to her, "I'm busy, and in any case, I believe you've made your feelings for me quite clear, Frau Meyer."

"I want to speak to you. I need to apologise."

Whipping his gaze to hers, he said, "I've told you I'm busy. Now go!"

"All right, be angry with me, if you like," she said, exasperated. "But don't take it out on your men, they're tired out."

He turned to meet her gaze. "Don't tell me how to run my command, Froggy."

This was not the first time she had tried to apologise over the last couple of days. He'd put a barrier between them, not just between them, but between him and the rest of the world. He'd worked his men since the lifeboat incident a couple of days ago 'til they were ready to drop. Drill after drill, for men already tired, and on top of that, he'd insisted that the U-boat be cleaned up. Spotless is how he wanted her. The men were left in no doubt that the old man was in a mood. He'd not bothered with sleep for the last forty-eight hours, and his meals had been taken on the move, on the bridge, in the wardroom. Anywhere away from her.

Paul Werner had voiced his concern later to his fellow officers over a meal shared by Frances.

"You blame me, don't you?" she said. "Well, I tried, several times."

There was a rattle, and Mueller's voice crackled over the intercom. "Well, men, Christmas Day tomorrow. What shall we do, huh? Have a party? Half a bottle of beer for every man not on duty and another half later with dinner. That's all."

From all sections of the boat came a simultaneous cheer. Mueller ducked through into the wardroom, saw her, changed his mind, and ducked out again.

Frances turned to Werner. "Well, a bit more human at least."

Werner nodded. "'Peace and goodwill to all men', maybe we can save him yet. Go and talk to him, Frances."

"I will not. I've done my bit," she said, "Christmas Day tomorrow... Who'd believe it?"

* * *

Christmas Day dawned brightly enough. There was a strong northerly wind blowing which made the sea choppy and headway slow. Frances woke from a troubled sleep and could not believe the transformation that had taken place during the night, as though the angels themselves had been at work. The boat had been hung with all manner of paper streamers and cardboard decorations; even an artificial Christmas tree had been produced from somewhere and set up in the wardroom.

"See," said Paul, "I told you we carried everything we needed for every kind of emergency. Even a Christmas Day emergency. Merry Christmas, Frances," he said, kissing her on both cheeks.

"The old man's still got a mood on him," Zeitler remarked. He took a swig of coffee. "Ever since finding them lifeboats." Then he stood, and he too kissed her on both cheeks.

"Where is he?" asked Frances.

"Up top. Why not go up? Talk to him?"

"I've tried, several times. He's not amenable." She decided against trying again and turned to Werner.

"What's in store today for us then? Special celebrations?" She broke an awkward pause.

Werner shrugged. "Prayers mid-morning. We thought of committing Schumacher to the deep, but Hengst seems to think the lad would want to be taken home."

"Well, I hope we get him out in one piece, that's all," said Zeitler.

"What do you mean?" asked Frances.

"Nothing." Werner shot Zeitler a warning glance, which he failed to see or ignored.

His expression turned sombre. "Cor, we had to cut one out once, remember? Volf, wasn't it? Swelled up something awful and got stuck in the tube."

Frances swallowed. She was grateful when Werner spoke up.

"That's enough, Chief."

"Oh! Look, sorry," said Zeitler, taking her by the arm. "Damn my mouth, I was forgetting."

She smiled wanly. "I'm getting used to all sorts of horrors, Chief, I don't think anything could shock me anymore. This journey has certainly been a baptism by fire."

"Toddler, what brings you here?"

Frances followed Werner's glance to the wardroom hatch. "Dieter, Merry Christmas," she said.

He smiled awkwardly and produced from behind his back a bouquet of intricately made paper flowers. Thrusting them into her hands, he said, "Me and the boys made you these, Frances. Merry Christmas."

Her throat narrowed. This was surely the least expensive present that she'd ever received, and yet the work and detail that had gone into each bloom was incredible. She was overcome, thinking of the men and the effort they had made, how they'd likely given over their free time to make something so beautiful for her.

"I don't know what to say, Dieter, really, I didn't expect..." She kissed him on the cheek, amused once more by his blush and the effect she had on him. "Thank you. Please give my thanks to all."

Later that morning, she gathered with the rest of the crew on the deck. The wind dropped; the sea calmed. Once everyone was still, Mueller led them in prayer for an end to the war, and for peace and understanding between nations. They also prayed for the souls of the dead and for those who had lost loved ones. Lastly, they prayed for themselves, that they might reach their port without further hazard. She went below in a thoughtful mood.

Mueller could pray so eloquently for peace and understanding between nations, and yet he couldn't find it within himself to meet her even halfway. He continued to give her a wide berth the whole of Christmas Day. He preferred his own company, it seemed. That evening, following the Christmas meal of tinned duck, carrots, peas, and potatoes, she was surprised when he joined the crew in their Lordship's cramped fore'ard quarters for an evening of entertainment. Taking up Dieter's violin, she led them in the singing of several carols and beckoned Gotz to stand next to her and sing the opening verse of *Stille Nacht* (*Silent Night*) in his beautiful tenor voice.

She watched Mueller covertly, noting that he sang with gusto, if off-key. Moments after the final notes of *Leise rieselt der schnee* (*Softly Falls the Snow*) faded, their gazes met. His expression turned stony and hard, and giving her one of his most withering looks, he left. She refused to be put off and launched into her favourite piece, *Meditation*, and then straight into a swing version of Irving Berlin's *Blue Skies,* which surprised them all. She ended on an even higher note with a medley of Hungarian folk dances.

The men showed their appreciation; they cheered and clapped and whistled, and she told herself that she didn't care where Mueller was, or what he was doing. He could go to the devil, he didn't matter.

It was 2000 hours and Frances made her way into the wardroom and was glad to find Paul Werner.

"So, what's next, Paul?" she asked.

"Celebrations until midnight, I believe." There was raucous singing going on from the front of the boat. "I reckon it will continue until then."

She stifled a yawn.

He smiled at her. "You're tired. Why don't you turn in?"

She shook her head. "Can't do that, the curtain's across. Your lord and master is in residence."

"No, he's not," replied Werner, "I've just been with him up top. If I were you, I'd get in there quick and put in your claim."

She questioned him. "Are you sure he's not there?"

"Of course, I saw him not two minutes ago."

"Then I'll wish you good night, Paul." She didn't read anything into his answering smile. But a moment later, stepping through the curtain and finding Mueller seated at his desk, she recalled it.

"I'm sorry, Kapitan Mueller. Paul said—I'll leave."

"Stay!" Mueller jumped up, deserting his partially eaten meal and a half empty bottle of wine.

"Is that an order, Kapitan?" She swung around, jaw tight.

"No. No, of course not. Stay, please. Have a drink. Sit down." He pointed to the seat and, grabbing another glass, poured her a wine and seated himself on the bunk.

"I don't think this is a good idea," she said, remembering his mood over the last few days.

"Why not?"

"Well, isn't this a time for peace and goodwill, Kapitanleutnant. I hardly think you are in the correct frame of mind for that, are you? You've made it quite clear since—"

"Since what?" She was wishing she had kept quiet, but he was looking at her, waiting for an answer.

"The men in the boat. I'm sorry. I shouldn't have brought it up. Not tonight."

Mueller was in a forgiving mood, helped no doubt by the alcohol. "Oh, for Christ's sake, Froggy," he said. "It's only a couple of days since you planted one on me, and now we can't even talk it seems."

She glared at him. "I beg your pardon; it was you who kissed me!"

"No, you definitely kissed me." He gave her a wide smile, and she wondered if he was a little inebriated.

"So, you are not responsible for your own actions, Kapitan Mueller?" she taunted. "Typical. What?" He was still grinning at her.

"I love winding you up and watching you jump, Froggy."

Despite herself, she laughed at her own reaction. "Pig!" He smiled his gap-toothed smile, completely disarming her.

"Come on, stay, and have a drink. It's Christmas, after all, and I could do with some company," he said.

She nodded and sat at his desk. "Why are you stuck in here on your own anyway? There is quite a party going on."

"You think they would want their old man gate-crashing? No, this is their time, they deserve it."

He poured her more wine and returned to sitting on the bunk. Music played over the speakers, compliments of Heinemann from the radio room, who Frances had noticed on the way in was still wearing his headphones. She lifted the wine glass.

"Thank you. I'm sorry. I really didn't know you were here. In fact, I was assured you were not."

"Werner?" he asked.

She nodded. "He told me you were up top."

Mueller raised his eyebrows. "We're on the bottom, Froggy, submerged." He laughed at her. "Werner has got some stupid idea about us being ... well, you know..." He gave her a thoughtful look. "He thinks we like each other. Something about electricity and sparks." Mueller shook his head. "Silly sod."

"Ridiculous," she agreed. "Silly man."

The sound of raucous laughter reached them from the fore-end, followed by loud singing almost drowning out the music, causing Frances to blush and look down, and Mueller to smile and softly speak the bawdy lyrics.

Sheikh Abdul, the randy old codger,
Had a new girl each night of the year,
And when there was none left to roger,
He pleasured himself with a queer.

"Looks like the party is set to continue for some time yet, huh?"

"Yes, I suppose so." She felt ridiculously nervous and looked to the floor to prevent his eye contact.

"So, Christmas night. What would you be doing if there was no war on, and you weren't stuck here with me?"

"Oh, I don't know." She paused. "I suppose I would have bullied Steven into taking me dancing."

"You like dancing?"

"Mmm." She nodded. "Steven didn't; he just went to keep me happy and then bribed all the young men he knew to dance with me." She smiled to herself at the recollection. "And you, what would you be doing?" she asked, managing to find the courage to raise her head and look at him.

He was smiling at her gently, as he had on the night that he had held her close and she had told him of their attempt to leave France. "Family first, then later into town, and like you, probably a dance hall somewhere. Or maybe a party with a group of friends." Through the laughter and singing, they both heard the opening bars of *Moonlight Serenade,* and in perfect unison they announced, "Glen Miller."

Mueller jumped from the bunk and made a stiff bow in front of her. "May I say you look ravishing tonight. Could I have this dance, Extraordinary Seaman Froggy?" He held out his hand to her, and she stood up with a laugh.

"This is mad, we've no room."

"Well, the whole bloody world has gone mad, so I reckon we deserve our own bit of private madness on a very small dance floor, don't you?"

She smiled, taking his hand, looking up into his eyes, and wondering how she had ever found them icy. She momentarily stiffened as Mueller placed his other hand around her waist, but as they moved to the music, she relaxed, enjoying the feeling of being close to him again, enjoying the strength and firmness of his body, the oil, the sea, mixed with the smell of him, male.

"We must be the oddest couple anywhere." She laughed again, and she thought she sounded a little hysterical.

"Don't you believe it. You haven't been to some of the parties I've been to."

Her brain was trying to think of something to say. Something sensible to cover the ridiculous nervous jittering she felt inside.

The words tumbled from her. "I still haven't apologised, have I? I am so sorry, I didn't understand. Paul explained everything. I'm so ashamed of what I said." She surprised him and herself as a sob caught in her throat.

He looked into her eyes. "It's fine. I didn't like myself much at the time either. It's taken me a few days to come to terms and accept my responsibilities. Some parts of the job are not always easy."

Before she could register what was happening, he'd lowered his head to hers. His kiss deepened as he pulled her to him. She felt trapped within his embrace, and when his hold on her loosened, her knees were weak, her head spinning.

~ 198 ~

Finding her glance, he said, "I'll definitely take responsibility for that though." She started to protest, but he stifled her with a fingertip to her lips, and lifting her arms around his neck, he murmured into her hair, "And this, I'll take responsibility for this." At first, when he again brought his mouth to hers, she struggled, but soon she gave in to the thrill, the way her whole body seemed to be vibrating. She stood on tiptoe, wanting more. No one had ever kissed her and made her feel this way. Steven's kisses had been pleasant, but Mueller was kissing her with passion, treating her like a woman. There were feelings shooting through her centre, primal feelings she had never experienced before, and she liked it. He was holding her close, and his body told her that he was liking it too.

Pushing away, she said breathlessly, "I'm afraid, Kapitan Leutnant, that I am going to have to hold you responsible for this, too," and she reached up, pulling his head down, initiating another kiss, "and this," she said, breathlessly kissing him again. "You see, I think I have completely lost my mind."

He trailed a fiery path of kisses down the curve of her neck, muttering hoarsely, "My God, Frances, I want you like I've never wanted anything or anyone before."

Her heart beating, hammering in unison with his, she said, "I want you too, so very, very much."

He set her a little apart, locking his eyes on hers. "Are you sure?"

She nodded. "Certain."

Sweeping her into his arms, Mueller, deposited her onto the bunk.

She giggled. "We can't, not here, can we?"

"Nothing in the rules that I know of says we can't, Froggy." He peered down at her. "Are you getting cold feet?"

"No, but what if...?"

"Stay there," he ordered and disappeared through the green curtains. She heard him talking softly to Heinemann, then he reappeared with an ear-splitting grin, "All sorted. Heinemann will prevent anyone from entering, not that they would—they know better—and anyway, listen to them, still going strong."

"Heinemann knows!" Frances felt herself blush.

"I don't know what Heinemann knows; you're blushing, by the

way." He smiled and climbed onto the bunk beside her and gave a bounce. "Time to test German engineering."

"What about your shoulder?"

"What about my shoulder?" He tucked some stray tendrils of her hair behind her ear.

"I thought you might—"

"No thinking, Froggy." He covered her face with kisses and found her lips once more. Kissed her eyes, the tip of her nose. She'd lost her breath when he stopped, and levering himself up, he searched her gaze. "Are you sure you want this?"

"Yes, Kristian, I'm sure. I am." Her use of his name made him smile. Sitting up, he pulled off her boots and then his own.

He pulled off his shirt and then unbuttoned hers, cradling her breasts, taking the nipples into his mouth and she fleetingly thought back to her lovemaking with Steven. Pleasant, yes but this...

Her back arched in ecstasy. She tangled her hands in his hair.

Shifting, he opened her trousers, sliding them down her thighs, running a path of hot kisses to her navel.

She heard his own trousers drop to the floor, and then he fitted himself alongside her, murmuring endearments as he ran his hand over the flat of her belly and along the contour of her hip. She traced the ladder of his back, numbering each bone, flattening her palms on his buttocks. She felt his fingers come between her thighs, and finding her ready for him, he lifted himself onto her.

"All right?" she whispered, feeling him wince.

"Yes," he growled, husky-voiced. "Better than all right."

She opened her legs, and he entered her slowly, gently, tenderly, and she felt his wish to make it last, but soon they were lost, rocking together on a wave of passion that wouldn't be denied. She bit her teeth together to keep from crying out when she climaxed, and she felt his release come at nearly the same moment. The silence was broken by their ragged breath, the entwined throbbing of their hearts. Now Frances heard the music again, faintly, as it drifted through the curtain.

"Does that happen a lot?" She ran a fingertip over his lips. She was gazing at him, and he noticed that the fire in her eyes was now a gentle glow.

"What, Froggy?" he asked, lifting her hand, kissing the inside of her wrist.

"That, you know, what just happened, both together like that?"

"Not always, and when it does, it's special."

"I never knew it could feel this way."

"Your husband?" Kristian lay alongside her now. His gaze was tender.

"He was like a father." She faltered to a stop.

"You deserve better."

"Gotz, when he—he was rough, his hands—and humiliating. Otto, too, he made me feel afraid. I've never felt anything like this before, not so deep, through all of me," she said, kissing him.

He crinkled his eyes at her, then shouted, "Wow!" as her hand caressed his balls and he jumped back into life. "So, you want an encore then?" he asked, grabbing her, and making her laugh.

"Can you do that then, can you do it twice?" She laughed.

He lay on his side and pulled her to him, lifting one of her legs and wrapping it round his hip. "Oh, I'd make love to you all day, given the chance, my lovely girl; twice is nothing."

Later, exhausted, they lay side by side. "That was some encore." She smiled.

"Encore? I think we just played a whole symphony."

"Really, Kapitan? And you told me you hadn't a musical bone in your body."

He laughed aloud and held her down. "And just where has a nice girl like you picked up such filth?"

"From listening to your boys, of course."

"Always got an answer, haven't you, Froggy." He looked at his watch. "I'm going to have to put in an appearance soon. It's 2230."

"Do you have to?" she asked.

"Yes, but I've got time for more wine before I go." He pulled on his pants and crossed to his desk, poured them each a glass and came back to sit beside her on the bunk, rebuttoning his trousers.

"How many bottles have you got there?" Frances asked.

"Oh, just a couple...things aren't what they were. I remember a time when we toasted our success with champagne."

"So that's what happened to all our champagne. I was wondering."

Mueller looked at her with disbelief. "You're not trying to tell me you can't get hold of champagne in Paris, are you?"

"No," said Frances. "You can get hold of anything you want in Paris, provided you know the right people and have enough money."

Mueller nodded. "I must say Paris is a beautiful city. Did I ever tell you I've been?"

"No." Sitting up, Frances drew the blanket around her.

"A couple of times on leave—when I couldn't get home. Phew! It was mad."

"I'll ask that you spare me the sordid details, Kristian Mueller."

He laughed, drank a swallow of wine. "Sensible girl!" Drawing her to him, he kissed her briefly. "You said before you'll go back. Do you still want to?"

"Will I be allowed?" Frances sipped her wine. She'd been wanting to ask, nervous about it. She had no clue what her status was.

"If that's what you want. Why not?"

"They'll let me go just like that?"

"They'll likely caution you, but I've assured them that you know nothing. And I mentioned how you nursed Schumacher. You'll be fine. The Kriegsmarine doesn't make war on women. Will you be all right there? Is there nowhere else?"

"No, apart from cousins in England who I don't know at all. My aunt is in Paris—at least I hope she is. My—my home is there..."

"And this Otto is, too, right?" Mueller's eyes were intent.

"But he can't hurt me now, can he?" she asked, trying to convince herself. "I can deal with him now that Steven isn't here."

"Your Steven," Mueller said, "he was a brave man."

"Brave? Yes, I suppose he was. I never thought of him as brave, and yet he never complained once about his illness. He kept his suffering to himself."

"He was sick then?" asked Mueller with surprise.

"Very. For some time. Tuberculosis, we think. That's why we were trying to get to England for medical care."

"I'm sorry," said Mueller. "It must have been dreadful for you, losing him."

"Dreadful, yes. Steven was my love."

"You met at the Conservatoire, you said before."

"He was my professor. He was a good deal older than me."

"And you fell in love with him?"

"Yes. He always took such good care of me."

"And a good lover?" Mueller bit his lip. Damn his mouth. She had blushed and looked away from him, and yet was continuing.

"We didn't have that sort of relationship… I mean …" She stumbled as she realised that she was talking of her marriage, talking of memories that should be sacrosanct surely. But she needed to talk, to purge herself of these mixed-up feelings. "We were very close. He didn't seem to need that sort of relationship, not often anyway. It didn't matter much to him. It was all about the music."

"Ah, if music be the food of love, play on."

She laughed. "Well, if that was the case, we should have been at it all the time."

"No, not at all. Do you know the story?" Mueller asked.

Frances shook her head, "Ask me about Beethoven or Mozart, but Shakespeare, no."

"*Twelfth Night*, quite fitting as it happens. Orsini asks for more music because he muses that an excess of music may cure his obsession with love. So, looks like it works, at least for Steven. What about you?"

"I didn't know until now what I had been missing."

Chapter 27

This wasn't the way he thought it would be. Shag and run—that's how it had worked for him in the past. Only it hadn't worked last time, and he was stuck with a wedding he'd rather not attend, and it hadn't worked this time either, because there was nowhere to run, and he wasn't even sure he wanted to. Truth was, hadn't he wanted her since he pushed that stray curl aside? The scent of her body, the sound of her voice had invaded his thoughts, and he didn't like it. It was a non-starter, he knew that, and she'd hinted as much. They'd enjoyed one another, and that was all. It was done, and now he could get on with the rest of his life, for as long as it lasted. She had filled his head for too long. When he got back to port, he would be able to hand her over to his C.O. and walk away with scarcely a second thought. Mueller pulled his hands through his hair and puffed air into his cheeks, letting it go with a sigh. That's the way it was going to be. No regrets.

It was almost midnight when he arrived in the wardroom. Werner was sitting, occupying his usual position. Heinemann had turned down the music to background noise, the partying had finished. All that continued was a tired, muttered conversation. Somewhere, a watch should be preparing.

"Exec, give the order, prepare to surface, standby watch!" snapped Mueller. "I'm getting a coffee."

He made his way to the galley with Paul Werner on his heels.

"So?" Werner asked when they were out of earshot. Mueller nodded at his Executive Officer; jaw set rigid.

"So what? Have you something to ask me, Leutnant?"

Werner shook his head. He knew that look on Mueller's face, it said back off.

"I've asked you to give the order to surface, Exec."

Paul Werner gave a salute and made for the control room, wondering what had happened between Mueller and Frances during the last few hours. It had been clear to him for some time that there was a chemistry between the two of them, but the reaction he had just gotten from Mueller was not the one he had expected.

As Mueller listened to Werner giving his orders over the intercom, he made his way back to the wardroom and settled on the bench with his coffee and his thoughts.

* * *

The following day was not without its difficulties, though he thought no one would have noticed except maybe Paul. Damn him. He carried out his command as normal. The only difference was that he spent a little more time with the lads. He didn't want to be on his own, he didn't want to give her a chance. He was stuck with having to see her over dinner and had hoped that maybe she would decide not to put in an appearance, but she had, and he found it difficult. He found himself guilt-ridden, and when she took her place at the table he averted her gaze.

"How's it going then, do you think, Exec, Chief?" he asked.

"How's what going?" Werner asked.

"Jesus! The damn war, what else?"

Werner shook his head, he wasn't going to make things easy for Mueller. The girl sitting beside him was thoroughly miserable, and he felt responsible in some way. She sat in silence with her head down, toying with the food on her plate, pushing it around, scarcely eating a morsel.

Mueller tried again. "Are we winning, do you think?" He took several mouthfuls of food, trying to clear his plate as fast as he could. What was left of the duck from the day before had been put into a stew, and he didn't want to waste it, but he was finding the meal tortuous. He was aware that a couple of times she had tried to meet his gaze, but he wouldn't let her. After ten minutes or so, he stood. "Where the hell's the bloody coffee?" he grumbled, making his way to the galley. He decided against returning, using the time to chat to Hayman about any remaining supplies. He had a coffee pot sent through to the others.

Later that evening, he got trapped in the wardroom with her and Werner. The watch had changed, and the wardroom was a thoroughfare of men. He sat waiting for the lads to disperse. This time she was straight in, her wolf's eyes boring into him.

"Won't you even speak to me?" she asked.

He noticed she was blushing. "What do you want me to say? I thanked you last night." He saw her wince and bite her lip. He thought he may as well have slapped her, and he felt churlish.

She stood. "That was unnecessary, Kapitanleutnant," she said and left, heading towards his nook.

Werner turned on him, scowling.

"What, Exec?" he snapped. "What? Oh, for Christ's sake!" Jumping to his feet, Mueller left too, pushing his way through the men, following in Frances's wake, dreading her recriminations like ice in his stomach.

"You're right," he said, stepping into the cabin, drawing the curtain closed behind him. "My comment was unnecessary, I'm sorry." She turned away in an attempt to hide her tears, he presumed. "Look, Froggy," he said, "I don't know what you expect from me. We had a good time last night, didn't we? It was Christmas, we enjoyed one another, didn't we? That's all. I thought you understood that."

"You mean like enjoying a Christmas present?" she murmured.

"Yes, like that."

"Then I think last night was one of my best ever Christmas presents."

He was confused; he expected her to play the blame game. "You don't regret it then?"

She turned, and he saw the fire in her eyes. "No, I don't regret it. There are twelve days of Christmas though, aren't there? What I do regret is that you don't want to celebrate the other eleven."

He moved towards her. "There are tears threatening, Froggy. I can see them."

"A few, but I decided they would probably be lost on you, and a more direct approach would serve my purpose better."

He raised his eyebrows. "Did you now?" She took a step back and looked him in the eyes, and then he gave her a very slow smile. "Then later we should celebrate the second day of Christmas. I wouldn't want you to have any regrets at all." He grabbed his cap and lambskin and was still smiling as he left. "I'm going up top. I'll be back later."

* * *

When Mueller returned around midnight, they quietly made love, and then fell into a wonderful, deep, warm sleep. Frances woke a couple of hours later to Mueller's caress as he trailed his hand along her naked body, following the gentle curve of her breast, waist, and flank. Opening her eyes, she asked him lazily what he was doing, enjoying the stirrings that were starting inside her.

"Looking at you, just looking and thinking how bloody beautiful you are," he said.

She suddenly became embarrassed and tried to cover herself, but he pulled the blanket back from her again, leaving her open to his gaze.

"What on earth would you do if someone walked in now?" she asked.

"Cry rape?"

"Oh, very funny. It's hardly fair, is it?" She pulled the blanket back to cover herself. "I think I would like to study you, you know."

"Ah, you mean play 'I'll show you mine if you show me yours?' I haven't played that for years."

"I haven't got a clue what you are talking about," she said.

"No, Froggy, of course, you haven't, because it's always been about the music."

He pushed back the blanket, brazenly letting her inspect him. She gazed at his body for a while, silently admiring the athleticism of his form, tracing her hands over his chest, following the smattering growth of hair, and then stroking gently across his abs and the flat of his belly following the line of hair which ran down inside his underpants. She pushed her hand inside to find his penis, which she gently caressed, and heard his intake of breath. She smiled, turning to look at him. His eyes were half closed, trance-like.

"You are an absolute wanton," she said and laughed. Lying back beside him, the thought kept entering her head that once back in port, it may all be over, and she couldn't bear the thought of letting him go. "Will I ever see you again after we get back, Kristian?"

He nodded. "I'll get to Paris, I promise." He kissed her gently, and she returned the kiss with mounting passion. He was unsure whether it was his cock or his conscience, but something inside him said that he wasn't ready to let her go. Not just yet.

"Look, forget Paris. Come to Brest." She looked at him, her eyes wide with disbelief. He repeated, "Come to Brest. The war's going to continue for some time yet, maybe years."

She shook her head. "It's too soon, isn't it? We should wait, surely, shouldn't we? Give ourselves time."

"Do we have time, Froggy? Who knows what will happen? Everything is uncertain. Life is uncertain."

"Do you realise what you're asking?" she said. "You'll be away for weeks at a time... You're asking me to be there." She shrugged and sighed. "I won't even know if you're coming back. They'll tell her, "She said, referring to Sophie Heyne, "but what about me? How would I cope, not knowing?" Mueller stroked her arm, and she sighed. "How much time will there be for us?" she asked.

"We'll have days...nights together, I promise. I'll have to go home to Germany, of course, and I'll marry Sophie, but there will be time for us too."

Frances swallowed hard. She wanted to ask him about the damn marriage, about Sophie, but he refused to speak of it to her, except to say that Sophie didn't matter. She took his hand and toyed with the strong fingers, thinking of raising the subject of his marriage again but not wanting to spoil the moment.

"You're asking me to be your mistress, Kristian," she said thoughtfully. "Do you know what they do to women..."

He felt suddenly guilty for even suggesting it. She was right—being with him could put her in a dangerous predicament. "I'm sorry. I had no right to suggest it. Forget it. It's madness. Go to Paris. It's safer. I'll find you there."

For a while, she was lost in thought, and then she spoke. "It is madness, but you said last night that the whole world is mad, and we deserved a little madness of our own." She laughed a little hysterically.

"Do you know I've always had a yearning to live in the country? Maybe if we found a cottage outside the city, away from those that pry—"

"My God, Froggy, what are you saying?" A wave of warmth flowed through him, filling him up with a feeling that he'd never experienced before. "Are you saying yes?"

"I think so." She bit her lip and stretched her fingers upwards to caress his face. "If that's what it takes. Then I'm saying yes."

Mueller took both her hands and kissed them, shaking his head in disbelief. "I'll make sure you're taken care of; kept informed. I promise."

She placed a finger on his lips. "Hush. I don't even want to think about that. I couldn't bear it," she said.

Chapter 28

Triumphant but wounded, the U-boat approached her journey's end. The dark coastline of France lay accented between the pearlescent grey of the sea and the dull grey skyline. It had been a slow journey. They limped back to port from their grid position with one damaged engine. The journey had grown in monotony, the excitement of their kills quickly forgotten, but now they were making for the approach into Brest. They would soon be back in port. There would be good food and drink, and of course, there would be girls.

The Brits had lately increased their screen of aircraft in the area, and it forced them to travel on the surface by night only, making headway even slower. For daytime hours in the depths, they crept along at a speed of only three knots. Day became night as they rested and slept. Then, under the cover of the dark, they surfaced, forcing Tommy to resort to his new radar to find them, which he did exceedingly well. They were forced to crash dive three times in two hours during that first evening's approach, having to suffer clusters of bombs, one of which lifted their stern clear out of the water. The bombardier, concerned, must have reported a direct hit, for after that things quietened down.

Returning to the depths again at dawn, they found themselves surrounded by the sounds of inexplicable explosions which set all of their nerves on edge. Mueller was relieved when the evening came and they resurfaced. He took to the bridge, taking up the voice tube to inform the men below.

"We're in the middle of a fishing fleet. Exec and Watch to bridge." Mueller listened to the sound of Werner's feet ringing on the rungs of the ladder, followed by those of the men on watch. There were shouts from the fishing trawlers, telling Mueller where to stick his submarine, as Werner joined him.

"Not very friendly," said Werner, laughing at their predicament. "So, what do we do? Dive and let them get on with their fishing?"

Mueller gave a sniff of derision. "Let the buggers suffer. I reckon they'll make a damn good shield for us from any air attack. We're lucky, Exec."

They stayed in the middle of the fleet until dawn, when they expected an escort vessel to meet with them at a predesignated spot. The vessel didn't show up, so without the cover of the fishing fleet, they were once more forced into the depths.

The escort vessel eventually arrived, approaching mid-morning. Mueller was in one hell of a mood: they had been in the right spot at the right time after a long patrol, he viewed the late arrival of the escort as gross inefficiency. Mad as he was, he couldn't help but get caught up in the festive spirit of his crew. The crew had missed Christmas with their loved ones and New Year's Eve and were now more than ready to make up for it.

With land in sight, the men were happy and relaxed. They changed into fresh fatigues and combed their hair and beards in an effort to look presentable. They had several more thousand tons of shipping to add to their list, and they'd come through an ordeal which should have finished them. On top of that, their old man of late had been strangely ecstatic and there had been mutterings amongst the lads that maybe he was dropping his anchor into Frau Meyer's lovely harbour. The overall consensus was, however, good luck to him; they reckoned to a man that Frau Meyer was a pretty good sort.

With the arrival of the escort, men spewed from the hull and onto the deck, gasping for the fresh air that they had been starved of over the last few days. A couple of them busied themselves hoisting white pennants, one to represent each vessel they had sunk.

Frances was satisfied she had found her niche in life. It wasn't to give her all to art and to thrill the world with her musical accomplishment, but to give herself to the man standing beside her now. To delight him with her body as he did her with his. She was back in her own country, secure again, and it felt good.

They were a couple of miles out of port. The escort would leave them soon so that they could make a victorious entry alone in the wintery afternoon sunshine. The officers and Frances were assembled on the bridge. As with the rest of the men, their mood was light-hearted.

"Well," said Werner, "today is the start of a new year—1943—let's hope it's a good year for us all, huh?"

"A new year and a new start," mused Mueller.

"Hey, and for some, a new wife!" Zeitler quipped.

Frances turned away; she hated it when they referred to Mueller's marriage. She decided that when they were alone later, she would insist that he tell her all about Sophie and why the marriage had to happen. She had questioned him in the past about the possibility of a pregnancy, but he had laughed at her and told her that definitely wasn't the case. She wanted to ask so many questions, but he never gave her the chance to ask; he wouldn't discuss any of it.

The only thing he had said was that the marriage would take place but that she needn't worry, as it would in no way interfere with their relationship. How couldn't it? she had wondered. He said when he had asked her to stay in Brest, that his life with her would be separate, nothing to do with the one he had in Germany. She supposed she would have to accept that, for now at least, but she baulked at the idea of being the other woman. He had told her earlier that day that he wanted her more than ever and that he needed her. He'd certainly shown that to be the case over the last few days.

Werner came to her side now. He always seemed to be aware of the way she was feeling. Over the weeks, she had grown very fond of him. He had shown himself so many times to be her friend.

"So," he said with a gentle smile. "What is the first thing on your agenda?"

"Oh, Paul, need you ask? Hot bath, a hair wash, and a change of clothes. Something nice and warm." She drew her old coat around her to keep off the chill January air.

Mueller walked across the bridge and joined them, rubbing at his beard thoughtfully. "I suppose I'll have to make time to visit Schumacher's family in Berlin," he complained.

Paul Werner shook his head. "Now, that part of your job, I don't envy you."

Mueller raised his eyebrows. "You mean there are parts you do?"

"Only your pay!" Werner slapped him on the back. "Your shout when we get to the bar."

"Oh, baths, beer, beds, and women." Zeitler sighed dreamily. "All ours tonight."

"I'll settle for one bed and one woman," whispered Mueller in Frances's ear, just a little too loud, causing Werner to grin and Frances to go hot with embarrassment.

The day was undoubtedly a grey one, but the spectacle of France rising out of the sea made Frances's heart soar. It was certainly an awe-inspiring contrast to the drab world of the last few weeks; she thought. It wasn't long before she could make out patches of green vegetation, and then the large granite complex of the naval college and the white houses with their colourful roofs of blue, red, and green.

"Quite a welcoming committee, by the looks of things." Mueller held his glasses out for Frances. "Have a look—a veritable hive."

Frances struggled under the weight of the glasses but managed to focus. She looked towards the quay, which she saw was busy with people.

"What's going on?"

"Nothing apart from us returning to base. All for our benefit, Froggy, you see. Brass bands, flowers, dignitaries, women. Christ, you'd think they'd have something better to do, wouldn't you?" He grasped her around the shoulders and gave her a quick hug.

"What are those?" asked Frances, pointing to the large concrete structures beside the pier.

"The U-boat pens. Home for the Old Lady while she's refitted. She needs time to recover too. Exec, assemble the men." Paul Werner disappeared with a smile into the hull.

They were approaching the inner harbour now, and Mueller gave the order to reduce speed. The crew struggled to find their legs on deck in the unaccustomed calm as the U-boat serenely floated toward the sizable crowd lining the pier. The military band struck up a rousing Teutonic march. The men stood to attention and Mueller gave a casual salute as they came to rest.

A tall, dark, middle-aged man in a double-breasted blue overcoat stepped forward, giving a formal salute. He shouted up to the bridge, "Welcome home, Kapitanleutnant Mueller!"

Mueller shouted back in reply. "Thank you, sir!" and turned to Frances. "That's our flotilla leader, Klaus Vormann. He's a good sort, you'll see." He turned to Werner, who was now down on the deck with the assembled crew, and gave him a nod, granting permission for the men to go ashore.

Frances smiled as she saw men had already tottered across the gangplank onto dry land. There was Toddler, struggling with one or two others to get rid of his sea legs. The immense frame of Gotz was easily recognisable in the melee; he was hugging a young nurse and no doubt planning already to try out his technique once again.

The pier had become a mass of thronging people. Sailors, nurses, admin girls, dignitaries and their wives all had entered the party spirit; it was a festive time. New Year's Day, and Tommy, it seemed, was sleeping off New Year's Eve.

Mueller was striding across the gangplank ahead of Frances. She noticed two men wearing the black uniform of the S.S., and a chill ran through her. Catching up with Mueller, she grabbed his arm. "Kristian, who are those men?"

"Where?"

She gestured. "There." She pointed out a car that was parked some fifty yards from the pier. In all the hustle, it hadn't been noticed, or maybe it had only just arrived. Two men were standing beside it. Their black uniforms were unmistakable.

His expression darkened. "S.S.," he muttered. "What the devil—"

Mueller helped Frances onto dry land, supporting her a little to give her time to find her balance. Vormann slapped him on the shoulder with a smile.

"Looking forward to your report, Kristian. We've got a good meal laid on for you and the boys, and as a bonus: three weeks' leave. I guess you'll be making straight for Berlin though, hey, some wedding that will be!"

Mueller didn't answer. He was watching the S.S. make their way across the crowded quay. He turned to Vormann, pulling Frances forward.

"This is Frances Meyer. You'll be interested to read about her in my report."

The newcomer wearing the death's head insignia and the rank of major cut him short.

"Ah, Commandant, Kapitanleutnant."

Vormann greeted the two men. "Major Kessel, Leutnant Stromburg."

"So..." said Kessel, smiling at Mueller. "You are one of our national heroes, one of our grey wolves." He indicated Frances. "And this is the woman you radioed about, Meyer?"

Mueller put his arm protectively around Frances's shoulders, causing Vormann to frown.

"It is! May I ask what you want with her?"

"Let us just say that we believe that Frau Meyer can help us with certain enquiries—"

"The devil she can," spat Mueller.

"Major Kessel, I live here. Well, not here, but in Paris. I'm French. Do you know who I am? I am a friend of Herr and Frau Abetz. Please contact them, ask them about me," pleaded Frances.

"She knows nothing of interest to you people. I'll stake my life on it," added Mueller.

"Please, Kapitanleutnant, the lives of our heroes are worth a great deal to us." Kessel smiled coldly. "Allow us to do our duty, please, and decide about the woman. Now, Frau, you will come with us."

"Don't you lay a finger on her!" Mueller warned.

"Stand to attention, Kapitanleutnant!"

Mueller turned in disbelief, meeting the expressionless gaze of his C.O. "I will not!"

"Stand to attention, Kapitanleutnant Mueller, or believe me, I will place you under court martial."

Frances's eyes were wide with fear, and her guts were churning. She was frightened of these men, but more fearful of what Mueller might do. His C.O. was threatening court martial; locked up, he could not help her at all.

"Please, Kristian, if they arrest you, what chance will I have? I'll be all right. Please, Major Kessel, please contact my friends in Paris. They'll tell you there's nothing I can help you with."

"Where are you taking her?" demanded Mueller, knowing that to argue outright would be foolish and that she was right, she needed him.

"The prison at Brest, Kapitanleutnant. You'll be able to see the woman later if that is what you want," said Stromburg.

"Prison?" Frances's heart slammed into her chest wall. "Please, I don't know what to say. I don't know what information you think I have."

Mueller didn't like the sneer on his face or the look of Stromburg; he was cold and calculating.

"This way now, Frau," the man continued, taking hold of Frances's arm.

Mueller spoke through clenched teeth. "Don't touch her."

"Kapitanleutnant," Vormann warned.

Frances realised at that moment that Kessel and Stromburg would not be swayed. Maybe later, she thought, after they'd talked to her. They'd find out for themselves that she knew nothing. She tried to smile. "I'll be fine, Kristian. They'll soon find they've made a mistake. Don't make matters worse, please."

Vormann placed a restraining hand on Mueller, and he watched helplessly as the two men marched Frances off between them, across the quay to the waiting car. She looked back for a moment before they shoved her into the backseat.

Locking her gaze, he shouted, "I'll get you out, Frances, trust me!"

At his elbow, Vormann spoke sternly. "Mueller, I don't know what your relationship is with that woman, but my advice is to walk away now and forget her."

"I don't think I can do that, sir," he replied.

PART 2

The Doctor

Chapter 29

January 1, 1943

From the harbour, the S.S. officers took her straight to the prison in Brest, squashed between the two of them, and then slung her into a cell with whitewashed walls, a bunk and table, that being the only furniture. There was a small, barred window in the cell, about ten feet from the floor, from which, if she stood on tiptoe backed up against the far wall, she could see a tiny sliver of sky.

Her mind was in a whirl of panic. What if Mueller couldn't get her out, or if he didn't bother to try? It should be inconceivable, and yet?

Was there anyone else other than Otto who she could contact? She was a famous musician—they wouldn't leave her here, not in a prison. Edie? Had Edie made it back to Paris from Fecamp? Would she know of the *Etoile*'s sinking? She would surely wonder where Jacques was, why he hadn't got in touch in some way.

Her relief when she heard long strides mingled with those of her fat warder, warning her of approach, weakened her knees. It had to be Mueller. She just had time to splash some water on her face and drag her fingers through her tangled hair. It had been only a few hours since she had left him at the harbour, and already it had seemed a lifetime ago. He'd been so angry then that she'd feared what he might do or say.

She stiffened at the sound of the keys jangling in the lock of the cell door. The bolt shot back. The warder, whom Frances had nicknamed Big Bertha, pushed the door wide and snarled, "You've got a visitor."

Kristian Mueller pushed past the woman. He looked the same as when Frances had left him, dishevelled and dirty in his old cap and torn sheepskin, the beard and long hair, and she thought how wonderful he looked.

He gazed at her with relief. "Are you all right? Did they hurt you?"

"No, no, but I'm frightened, Kristian. I don't understand. You said I would be safe—"

"You can leave us now." Kristian spoke to Big Bertha, not taking his eyes from Frances.

"I'm sorry, Kapitanleutnant, I can't do that," the warder replied.

"No?" He turned, and taking the woman's arm, he shoved her out the cell door, clanging it shut behind her. Seizing the bars, Bertha threw her weight against it, but the warder was no match for Mueller's strength, and Frances joined him, adding her weight to his.

"I'm reporting this," Bertha said, backing away. "This is not permissible." Her footsteps had scarcely faded before Mueller had Frances in his arms, kissing her.

Releasing her after a long moment, he said, "Wow, what a team."

Frances smiled up at him and burrowed against his chest, enjoying the feel of his body, of his strength, until he gently pushed her away.

"I've got you these," he said, delving into the pockets of his tatty jacket and pulling out a comb and some chocolate. "You're going to have to wait a bit longer for that bath of yours."

She frowned. "How long?"

Mueller shrugged. "It's not going to be as straightforward as I thought. It seems the Kriegsmarine has little jurisdiction here, you see."

She swallowed hard, feeling her heart fall against her chest wall. "You mean I'm stuck here?"

"Just for a while," he answered, stroking her hair. "Don't worry, I can contact some pretty powerful people. It'll mean a few phone calls, that's all." He lifted her chin, holding her gaze. "Trust me, I won't let you down. Have you eaten?"

"They brought me some soup and a piece of bread hours ago."

He shook his head, cross with himself. "What a bloody fool I am bringing you this rubbish. I should have brought you some proper food."

She smiled, wanting to reassure him. "I'm not hungry, Kristian."

He ploughed his hands through his hair, unconvinced. "I've been stuck at our homecoming party and debriefing," he explained. "Regulation, or I'd have been here sooner; the lads are still enjoying themselves."

"I bet they are." Her laugh was sharply bitter, truncated. It burned— the notion that while he'd been celebrating, she'd been locked in here, exhausted, and terrified — But now there were footsteps approaching— two, maybe three people.

Mueller found her gaze. "Here comes trouble."

A jolt of panic paused her heart. "Promise you won't lose your temper." He didn't answer. She had a bad feeling. "Kristian, should anything happen, you will find me in Paris. 159 Rue Moncey, Aunt Edie's."

"159 Rue Moncey," he repeated and nodded.

The footsteps stopped, and keys jangled once more in the lock. "This is Leutnant von Stromburg, Kapitanleutnant!" barked a man's voice. "Stand back from the door, if you please!"

Frances darted a frightened glance to Kristian. "He's one of the S.S. who brought me here from the harbour."

Sitting on the bunk, he pulled her down beside him. "Shush. It'll be all right." Looking toward the cell entrance, in a parody of politeness, he called for their visitors to enter. "I'm away from the door! Come in and join the party."

First, Big Bertha appeared, followed by von Stromburg and another unknown S.S. officer.

"Just what do you think you're doing, Kapitanleutnant?" Von Stromburg was not happy.

Mueller raised his eyebrows innocently. "Visiting a friend."

"The prisoner is not allowed visitors without a warder present!" snapped von Stromburg. "Please, Kapitanleutnant, don't make things difficult for us."

Mueller set his arm around Frances's shoulders. "I don't want a warder present."

"I don't care what you do or do not want." Von Stromburg raised his voice. "It's the rule, Kapitanleutnant. This woman is a high security prisoner."

"On what grounds?" Frances asked, half standing.

Mueller pulled her down. "High security, my arse, she knows nothing!"

The second S.S. officer, a wiry, mean-looking type, had kept quiet until then, though he carried a riding crop which he flexed from time to time.

"I think you should leave, Kapitanleutnant. It would be best. You've outstayed your welcome," said the officer.

"I'm in no hurry," Mueller stated easily. Frances's blood cooled. His attitude, his failure to respect their orders, was angering the officers. *You aren't helping!* She wanted so badly to say it. She clenched her teeth together.

The S.S. officer smiled, uncovering small yellow teeth. "I don't think you understand my meaning, Kapitan; it would be best for the woman." He slapped the crop hard against his boot.

Before Frances could stop him, Mueller lunged at the man. Frances half rose.

Von Stromburg set heavy restraining hands on Mueller's shoulders, blocking his attack. "Didn't you hear what Leutnant Hoess said, Kapitanleutnant?"

"Don't you touch her!" Mueller warned.

Frances caught the movement when Big Bertha raised her truncheon. "Kristian!" she shouted, but she was too late. The warder brought the weapon down on Kristian Mueller's skull. He crumpled to the floor, bringing the officer with him.

Frances flung herself to her knees beside his prone body, only to feel the warder grab her arm, her thick fingers digging into her flesh and making her wince.

"Sit down, Frau." As von Stromburg spoke, Big Bertha shoved Frances onto the bunk, holding her there. "You know this is all very unpleasant and quite unnecessary," von Stromburg said.

He kicked Mueller, and she cried out, "He's hurt! You have to help him. He needs a doctor."

"Come, come," von Stromberg said, and flicking a glance at the second S.S. officer, he issued an order. "Move him."

Fear raced down Frances's spine.

"Our gallant Kapitan will be all right. When he wakes, he might have a bit of a sore head, that's all, I promise you. He's one of our heroes, after all. In the meantime, we don't want him causing more trouble, now, do we?" said von Stromburg.

"Please, let me tend to him." Frances was frantic, begging, giving any reason she could think of that they'd leave Mueller with her, but her pleas fell on deaf ears.

"Carry on, Leutnant Hoess," ordered von Stromburg.

Hoess saluted sharply.

"Please." Frances's voice slipped and caught. She flinched when Hoess smiled at her. He crossed the cell floor toward her, kicking Mueller's inert body as he passed him. Before she could register it, he had wrenched her arm behind her back, pulling it so high she feared it would break. Her knees weakened; her stomach heaved. She was afraid she would vomit. What would they do to her? She felt so helpless. Now Bertha grabbed Mueller by the ankles and dragged him from the cell, returning a moment later for his old, battered cap. That was the last time Frances saw him. It was also the last time she cried.

Chapter 30

January 3, 1943

They moved Frances that same night back to her beloved Paris, a distance of nearly 600 kilometres. They had told her at the prison that it was the French authorities who wanted to question her, and she was relieved, thinking that maybe her trials were over, that they would set her free. But in the early hours of the morning two days later, the police van in which she was travelling alone drew up outside the Prefecture of Police opposite the Hotel Dieu. They hustled her through colourless corridors to the fifth floor and into a room containing several benches and a bed. A bed in a waiting room, what nonsense, she thought.

By eight o'clock, others had joined her on the benches, and she could smell their fear. A gendarme stood guard, and they were forbidden to talk to one another. She had only heard whispers of what went on in room 35 of the building, and she wished now that she hadn't listened to the rumours spoken of Fernand David, head of the Special Brigade who worked hand in hand with the Gestapo and S.S.. Her pulse was racing, and her stomach was churning—not through lack of food, she realised, but terror.

Then the door of the adjacent room opened and a tall man in a grey suit said softly, "Commissaire David will see you now, Madame Meyer." They knew who she was. Surely that was a good sign, she'd soon be free.

As she stepped shakily forward to the door, one of those in the waiting room whimpered, and another muttered, "David le Rouge. Jesus, have mercy on us."

She could remember little of that room, or little of the interview with the infamous commissaire. There had been three men who had repeatedly questioned her over and over for the names of those who had helped in the exodus from Paris.

"I don't know any names. I don't know any of the places that we went to," she had told them again and again.

"You have links with the Resistance. Give us names now, and maybe we will let you go home, Madam Meyer."

She repeated, "I do not know about the Resistance. I don't know what you want me to say."

At first, they had been patient, treating her with kid gloves, as one would a child. Then the blows fell. They pushed her forward over the desk and ripped the shirt from her back. To start, when she had failed to give them the information they wanted, they had whipped her with a belt.

"Please," she begged, "contact my friends, the German foreign minister, Monsieur and Madam Abetz. They're my friends. I visit them—"

She felt the metal bar hit her spine at the same time as she heard Ferdinand David shout out, "Liar!" Having little previous experience of physical pain, her pain threshold was mercifully low, and she passed out.

She had no idea how much later it was when she finally regained consciousness and found herself lying prone on the bed in the waiting room. The bed which was reserved for the last person out of interrogation. She groaned from the pain in her back and then retched, and a man's voice, decidedly French, spoke gently to her. "You're lucky they finished with you so quickly. They've got some other poor sod now. Resistance—he'll not get off so lightly."

As if to underline his last statement, an agonised scream came from the interrogation room. The speaker slid his arm beneath her shoulders. "Come on, Mademoiselle, I think we had better get you to the hospital, they're going to need this bed for someone else before too long." She peered up at him, tears brimming in her eyes.

"Will they question me again, or are they letting me go?" She came face to face with the voice. A plump, jolly looking gendarme was standing beside her, his soft brown eyes filled with pity.

"You're lucky," she heard him say again, and then she lost consciousness.

* * *

She spent several days recuperating at Hotel Dieu Hospital. She had tried talking to the doctor and the nurses, but they wouldn't speak of anything other than her wounds, which were well tended. There were baths, clean clothing, and good food. All to prepare her, to make her strong again so that she might withstand her next ordeal—Drancy!

Her mind jumped back to Steven's internment, it hadn't been for long, but he'd come home a shadow of his former self. Was that going to happen to her? Surely they would soon realise the mistake they had made. There had been a mix-up, that's all. She'd be able to explain everything, and they'd apologise and let her go home. Kristian would come and take her back to Brest, to the cottage he'd found for her.

The police van drew up in front of the enormous, half-finished housing complex on the east side of Paris, which in 1941 had been enclosed within a barbed wire fence complete with watchtowers. Drancy! Non-secret, in full view of the neighbouring working classes, staffed almost entirely by French authorities, none of whom wanted the responsibilities of its running, and whilst those authorities fought, conditions deteriorated. And yet it had been in such conditions of hardship that Frances had found dignity and friendship.

She arrived in the police van that had transported her the short distance from Hotel Dieu Hospital, along with four other women, on January 16.

A gendarme met the van and ushered the women out. "This way, ladies, this way. Come along." They followed him to an office in one of the high-rise buildings surrounding the U-shaped prisoners blocks.

"Name?" a hard-faced, middle-aged woman questioned Frances.

"Frances Meyer. You may have heard of me;, I am also known as Frances Lamont. My maiden name, I use—"

The woman looked up, hard eyed. "Frances Meyer. Date of birth."

"August 3, 1918." Frances tried again to explain who she was. "I'm a violin virtuoso. I trained at the Conservatoire. I'm—"

The woman looked at her stony-faced. "This is all information that we don't need, Madam Meyer. You're a Jew, correct?"

"No, I'm—"

"Please wait over there with the gendarme until we have finished with the other women, Madam Meyer." She pointed towards the gendarme waiting by the door.

After taking down their details, a gendarme took the group to the four-storey prisoners' quarters. The poor man was almost apologetic as he left them in the stinking surroundings. There was no furniture, no plumbing, and no sanitation in the block they were to share with hundreds of others. All they could call their own was the small place they had found to sleep in. Some longer-standing internees had bartered for poor quality mattresses or had been lucky enough to have been left them by others moving on, but for most, bedding consisted of foul-smelling straw.

She chose her spot carefully, at the far end of the block away from doors, windows, and draughts. As she gathered a small pile of mucky straw to act as bedding, she watched for a glimmer of interest from her neighbour. Next to her, a woman seated on a filthy mattress, head bent, and shoulders hunched, covered in a thick coat, showed no interest at all in her arrival.

She made the first move. She held out her hand to the woman.

"Frances Meyer," she announced, and when the woman looked up, her breath went down hard. She jerked her glance away and immediately wished she hadn't. The woman's cackle mocked her, but the vision of her face—one side was badly deformed. The cheekbone appeared to be smashed in. Whoever had done that must have hit the woman with tremendous force, thought Frances, thinking back to Ferdinand David and the metal rod that he had smashed across her own back. The injury to her neighbour's cheek had pulled the eye downwards on that side of her face so that it pushed her nose off-centre. When she spoke, her lips pulled in differing directions.

"Do I really look that bad?" she asked.

Steeling herself, she turned back to the woman. "Yes, I'm afraid you really do look bad," she said, and her horror was mixed with pity

"Well, thank God, at least you're honest." The woman's smile was more grimace. "Here, sit down." She scooted to one end of the thin mattress, and when Frances had seated herself, she said, "I would offer to shake hands, but—" Uncurling her fist, she revealed her bloodied and torn fingertips.

Without thinking, she cradled the woman's damaged hand in her own two hands, throat closing in compassion and no little commiseration, for she, too, knew the brutality of their captors. Raising her gaze, she met the woman's eyes. "How?"

"How?" the woman demanded. "My God, where have you been for the last three years? Are you staying?"

"I'm staying. What's your name?"

"Oh, the Krauts have several for me." The woman cackled. "My real one, though, is Miriam Rosenburg."

"You're a Jew, then?"

"Aren't you, with a name like Meyer?"

"My married name. I really shouldn't be here," she explained. "It's all a mistake."

"Oh, and I should?" Frances realised what she had said and was about to apologise, but Miriam continued. "So, Frances Meyer, even being married to a Jew is enough these days, isn't it?"

Frances shrugged, refusing to acknowledge the fear that was in her belly, that Miriam was right. "I think I'm here because they thought I had information."

Miriam straightened. "About what?"

"The Resistance."

"And have you?"

"No, none."

"And if you had," Miriam pressed, "would you have given it to them?"

"I don't know. I didn't know anything, but if I had information," Frances said, shaking her head, "if I'm honest, then probably yes! My God, Miriam, what on earth did you do to deserve this?"

Once again, Miriam barked out her hard laugh. "Deserve, what a strange choice of word, Frances Meyer. Does anyone deserve this, do you think? Did you?"

"No, of course not. I'm sorry, I didn't mean—"

"All right, forget it. I know what you're trying to say."

They shared a brittle silence. Miriam broke it.

"My family were all arrested in '42. I have never seen or heard of them since. We never hurt a soul, not one of us. I suppose I was the lucky one, I was out when the pigs raided our home. After the disappearance of my family, I swore revenge and began working for the Resistance.

They got me a new identity, new papers—the lot. I made sure the Krauts really paid for what they did to us. And then I was betrayed—by a lover." Miriam gave a parody of a laugh. "Hard to believe I could have had a lover, isn't it? The gestapo did this, they hit me so hard they smashed my cheek bone and pulverised my left eye socket. Not content with that, they also practised a little dentistry and finished with a first-class manicure." She looked down at her mangled fingers. "They have such a way with them, don't you think?"

"I'm so sorry." She had nothing else to offer.

"Hah! Don't be sorry." Miriam laughed, "They didn't learn a thing from me, not a bloody thing." Miriam had paused and then asked, "How old do you think I am?"

Frances had shaken her head. It was impossible to tell from the face, though the body still appeared slender and firm.

"I'm twenty-three," said Miriam. "Twenty-three and glad to be alive, and I'll tell you something else, I mean to stay alive 'til the end of this bloody war 'cos if you give in to them and die, the bastards have won."

As they lay side by side that night, Frances found it impossible to sleep. There was a constant hum of chatter from others in the same predicament as herself, mixed in with coughing, babies crying, and the stink of too many people packed into a small space. In the end, she took hold of Miriam's arm and gave it a shake.

"Miriam, Miriam. Are you awake?"

There was a sigh from beside her. "I am now. You need to get some sleep," Miriam said.

"I can't. Miriam, what's going to happen to us?"

"Deportation."

"Deportation?" She remembered what Otto had told her, that Jews were being rounded up and deported. Steven, too, when he returned from his internment, had said that a thousand or more people had disappeared, and taken somewhere by train.

All of this she had swept aside, refusing to accept that such a thing could happen, refusing to believe even her own husband.

"Every few weeks the names are called, the transit fills up and off you go. What did you think was going to happen?"

"I don't know. Where will they take us?"

"Who knows?" Miriam shrugged. "Got to be better than this place though, hasn't it? I hope you don't smoke."

She shook her head, "No, I don't ... why?"

"One Galois is ten to thirty francs, more just prior to deportation. Anyway, tell me about your past, since we're not going to sleep."

Despite everything, she smiled. "What do you want to know?"

"Everything. I'm just a kid from the poor quarter. I bet you lived like a princess."

"Well, not quite." She laughed, and she told Miriam about her life up to the departure for England, cutting things short and merely saying that Fecamp was as far as they got.

She recognised Miriam was filled with such hatred for the Germans that she would never be able to understand her relationship with Kristian Mueller. She thought that she would like to tell her one day, but the time wasn't right now, and Miriam would view it as a betrayal. She also knew that Miriam had kept some of her own past to herself and so there came to be an understanding between them and neither pressed the other for information they were reluctant to give.

"Fancy me rubbing shoulders with someone famous," Miriam said when she had finished her tale.

A most peculiar friendship began that day in January at Drancy. Miriam Rosenburg was glad to find someone intelligent to talk to who was not repulsed by her injuries. She recognised Frances's innocence and, as a thank you for her honesty, decided she would take care of her. Frances, on the other hand, was glad of the company and happy to accept any advice on the art of survival, something which she found Miriam was particularly good at. By the end of that first day, she had learnt that food comprised a starvation diet, usually of cabbage soup, and that there was no plumbing or sanitation. Toilet paper was a thing of the past, and diarrhoea and dysentery abounded. To make matters worse, because of the gross overcrowding, a visit to the latrine was only allowed once every sixteen hours. On the plus side, she found out that many things were available if you had the money on the very extensive black market. By the end of the third day, she found herself to be starving. She had always loved her food, and cabbage soup and a hunk of bread did little to stave off the pangs of hunger.

"You'd better write to your aunt—see if she's alive—and let her know you're safe; get a few extras too," said Miriam following one of Frances's many complaints.

"Write?"

"Sure. You're allowed to keep in contact with the outside; parcels once a week, too."

"You're joking."

"I most certainly am not. I wish I dared write to someone, but there's no family now, and they keep watch. Anyone else could be linked to the Resistance. I thought of trying to smuggle a letter through the wire once, but you don't know who you can really trust." Miriam had paused thoughtfully. "Concerts—we must arrange for you to play concerts. It would keep the people's spirits up. A real virtuoso, they'd love it. What do you say?"

"What I say is I don't have a fiddle, do I? And where do I get some paper to write this letter?"

"Watch this, Rich Girl, I'll sort the fiddle and the paper. But mind what you say, they'll read the lot before they send it."

Frances carefully considered all that Miriam said and decided there would be no harm done by letting Edie know what had happened during the attempted crossing to England, though she was careful not to mention that her aunt had been part of the escape plan. She also couldn't see any point in not mentioning that she had been found and picked up by the U-boat. Since they had imprisoned her on her return from that patrol, she was certain that all of this information was already known.

* * *

Edie's response and parcel arrived less than a week later. It contained all that Frances had asked for, and more. The letter had been torn open, read, and replaced, but holding it to her nose she could still distinguish Edie's perfume, and her eyes had filled with tears that she refused to shed knowing that her dearest aunt was still alive. That first wonderful letter—a link with the outside world.

My darling niece,

I now have a reason to live again. I feared the worst when I received no word, fears which I find now were thankfully unfounded for you, at least now that I have received your letter.

I have wept many times over the last few days since hearing from you, for Steven and dear Jacques, though mostly I have wept for joy in the knowledge that you are safe. How you must have suffered all those hours on your own in the cold.

I thank God for the men who picked you up, that they were decent, though lately I find it more difficult to believe that there are any decent men left, and I do not mean just German men... there are such goings on now.

Speaking of Germans, I have had a visit from Otto. He would not believe me when I told him I feared you dead. He said that if you were, he would know himself, that he would feel it, and he did not.

He made me promise I would let him know the moment I had word from you, though, of course, I will not if you do not wish me to. Think carefully, Frances, I believe the man truly cares for you, though because of this damn war, his feelings are a little confused and warped, and he has, at times behaved badly. I am sure that a man in his position could get you out of Drancy.

Please let me know what I should do.

Your loving aunt.

She read and reread the letter and, being sure that there was no mention of Mueller to incriminate her, she showed it to Miriam.

"Well, what will you do?" she asked.

"I'd rather stay here than owe Otto a favour, which I know he'd collect on. I hate him, the bastard," she said, though secretly she still hoped that Mueller would keep his promise. *He'd be married by now,* she thought, *setting up house with his new wife,* and she wondered if he had any time at all for her in his thoughts.

Miriam had given her a hug. "Good for you. How I hate these bitches that fraternise. They'll get what they deserve at the end of all this. We'll make sure they do, won't we?"

Frances was struggling to answer, knowing that any answer she gave would be riddled with lies, but thankfully, Miriam's attention was on the large hamper that had arrived alongside Edie's letter. The two women spent the next half hour looking at and discussing its contents, and then deciding what to eat first. Miriam insisted that one of them should guard the food constantly, and if for any reason they both left the small area of the building which had become their home, then they took the hamper along with them.

The second letter and another food parcel arrived from her aunt just over a week later, in the first week of February, and contained information which had nourished and warmed her more than any food contained in the parcel and had made her heart soar.

Dear Niece,

Imagine my surprise, today, January 30, when I opened the door to find a German Naval Officer standing outside. I assumed him to be the young man that you wrote of. He is exceedingly handsome. He spoke of you with great warmth, my dear, and begged me for any news of you. I understand you're not wanting Otto to know of your whereabouts. I don't know what I should have done, but I told my visitor of your internment in Drancy, at which point he picked me up and kissed me.

He told me he had been trying to find you for some time, and that you would understand the difficulties that he has had. Evidently, I was his last hope. He asked me to tell you that by the time you received my letter, he would be back at sea and wanted me to assure you that before he left, he would make sure that the wheels were in motion for your release.

I am to tell you, too, that by the time he gets back from his next patrol, he expects to find you installed in that little cottage in Brest.

My dearest girl, I can only guess at what he meant. I like him immensely, but if what I think has happened, has happened, then I urge you to take extreme care. There are those that would not understand, though let me reassure you I am not one of them.

Your loving aunt.

Frances knew Miriam was waiting with anticipation for some inkling as to the contents of that letter, but if she ever found out what was in it, their friendship would be at an end. She was totally unable to hide her excitement, however, which Miriam at once picked up on as they sat side by side, rummaging through the contents of the second food package.

"So come on, Rich Girl, spill the beans," she said.

"What?" Frances couldn't prevent the threatening smile from creeping across her face and sat, just grinning at her friend, so full of joy that Mueller had visited Edie. She was unable to speak for fear of sharing it.

"Must be good news, anyway, for you to be so happy in this place. Unless you've just gone insane, of course."

Frances decided she had to sate Miriam's curiosity. "I'm getting out."

"You have gone insane, no one gets out of this place."

"Yes, they do. Steven got out. They rounded him up, and then he got out."

"That bastard Otto, I suppose. You said there was no way you'd accept help from him, didn't you?"

"No, Miriam, it's not Otto. Look, suffice it to say I'm getting out of this dung pit, and I'm going to get you out, too."

Miriam wouldn't let things lie. "How?"

"Leave it, please." She grasped Miriam in an embrace and kissed her. "We're getting out, that's all you need to know for now. Yes?"

Frances left Miriam to guess. She thought the effect that the letter had on her friend was strange indeed.

The weekly food parcels were always shared. At first, she had wanted to play Madame Bountiful amongst the others. The children's need for food particularly upset her. She and Miriam had their first argument because of this.

Miriam had found an old man with a reasonably good violin in his possession who was willing to lend it to Frances, and she then set about organising a concert at the beginning of March with the blessing of the French gendarmes who guarded their block. It was following this first concert that Frances suggested to Miriam that they might share the contents of their hamper with those most in need, particularly the children.

"Do you think these people would do anything for you if the position was reversed?" Miriam asked.

Frances turned away from her.

"You think I'm cruel," said Miriam, touching her shoulder. "I'm not. Look, Frances, feel sympathy, but feel it inside. Keep it to yourself, or it will be looked upon as a weakness. If you're seen to be weak, you will be easy prey."

Frances had done a lot of thinking that day. She had thought back to the situation on the U-boat when she had attacked Mueller for not helping the British sailors on the life raft. Paul Werner had brought her up short by asking her how she expected him to choose which sailors to help. Hadn't Miriam hinted at the same? How could she choose out of the hundreds of children who should receive a tiny morsel from her hamper? At the end of that day, she admitted Miriam was right.

The once-a-week food parcels were wonderful though, as they relieved the boredom for two or three days by creating a dilemma (should they gorge themselves and feast, or should they ration the food out?), also created immense stress for the women. If they chose to ration the food, where could they hide their store so that it wouldn't be stolen? There was constant looting on the block, mainly for food, and often angry arguments would break out. Thankfully, they were spared this additional stress, and Miriam suggested it was probably as a thank you for the music that Frances was giving everyone. Even in the dung pit that was Drancy, there appeared to be a sense of honour.

After six parcels, there were no more; they stopped, along with the letters, and Frances had waited, expectantly, certain that the non-arrival of the parcels meant she was to be released. It made sense to her.

"Hey, isn't there a possibility that something could have happened to your aunt?" Miriam pointed out one day.

"Something happen to Edie? No." Frances dismissed the idea straight away. She wouldn't even consider such a thing.

Then another entire week passed, and Frances waited every day for news of her release. Edie would come, she was convinced, or maybe even Mueller himself would turn up. Her knight in shining armour. There was nothing though, except that they learnt of their deportation.

* * *

At first light on the 20th of March, they had marched the deportees with Frances and Miriam amongst them, down to the barbed wire enclosure in the middle of the courtyard. There they were lined up to wait in the freezing icy drizzle. Then instructed to hand over any monies that they might have. In return, they were given a receipt, a promissory note printed in German which would enable them to be reimbursed with an equivalent number of Zlotys to Francs. Pathetically, those still in possession of money gave it up; it was so reassuring to not have to bother about transporting cash and to have something in writing for the other end.

Next they had all to suffer—men, women, toddlers even—the indignity of a search. Then, as their names were called out, they were marched off to the South gate and loaded into the familiar green and white city buses.

The organisation was impressive. There was little resistance, why should there be? It was a relief, after all, to be getting out of Drancy.

Chapter 31

March 21, 1943

Frances turned back, heart pounding, searching vainly for Miriam. The shrill cries of a child pierced the angry shouts of armed men, "Maman! Maman!" Frances's heart broke for the baby. But she was as helpless to come to the child's aid as she was to find Miriam in the heaving crush of bodies. The air smelled of sweat, fear, and desperation. When an old man in front of her stumbled, she steadied him even as the butt of the sentry's rifle crashed down onto his shoulder. The blow nearly took them both to the ground. Somehow, she kept their balance, and they were pressed forward. The old man clutched her arm, his gnarled fingers blue with the cold. Up and down the endless line of rail trucks, she saw younger, stronger people helping the older and infirm ones.

"It will be all right," she told the man, but now a push from behind wrenched him from her grasp. She lunged for him, but at that moment a hand appeared, a lifeline, and her gaze locked with those of a younger man standing above her in the cattle car doorway. "Come, come!" he shouted.

Instinctively, she grabbed hold and felt herself lifted, blinking, and stumbling into the railcar. Releasing her, the man, her saviour, grinned before turning from her, and again reaching outside the cattle truck door. It was reflex when Frances joined him, leaning down to offer her hand to a young heavily pregnant woman holding a canvas-wrapped bundle nearly as big as her.

"Leave it!" Frances shouted, gesturing. Her glance jerked from the woman to a sentry, making his way over to them. He was the same one who had struck the old man. A pregnant woman would mean little more to him. Frances's blood cooled in her veins. She brought her frantic gaze back to the woman. "You've got to put it down. I can't lift you—the extra weight—"

"No!" The woman clutched it to her chest. "I need it—things for the infant."

"Get a move on there, or I'll give you some help you don't want!" The sentry raised the butt of his rifle.

Frances grabbed the man who had helped her. "Quickly! Give me a hand, she's too heavy for me."

Stepping to the railcar door, he shouted at the woman, "Sling your bundle up here, and I'll pull you up."

But stubbornly, she clung to it. "No! It's all I have."

The German sentry stepped closer.

"For God's sake, give it here!" Frances yelled, then shifting her glance to the sentry, she shouted at him. "One second, please, we have her!" Their lives seemed to hang in the balance in the moment before the woman gave in and hurled the bundle through the truck door. Frances and the young man took one arm each, hoisting her up and onto the fusty straw-strewn cattle car floor.

"Thank you! Thank you!" She panted as Frances collapsed beside her.

Whatever relief they shared was short-lived as others were helped into the truck, forcing them further into its murky depths. Minutes later, the doors were jammed shut against the swell of tightly packed bodies, condemning them all to an airless, stinking gloom. As Frances's eyes adjusted, faces swam at her in the thin shafts of wintry sunlight which dared to find their way through the slits in the planked walls. She recognised many of them, who, like her, had been at Drancy for some weeks. Their eyes were lacklustre, their skin had the same greyish tinge. Others who had suffered Drancy for only a few days or less were in much better shape. They still had good clothing and full hampers of food. Frances cast her eyes over the hampers enviously; the last week or so with no hamper from her aunt had left her starving.

Her gaze rested on one family in a corner of the railcar close to her. The woman was about forty, Frances guessed, and expensively dressed in a fur coat and fur-lined boots. She held her arms protectively around her two youngest children, a boy of about eleven and a beautiful girl who looked to be about seven. An older boy, in his mid-teens, was arguing with his father. Interested, Frances strained to hear their conversation above the rest of the hubbub.

"You'll do as you're told, boy," said the father, "and that's an end to it."

"But Papa, the floor is loose here, we could pull up a few planks and get out."

"What about your mother?" the father continued. "Think for a while, my son, do you really believe your mother is up to a cross-country dash?"

"She's stronger than you think, Papa, we could at least try," the boy insisted.

The father shook his head in exasperation. "And what do you think would happen to the rest of these people? You heard what they said. One escape and the rest will pay."

"Yes, that's right!" said a brawny man in a homburg-style hat. "You're staying put, lad. We're going to a work camp, I heard. Now I reckon a bit of hard work never hurt no one, son."

"I'd rather risk an escape than work for the damn Krauts," the boy argued. Frances considered his response and wondered if the opportunity arose, whether she would risk an attempted escape.

"Well said, lad!" another man called. Still another male voice piped up. Frances couldn't see who it belonged to.

"We're all gonna be shot anyway," he said. "They'll take us somewhere out of the city and shoot the bloody lot of us, just you see."

"Don't talk rot," retorted the man in the homburg. "We're not living in the dark ages; we're all civilised people, for goodness' sake."

Exhausted, Frances turned her attention away from the dispute, wondering how she might make room to sit down, wanting only to close her eyes. There was a jolt as the train finally started to move, and she widened her stance to keep her balance, but a second, more ferocious jolt threw her against the pregnant woman.

"I'm sorry," she apologised. The woman smiled up at her, and it struck Frances how pretty she was. An eerie quiet fell as the train pulled away. Feeling a tug at her skirt, Frances looked down.

"Sit," the pregnant woman said, scooting over. "There's room."

Frances sank down gratefully into the sour-smelling straw, murmuring thanks to others who obligingly rearranged themselves to accommodate her.

"When is the child due?" she asked, wondering how this poor woman was going to cope with a babe in arms at a work camp.

"Anytime now," the woman replied, patting her swollen belly. "I can't wait. I love him already."

"Him?" Frances smiled.

"Oh yes, I only wish his father could be with me."

"Where is he? He's not—"

The woman finished the sentence. "Dead? No! They came for him some time ago. When we get to this camp, we'll be together again, I'm certain of it. Are you married?"

"I was," Frances said, realising that this was the first time she'd thought or spoken of Steven for a good while, and it filled her with shame. "My husband was killed some months back, in October. We were trying to get out of Paris to England. We nearly made it too—got as far as mid-channel..." She trailed off as the memories of that exodus came flooding back.

"What happened?" the woman coaxed and immediately apologised. "I'm sorry, it must be painful to talk about it."

"Not now. I've had time to come to terms with it. They were all shot! An 'E' boat."

"An E-boat?"

"One of the German patrol boats. There were soldiers on board."

"So, the men on this E-boat killed everyone apart from you and later picked you up?"

"No," Frances said with a smile and a memory. "I got picked up by a U-boat. I managed to get off our boat; it was burning. I lowered a lifeboat."

"A U-boat picked you up? And the pigs brought you back. Oh, you poor dear." The young woman patted her hand sympathetically, and Frances noticed how cold they were.

Frances turned away. How it hurt her. She wanted to explain, to talk of him, to share him. But how could she talk of her love for a German U-boat Kapitan surrounded as she was by all these people, her own countrymen who had suffered, were suffering still, at their hands?

Where was he now? She wondered. Was he safe in Brest? He'd promised to get her out of the prison there, but they'd moved her later that day. Surely they would have told him where they had taken her. Something must have gone wrong; he wouldn't just leave her. Maybe those S.S. pigs—but no! They'd surely not have hurt him. They were his countrymen, after all.

Chapter 32

"Frances?" She heard a voice calling her name and felt warm breath near her ear. Part of the dream she was having—she and Kristian were on the bridge of the U-boat. There was no war and no one else on the boat. Just the two of them drifting, and they looked into the night sky together, wondering at the enormity of it.

"Frances! Wake up!" The voice rose, insistent and shrill.

Although she wanted to cling to it, the dream skittered into the closet in her mind. She half rose, blinking in the gloom. Was it day? Night? She had no idea. She'd lost track. She wanted to lie down again, to lose herself in her dreams.

Ruth peered anxiously at her. "The baby, I think the baby is coming."

"Are you sure?" Frances asked. "Maybe it's another false alarm like yesterday." Frances prayed it was. She knew nothing of delivering babies.

"No, this is different. I've been timing the contractions, they're coming more frequently now."

"But you can't have him here for God's sake!" Frances protested, even though she knew it was absurd.

The ghost of a smile flitted across Ruth's face. "I don't think I've got any say in the matter."

But I don't know anything about delivering babies. Frances wanted badly to say it aloud. Wounds, blood, I can deal with, but babies? She bit back the words, seeing the fear in Ruth's eyes.

"You've got to help me," Ruth begged. "Please."

"Yes. Of course, I'll help. Don't worry, everything will be fine."

Frances raised her voice above the general hubbub. "Listen, everyone. Is there a doctor or a midwife on board?" She thought back to the excitement of her father when he returned home after delivering a baby. He never lost his excitement for that, bringing new life into the world.

A frail elderly man pushed his way from the rear of the cart; he raised his voice. "Here, young woman, I am a doctor. How can I help you?" Frances looked into the still sharp grey eyes nestling under the silvered brows.

"Thank goodness," she said. "Over here, there is a woman about to give birth."

There was general chatter as people moved aside as best they could, allowing the old man to join Frances to the side of Ruth.

"Doctor Charles Solomon," said the old man, patting Ruth's hand. "Now let's see how you're doing."

"Will you manage in this light?" questioned Frances.

"We'll see, my dear. I can do my best and no more, though we'll need more room than this."

Frances stood and jostled people into even more cramped positions. "Please, everyone," she implored, "could we make a little more room, please? We have a woman in labour over here."

"Yes, yes, we can move over more this way to make more room," a voice came from the rear of the cattle truck.

There were others. "My daughter can sit on my lap for a while."

"If we pull our legs in a little, there will be more room." Most complied helpfully, but one or two selfishly complained.

"That's better," said the doctor. "Now let's see if my old bones will let me get down." He sighed painfully as he knelt on the floor. "Arthritis," he explained. "I'm riddled with it. Still, no matter." He turned to Frances. "I will need your help, my dear. Are you up to it?"

Frances nodded, swallowing her panic, rising to the challenge. "What can I do?"

"Well, we have no instruments for you to hold and no water for you to boil. What we do have is a young woman who needs a great deal of encouragement." He made a well-practised examination of his patient. "She's doing fine. I don't think there will be any complications.

She's well into the second stage, dilating nicely," the doctor explained, withdrawing his hand from beneath Ruth's skirt.

Kneeling, Frances cradled Ruth's head in her lap, aware of the filth and the rough straw floor. "What's in your bundle? Anything that may help us?" she asked.

"Clean cloths and a couple of warm shawls, some clothes for the baby and some nappies."

"Here, this may help." A woman in a fur coat offered a pair of delicate linen handkerchiefs and a half full bottle of vintage champagne. "It's all we have left, I'm afraid."

The doctor suggested that Ruth lay on some cloths, took one of the handkerchiefs from the woman and wiped his hands. Frances took the other, and the champagne, smiling her thanks. Making a pad with the handkerchief, she dampened it with the champagne and mopped Ruth's face.

"Better?" she asked. Ruth sighed. Suddenly, she stiffened, grabbing Frances's hand.

"I think there's a big contraction coming."

"Take deep breaths," the doctor advised, "then, as it peaks, push hard. Now," he urged, watching her.

Ruth's face contorted, and even as Frances urged her, "Push, Ruth! Push!" she half rose on her elbows, grunting, then bellowing with the effort, and moments later, collapsing against Frances. Amazingly, as Frances looked on, Ruth's eyes closed, and she slept. Frances met the doctor's gaze.

"She's exhausted," he said.

Frances looked around and faces loomed at her. Pairs of eyes glimmering with wonder. There was quiet in the truck, many looked upon this imminent birth as a sign of hope. They waited in silent anticipation, scarcely daring to breathe, awaiting the coming of a possible messiah.

The sobbing renewed with each contraction, as Ruth prepared to ride out its rigours. It seemed an interminable time until the doctor smiled and said, "You're nearly there, my dear. I can feel the head."

"I can't do it!" Ruth panted. "I can't do any more."

Frances gripped the woman's shoulders tightly and shouted, "Yes, you can, Ruth! Just once more. Come on, push!"

With one last effort from his mother, the tiny infant was born. The doctor expertly cut the umbilical cord with a penknife that someone had produced, and then he laid the baby in the mother's arms. Ruth and Frances both burst into tears, and from somewhere in the truck, they heard the voice of a woman singing a Jewish lullaby.

In a filthy cattle truck, somewhere between Drancy and a place they knew only as Pitchipoi, the miracle of life had occurred, and for many, for a few moments, at least, the fear had lost its grip.

* * *

March 24, 1943

It was a little more than twenty-four hours later when Frances felt the truck slow down. Possibly the changing rhythm woke her.

"We're stopping again," said Frances to no one in particular. She hoped they could empty the stinking pails of excrement and be given a small amount of water to drink as they had a couple of days earlier when the train stopped to take on more coal and water for the engine.

"Thank the Lord," said the woman in the fur coat. She shook her husband awake. "Lucien, we're stopping. We'll get food and water now. See, children, all will be good."

Other families stirred. A tangle of voices rose, muttering, anxious. Several men shifted about, trying to get a view of the outside through the planked walls of the truck.

"There's lights," one said. "We're definitely approaching a station; I can see people outside."

"Where are we, do you think?" Ruth Peton looked worriedly at Frances as she rocked the baby back and forth. In the few hours since his birth, he'd been remarkably well behaved, but with the noise and agitation, he'd begun to fuss.

"It must be almost four days since we left Drancy." Frances stroked the baby's cheek, and he fell silent, keeping her gaze as if fascinated. "We could be anywhere."

A horn blared, and Ruth's baby, whom she had named Nicholas, howled.

"Shut that bloody brat up!"

Frances craned her neck but couldn't see the man who'd yelled.

"There are loudspeakers," he explained. "We might find out something if you all keep quiet for a bit." And just as he'd said, when the truck shuddered to a stop and the driver cut the engine, a heavily accented German voice was sharply audible.

"When your doors open, exit your truck quietly and quickly. Fall into line. Do not panic. Leave your belongings behind. They will be returned to you later. I repeat, leave your belongings."

Ruth's free hand clutched the canvas-wrapped bundle. She raised a stricken gaze to Frances. "I can't go without Nicholas's things."

"They'll bring it all to you later. It's all right," Frances said, although nothing about any of their journey from Drancy felt the least bit all right. She held out a hand, helping Ruth to her feet, and they huddled together in the warm press of bodies, listening as the sentries' voices rang out, rapping out instructions in a language which, for many, was unfamiliar. But the message was obvious, Frances thought. *Do as instructed, do not dare to disobey!*

The shouts, the grating of metal on metal as other trucks in the convoy were opened, came nearer and nearer. Still, Frances flinched at the sound when the butt of a sentry's rifle banged against the side of the truck that housed her. The crack of the metal bolt sliding from its housing rang out like a gunshot. The door was flung open. Although it was night time, it was almost as bright as day as there were floodlights which lit up the surroundings. Frances shrank from the glare, throwing up an arm, shielding her eyes. She felt rough hands grab her and lower her to the ground.

"Off! Off! Quick! Schnell!" The sentries' shouts rose around her.

"Frances!" Ruth's shriek rose above the cacophony.

Even as the sentry attempted to stop her, Frances jerked free of his grasp and turned, reaching up for baby Nicholas.

Somehow now Ruth was beside her, both panting, fighting to keep upright in the mass of people being jostled forwards towards enormous gates over which Frances could just see written in wrought iron lettering *Arbeit Macht Frei*: Work makes you free. *So, it is a work camp,* she thought. They were now being shoved into rough lines to gain some sort of order.

"My God! Frances, look!"

The line they were in had come to a temporary stop, and Frances peered toward Ruth's disbelieving gaze.

"Is it what I think?" she asked. "Are they carrying the dead?"

Frances stared, trying to make sense of the scene. There were groups of skeletal figures dressed in baggy striped clothing moving from the open cargo doors of several of the trucks, bearing what appeared to be lifeless bodies. But possibly her eyes were playing tricks. It was difficult to make out what was real from the spectre of night shadows. Frances couldn't discern where the bodies—if that were indeed what they were—were being taken. She jerked her gaze away.

"Who knows what it's about?" she said, even as the truth twisted in her stomach. She'd heard the rumours, hadn't she?

"Who are they, do you think?" Ruth asked, horror clear on her face.

"Convicts, by the look of their clothes. We must be near some sort of prison," Frances answered. "But don't worry. We won't be staying here, we'll be moving on." *Surely we will,* she thought to herself.

The baby mewled. Ruth jostled him gently. Around them was the uneasy mutter of conversation.

"Listen, I can hear music." Frances's heart soared. As the plaintive notes of a violin reached her, she pointed with her finger, and the surrounding group strained their ears.

They were moved along slowly towards the iron gate. On a raised platform, just in front of the gates, they could make out a group of female musicians smartly dressed in blue skirts and white blouses.

"See, I told you," Frances said with a smile, which she wasn't feeling inside. "They have music. We'll be fine."

The sentries were getting agitated. There was much stumbling. People were dazed and confused, the ground uneven and lumpy. As they fought to get their bearings, they were shoved and roughly pushed into columns, all the time moving forward towards those gates.

"Frances! Frances!" She swung round as she heard the familiar voice call her name, straining to see where it came from. "Over here!"

"Oh, I don't believe it!" Frances laughed despite herself as she saw Miriam's head bob up from the crowd and disappear again. "Miriam—

it's Miriam!" Squealing with delight, Frances swept Ruth before her. "We were in Drancy together; we must get to her. Come on!"

The two women, Ruth with Nicholas clasped protectively to her breast, pushed against the flow of bodies, both ignoring the mutter of complaints. "Shift out the way—you're going in the wrong direction."

A sentry grabbed at Frances, shouting, "Hey, you!" Evading him, she linked elbows with Ruth, and they fought their way to Miriam's side. The two friends embraced warmly, laughing and crying at the same time.

"Thank God I have found you," Frances gasped, stepping out of Miriam's embrace.

"What happened?" Ruth asked, staring at Miriam.

Miriam returned Ruth's stare. "Who're you?" she asked.

"Oh, forgive me," Frances said, flustered. "This is Ruth. Ruth, this is Miriam. We are old friends from Drancy." Frances shifted her glance to Miriam. "Ruth and I are old friends from the journey."

"Well, I can assure you I am human," Miriam addressed Ruth, her tone caustic. "At least, more so than these Kraut bastards."

Ruth's eyes widened; her mouth fell open. Frances laughed.

"You'll get used to Miriam. She's not dangerous, I promise you." A tense moment passed as Miriam and Ruth eyed each other, and when they smiled, Frances relaxed.

Reaching out, Miriam touched Nicholas's cheek with her fingertip. "He's beautiful," she said.

"He was born during the journey," Ruth said. "He's scarcely a day old."

They were close to the gate now, and they could see several officers on a second raised platform in front of the musicians. Frances's blood ran cold in her veins, and her heart pounded at the sight of them. And then, beaming into the orchestra, she began to giggle hysterically. "What an orchestra!" she said, listening to the strange mixture of sounds as guitars, violins, mandolins, and percussion blended fantastically in a stirring rendition of a Strauss waltz. "I've never heard anything like it, what is this place?"

As they got nearer to the platform, they became more aware of what was going on in front of them and why it was taking so long to move forwards. There were people crying, pleading, and screaming as families and friends were separated. The S.S. were showing some to the left and some to the right. The three women tried desperately to make some sense of it, but it made no sense. They linked arms, Frances in the middle. "See, we're like the three musketeers," she said. "All for one, and one for all. We'll stay together, you'll see."

"But there are four of us." Ruth reminded Frances of Nicholas, who was stirring and whimpering in her arms.

"D'Artagnan, of course," said Miriam, and Frances gave Ruth a nod.

The three women moved ever forward, offering words of encouragement to each other.

"It will be all right—you just see."

"It's just because there are so many people, they have to separate them so that the food goes round."

"It's just their way of organising things—that's all."

Ruth began to cry as she realised young people were being split from old, they separated mothers from children, sick and infirm were sent one way, able-bodied, another. And the band played on.

"Age?" a tall, beautiful woman with shorn hair, obviously a Jewess, asked in French, looking down from the ramp at Miriam, seemingly unconcerned by the presence of the two German soldiers standing nearby, engaged in conversation. Members of the S.S., Frances thought, if the lightning bolts on their collar patches were anything to go by.

"Twenty-three," Miriam replied.

Frances saw the Jewess look across at the pair of S.S. as if awaiting a signal. When the shortest of the two turned his attention to the woman, Frances was struck by his style. He was more than immaculate; good looking in an Italian sort of way. His hands with long tapered fingers held a pair of white gloves, which he slapped against his thigh as he asked, "Well?"

"Twenty-three, Herr Doctor," informed the Jewess in German.

With a flick of his thumb, the doctor showed that Miriam should join the shorter right-hand column. Ruth wasn't asked anything. Clasping her child to her, they sent her to the left, where a long line of waiting people were being loaded onto waiting trucks. She looked back, as the Jewess asked Frances, "Age?"

"Twenty-four," she answered. Her heart pounded so loud in her ears she thought the Jewess must hear it. "Please," she whispered, "what is this place? What is happening?"

The woman ignored her, looking again at the doctor for instruction. He held up his thumb, signalling her to go to the right, behind Miriam.

"Frances!" Ruth's shout was shrill, bordering on a scream. "I want to come with you and Miriam."

"Herr Doctor," Frances addressed him in perfect German.

He looked up sharply. "What is it, Fraulein?" he asked.

"Our friend...please, can she come with us?"

"Impossible!" He barked the word, making her step back. Then he smiled the same smile that she'd seen on so many people's lips lately, the smile that lit the mouth but not the eyes. "Don't worry, Fraulein," he told her. "You'll catch up with your friend later, I promise you. It's better for her to take a ride in the truck with a child that young."

Frances nodded in agreement. After all, it was only a couple of days since Ruth had given birth, and she must still be exhausted from the effort. The man was a doctor after all, wasn't he?

The lines of people began once more to shuffle slowly forward.

"What did he say?" Ruth called.

"He thinks it's best you ride in the truck because of your condition. I agree. Go on, go in the trucks. We'll find you later, and don't worry."

"If you believe that, you're mad," said Miriam.

"The doctor, he said so, didn't he?" Miriam shook her head as Ruth waved and shouted.

"And maybe we'll find my Abram as well."

The people moved faster now as those to the left were loaded into the trucks and the men on the right were ushered through the huge gates.

"Keep your fingers crossed for me..." Ruth's last words were lost as she climbed into the truck with Nicholas clasped safely to her breast. Frances and Miriam swung round as in the hubbub they heard a woman admonishing her three children and advocating good behaviour.

"Now you make sure you behave, Jacob," she said. "I don't want to hear from any of these soldiers that you have been rude or disobedient. Go now—go with Greta and Marta and take a ride in the truck. I will find you all later, before bedtime, I promise."

~ 248 ~

The children, the eldest of whom must have been less than ten, Frances thought, held hands and ran towards the trucks, turning to give their mother a wave. "Love you, Mummy. See you soon," they shouted.

Behind them the lines of people seemed endless, the voice of the Jewess interminable. "Age? Age? Age?" She repeated the demand over and over. What did it all mean? Frances had no idea. She turned to Miriam, looking for consolation as a feeling of dread iced her stomach.

Now a voice rose, a woman shouting, "No! No! I will not leave my parents. We will all stay together."

Looking back, Frances saw they had moved an elderly couple off into the left-hand column and the young woman who had shouted was standing by defiantly, refusing to move to the right.

"You wish to stay together, Mademoiselle?" asked the doctor in passable French. "Very well. Go to the left if you wish." The woman thanked him as the doctor stifled a yawn.

Miriam grabbed Frances and pulled her forward as they were herded through the gates with the other women, many of whom had been separated from their menfolk. A few, remained optimistic, but the majority were sobbing, crying out to the guards for information. When would they be reunited with their families, children, and partners? When would they be given food and water? No answers were given, and the march continued round the perimeter of what appeared to be a large camp, enclosed behind electric wire and watchtowers. After all, they had been off the train for hours now and the weather was starting to bite. Both Frances and Miriam were feeling the cold and feeling their hunger but were determined not to be downhearted. They were out of that shit hole Drancy, weren't they?

"For once," said Miriam, "I'm actually glad that there's just me to worry about."

"Me too," Frances agreed. "Are you worried, though?" she asked.

"Yes, I'm bloody well worried. You?"

Frances nodded. "It's the not knowing. Where the hell are we, Miriam? None of this feels right."

They were driven on, arm in arm, for about a mile, and as dawn approached, they found themselves in a wooded area of birch trees. A sentry, a tall handsome lad of no more than twenty, had been walking to their left and, from time to time, had cast covetous glances in their direction. He approached them now, as Frances blew on her hands, trying to fight off the cold.

"If you have sex with me over in the woods, I will get you a coffee," he said in broken French. The two women looked at each other in disbelief.

"My God where are we, that coffee is so expensive?" gasped Frances, wide-eyed.

"Or maybe it's sex that's cheap." Miriam laughed. "What about me, sonny?" she asked, leering at him.

"Sod off, you ugly cow. I'm not that hard up."

"Neither are we," Frances said with a coquettish gaiety that she wasn't feeling as the boy fell back in line. "Let him try his luck elsewhere," she said to Miriam.

That incident kept Frances and Miriam amused until dawn broke. They dwelt on it over and over, and by so doing, were able to control the screaming that was tearing away at their insides, trying to find a way out.

They were halted in front of another gate and guardhouse, which was shrouded in a thick grey mist that turned their stomachs with its fatty cloying smell. Frances's stomach twisted as she realised they must be in some kind of prison.

They were marched through the second gate past the guardhouse and into an immense area, the older and infirm amongst them staggering with exhaustion. Rows of rectangular shaped huts rose on either side of them. The sudden shriek of whistles broke overhead. Frances stabbed her fingers in her ears, watching in trepidation as people came out of the huts, most of them emaciated, white-faced and hollow-eyed. They were dressed in the same stripes she'd seen at the train station, the ones she'd known prisoners to wear.

Commanding voices called out, "Zahlappel!"

Miriam looked at Frances.

"German for roll call," muttered Frances to Miriam, who was standing still, a look of shock on her face.

"A roll call. It must be a prison. But a roll call at this time? It can only be five or six a.m."

Frances had little time to speculate before she and the others were driven into one building she would later hear referred to as the sauna. Short-haired women wearing baggy striped trousers and jackets marked with a green triangle shrieked out their orders. "Strip now and into the showers!"

The women, at near one hundred or more, Frances guessed, jostled against each other in a state of anxiousness. She stepped out of line and approached a woman wearing a green badge.

"Can you tell us please what's going on? Where are we?" The woman swung her arm, catching Frances across the face with a glancing blow, and she was told to get on with undressing.

A second woman approached her.

"What's going on? You load of shit; you'll soon find out what's going on!"

"Just do what they say," Miriam advised, as she and Frances removed their clothes. "Don't draw attention to yourself."

"Bloody hell! Have you seen what we've got here?" A short-haired guard approached, and grabbing Miriam, dragged her forward, calling to some of her workmates in German. "Hey, girls, just look at this for ugly. Just come and look at this ugly Jew sow."

Frances's initial shock boiled into anger. She felt it heat her blood, the space behind her eyes. She opened her mouth, but words of protest died on her tongue as she took in the look on Miriam's face. *Let them have their fun,* her look said. *After all, words don't hurt.* Frances clenched her jaw. If Miriam could choose her battles, so could she.

Others came gathering round Miriam, ogling her. "Christ, I reckon a trip to our hairdressers can only improve this one, eh, Machtilda?" one said.

"Surprised she's even got to keep the appointment," replied another. They all laughed, and Miriam was pushed back into line.

"What were they saying?" Miriam asked Frances.

"Oh, a load of nonsense about hairdressers and such like. Nothing important." Frances said, teeth chattering. "My God, it's cold in this place."

The women, now all naked, stood, eyes downcast, trying to cover themselves with their hands. Frances was glad for the interruption when a woman who seemed in charge appeared and blew a whistle.

Beside her, an opening Frances hadn't noticed before was lined with shower heads. At the woman's command, water poured from them. She gestured, ordering them into the concrete-walled chamber in broken French. Shrieks of protest erupted as the frozen water pelted bare flesh. The woman next to Frances, more a child, really, flinched from the stream, bumping into Frances, and was swatted across the buttocks with a paddle for her actions. A sob broke from her mouth. Frances wanted to comfort the girl but was afraid to do anything. After an interminable time, at least fifteen minutes, Frances thought, the water shut off, and they were marched into yet another concrete room.

"Where are our clothes?" whimpered the girl.

"Hush," Miriam warned her. "They're gone. They've taken them."

While their clothes and last belongings were gathered up, they were taken and dipped in a foul-smelling blue-green liquid, which made their skin smart. The young girl cried out for her mama, and as she was forced into the vat of liquid, screamed as it stung her young skin.

Again, they were made to line up, still naked, many of them blue-skinned, and pushed towards a line of women clad similarly to those giving the orders, only this time they wore a scarf on their heads that bore a yellow triangle, the Jewish colour.

"See how we look after you?" taunted the woman, Machtilda, as she prodded them into line. "First a beauty treatment, now a visit to the hairdressers!" She laughed raucously, enjoying her own joke. "Arms and legs out. NOW!" she ordered.

Frances and Miriam exchanged a horrified look whilst a few of the other girls, mostly the younger ones, sobbed as the hairdressers got to work on heads, armpits and pubic regions with razors grown blunt from use which nicked painfully at the skin with each stroke. Frances felt her own hair tumble down her back and looked down at it, biting her lip, as she remembered how much Kristian had loved tangling his fingers in her wayward tresses that now fell about her feet in a lifeless mass.

As the woman started on the other parts of her body, she thought she would risk questioning her. "Where are we?" she whispered, but the woman stared at her unblinking, leaving her unsure as to whether she had even been heard. She looked around her at the other women, recognising the fear in their eyes, fear that she was feeling too. The feeling of being cornered like a rabbit caught in a trap. That fear in that building, she thought, was almost tangible.

Once finished, Frances and Miriam were reassembled into the line. For a few seconds, they stood unsure of what to say to one another, embarrassed by the completeness of their nakedness. As they caught each other's eye, Frances giggled. "Well, if this is the latest fashion, I don't think much of it!" She fought to suppress her laughter, which was in danger of becoming panicked and hysterical.

Miriam shook her head, not sharing in Frances's humour. "I saw you talking to your hairdresser. What did you learn?"

"Not a thing... and you?"

"Mine told me we're in a place called Osweicium, the Krauts call it Auschwitz. We're in the second camp, Brzezica–Birkenau, after the birch trees in the wood outside."

"Birkenau," mused Frances. "It sounds like a holiday resort, doesn't—" She barely registered the hand that came, the slap it delivered across her face. "Hey!" she cried, raising her own hands protectively.

"You wait in silence, Jew slut."

"She's no Jew!" Miriam said sharply. "You've actually made a mistake—"

"You shut your mouth," hissed the woman. "Otherwise, you'll find yourself on Himmel Commando sooner rather than later."

"Himmel Commando! So, what!" retorted Frances angrily. The woman closed in on them and grinned, showing broken teeth.

"So what?" she repeated. "Pffft... Sky work... Your sort always ends up there sooner or later. You leave by the chimney. Don't tell me you can't smell it?" she said in passable French.

"What?" asked Frances.

"The pig roast," the woman said with a laugh as she moved away from them.

Miriam circled her finger around the side of her face. "Round the bloody twist," she whispered.

Chapter 33

Ruth stood near the front of the horde, outside a large concrete building, holding Nicholas in her arms. She guessed the crowd must have been near a thousand, comprised mainly of women, children, and the elderly. They'd been unloaded moments ago from a convoy of trucks and herded to this building. No one had told them why, or what to expect. Ruth's arms ached from Nicholas's weight, and her knees wanted to give way beneath her from fatigue. When Nicholas cried, she put him to her breast, hoping that before long they might give her some food herself, worrying that without nutrition, her milk supply would dry up. Now a voice burst over a loudspeaker, noisily explaining in passable French that they were all to be showered and disinfected. Ruth's own sigh of relief was joined by others. After such a journey as they'd had, a shower was something to be relished.

S.S. guards ushered them over a wide threshold and into the building that was divided into two chambers. Benches lined the walls where she stood, and when the order came that they were to strip off their clothing, Ruth, like nearly all the others, complied without reservation. Any show of modesty after the indignity they'd suffered making the hellish journey here would have been false. The loudspeaker voice bade them to make a neat pile of their clothes and advised they would receive clean, warmer clothing.

Ruth noticed several grey-faced men in striped uniforms moving silently amongst them. Some gathered the stacks of worn garments. Others distributed soap and towels. These men were clearly prisoners and were carrying out tasks for their S.S. masters. In return, they received better food and accommodation until they outlived their usefulness or conscience made martyrs of them. The confused, naked people were then led like lambs to the shower room, and there were those amongst them that gave thanks for their safe arrival at such a place; and perhaps it was just as well that this was the way it was.

She couldn't take little Nicholas in the shower with her, Ruth thought. She searched the crowd in vain, hunting a familiar face, someone to hold him for her. A man stood a few feet away, his head sank and his shoulders bowed. Somehow, he seemed less threatening than the others, and strangely familiar. Was it the line of his brow? The slope of his nose? She didn't know, couldn't quite place what drew her to him. He didn't look up at her approach. Only when she spoke to him, when she asked, "Do you know of a place where I can leave my child?" did he glance at her and shrink away. It was as if he had seen a ghost.

But now, seeing his eyes, she knew him, though he was dressed as one of them, the Sonderkommando, and like them, he was a spectre, a ghoulish caricature of the man he'd been when she'd called him husband.

"Abram?" His name came from her mouth on a shallow breath of shock and disbelief. "Abram!" she cried more loudly, "it is you!" But he shook his head and pushed his way from her, losing himself in the sea of humanity. "Abram! Abram!"

Plunging into the crowd after him, she screamed his name until her throat was raw. Had she made a mistake? Surely that pathetic creature could not be her Abram, the man she loved, the father of her child. And yet, she knew it was him, and thanked her God that her prayers had been answered, that she had found him. Still, he had backed away from her, deserted her. Desperately, she shoved people aside, determined to reach him, ignoring the threats of the guards, their growling dogs, the frightened cries of her own child. Now she spotted him again, crouching against a concrete wall. "Abram!" She fell to her knees beside him, staring into his expressionless eyes. "What have they done to you?"

"Get away from me," he hissed, roughly shaking her from his arm. "You don't know me; I don't know you."

Still, she insisted, "Of course you do! Look!" Ruth exposed Nicholas's tiny face. "Look at our child, a son, perfect, as we dreamed—"

"Get away from me!"

His angry shout attracted the attention of an S.S. guard, and he approached them, dog straining at the leash. "What's the problem here?"

Abram shook his head wildly, keeping his gaze on the floor. "Nothing. Nothing's wrong, sir," he muttered. "A mistake, that's all."

"Stand up," the guard ordered, and as Abram obeyed, to Ruth's horror, the guard brought his knee up hard against Abram's genitals, causing him to groan, to double over.

"Your job's to make sure there are no mistakes. Get on with it or join the line." He towered over Abram, unmoved by his obvious pain, watching until he rose, unsteady on his feet, and lurched into the mass of people. Ruth looked after him, tears tracking her cheeks, blurring her view until she lost him completely. The S.S. guard prodded her with his rifle. "Get into line."

She was barely aware of her surroundings as she resumed her place, shuffling with the rest of the solemn herd, scarcely noticing as they approached a second threshold, where a thick, heavy-looking door stood ajar. Neither did she more than subliminally register the ruckus moments later when an elderly woman near her, who had continually complained, demanding to see the person in charge, was pulled from the prisoners' ranks and callously beaten. Ruth watched, unseeing, as the guard set his dog upon the old woman, allowing it to tear at her flesh and shake her like a rag doll until she ceased to struggle and lay quite still, a pulpy mass of mangled tissue and blood-slicked bone.

She was indifferent to the others when the air around her erupted with their screams of protest and terrified wails, and it was with only subliminal interest that she registered how the guards responded. Becoming further agitated, they struck at the dissidents with their rifles, pushing and shoving the throng toward the second opening, forcing them through the narrow passageway into a more confined space. One that Ruth thought, vaguely, could not possibly hold them all.

Standing with the others, she blinked through her tears and gently stroked Nicholas's downy velvet head.

She was not aware when the door closed, nor did she mind very much when a mist came, muffling sight and sound so that eventually, it all faded away into nothing.

Chapter 34

"You are quite certain there is no Jewish blood on either of your parents' side?" The girl, taking down the information, questioned Frances a second time about her parentage.

"Quite sure." Frances studied the number tattooed on her arm. What was its meaning? She still couldn't grasp it had happened.

"Grandparents, then?" the girl suggested.

Frances looked at the girl. "No... I have no Jewish blood whatsoever."

The girl scribbled notes as if it didn't matter that Frances was in the wrong place. She doubted that the information was ever used. It was for file purposes only, to keep everything neat. How had this happened? That she was here, naked, shorn of her hair with lots of women, all in the same position, being herded forward to this desk and questioned?

Next to her, the tattooist spoke quietly. "You'll get six weeks of quarantine. Most don't make it past the first three. Learn to become invisible."

It was the same advice Miriam had given. Still, Frances asked in a low voice, "What do you mean?"

"Do nothing to draw attention to yourself. Memorise your number, 35921. You haven't a name anymore. Forget this number and you're dead." Even as Frances stepped away, half dazed, she heard the tattooist whisper again, "Remember, become invisible."

From that room, the women were taken, still naked, out into the freezing cold to block twenty, the quarantine block. As they were marched along the lagerstrasse, the main road of the camp, Frances noticed S.S. guards smirking with amusement, as she and all the women fought to keep some sort of modesty by trying to cover themselves with their hands. The freezing Auschwitz mud, which sucked at their feet, made their march even more difficult, sometimes drawing them in up to their ankles. Frances had to catch hold of Miriam at one point as she tottered awkwardly, all modesty forgotten, and Miriam steadied her. They continued walking in the line, watching as others grabbed out wildly at one another to keep their balance. They were frozen.

A stocky woman, reasonably well-dressed, met them at the door of a dark, low-built hut. "All right, you filth!" She spat the words. "Off into the meadow." Strange how the word meadow can conjure up such lucid happy memories. Frances thought of a summer's day from her childhood in middle England. The meadow next to the park, a field of green, dotted with buttercups and daisies, smelling sweetly of clover. Not this time; the meadow was a patch of mud behind the hut, crawling with remnants of females in varying states of abomination, but none as naked as those born fresh to Auschwitz.

Minutes after their arrival in the meadow, the woman from the front of the hut arrived with a dozen or so others, laden down with clothing, which they roughly distributed throughout the group. Frances was given a thin white shift and a lemon cotton dress. She also received a small kerchief to cover her newly mowed head and a pair of rough men's brogues, which completed her outfit.

"But I'll freeze to death in these," she complained to the woman who appeared to be in charge.

The woman looked her in the eye. "And who's here to care, you Jewish slut?" She turned and walked back towards the hut.

"No, you see, I'm not Jewish. You've made a mistake. I'm not Jewish!" she called.

The woman turned, fixing her eyes on Frances again. "And who's here to care?" she repeated. "Slut."

Frances dressed herself in the shift and lemon dress and tied the kerchief around her naked scalp. She looked around for Miriam but couldn't see her anywhere, and a sudden feeling of loneliness overwhelmed her. Sitting down in a drier patch of mud, she set about putting on the boots that she'd been given. Luckily, they were not huge, unlike some other poor sods, who, having size 36 feet, found themselves issued with a pair of size 44 men's boots. As she knelt in the soft mud to tie her shoes, someone suddenly blanked the daylight out.

"Hey, cop hold of this—a Madeleine Vionnet special," joked Miriam.

"Where on Earth?" asked Frances as Miriam uncovered herself from underneath the Russian ex-conscript's greatcoat, offering her a second one.

"Didn't you notice?" asked Miriam. "Those lousy cows giving out the clothing were hanging onto the coats. I nicked a couple while their backs were turned."

Frances's laugh was sardonic. "Talk about all dressed up and nowhere to go. Where do you think, my dear, the nearest restaurant can be?"

Whilst they continued to poke scornful fun at each other's appearance, a gaunt figure moved in on them. "Too late for breakfast lest I organise for you."

Frances looked at Miriam, who looked at the newcomer. "What do you mean 'organise'?"

"If you want anything here, it has to be organised. I can barter for you."

"What's in it for you?" asked Miriam.

"Bread... bread's the currency, see, or maybe I can change things around a bit for you. Hungry, are you? Well, maybe them coats you're wearing will get you some food."

The temptation was great, for Frances's stomach was churning, she couldn't remember the last time she had eaten. She began to take off the coat.

Miriam put a restraining hand on her arm. "You think they're going to fill you up? Open your eyes, gal." She turned to the woman. "How much bread for the coats?"

"Two slices... maybe three, if I drive a hard bargain."

"No deal," said Miriam. "We'll hang on to the coats for now."

The woman spoke as she moved on. "Ah, well, let me know if you change your minds."

"How will we find you?" Frances asked. Her hunger was so intense that three slices of bread, even two, seemed a feast.

"Ask anyone for Lizette. Then I'll find you," said the woman. "We French have to stick together. By the way, if they come on a round-up for work detail, make yourself scarce, keep moving. Outside work will kill you off in no time."

As Lizette moved off towards another group of women, Frances turned to Miriam. "Work? Outdoor work? I don't understand, Miriam. What the hell's going on here? There must be someone that we can complain to, surely."

Miriam took Frances's arm and shook it. "Frances, look at me. You say nothing. Particularly, you don't complain. I have the feeling the people running the show here are capable of anything. We lie low and don't draw attention to ourselves. Do you understand? She gave a caustic laugh. "I know it's hard for you, having lived in the limelight, but it's time to forget the limelight, Rich Girl, and just concentrate on the living part."

"But they've made a mistake and—"

"And they don't give a shit. Remember what the girl who tattooed you said? Disappear."

"I wish I could bloody well disappear."

"Frances?"

In frustration, Frances made to pull her hand through her hair, knocking the kerchief to the ground instead. "All right, all right, Miriam. I'll keep quiet."

Miriam gave her a hug. "Good."

* * *

At what they guessed to be about midday, great drums were carried out into the meadow by several women. Frances looked at Miriam, a grin of relief on her face; she could smell food.

"Looks like there's a meal on its way, thank God."

"About bloody time," Miriam smiled.

Each woman was issued a red enamel dish and ordered to line up before receiving a ladle full of the steaming, semi-viscous concoction, in which, if you were lucky, you found a bit of potato peel and swede. It was their turn. They held out the bowls and received the food, which warmed their hands until they found a patch of mud that was drier than the rest and sat down, side by side. Frances lifted the dish to her lips and quickly thrust it away, gagging on the stench.

"I can't eat this. I'll throw up." Glancing at Miriam, it amazed her to see her tip back her bowl and swallow down some of the contents, her eyes closed as if in ecstasy. "How can you do that?" Frances demanded.

Miriam put her dish down into the mud of the meadow. "You have to eat if you want to live," she said seriously. "Listen, pretend it's the finest French onion soup you've ever tasted, okay? Close your eyes and believe it. You've tasted nothing better."

Frances took a sip and swallowed hard, concentrating, willing her stomach to accept the insult. "Oh God, I can't," she muttered.

"Come on, now," Miriam encouraged. "It's the finest soup in Brittany. Mmm, smell it. Smell the onions, taste the croutons."

Frances peered into her bowl. "Bacon aren't they?" she said, screwing up her face but trying to enter the spirit.

"Well, yours might be, but mine are garlic," Miriam said. "See, Frances, that's the beauty of this stuff—it can be whatever you want it to be."

"All right, show off," Frances said. "Mine isn't soup at all. It's mouth-watering chicken cooked in wine, and with it, I have potatoes and green beans."

Some of the other girls had heard what was going on and a small circle had gathered.

"I'm making a gateau," said one girl, who introduced herself as Madelaine. "See, I'm mixing the butter and the eggs."

"What now?" piped up another as Madelaine mimed perfectly breaking eggs and mixing them in a bowl.

"Now? Now I'm adding the flour, sifted, of course, and the chocolate. Ahhhh, smell the chocolate."

The women all sniffed ecstatically, and almost in unison, sighed. "Ahh."

"How long will it take to cook?" asked Miriam.

"An hour," came the reply from Madelaine.

"That long?" everyone protested.

"Well, maybe I can speed things up a bit, forty minutes, let's say."

"Yes, let's say forty minutes," another girl named Katrina agreed.

That pretence on the field encouraged more than just Frances to eat, and it also became a way that many hours were spent over the coming days. Madelaine made a good deal of gateau, Frances became proficient at dicing onions and potatoes, and Miriam kept them all laughing by stirring all the pots and describing the wonderful smells.

That evening, they were lined up in fives in front of the block and experienced their first roll call at Auschwitz. It took two hours standing still in the freezing air, then they were allowed into their hut.

"My God, Miriam, I've never been this cold, thank goodness they've let us inside." Her eyes swept the stark building which had originally been built as a stable and was now to house eight hundred women.

Frances noted the brick heating channel running down the centre and wondered how cold it would have to get before it was used. At the far end was an office for the Blockawa, the woman in charge of the hut, the same one who had introduced them to the meadow and had overseen the roll call; her office also served as her bedroom. For the rest of the women on either side of the heating channel, there were rows of three tier bunks. Each section had been intended to sleep one, but now each bunk was to sleep four or maybe five women, head to toe. They slept on stinking straw mattresses, the two on the outside hanging onto the edge of the bun and if one turned in the night, they all turned!

The morning roll call was interminable. The women were made to stand in silence, teeth chattering, until every one of them, some eight hundred, had been accounted for. Frances was thankful that Miriam had got the great coats. She reckoned without them, she would have frozen to death, some had already. They soon learnt that if someone made a whispered comment or thought they might pass the time by humming or singing, then the entire group would suffer by being kept standing out in the cold for a further hour.

Frances would mostly spend the time in deep thought. She would often daydream of Mueller and then her thoughts would flit back to the *Etoile* and she would inwardly chastise herself for having such beautiful thoughts regarding a German. Hadn't the Germans killed Steven and Jacques? Hadn't Otto forced her into the exodus from her home, her wonderful Paris? And now they had forced her here, to this dung heap, this fucking hell on earth that was likely going to be the death of her. Of her! Frances Lamont, virtuoso. And then she would go over and over all the things she had done wrong. The things that she needed to take the blame for. The times she had pushed Steven into doing something he didn't want to do, such as the concerts in Germany, eating out and partying, fraternising. The times she knew she had flirted with Otto and the time she had allowed herself to fall in love with Mueller. Maybe then this was her punishment.

* * *

After morning roll call came breakfast, which comprised a drink of hitherto unknown brownish-blue liquid. The quarantine block was then once again turned out into the meadow. It was out here and back in the block in the evenings that the talk always seemed to revert to food. Food was the favourite topic of conversation, as each took it in turn to describe the cooking of their favourite dish, and those who couldn't cook, like Frances, described the decor, tastes, and the smells of their favourite restaurants.

Miriam soon proved herself to be a natural survivor, and Frances thanked her lucky stars on more than one occasion that she'd formed such a strong bond with her. It was Miriam who warned Frances of the dangers of drinking too much water, which would have resulted in diarrhoea, and she who caught on that at roll call as you left the hut at the double to line up outside, it was better to be in the middle of the group rather than the outside. You might risk getting a bit crushed in the centre, but those on the outside were more likely to be beaten by the Blockawa and her helpers, the Kapos.

It was also Miriam who, having been caught for the gardening work detail, thought of an ingenious way of bringing back a few potatoes. She'd find Frances out in the meadow and, drawing her away from the prying eyes of others, would open her coat to reveal potatoes hidden in the lining. Without a doubt, it was these few extra rations that kept them going. Remembering back to Drancy when Frances shared her food parcels with her, Miriam shared all that she could steal or organise with Frances.

While Miriam was away on work detail, Frances tried to keep warm in the meadow, her thoughts dwelling on the woman who had become such a close friend in such a short time. Each roll call of sometimes four hours standing in the freezing icy rain seemed only to strengthen Miriam's resolve to survive. Frances struggled to keep her own resolve to be like Miriam's and watched as other women sank to their knees, physically or mentally beaten. But not Miriam—she would not let them win.

It was she who taught Frances to survive, to eat all the mouldy rations, the few ounces of bread and the smear of margarine that did for their breakfast and evening meal. To swallow every last drop of the viscous concoction masquerading as soup that tortured the taste buds each lunchtime. Miriam had also worked out that if you waited until near the end of the queue, you were more likely to get a few bits in your soup that had sunk to the bottom of the cauldron, though exactly what the bits were was never quite clear.

"Eat everything and conserve energy when you can," Miriam told her.

Chapter 35

Missing the work detail could not last forever, and eventually, like Miriam, Frances was selected for the Hausenkommando, who carried out the outside work. They had taken Miriam from the potato field, and the two women found themselves working side by side on the construction of a railway. They were marched out of the camp immediately following roll call at six-thirty a.m. at the double, in time to the laughable orchestra, which Frances now didn't find all that funny. As her column passed through the gate, she imagined she caught the eye of one of the string players. She yearned to be up there with them, to hold an instrument again. How clean they all looked in their white blouses and blue skirts.

The women found the Hausenkommando hard work. It seemed the S.S. were aiming to extend the railway track into the camp. The women were each given a heavy shovel and ordered to dig over the frozen ground, still solid following the hard winter frosts. Kapos screamed and shouted, trying to bully the women into performing the near-impossible task.

"Why don't you try it?" someone dared to suggest and was struck a heavy blow across the face and sent sprawling to the ground by one of the Kapos. What members of the S.S. were about, seemed content to leave the bullying to others.

Frances bore down on the shovel with all her might and tried to ignore the tugs in her belly that warned her that building work was no fitting occupation for a pregnant woman. She'd had her suspicions for some time as to her condition, there had been times earlier on when she had felt nauseous, but then so had many others, old, young, female and male, and so she had pushed the thought to the back of her mind. There had been plenty of reasons for vomiting in Drancy, pregnancy being one of the least likely. Her cycle hadn't helped her; it had always been erratic, and since the horrors of the exodus from Paris, she hadn't menstruated at all. Now, though, she was certain. Despite the starvation diet, her girth was expanding, and a couple of days previously she had felt the first fluttering. Like a butterfly beating its wings against her insides, the child had let her know of its existence, letting her know it did not agree with its mother carrying out such strenuous work.

She had felt the joy in her body and her soul with those first stirrings. Joy felt in Auschwitz was a miracle, and she had wanted to tell Miriam, to share its wonder with her. She was desperate to confide in someone, but she really didn't need anyone to tell her the tales of what happened to pregnant women in Auschwitz, or women with babies like Ruth. They'd been told early on. They knew, they all knew.

Maybe Miriam would have an answer. Miriam was all-knowing, and she was afraid that she would guess that the child growing inside her was not her husband's. Then there would be questions, followed by answers that Miriam would never understand. Recriminations would follow those, and she wouldn't be able to bear them. There was only one kind of German—a bad one. Would she listen while she told her story of how she'd been rescued, how she'd been accepted by the crew of the U-boat, how she'd fallen in love with Kristian?

Shouting and a gunshot jerked her gaze. A few feet away, Miriam shot her a warning glance. Frances could hear Miriam's voice in her brain. *Pretend you haven't noticed. It's only the S.S. playing their favourite game. Carry on with your work, don't draw attention to yourself, or you will be next.* Frances remembered a week ago when a guard was looking for amusement. He'd chosen an overweight woman, and throwing his cap, he'd had her chase it like a dog. If she'd refused, Frances knew she'd have been shot for disobeying the order. But even compliance was a risk. They had shot dead another young girl, who Frances knew as Aline, after chasing a cap for trying to escape.

The S.S. were such bastards! How could Miriam be expected to understand that she was in love with a German, and that the child she carried was his and that she desperately wanted it?

She bent over her shovel. To have a baby in Auschwitz was almost impossible. To keep it was even less of a possibility. Maybe she should end it now, break from the ranks. Run and finish it all. Wouldn't that be the easiest, the most sensible thing to do? Unlike Miriam, she didn't feel that she was a survivor. Miriam would never have got herself into such a fix in the first place, much less cling to the desperate hope that Mueller would come.

Perhaps he was dead. The thought sickened her. She couldn't, wouldn't think about that. She would know if he were, she would feel it, and she didn't. She felt him with her, felt his arms around her, the fabric of his shirt beneath her cheek when she lay her head against his chest. She heard his voice telling her she was leaving the camp, that it had all been a mistake and that now it was sorted. That he had found a cottage for them in Brest, removed from the town and those that pry. It had a garden where she could sit and wait for him to come home after patrol. And she imagined his shared joy when she told him of the baby.

Her hunger brought her back to reality. She wished it were lunchtime. She thought it must be approaching midday. Her guts felt empty, but worse than that, her bladder felt full. At least after lunch, they gave you a couple of minutes to squat in the field and defecate. Other times of the day, if the need arose, you did it where you stood. She wondered how much food she would get. Looking at the amount of earth she had shifted, she suspected not much.

In the distance, she caught the sound of a whistle blowing its high-pitched shriek, and her jaw tightened. There were always whistles blowing. A whistle for roll call, a whistle at the end of roll call, a whistle when the food arrived, a whistle when it went away and another ordering you to squat. What the hell did this whistle mean? She wanted to close her ears to the damn whistles.

Looking around, she spotted the other women, including Miriam, standing to attention. It was an inspection then. She saw a male S.S. officer had arrived on a motorcycle together with a woman, also S.S., leading two dogs. They'd come to check the work. Frances caught the sound of their voices as they berated a young girl who looked to Frances to be no more than fourteen. It was evident that by S.S. standards, her performance had fallen short. The male was slapping her face with his gloves. Frances kept her eyes averted, knowing it was best not to look, not to show any interest.

The S.S. were moving along the line now, getting nearer. Frances flicked a quick glance at Miriam to her right and saw that, like the rest, she had stopped working and was standing with her eyes cast down. Frances copied her, studying the ground. She could hear the dogs panting, straining at their leashes. The S.S. woman seemed barely able to contain them.

Oh God, please don't let them stop here. The prayer raced through Frances's mind, a heated streak. She could hear their conversation now. They were cordially passing the time of day. She caught their words, something about the weather, the brilliant blue of the sky. They must have passed Miriam. Frances wanted to look up at her friend for support but dared not. Now the footsteps stopped. A pair of black boots, toes gleaming, appeared in the dust inches from Frances's own filthy boots.

She could smell the leather of the motorcyclist's jacket, a fainter odour of aftershave and sweat. He idly slapped the gloves against his thigh. Frances wondered if he would use them on her like he had the girl. She braced herself, waiting. Fear bricked her throat. But he seemed to be paying her little attention. He and the woman were talking about their social life, where they were going on leave. The subject changed to the arrival of the new camp doctor.

God in heaven, why had they stopped? Frances raised her eyes ever so slightly to the level of the motorcycle rider's knees. Beyond him, one of the dogs was delivering a stream of urine over the mound of earth she had shifted. The woman yanked on his leash. She and the motorcycle rider moved along. Frances's knees weakened, and for a moment, she thought she would faint with relief.

Chapter 36

Little changed for days. At six-thirty a.m., they were marched out of the gates to the sound of the orchestra. At midday, they stopped for half an hour, if they were lucky, for something to eat, then at six thirty p.m., they marched back through the gate, this time at double time and carrying their dead. The mortalities were high, either through mindless killing or through suicide, and more often just from the rigours of the work and the starvation diet. They were always hungry, but never at night did those pangs keep them awake. They sank gratefully onto the filthy pallet, totally worn out, only to be roused again when the whistles blew. The whistles could blow anytime. In the middle of the night, when the weather was at its fiercest, if the S.S. on duty was particularly sadistic. The whistle would blow, as it was blowing now for Zahlappel.

"Out, you lazy pigs! Out, you loads of shit!" The Kapos were screaming and beating the women awake.

Frances felt Miriam shake her. "Come on, quick, up."

The two women made for the door to line up, ducking blows. They reckoned they had only been in bed for a few hours, it couldn't be long after midnight. Outside, the rain fell in sheets.

"Just you wait!" snarled the Blockawa. "A treat for you all. A nice little shower. Strip! All of you, strip now!"

Miriam looked at Frances, she was worried that if they removed their warm coats, chances were, they would be stolen. Frances worried for a different reason. Whilst she had kept herself hidden under the greatcoat, her pregnancy had gone unnoticed. Without it, though, she wouldn't stand a chance. She was approaching five months pregnant, and though not big, against the rest of her starving body, the swelling of her belly would be obvious. True, others had the swollen belly of famine, but that was not to be confused with pregnancy.

"Raus, Raus! Out, out!" The Kapos were approaching, truncheons at the ready. The women hurriedly stripped, carrying their thin shifts across their arms.

Miriam caught up with Frances at the outside door. "Christ, Frances, why didn't you tell me?" she asked reproachfully.

"I didn't think you would understand."

"Understand pregnancy? Why not, you fool? How far are you?"

"Quite far," said Frances, not wishing to give too much away.

"And I suppose you want it?"

"Of course, I want it!" Frances snapped.

"Even in this place?" Miriam asked softly.

Frances didn't answer. Clearly, Miriam thought her mad. But what did she know? The child was hers, something that belonged to her in this damn place, where everything was taken from you. Well, they'd not take her child from her, not if she could help it, not without a fight. It was hers, and it was part of him.

"Frances, you know what they say happens to women with babies. Have you forgotten Ruth so soon? There are enough whisperings. We all know what happened to her, don't we?"

"It's not true, it's only hearsay, I don't believe it happens. They're taken to family camps." Miriam raised her eyebrows. "They are!" Frances insisted above the icy knot of her doubt.

"You're only fooling yourself. You know—we all do—what that thick black soot is that lies everywhere. We all know what the stench is too, do you really want to become part of it? Do you want to die that way, and your child, too?"

A sudden icy foreboding came over Frances, and she grabbed Miriam's arm, eyes wild. "What'll I do?"

"Keep calm, and keep close, and pray they don't notice you. Keep your shift across your belly. You're not too obvious yet, perhaps."

"And what if I do get away with hiding it? What then?"

"Then we'll have to get rid of it. It's a bit late now, but I've heard that one of our doctors at the Revier will help girls in trouble."

"An S.S., help?" Frances queried.

"No... not an S.S. I told you, one of ours."

The Kapos had been beating the women, hurrying them through the door from the hut into the stinking weather outside and the searchlight, which had been directed at their hut by a guard. Miriam had grabbed the woman in front of them by the shoulder.

"Irene, keep close to Frances." The gaunt woman turned round to question. "Swollen belly," Miriam explained. The woman nodded in understanding. They were outside now, already sodden, and cold. They were making to line up in their fives to be counted, but this was different.

"It's a bloody selection," muttered Irene. My God, thought Frances, they all knew it happened, but their hut had so far not been through it. They had such a way with words, these Nazis. The meadow, and now a selection. Selected, made to feel special. Well, you were special all right—any show of physical or mental weakness, and you were one of the chosen sent to Block 25, and then where? To the ovens. Surely hearsay or something put about to make them submit.

Several S.S. guards were making the women form a circle and jog round past three high-ranking officials. Frances shuddered involuntarily as she recognised the fat face of Taube, one of the most feared and sadistic of the S.S. It had probably been his idea to make them all strip. Then again, she thought, maybe not, for also present was Irma Grese, instantly recognisable—blond, beautiful, impeccable, dressed up to the nines, dressed to kill, some might say. The woman she saw with the motorcyclist, planning a night out. Of all the female S.S. at the camp, she was the most feared. Only twenty-two, with the form and face of an angel, yet she was known to have beaten some women to their deaths. The third official Frances recognised, too. A lean man, immaculate, he stood at ease, swagger stick beneath one arm, sporting a soft hat rather than the hard cap usually favoured by the S.S, showing the badge, the caduceus of a doctor on the front. The man she had addressed regarding Ruth the day they had arrived at Auschwitz. Dr Mengele.

"Cor!" whispered Irene, "what I'd give for a night between the sheets with him." A few of the other women giggled nervously, some muttered in agreement. Most, like Frances, were too afraid to do either.

Frances had learnt from others that during a selection, the S.S. would be on the lookout for three categories of women. First, the Musselman—

those who had lost hope and with it the will to live. Sunken eyed, they shuffled around the camp, heads wagging. She knew of a few in their own hut, but she didn't think they alone would be enough to satisfy the appetite of the S.S. They'd be wanting more this night; they'd be looking to the second group.

Second, there were the sick, those too ill to work, too weak to run as they were being made to run now. Come on, she said to herself, you are not one of them. You're young, you're healthy. Maybe the weak and sick will sate their hunger. Maybe they will look no further, maybe the pregnant will be overlooked this time. Run, you are young. Run! You are healthy, and in your belly, there is a child to protect, his child, a child that you want.

As the women ran past, the doctor signalled as he had done before—some to the left and some to the right, others to keep on running. She knew that to stand any chance she had to keep up with Irene in front of her, hoping that if she kept quite close, maybe they wouldn't notice her condition, frightened that if she got too close, she may stumble and draw attention to herself. Right, left, right, left. Like a metronome, never falter.

It was still raining. Soon the clay soil would soften and drag at her feet, drawing them in, making the drudgery even more tortuous. Frances saw that many of the women were dropping, making the going for the rest of them difficult with the added danger of tripping over one of them. She estimated that over half of the women from the hut had by now been sent to Block 25; from there, there was only one way out. But she was still in the circle. The circle of grotesquely bobbing females who quite literally were running for their lives. She sensed she was going to get away with it. This time, at least. She heard Miriam breathing heavily behind her, reminding her she was going to have to face the pressure from her and others to abort. Well, she would face that when and if it happened. The infant inside her gave a hefty kick, as if to let her know she was doing fine.

A whistle blew another damnable whistle.

"Line up!" The order was issued from one of the guards. The gasping women were roughly moved into rows of twenty. Frances found herself at the end of the front row, next to Irene, which meant that Miriam was at the far end of the row behind her.

Please, God, let them be finished with us, she prayed, and she knew she was not alone in her petition. She had no idea of the time, no idea how long she had been running. There was no vestige of dawn showing to the East, there was just the interminable rain.

Taube led the inspection, beginning at the end of the line farthest from Frances. He lifted women's breasts with his cane, leering. Frances stood stock still, not daring to move, hardly daring to blink, disassociating herself from her body, refusing to feel the degradation, remembering a happy time from her childhood. The cottage garden in England. The lilac would be in bloom now, she thought.

Grese seemed to have lost interest. She had wandered off and was talking to one of the guards whilst Taube and another officer she didn't recognise continued down the line.

Frances hardened her jaw, trying to control the involuntary twitches of fear that her face made as Taube drew nearer. Suddenly, she felt his cane prod in her belly. Startled, her gaze jerked to his, and he held it, waiting for her to flinch, enjoying her terror.

"Ah, one for you, I think, Herr Doctor. Hardly the bloated swelling of famine, I think. Too neat."

The doctor joined Taube and, looking Frances over, agreed her condition was indeed due to pregnancy.

"I'll take her," he said. At his gesture, a guard stepped forward and smeared a great red cross in paint on her abdomen. And before the humiliation had registered, they had passed to the line behind.

About ten minutes later, Frances found herself separated from the rest of the women from her hut and alongside five other women in varying stages of pregnancy. She was ordered into the back of a truck. "Where to?" the driver asked the guard.

"The doctor wants them, poor cows," came the reply.

Chapter 37

A short time later, the women, who Frances had learnt on the short ride were all French—were unloaded and taken into what appeared to her to be a large hospital block in the main camp. She blinked in the light. Her senses were so dulled by filth, that it was a moment before she could identify the smell of the soap. That and the stark white of the walls blinded those senses that were now used to filth.

A nurse, German by her accent, handed Frances a towel and a starched white surgical gown. "The doctor will see you all shortly," she snapped.

Frances interpreted for those who couldn't understand.

As they showered, she noted that, compared to hers, the other's bodies appeared reasonably well fed. They could not have been long at Auschwitz, she thought.

"You'll see, we'll be fine," said one, a pretty brunette. "They won't harm a pregnant woman. We've been taken off work detail and brought here to be looked after."

Looked after. What did that mean in Auschwitz terms? Frances wondered. The initial relief that she had felt on realising she was in the hands of a doctor was now wearing off. This place, this hospital, was a pretext for something else, she was certain, but what? A chill ran down her spine.

A second nurse, an inmate, judging by her skeletal appearance, was gently ushering them through the showers. Frances guessed from her accent that she was a Pole, but her head was unshorn, and Frances had learnt if women kept their hair, they weren't Jews.

"Come now, girls," the nurse gently chided. "Come with me and wait for the doctor. He will be here shortly, and he doesn't like being kept waiting." The towel she threw over Frances's shoulders as she left the shower was rough. "Please," she continued speaking in broken French, "for your own good, for the good of us all, don't keep him waiting."

The women prattled on, talking about when their babies were due, and whether they were going to have a boy or a girl, and what they would name them.

Frances felt annoyed, she needed to think. It was obvious that she was in some sort of hospital, but different to the Revier at Birkenau. Here there was no stench of disease.

She touched the nurse's elbow. "What's going to happen to us?"

"Nothing. You'll be fine," the woman answered.

But Frances knew from the way she averted her eyes that she was lying. She and the other five women were led fresh from the shower to an adjacent room, where they were given clean white gowns to dress in. From there, they were taken to a waiting room, which made Frances shudder as she remembered that last time she'd sat in such a room, before being beaten, hospitalised, and eventually ending up in Drancy.

"Well, at least we've got a shower out of all this," said one girl in an attempt at being jovial. "I wonder who the doctor is. Do you think he's that really handsome Kraut, the dark one from earlier on? Don't you think he looks kind?"

The door opened to reveal the doctor, and Frances recognized he was indeed the dark, handsome man, Dr Mengele, from the selection. He smiled at the women, and Frances felt a pang as his lips uncurled to reveal a small gap between his front two incisors reminiscent of Mueller. There, all similarities stopped. This man wasn't nearly as tall, and he was swarthy with Italian-like features.

His glance swept over the women as he said, "Ah, ladies, good of you all to come. Do as you're told, and you'll be fine, huh? Carry to full term. If you don't do as you're told, Fffttt!" The doctor waved his arm nonchalantly in the air. "You'll leave by way of the top floor, so to speak."

The women looked at each other questioningly, but Frances's blood cooled. She had no doubt about what he meant.

"Now, who shall I see first?" His eyes scanned the group hungrily and locked on Helene, the most heavily pregnant of them. "You, come!" he said.

Her eyes closed briefly, and Frances heard her soft grunt as she struggled to her feet. Helene followed the doctor through the door without a glance backward.

Frances exchanged glances and a nervous smile with the others. But they kept still, straining their ears, listening for a clue of what was being said behind the closed door. As hard as she tried, Frances could make out no words. Now a sound came—a sob?—too quickly stifled to be sure. Frances felt her pulse tapping at her temples. The interview lasted about ten minutes, she guessed, then the door opened, and Helene appeared, red-eyed, pale, and shaken, in the company of a nurse, who took her from the room. Minutes later, the nurse returned, and the doctor appeared and made a second selection. The process was repeated until finally he pointed to Frances.

"You!" he announced, singling her out with his pointed finger.

She rose, feeling the heat of the doctor's scrutiny as she closed the gap between them. She sensed he was strangely excited, and as the door closed behind her and the nurse, she felt trapped, a fly in a spider's web.

Mengele sat in the black leather chair behind a large desk. Spread out before him were the notes he had taken from the interviews with the other women. "Country?" he asked.

"France!" Frances spoke through jaws tight with the effort of keeping her voice steady. She kept her gaze level; how, she didn't know.

His mouth went slack for a moment, as if in surprise, and then he straightened. "Strip!" he ordered.

Frances stood stiff-spined; eyes unwavering. She heard the sharp intake of his breath as he leant towards her across the desk.

Pounding it, he shouted, "Strip, Jew whore!"

Frances slowly undid the tapes of her gown and let it drop to the floor. Remember, she told herself, this is not you he's seeing, just flesh and bone, not really you. "Why am I here ?" Her brazenness shocked her, but she took strength from it.

The doctor drew himself up in his chair. Ignoring her question, he demanded, "How far are you?"

"About five months."

"Any twins in your family?"

"No."

"The father's family?"

"I don't know. Why am I here?"

Without responding, the doctor left his chair, moving towards her, stealthy, a panther waiting to spring. She could smell his lavender perfumed soap. He was immaculate in his appearance, and somehow she felt filthy, degraded in his presence. *No!* Denial shot through her brain. She was intelligent, a talented human being. The world had been her oyster. She would not give in to him that easily.

Again, she asked, "Why am I here, Herr Doctor?"

The doctor rubbed his chin thoughtfully. "You speak good German." His smile did nothing to warm the ice in his eyes. "You are here because I want to know your details."

They had taken her details many times over, and she wondered if it could be some sort of test. He was playing cat and mouse with her, toying with his prey.

"I have only a number, Herr Doctor," she answered. "I have no other details."

"Bravo, well remembered, Frau. Or is it Fraulein? No, it's not your number I'm interested in. It's this. How did you come by this?" He prodded at her belly with his pencil.

Frances felt her face warm, and it surprised her that she could still feel embarrassment. She decided to play him at his own game. "You're a doctor," she replied. "Surely you don't need me to explain?" Before she had time to register the rise of his arm, he'd struck the side of her head, knocking her off balance into the corner of his desk. Her ears rang as she pulled herself back up to her feet.

The doctor continued, "Let me make myself a little clearer. It's the intimate details I want of you and your mate copulating. The filthy, intimate details of how you Jew animals make more of your vermin."

Frances watched as he wiped flecks of spittle from his mouth. Clearly, he was demented, perverted. Her eyes flashed to the nurse, hoping for some support, but the woman stood motionless, eyes on the floor, like stone.

"Come! Speak up, Jew whore." Frances's head reeled when he hit her yet again, backhanding her this time. "Otherwise, the bastard in your belly will be food for our ovens."

"I may be a whore, Doctor, but I am no Jew," she spoke quietly, fighting to keep the tremor from her voice. "I'll tell you nothing," she assured him, bracing herself for another attack.

But the doctor merely raised his eyebrows. "Very well, the choice is yours." He picked up the phone and issued an order for guards to collect her, then he turned to the nurse. "Get her out of here and wait." The nurse grabbed Frances by the arm.

"I'll look out for you as you leave by the chimney," he said to her, his voice shrill, taunting.

Her blood curdled as the cold realisation of what her defiance could cost her. She thought of Ruth. So, she had died and then went to the ovens. It was true then, real. She remembered Miriam's preaching that survival was all that mattered. She wrenched free of the nurse, wheeling to face the doctor, shouting, "All right, all right! I'll tell you anything, everything. Please... please don't kill me. Let me have my baby."

The doctor's smile was twisted. His eyes glittered with something like enjoyment. "Too late, Fraulein," he said, switching his glance to the nurse. "Get her out of here," he said.

"No!" Frances jerked again from the woman's grasp. "I'm not a Jew."

He opened a drawer, removed a pistol, and raised it to her face.

"I'm not!" Frances cried.

"Possibly, but you no longer interest me," he told her, his tone bored. His finger bore down on the trigger. The click of the hammer was loud in Frances's ears.

"Go ahead, then, shoot me, Herr Doctor, and you will be killing a good German child."

His gaze narrowed.

"The father is one of your own, one of your war heroes, one of your grey wolves."

The doctor let his arm drop and stared unblinkingly at her. She wanted to look away, but knew she had to hold his gaze.

"If you're lying to me, you'll wish you had gone to the ovens," he told her.

Chapter 38

Frances shook uncontrollably from the moment she left the office. The man seated behind the desk was a monster. It was clear, and yet she couldn't help thinking what she might have made of him had she met him in different circumstances. He was handsome, debonair, cultured. No! Surely, just a monster. From the office, the nurse took her back into the waiting room and found it deserted except for herself and a female S.S. who stood beside her, a face of stone which threatened, *Sit here. Say nothing, do nothing, or else!*

Frances sat quietly, lost in thought over the interview.

The doctor eventually lowered his pistol and returned it to the drawer of the desk, seating himself on the black leather chair.

"So, Frau, let me hear your story."

He sat and listened patiently, scratching his head from time to time and not interrupting until she had finished.

"So, what do you think has happened to your Kapitan?" he asked. She stood for a while, uncertain of what to say. Uncertain of what she thought. He pushed her to speak up. "Come, do you think he's dead?"

She sighed. "I don't know, Herr Doctor. He didn't come for me as he promised. He was to be married."

"So, he doesn't know of the child?"

"No!"

"No matter. I have decided to let you have this child, Frau Meyer. When your time comes, I will deliver it myself. I will be interested to see what colour eyes the child has. What colour were its father's?"

"Blue, Herr Doctor." *Wonderful deep blue,* she thought.

"Ah good. We will find a good German family to bring it up."

She panicked. "You mean you will take the child from me?"

"I can reconsider…"

"No!" She recognised the danger signs. "No, Herr Doctor, thank you."

The doctor smiled. "That's better. Now, a change of work for you, I think. I hate talent to be wasted, and I'd like to know where you are so that I may take good care of you." Inwardly, she shuddered at the thought.

Josef Mengele lifted his phone and arranged for a guard, the one who was with her now, the woman they had seen earlier at the selection, the one they all feared. Blond, beautiful Irma Grese.

When she first appeared, Frances noticed she had smiled at Mengele intimately, which he ignored. "Take her outside and wait for the Lagerfuhrerein," he ordered.

And so, they waited now, she and Irma Grese, together. Sitting for what felt like an age, while the woman Grese slapped a whip against her own silken leg.

Suddenly, the slapping stopped, and Frances felt fingers digging into the flesh of her arm as she was yanked to her feet as footsteps approached. There was a tapping of heeled shoes, something unusual in Auschwitz. Frances dared to turn her head, and her eyes met the searching China blue stare of one of the most elegant women she had ever seen.

The woman was tall and slender, dressed to perfection in a finely tailored grey uniform. Her face was free from all traces of makeup, its use being banned by the S.S. and yet Frances thought this was a woman who was so perfect that the addition of makeup would have added nothing. Frances took in the two thick, golden coiled plaits wound round the woman's head and wondered what on earth the likes of her could be doing at Auschwitz. Then she spoke in deep Dietrich tones, it would have been wrong for her to speak in any other way.

"Is this my virtuoso?"

"Yes, Lagerfuhrerein," replied Grese.

"Very well." She turned to Frances. "You will be in my orchestra. I will hear you play. Have you anything to say?"

Frances stared at her stupidly as the words rang in her head.

"Well?" said the woman. "You don't look very pleased."

"I... I have no instrument." Frances stumbled over the words.

The woman's laugh was trapped in her throat. "Is that all? Never you mind. We will get you back to Birkenau, to the musician's hut. We'll sort you out an instrument." She turned to Grese. "See to it!" Then she left, long legs gliding, taking her away.

Frances wanted to chase after her, to question her, clarify. Check her understanding. She would play in the orchestra, she would hold a violin, caress it. Her heart rose, despite her fear. She was almost glad to be returning to Birkenau, but what of Miriam and the others? How could she let them know she was still alive?

The woman Grese slapped her whip against her shiny shoe, making Frances jump, "Well, aren't you the lucky one?"

"Perhaps," said Frances, looking into her frozen face, "though I thought luck had run out of this place long ago." She felt the sting of the whip across her breasts.

"I'll be watching you, whore! Lower your eyes."

Frances winced as the whip struck her again, and she looked to the floor. *One day, Irma Grese, you'll get your due.* The promise, a threat, really, seared the walls of her brain.

The journey back to Birkenau in the back of the truck was uneventful. Frances tried to work out the time and guessed it to be about midday. Her gut was telling her she was even hungrier than usual, she hadn't thought that could be possible, but her stomach had obviously missed the insult that passed for breakfast. Maybe, she thought, she might be in the musician's hut in time for the midday meal. She wondered what those lucky girls had to eat and hoped that there would be plenty left over for her.

The truck bumped its way into Camp B where those of importance lived. The women who worked in the place known as Canada, the administrators, those who occupied positions of trust. She rubbed her shoulders against the cold; all she wore was the thin cotton gown that they had given her after her shower. The sun was shining over the flap in the back of the lorry, but early May in Auschwitz could still chill you to the bone. The infant inside her gave a hefty kick, and as she rubbed at the pathetic little bump, she wondered how it found the strength and nutrition to carry on growing.

The truck pulled up outside a hut that looked like any other, and the guard ordered her to get out. As she jumped to the ground, she saw the gaunt faces of young women pressed to the windows. Then the door opened, and the bulky frame of a middle-aged woman appeared.

"You, violinist, come here now!" she snapped with a harsh Slavic accent.

Frances stood for a while on what she hoped to be the threshold to heaven until the woman gave her a hefty shove through the door and she heard it slam behind her. Forty or so pairs of eyes turned upon her, some with distaste, all with interest. A Jewish girl approached with the traditional welcome of salt and bread.

"I'm Ewa," she said in French.

Frances gave the girl a smile and held out her hand to her.

"Frances."

"I know," said the girl. Then, much to Frances's astonishment, she threw her arms around her. "Thank God, I thought you would be dead by now." A few of the other girls had gathered round, some were smiling,

Frances turned to Ewa in confusion. "Do I know you?"

"No, but I know you. You were much talked of, in the Conservatoire."

"Ah, so that's it." Frances laughed. "Tell me, what were you studying?"

"Cello," Ewa replied.

"But you can't have found out about my being here from the Conservatoire. How?"

"Oh, I saw you marching through a couple of mornings. I recognised you straight away. I told Alma about you, but she would have none of it, said we had more than enough violins."

"Alma... who is Alma?" Frances asked.

"Alma Rose, she's our conductor, a marvellous violinist too, though not in your class, but brilliant all the same."

"Wasn't there a Rose in the Berlin orchestra—first violin?"

Ewa nodded. "Alma is his daughter."

"Then she must also be a relative of Gustav Mahler," said Frances.

"His niece, to be exact."

Frances turned, searching for the voice that had spoken behind her. She noticed that all the girls had stopped chattering and were almost standing to attention. She found herself face to face with a tall dark woman whose body appeared so rigid that Frances feared it might snap.

"I am Alma Rose," the woman said. Frances extended her hand. "Frances Meyer."

Alma ignored her outstretched hand. "I know who you are, though I confess I thought your name was Lamont."

"My maiden name. I kept it for performing," Frances explained.

"I never saw you. My father was looking forward to you joining the Berlin Orchestra a few years ago. Nothing came of it."

"I was thrown out of Germany by the damn Nazis."

"Well, no matter," said Alma. "I myself am a good German."

Frances was unsure how to reply to this latest piece of information, Alma seemed proud that she was one of them.

"Well," said Alma, "I suppose we had better get you some clothes in case I decide to use you."

"What do you mean?" Frances asked, horrified. "Surely I'll play?"

"We'll see. Like Ewa has already said, we have plenty of strings, I myself am a soloist."

She's jealous, thought Frances, *that bloody stupid woman is jealous.* The interview with Alma, it seemed, was over. She was already ordering the large woman who had let her in to get clothes, then she turned and walked the entire length of the room and disappeared through a door.

"Come on," said the large woman, prodding at her. "Let's see what size you are beneath that gown."

"You'll have to leave a bit of space, I'm pregnant," Frances announced. The girls broke into a gaggle.

"Pregnant, is it? Well, we'll have to put a stop to that before the Krauts find out."

"No, they know, it's all right."

"They know, and they're letting you keep it?" asked one girl incredulously. "How come?"

Frances's mind raced; she couldn't tell her tale here. "The doctor said I could carry to full term. He knows a German couple who will give it a home."

"The new doctor? They say he experiments on pregnant women," stated Ewa. She paused and then continued, "And babies." Frances felt sick, then dizzy, she saw the floor coming up to meet her as she fell into a faint.

Chapter 39

D octor Josef Mengele sank back into his chair, well satisfied. He had only been at Auschwitz for weeks, and already he was making his presence felt. He had power, and why shouldn't he have? He was, after all, an intelligent man, and he wondered how those idiots from his school days were faring now. While they had wasted their time playing silly games, he had worked at his studies, and because of that, they had never accepted him; they had thought him weird.

Now he could afford to be a little magnanimous. Perhaps it hadn't been all their fault; he had been a rather sickly child, and his mother had fussed. His father Karl was a bitter man, he cared more for his factories than his son. Well, he'd shown him, he'd shown the bloody lot of them—a doctorate in medicine under no one less than the venerated Doctor Otto von Vershuer, the leading expert on the new science of race. He had picked up the antisemitic virus from von Vershuer, and Hitler had stimulated it.

He joined the Nazi party, and finding the atmosphere much to his liking, took it one step further and joined the S.S. Not long after that, he had met the love of his life, Irene Schoenbein, and despite a great deal of hassle from his mother, he had married her. Dear Irene, he wondered where she was now. She had been so beautiful, so intelligent, and independent. That had been her undoing. Hardly the archetype of the German hausfrau. Their relationship had been doomed from the start; she was out of his control.

That woman, the French one—she had reminded him of Irene. She was clever and attractive, and her amber eyes fascinated him. She had stood up to him the way Irene would have done. And her story? Too fantastic to be made up, surely. Well, he'd see—it was easy enough to check out, and after all, it didn't hurt to be magnanimous occasionally. It showed strength, not weakness, and if the whim took him.

Frances tossed and turned her way back to consciousness. At first, she was only aware of the music. That was "The Blue Danube," surely, that stopped and started again. The sharp staccato commands of the woman, Alma Rose, punctuated the melody. Frances remembered meeting her. She remembered fainting a short time later. Daring to open her eyes, she looked around and found she was on the dormitory side of the music room in the end bed of a row. A bed with a sheet, all to herself. It had been months since she'd had such luxury, except in a dream.

"No! Why are you all so stupid?" Fraulein Rose's voice lifted. "Not one of you is a proper musician. Why can't I have real musicians?"

Frances rose on an elbow to see the girls gathered in the larger side of the hut, which did as the music room. Along one wall was a table around which sat the copyists, transcribing scores, not daring to look up. In the middle of the room was a small platform which Alma stood on, taut as the strings on her violin, and red with anger. Girls and music stands surrounded her.

Frances turned over, and thinking of the doctor, she stifled a moan. Mengele—he promised he would let her carry her child full term and that he would find it a suitable home. Would he keep his word? How could she trust him? How could she believe him? And yet, to keep her sanity, she had to. The door of the hut suddenly burst open, admitting a runner.

"What is it?" snapped Alma, annoyed by the disturbance.

"Lagerfuhrerein Mandel is on her way!" warned the woman, quickly pulling the door shut behind her.

"Quick! Line up, girls!" shouted Alma.

"Over by your beds!" squawked the plump woman. "Get the new girl up and dressed, quick!"

Too late, the door opened, framing Lagerfuhrerein Maria Mandel, Chief of the women's camp at Birkenau—the woman she had met earlier.

"Where is my virtuoso?" she demanded huskily. "I want to hear her play." She turned her porcelain gaze on the women standing at attention by their beds and scanned the ranks.

Frances, still shrouded in the white surgical gown, pulled herself from her bed to her feet and felt the heat of Maria Mandel's gaze.

"What, no clothes yet?" the woman demanded.

"I'm sorry, Lagerfuhrerein. I have been unwell."

Mandel's face softened as much as it was able. "Not well, then perhaps this will make you feel better." She turned to a second S.S. woman who had accompanied her and took a violin case from her.

Approaching Frances, she said, "Open it up. Here, sit on your bed." Frances's hands shook as she fumbled with the latch.

"Here, if you're not well, let me do it."

The forty or so other girls looked at each other in astonishment. Mandel had seated Frances on the bed and had sat beside her, the long, silken encased legs carelessly crossed. The catch snapped back on the violin case, and she lifted the lid, releasing the unmistakable odour of a quality piece of seasoned wood.

Frances gasped. "It's a Galliano!"

Maria Mandel frowned. "You do like it, don't you? I was told it was exceptional."

"Oh, yes, one of the best, Lagerfuhrerein."

Mandel smiled with relief. "Take it then and play for me. It's yours for as long as you're here."

Frances looked longingly at the spruce and maple body lying lifeless in its case. It had been a long time since she had played back in January or February at Drancy. She held out her hand and gently caressed the sleek neck and curved body. Then she took it from its case and rested it beneath her chin, reverently placing her cheek upon it, lifting her shoulder to support it.

It felt good, and she sighed. Then she checked the pitch of the strings, which hardly needed any adjustment. She should have known that Maria Mandel would leave nothing to chance. She took the bow, balancing it in her hand for a moment to get the feel of it and to think what she should play, and then she tensed it and added a little resin. Touching the bow to the strings, she released the haunting melody of "Scheherazade," and it seemed strangely relevant, the tale of a girl who had to live by her wits to stay alive.

After several minutes of listening, Maria Mandel stood up and said, "Well, at least I haven't wasted my time. Kramer is going to love you." She nodded her head at Frances and swept out of the hut.

Alma went to her room and wasn't seen for over an hour. The girls didn't know what to do. It was rehearsal time, nothing had ever got in the way of rehearsal time.

The plump woman who Frances had learnt was called Tchaikovskowa and who was the hut Blockawa, had left straight after Mandel and had since returned with clothing for Frances. A blue skirt, white blouse, woollen stockings, underwear, a slip, and a pair of women's shoes that fitted. To top it all, she was given a warm woollen coat.

She placed the lot down on Frances's bed. "Dress," she said. "If Mandel comes back and you're still in that gown, she won't be amused."

As Frances dressed herself, the rest of the girls drifted away into small groups. Some chatted harmlessly, but Frances was already aware of the hostility brewing inside a few of them. Ewa was the only one who had openly shown her friendship. She was standing now with another girl, who she introduced as Lily.

"Take no notice of the girls," said Ewa. "Some of them are jealous. The Poles in particular hate us Jews. By the way, I didn't know you were Jewish."

"I'm not."

"But your hair; they only shave the Jews."

"Isn't it nice to know that even the Krauts make mistakes from time to time?" asked Frances. The three women laughed and some of the other girls turned on them.

"Yes, Frances Meyer, it's all very well for you to laugh," said one. "You've found a cosy nest here. I wouldn't be at all surprised if you're not spying for the Krauts."

"That's ridiculous!" Frances said defensively. "I hate them as much as the rest of you. I'd never spy."

"Not even to keep that child in your belly alive?"

"No!" She saw Mueller fleetingly in her head.

"Well, then, exactly what did you do for the good doctor?" challenged another of the girls.

"Nothing!"

"For goodness' sake," said Ewa. "Why should she have to do anything other than play? We've all heard her, haven't we? We all know how Mandel and Mengele are about music, her talent is enough."

"Enough for her, maybe," said the first girl, "but what about the rest of us? We're not soloists. We're the orchestra. We need to practise, to be good enough to stay alive."

"Yes!" said another. "Now she's come here and annoyed our leader. God only knows what will happen."

"Why did you have to come and upset the apple cart? We didn't need you!" someone else commented.

"Look, I'm sorry," Frances apologised. "I don't know what to say to you all. I don't know what to do."

The women were in groups, talking under their breath. Frances turned to Ewa. "God, Ewa, I don't know what to do. I didn't mean to upset Alma. Mandel asked me to play, I could hardly refuse, could I?"

"No, of course not. The girls are frightened, that's all. Mandel and Kramer set up this orchestra, and they're proud of it, but they'd destroy it on a whim—we all know that. We have to keep the S.S. happy, and it's Alma that has made that possible."

"See," said Lily, "she hasn't been here that long. Before it was Tchaikovskowa. She reckons she's some relative of Tchaikovsky's, but she's about as musical as a hall of deaf mutes. You should see her conduct."

"I'll talk to her," said Frances.

"Who, Tchaikovskowa?" asked Lily.

"No, Alma."

"I wouldn't," Ewa warned. "You don't know her, she's one of them, really. German and proud of it. Weird, don't you think, that she can be in here, live like this—"

"I'll go and see her," Frances repeated. She walked the length of the room, uncomfortable in the knowledge that the other girls were watching, feeling the weight of their eyes crawling up her spine. She stopped at the far end, noting that Alma's door was closed. She knocked gently. There was no reply.

"Alma, it's Frances Meyer. Please, could I speak to you?" She kept her voice low, not wanting the others to hear.

"Go away!"

"Please, Alma," Frances tried the door and was surprised to find that it wasn't locked, though only fleetingly, for a lock in Auschwitz and on the inside of a door was unthinkable. She ventured into Alma's room. It was small, just enough space for a bed and a cupboard.

Alma turned, and it was obvious from her red-rimmed eyes she had been crying. She set her lips in a hard line. "I thought I told you to go away."

"I'm sorry. I need to speak to you."

"Huh! You see? Already you're taking away my authority."

"No!" Frances was adamant. "There's been a misunderstanding. Why should you think that?"

"No misunderstanding!" Alma jumped to her feet, her slender body straight as a die, her face set in a hard line. "I could have been as good as you! Your talent could have been mine! I do have your talent, but I never had the support of my family. They were disappointed because I wasn't a boy, I never had the chances you had!"

"The others have told me how well you play, Alma," ventured Frances.

"Yes," said Alma, turning away. "It's all I live for. My music is my life. My violin, my lover."

"I don't know what to say to you," said Frances. "I can identify with what you've said. I understand what you are saying, but I don't know what I've done."

"Don't know what you've done? You have destroyed me! They don't need me anymore, you're the rising star."

Frances searched her mind for something to say, a way to soothe Alma's feelings. Alma gave a harsh laugh. "Ha! Who do I think I'm fooling? I've never been as good as you." Turning her back on Frances, she went to her cupboard, taking from it her conductor's baton, which she offered to Frances. "Here, you'll be needing this."

"Whatever for?" Frances asked, shaking her head in confusion.

"You can't conduct without one, and I'm sure the girls are ready to begin."

Frances held out her hand but instead of taking the baton, she took Alma's hand and held it, her clasp gentle but firm. "So that's it." She smiled. "Alma, I couldn't conduct the orchestra with a baton or without one. I wouldn't have a clue where to begin."

She left that room, believing that she and Alma now understood one another.

Chapter 40

Frances never really became accepted as part of that orchestra. After that one moment of near friendship, Alma raised a Teutonic barrier, and Frances was never to see a crack in it again. She was Alma Rose the Kapo, the leader of the music block. She was in charge, everyone did as she said, or they were made to suffer for it with a resounding slap across the face from the flat of her hand.

Frances spoke to Alma on one occasion about her striking the girls if they played a wrong note, but Alma turned on her. "My God, they are so slow. I beat them to make them learn. If they don't learn, the orchestra will be useless, and that will be the end of us all."

She had thought about that. Well, why should the orchestra be any different from the rest of the hell? The beatings, though fewer, still happened, if not from Alma, then from one of the S.S. women. As for the food? The same as the rest of the camp. Still, she had to admit she was lucky. The music block was warm. She had a bed to sleep in at night, a shower most days and a chance to go out and about in the camp from time to time just for the sake of going out. For them, roll calls were inside and because of the mistake they had made regarding her background, they let her grow her hair again.

Sometimes it would happen that they were instructed to stay in and keep away from the windows. At those times, they knew there was to be a selection. The orchestra girls were among the lucky few not to be included. Like the girls in Canada and in admin, they were virtually free from the degradation that the others were put through. At such times, Frances's thoughts would whip back to Miriam. She was desperate to see her, to let her know she was still alive, that the child in her belly was still alive—and better than that, appeared to be thriving. She was at a loss though of how to get a message to her.

Apart from rehearsals, they were expected to play twice a day outside for the work details and inside for the S.S.. Besides these regular performances, there were also irregular ones for the incoming deportees. When she was told to play at these times, Frances found she could bear these more easily than some others. She told herself that at least these people had suffered little, and for most, any ordeal would be over and done within a couple of hours.

It was the work parties that tore her apart. Watching, she found, was worse than being part of it. Thousands filing past, women whose bones were wrapped only in a loose covering of cracked, wrinkled skin. They were suspicious of the orchestra girls; some even went as far as hating them. You could tell from the scornful looks. Some dared to shout abuse, and how could anyone blame them? How could they be expected to know that they did have one thing in common with these girls—namely, hunger?

Following the selections, some members of the S.S. would often go to the music hut to forget their cruelty during the selections or, in some cases, to celebrate it. The majority would always turn up for the Sunday concerts. It was then that they expected the girls to shine. They had to make an effort with their appearance: impeccably cleaned shoes, freshly laundered garments. Then they were taken to the huge concrete building known as the sauna.

Its purpose was unknown. Its interior stood stark and cold, lit only by bare bulbs. Here the camp aristocrats would assemble. Often Kramer himself would appear. Kramer, the overall commandant of Birkenau, who had set the orchestra up with Maria Mandel. All the girls were terrified of him and rightly so, for even though he was always proper with them, they had heard stories of his abuse and were only too aware that he was capable of bashing in a woman's skull should the fancy take him. He was a stocky man with huge ears and a bulging chest and the supple tread of an animal. His presence was crushing. It was he, along with Maria Mandel, who kept the orchestra alive, for he was a great lover of music.

On one occasion, Kramer appeared with a film crew, and the sauna was filled to maximum capacity with hundreds of S.S. and inmates. They wheeled even the sick from the Revier in on their beds. How civilised it all was. The S.S. clapped politely after each orchestral selection, and the inmates joined in or clapped along. Little did the cinema audience realise that by the time the film had reached them, most of the cast would have been disposed of.

* * *

It was hard for Frances. Since moving into the music block, she had no close friends; most of the girls merely tolerated her, except for Ewa and Lily, but they were so young and held her in awe. The problem was made worse because she had replaced Marianne Kolzinsky, and Marianne was a favourite amongst the other girls. The situation was exacerbated when she and her violin were sent for one evening to play for Mengele. Some already thought that she must indeed spy for the Krauts. Why else was she allowed to keep her pregnancy and her hair?

A runner arrived, and Frances was taken to the main gate of Birkenau and from there transported to Auschwitz One. The S.S. had their own village there, complete with a bakery, a sausage factory, and a swimming pool. On reaching Mengele's quarters, a smart, detached residence, Frances almost vomited. The smell of the fresh food, mixed with her intense apprehension, was almost too much for her gut to take.

She was taken into the largest room, where Mengele was throwing a party. She recognised various members of the S.S.—Taube, Grese, Mandel, Kramer, and several others. Mengele took her to one side and set her out of the way, instructing her to play for them. It was a couple of hours later, nearing midnight, when Mengele finally signalled for her to stop and follow him into the kitchen. A young Jewish girl was frantically cleaning as they entered. She didn't look up from her task.

"Well, now," said Mengele with something approaching concern in his voice. "How is my mother-to-be?"

That he should ask after her well-being dumbfounded her, and she found she couldn't answer. She knew he wouldn't suffer fools, and she cursed herself for appearing such an idiot.

"I think I have tired you," he continued. "Too much playing for a woman in your condition." He offered her a hunk of freshly baked bread and a piece of cheese. "Here."

At first, she thought maybe he was playing one of his sick jokes until he said, "Take it with you, you deserve it. You've played well. Now to get you back to your hut."

She just managed to utter a thank you. She made that piece of bread and cheese last for the entire journey, savouring every crumb.

It was very late when the truck dropped her outside the music hut. The girls were all quiet. Some were asleep, but many of them were just pretending to be. She crept past them, trying not to disturb anyone, and as she reached her bed, Ewa crept across to her.

"Frances, are you all right?"

"Yes, yes, I'm fine," she whispered.

"What happened? Where have you been? With him, Mengele?"

"Yes, I have." Frances heard Ewa catch her breath.

"Then what they're saying about you is true," she said reproachfully.

"What are they saying, Ewa?"

"That you've slept with him."

Frances's mouth dropped open in disbelief, and then she laughed. At first, just quietly, then louder, hysterically. She laughed until she cried. And then, finding her voice, she shouted, "Oh, Ewa, for goodness' sake, look at me!" Frances tore her gaze from Ewa and cast it over the rows of beds. "Wake up, you stupid load of bitches. Wake up and look at me. Do you really think he's interested in me? I've played for them, and that's all—for Mengele and his cronies."

"I knew it!" said Ewa. "I knew you couldn't ever;. I'm right, aren't I? You would never betray us. You would never lie with him?"

"Yes, Ewa, yes, of course, you're right. I could never let a German touch me." She felt the lie stick in her throat.

Ewa grabbed hold of her then, hugging her, and Frances held onto her tightly, burying her face in Ewa's shoulder, feeling the child kick between them as if to remind her of her shame, that once she had.

* * *

The first visit to Mengele's quarters heralded many that were to follow. Sometimes, he expected her to entertain his cronies. At such times, she sat out of the way in a corner. Other times she was taken into his private sitting room and found him there alone and would play just for him. He would sit in his favourite chair, eyes slightly closed, sipping wine, smoking a cigar, enjoying her music and, increasingly, her company. Sometimes he would have a conversation with her. Not the sort you would have with a friend. No. He spoke to her as if she were a favourite pet. It was a one-sided conversation. He'd go on about his ideas and theories, unburden himself of his doubts, but never did he expect an answer. And Frances took care never to give him one. She would have loved to question him, to find out what made a monster such as him tick. But she had learnt her place at Auschwitz, and if she wanted to survive, wanted her child to survive, she must not forget it.

Chapter 41

Mid-May 1943

It was a month before she spotted Miriam. From her perch on the orchestra platform, Frances had searched the masses daily as they seethed past for a glimpse of her. It was quite ridiculous, her better sense told her that. Like searching for the proverbial needle in a haystack, but she couldn't stop looking, and now her diligence had paid off.

Miriam was among those who worked outside, only some twenty metres away. Close enough so Frances could see her weariness. But she had survived! Incredible! She felt her heart soar. Knowing Miriam, maybe her survival wasn't so incredible. She wanted to call out, "Miriam, look, I'm here, I'm all right, see I'm up here!" But to do that would be to risk a beating, or far worse. So, she sat, violin to her chin, and willed her friend to look up. But in seconds, she was out of view, lost in the teeming horde. She'd look out for her now on the way back, and she would find a way to draw Miriam's attention.

The rest of the day was endless. Endless rehearsals, endless chatter, endless bickering. And then it was time to play the workers back into the camp. A couple of hours before dusk, a truck came, bringing the workers back to the gate, where they were left to wend their way back into the camp of Birkenau, to the familiar strains of a Strauss waltz. Dragging their feet, dragging their dead. One waltz followed another as she kept her eyes peeled for a sight of Miriam. Finally, she spotted her familiar figure, and she stared, frightened to take her eyes off her for a moment. Frightened even to blink in case she lost sight of her. She muttered to herself, "For God's sake Miriam, look up." Immediately feeling guilty in the knowledge that if Miriam did and was caught, she would be punished.

Still, she had a plan and was determined to implement it. She followed Miriam's slow progress towards the gate, catching sight of the prisoner's staggering and an S.S. guard beating time against his boot with his swagger stick. She waited until Miriam was little more than ten metres away, then, counting to ten, she caused the Galliano to produce a hideous wail.

That such a beautiful instrument could make such a beastly sound was quite amazing. She was instantly aware of Alma's stony features turning on her in such a way that her eyes cut into her flesh. She was aware, too, of the other girls and the S.S., some of whom were pointing and laughing, but most of all, she was aware of Miriam. For a brief second, their eyes met, and Frances saw Miriam smile and nod, and then she was past and through the gate.

For her trouble, she felt the measure of Alma's hand not once but several times. On the journey back to the hut, Alma restrained herself, but once inside the hut, she caught Frances with such a resounding blow across the head that she fell to the floor.

"Stupid!" Alma cursed. "You are stupid. What in the devil's name were you up to? That was no mistake. You did it on purpose!" Then she dealt Frances another blow. The other girls were mad at her too, not even Lily nor Ewa sprang to her defence. She supposed she couldn't blame them.

"Look, I saw a friend. I had to let her know I was all right. I could hardly shout, could I? It was the only way I could think of. I'm sorry."

Alma's face was red with anger. "What will I say, do you think? Mandel will get to hear of it without a doubt. I'll not protect you. I'll tell her the truth."

"What, that I have a friend? I suppose that's not allowed."

It wasn't until bedtime that things settled down, until everyone had turned in for some sleep. As Frances drifted off, she congratulated herself that she had carried her plan through without harm to anyone else and with little harm to herself. It came as a surprise, therefore, when a runner appeared to warn them all a little before midnight that a visit from the S.S. was imminent. They all shook themselves awake and put their beds in order as Irma Grese and two others swept through the doorway.

Grese was flushed, and it was obvious that she had been drinking. Her pitiless eyes swept the women until they found Frances.

"Was that some sort of joke?" The shrill voice cut the silence as sharp and cold as a surgeon's knife.

Frances lifted her eyes and investigated the chill that was Irma Grese. The woman didn't like her, that was obvious. She harboured an insane jealousy over Frances's relationship with Mengele. Stupid bitch to think that she, with her short hair and her grey skin, could present her, the golden angel, with any threat.

Mengele did like her though, as much as he could like anyone. In his own strange way, he was taking care of her. The small offerings of food he made her, even though they were table scraps, had made a difference to her meagre diet, had enabled the child to grow, and just for that, Grese's blood boiled.

She flinched as she felt the sting of the riding whip across her breasts, a favourite punishment of angelic Irma's.

"You dare to look me in the face, whore? I've a mind to send you to the bakers."

Despite her fear, Frances kept her eyes level, and she felt her lip curl with contempt for the woman. Then she felt the sting of the whip for the second time, cutting through the cotton of her flimsy nightdress, which offered her little protection.

"Don't think he'll protect you. He's gone. You didn't know that did you? You must have wondered, though, why he hasn't sent for you the past few days." She gave a coarse laugh. "He's sick–typhoid. I wouldn't be surprised if you didn't give it to him, and more besides." She turned to go, strutting the entire length of the hut, followed by the other two women who had remained, silently sneering.

Frances relaxed. She had survived yet again. Then, just as Grese was about to leave, she turned.

"This bitch has a yearning for good German men, did you women know that? The child she carries. Have you ever wondered why she has been allowed to continue with her pregnancy?"

Aware of the enormity of the damage she was about to inflict upon Frances, Grese's gaze was triumphant.

"The bastard she carries belongs to a good German man!"

With that, the door slammed shut behind her, leaving Frances entirely alone. Not a word was spoken as the other women returned to their beds.

Chapter 42

Late May 1943

A week or so later, Frances craned her neck to see over the heads of the women in front of her. She hadn't imagined it; she had heard Miriam's voice. She even thought that she had caught sight of her entering the latrine block, and she most definitely had not seen her leave. Somehow, Miriam must have got to her part of the camp, of that she was certain.

Trust Miriam. Since the episode at the gate, the pair had managed to get messages to one another. Well, it had been Miriam's doing, really, she seemed to have the knack of sorting these things out. Her relentless energy and survival techniques had earned her the esteem of fellow prisoners and certain kapos.

Frances felt elated! Miriam was there. She had said in the notes that she would get there at some time, and now she sensed it. She also sensed the excitement that was amongst the other women. Somehow, that which belonged to herself and Miriam had rubbed off on the others. Women like Ewa and Lily, who were standing behind her now and having a job to keep still. No one had said anything since the incident with Grese, but Frances had felt obliged to try to explain to Ewa, at least, who was the closest person to her since her separation from Miriam. She'd tried to tell Ewa the way it was between herself and Mueller, and strangely, as she had tried to explain, she had baulked at the emptiness of her explanation. What were her feelings now? This place had killed any passion that had been there, any bond had been severed, because in Auschwitz you were allowed no human emotion. So, all that was left was the swelling in her belly and the certain knowledge that she had fraternised with the enemy.

They had killed her husband and her friends, and she had mourned for them by sleeping with Mueller, who had promised to save her and hadn't. She should be ashamed but couldn't, because she had loved him.

Ewa had made a few choice sounds from time to time during her explanation, and from then had remained as she was now, as the whole damn orchestra was—aloof!

The queueing seemed endless; she thanked her lucky stars on this occasion that she was pregnant. The pregnancy had corked up her bowels, so that she had at least got some control, unlike some who were shitting where they stood, whilst the women in charge of the latrine only added to their discomfort by verbally abusing the poor cows.

As her turn came, she took her place, seating herself on the two wooden bars that ran across the foul-smelling pit. She, being smaller than most, had to hang on to the third bar running in front at waist level and covered in excrement. Some women had lost their balance and had fallen in the pit, never to be seen again. Some poor, demented sods had committed suicide by jumping into it! Ah well, she thought as she clung on tight, just like the Krauts. Everything to order. Sleep to order, eat to order, even shit to order.

As she slithered to the floor, she thought she caught sight of Miriam once again. She was taking some chance hanging around for so long, besides, no one in her right mind hung around the latrine longer than they had to. She made her way through a group of women to where she thought she had seen her friend. She saw it was Miriam, talking to a group of the orchestra girls, mostly the Poles.

"Miriam!" she cried, flinging her arms wide and pushing her way through the centre of the group. Reaching for her friend, she threw her arms around her. Realising the lack of response, the lack of warmth, she stood back.

"So, Rich Girl," sneered Miriam. "I should have known."

"Known what, what's wrong?" asked Frances, eyeing the other girls suspiciously as they closed in. These, the women of the orchestra, the women who didn't like her.

"Traitor!" muttered Miriam. Frances shook her head.

"No, Miriam, please let me explain, you don't know the way it was."

"Explain? You had plenty of time to explain. Now you've had time to think up a good story, is that it?"

"It's not a story."

"Are you going to deny that you're carrying some Kraut's bastard?"

"Yes! No! It's not like you think—"

"Collaborating bitch! Up the stick and still at it, according to this lot."

Miriam's gaze swept over the orchestra girls. "So, what is it about these Krauts, then? Super big pricks?"

"I've had enough of this," said Frances, pushing against the women. "Let me pass."

Miriam barred her way. "You're not going anywhere, Frances. I've come all this way to help you. After all, that's what friends are for, isn't it?"

"If you were still my friend, you'd let me pass, Miriam. I knew you wouldn't understand, that's why I didn't tell you. You're so filled with hate."

"Too bloody right. I am filled with hate. So should you be. You need to come to your senses and get rid of that." She poked Frances in the belly. "And like I said, I've come to help."

Miriam moved in. Frances's eyes widened in horror as she took the first of two well-aimed kicks, one to her stomach, the other to her crotch. She heard other women shout encouragement, felt hands grabbing and punching and feet kicking as she sank to the floor.

Chapter 43

July 1943

It is extremely rare for a man to be a complete angel. It is even more rare for him to be a complete devil. Four months in Auschwitz made you doubt the latter part of that statement. And yet, thought Frances, Josef Mengele had treated her well, at least by Auschwitz standards. And she wasn't the only one. He had a youth for running errands, a Jewish boy who he sometimes showed kindness to. Then there was the male interpreter; she had heard Mengele pass the time of day a few times with him. He was said on occasions to pass the night with his lovely blond Jewish secretary.

The contradiction that was Mengele. The man who could let a woman carry to full term, sever the umbilical cord with such care, only to carry out the most diabolical of experiments on the new-born. In the name of science, he always insisted. But she knew, they all knew, that his work had no medical foundation whatsoever.

What would have happened to her child had it been allowed to live? Like God, he had decided to give her child a life? Maybe it was because of its impressive lineage, a virtuoso mother, and a German war hero for a father.

He'd been angry when he'd returned to the camp after the bout of typhus. He'd returned in a vindictive rage, determined to tackle the source of the infection. He immediately arranged for the entire occupants of a woman's barracks, some thousand women, to be gassed. That barracks had then been fumigated and the occupants of a second barracks moved in. After being disinfected, the second hut was deloused and so on until typhus in that part of the camp had been eradicated—no mean feat— but at the cost of a thousand. Not content with that, he had questioned

Frances endlessly about what she insisted had been an accident, a tumble.

"Just tell me who, and I'll make them pay!" He shook his head at her. "I don't understand you, Frances. I'd have thought you'd have wanted them punished for what they did. They killed your son, you almost died yourself. Really, you're very lucky someone bothered to report your—what did you call it? An accident?"

She laughed when he mentioned luck, and he raised his eyebrows at her quizzically, asking what her laughter meant, and she'd told him. That was the first time she had spoken to him without quaking, without feeling like a mouse inside the jaws of a cat. Because she'd lost her child, her lifeline, and both her body and her soul had taken enough.

"No, Doctor Mengele," she said, "luck has nothing to do with my being alive."

After that, she didn't see the doctor for some days. After a ten-day stay in the infirmary, she was sent back to the music hut and made to suffer the silence of the other girls. All ignored her, even Alma and Ewa. A few times, she caught Ewa looking at her, and she thought she could perhaps make the first move, but she didn't particularly want their company, anyway. She hated the whole of humanity and wanted no part of it. The more than usually meagre rations they were serving her didn't even hurt, starving would just speed up her departure from the bloody hellhole.

She was more than a little surprised when Mengele sent for her again. Now that her pregnancy had ended, and she'd given him no chance of taking revenge on her behalf, she was certain his interest in her would cease. She was taken once again to his quarters in the S.S. village, part of Auschwitz One. It was early evening, and the day had been oppressive. Now the air hung heavy with the sickly stench from the overcrowded crematoria, the glow from which lit the skyline over Birkenau. Frances noticed as she approached his door that even at that distance, the thick fatty soot deposits built up on the window ledges.

She was shown into Mengele's living room by his house-girl, and she found him seated in a large comfortable chair with the remains of his supper laid out in front of him. Bread, cheese, a decanter of red wine, and two glasses. He stood as she entered.

"Ah, come in," he said and pointed to a second leather upholstered chair opposite his own. "Here, sit down." Frances nodded and sat, unclipping the catches on her violin case.

"What would you like me to play for you, Herr Doctor?"

"Nothing," he said simply, taking the case from her lap and laying it on the floor beside her. Then he sat down again and leant slightly forward towards her, causing her to look to the floor.

"This could be our last meeting, Frances," he said.

"You're leaving Auschwitz, Herr Doctor?"

"No, you are," Mengele said, and observed her.

Frances felt the pace of her heart quicken. This was one of his gross games, the ones he loved to play. Taunting people gave him pleasure.

"Well?" he asked.

She thought for a moment. "I thought there was only one way for us to leave, Herr Doctor." She raised her head slightly.

He laughed, and not for the first time, the richness of the sound struck her. "What's the matter? Don't you trust me? I thought we were friends. Look up, meet me eye to eye, like you did that day in my office. That's what I liked about you, that's what probably saved you. It doesn't suit you talking to the floor like this."

"It's what I've been taught, Herr Doctor."

"The devil it is! Meet me on equal terms."

Frances raised her head slowly to find Mengele smiling at her. She wondered what atrocity he was hatching in his head at that moment.

"You're terrified of me, aren't you?" he asked.

"I'd be a fool not to be, Herr Doctor."

"Maybe, and you're no fool, are you? Well now, aren't you going to ask me where you are going?"

"I'm not sure I want to know."

Mengele stood up and padded over to her chair. Standing behind her, he placed his hands on the side of her head, pushing the short curls back behind her ears. A tremble of fear shot through her body as he touched her. The smell of the lavender soap he used filled her nostrils. Her stomach heaved.

"You're still very lovely, Frances. You must have been beautiful before. What would you do, I wonder, if I tried to make love to you?"

"I could hardly stop you, could I?" She fought to keep her voice level.

"You could ask me to stop," he teased. "Go on."

"Very well... please stop, Herr Doctor."

"Bravo! So, there is spirit in you yet. I thought the last time we met that you had given up."

Frances fought to control her fear. Mengele was a loose cannon; he could detonate at any time. "I thought I'd given up too. All right, Doctor Mengele," she said tiredly, "where are you sending me? Where am I going and why?"

"The where," he said, "is to the front. The why–there are two reasons. First, our boys could do with some first-class entertainment, and secondly, for your own safety. It was Fraulein Grese, I think, who made common knowledge of the finer details of your pregnancy. She told of your liaison with our grey wolf."

"Who told you that?" Frances asked.

"No need to be told. Grese made no secret of her jealousy; you're not the first. Well, do you still think your luck has run out?"

Frances rubbed at her face in disbelief. "I'll send you a postcard and let you know," she said dryly.

Mengele laughed again, the laugh denying the monster that he was. "There's bread and cheese here, if you would like, and a sip of wine would not hurt you either. Frances, you're looking at me in disbelief." He raised his hand in submission. "Very well, talk to me, question me; your only chance."

She took a deep breath. "Why the Jews?" she asked.

He sighed and tapped his fingers on the chair. And at first, she thought maybe she had gone too far by asking him that question. Then he spoke.

"If Germany is to be certain of victory, we must eradicate those others intelligent enough to rule the world. Namely, my dear, the Jews."

"Then you don't believe the Jews are animals?"

"Come now, Frances, animals that write, compose, become some of the most eminent doctors? Now, the Poles are something else." Josef Mengele took a sip of wine, paused a moment, then drained his glass. "Did I tell you about the group of Poles?"

Frances shook her head. "I don't think so." Mengele poured himself another glass of wine.

"Stupid bastards thought they'd found some meat boiling away in a vat at the back of our laboratories. They had, but it wasn't until they'd gorged themselves that they caught on they were eating some of their block mates." He laughed and wiped away a tear of mirth.

Frances felt the bile rise in her stomach.

Mengele continued, "We were boiling the flesh off, see, to send the skeletons to Berlin for research. You should have seen them when they found out. Sick as pigs—why, my dear, you've gone pale."

"I'm sorry, Herr Doctor, I think..." She stood up, reeling slightly. "The wine, I think. Could I use the bathroom, please?"

"Of course." Mengele took her arm to steady her, and her flesh crept beneath his grasp.

"Really, I can manage."

"Well, if you're sure."

She tottered uncertainly towards the steep staircase, up the stairs and to the bathroom, scarcely making it to the toilet pan before she lost the contents of her stomach. The sweat and tears from retching ran down her face, and she wondered how long she could stay in the bathroom without him growing suspicious. The last thing she wanted was to annoy him. She was going to leave Auschwitz—that's what he had said. He had arranged it, though, for what price? She was going to the front, he'd said. Which front? Surely there was more than one. She became aware that he was calling her from the room downstairs.

"Frances, are you all right?"

"Yes," she hurriedly replied. "Yes, I'm fine, Herr Doctor. I'm just coming."

She opened the door to find him standing at the bottom of the stairs, concern on his face. He held out his hand to her as she descended the stairs, and she forced herself to take it, to smile her thanks. He returned her to her seat and seated himself opposite her, correct, upright, proper, soulless. She regarded him levelly. How could he do it, commit such atrocities? The question burned, a fiery streak on her tongue.

"How can you do it?" she heard herself ask.

"Do what?"

"The selections. I know there are some guards and officers even, who beg not to be involved. Others rely on drink and the orchestra to forget, but you, Herr Doctor?"

Mengele stretched out his legs and settled back in his chair. "I like to think, you know, that I am not sending thousands to their deaths, but that I am saving the few."

Did he really believe that? She wondered. Was that the way he managed his guilt by convincing himself that he was a saviour? Yes, she decided. He was indeed demented enough to think that.

He stood up. "Now, Frances, back to the music block for the last time." He took her hand and shook it, as if she were an old friend. He was letting her go. There was to be no payment, no sex. Maybe tomorrow there would be no freedom from Auschwitz. Maybe there would not even be tomorrow.

Chapter 44

May 1944

The picture! Remember the picture the morning following that first solo performance in the Theatre Champs-Élysées. The picture in the newspaper of the man a few feet away from you. The man, Adolf Hitler, smiling and shaking people's hands. But not your hands. Only the hands of those in uniform, the S.S., the Wehrmacht, the richly clad women. Smiling, talking, but see how his hands carry on shaking even when they're not clasped in someone else's, and even your nostrils, used to all manner of human shortcomings, can recognise the odour of a sick man.

See how now he congratulates Frieder. Frieder who has organised this entertainment so well. Listen, hear him. "Well done, well done. The violin was particularly good."

Why don't you shout at him, tell him it was me who played, me who was good; a woman you had incarcerated, who has been made to perform at the drop of a Zeig Heil. Whenever the whim took you. First at Auschwitz. Ah, Auschwitz!

* * *

July 8, 1943

They took her from Birkenau by car to the train just outside the camp gates. The last time she had been there, she had been with hundreds of other people being forced forwards through the gates of Auschwitz. But on this day, it was quiet. There was no Jewess asking "age?" No doctor signing people left or right with the wave of his hand—just her, a guard, and the train. There were a few soldiers on board making for God knows where. They were probably going on leave, she thought, and wondered what they would do to remove the stench and the guilt of Auschwitz. Until the moment that the train drew away from the camp, she had expected Mengele to appear and announce that her leaving was just one of his sick jokes, but he hadn't. As the train drew away, her spirits momentarily soared, knowing that never again would she see Auschwitz.

Fool! Every time she closed her eyes, she saw it. Saw the suffering, heard the crying. Only now, as her journey continued, these images in her mind were alongside those she saw from the window of the train or car. Burnt-out Polish or Russian villages, hanging patriots, and dead and dying troops from both sides.

The trip from Auschwitz to Kharkov near the Eastern front took over two days to complete. A journey of almost one and a half thousand kilometres. At Krakow, a car journey replaced the train journey. Thankfully, the young man who had the job of getting her to her destination proved quite pleasant, and he reminded her a little of Dieter. Even though he guarded her well and took no chances, he was open to conversation on a shallow level as he drove. At first, Frances was determined to make the entire journey in silence, but she found sometimes she had to speak to him, when she had to relieve herself or needed food or a drink, and then she found him kind and co-operative, which had led to some sort of relationship between them.

To pass the time of day, she asked about his family and where he lived, and she told him about her glittering career before the war and how she was being sent to lift the morale of some troops. She, with her near-shattered spirit, was being sent to lift the morale of men with her music.

And so, to Kharkov, which had recently fallen for the third time in eighteen months and was once again in German hands. Kharkov, the third largest city in the Soviet Union, and despite the heavy fighting, you could still see the beauty of the city, prestigious, lovely still.

She found herself not playing for the troops as she had expected to. Once again, she was the showpiece for the occupying forces officers..

The officers of the Wehrmacht were pleasant to her, although it was made clear that she had prisoner status. She received reasonable food and lodgings in a third-rate hotel, and once they realised she would have none of them, the men left her alone. They didn't need her for that, anyway.

In the daytime, she knew there were endless discussions, spent bent over pathetic little maps. Then in the evening, when she entertained them, there were plenty of women to go round. Russian women mostly, some very young.

How could they? She wondered. Many of them were older men and had told her about their children. General von Manstein himself had spoken to her about his daughter Gisela. Von Manstein, though, had shown himself to be charming, setting the standard, which he expected the rest of his officers to follow. When she performed for them, she was treated like all the women: with respect. She could even walk out in Kharkov as long as she took an officer with her. "To keep you safe," she was told, and that was probably the truth, as there were places in the city where the snipers still hid, and it wasn't unusual to hear odd gunshots.

By August 5, the Soviet forces had renewed their attacks and on the 21st of August, the Red Army made a huge push to retake Kharkov. The sound of gunfire increased in and around the city, and all walks out for Frances ceased. As did her performances, as the Russians moved forward. She found she had a great deal of time on her hands, and spent most of it in her head, back at Auschwitz or thinking about Mueller. He would be married to Sophie Heyne, now Frau Mueller, and she would be just a distant memory to him. Or perhaps he never thought of her at all. When she had tried to explain things to Ewa, it all sounded so ridiculous. After all, he'd never spoken to her of love, not once.

Before she left the music hut, the morning after her meeting with Mengele, she had made the girls a promise to take revenge if the opportunity occurred. Easy to make a promise, still easier to break one. What could she do? What did they expect her to do? She knew the answer to that, all right. Many of them, like Miriam, had become fanatics. Their hate would overcome their fear. Given half a chance, they would sacrifice their lives if they thought they could take a few of them with them. But she wasn't like that. She wanted to live, yet the promise played on her mind constantly. Well, she would bide her time, and if the opportunity for revenge should present itself, then perhaps she would remember her promise.

* * *

Frances wasn't long at Kharkov. It surprised her when, on Field Marshal Erich von Manstein's orders, she was flown out in early September along with several high-ranking officials and some German women. He appeared to want to make sure that she was safe and away from the city, and she was thankful for that.

In September 1943, Manstein withdrew his troops to the west bank of the Dnieper River.

Set down once again somewhere in Poland in a military airfield, Frances found herself once more with a guard and loaded into a train. She convinced herself that she was on the way back to Auschwitz and felt a mounting horror. She considered questioning the man who sat opposite her, but then decided she didn't want to give him the pleasure of telling her that that was exactly where he was taking her. She found him to be a surly bastard, and she wondered what had happened to the young man she had travelled to Kharkov with just weeks before. She played him at his own game and sat the entire time in silence, only breaking it to ask if she might relieve herself, whereupon he would accompany her to the toilet without a word. On the very rare occasions that he needed to go himself, he merely press-ganged some other member of the armed forces into watching her for the short time with strict instructions that she was a prisoner and they were not to communicate with her. When he decided it was time to drink or eat, he would reach into a bag he had with him and pull out some rye bread and sausage or cheese, and give her water to drink from a canister.

Those few days on the train she scarcely slept, firstly for fear of him. He never smiled, he never spoke, he just stared. Then a greater fear overcame her, the fear of the unknown. As the train continued its journey, the realisation came that she was not returning to Auschwitz at all. So where were they taking her? What now?

As the journey continued, the train filled up with more and more young men, mostly Wehrmacht, but there were also naval and air personnel amongst them, and from their talk she realised they were going on leave. She was going into the Fatherland itself. Germany, the Reich. Right into the monster's belly to Munich, and then she went further into its bowels, where she joined the rest of the discarded shit in Dachau!

The Dachau camp was situated in a swamp area about sixteen kilometres north-west of Munich in a place known as Prittlbach. At

Dachau station, she was immediately made aware of different, but no less distasteful, methods of human degradation. A team of worn-out men shackled to a huge cart loaded with all sorts of heavy provisions for the camp met the train. Her guard, that "friendly" companion from the journey, took great delight in ordering her to clamber in amongst the heavy boxes and to ride in style, as he put it, to her new lodgings. She had no idea where she was, or where she was going, but she was to be rid of him, at least, and that was a blessing. However, the journey turned out to be one she would never forget as the men, already weakened by a lack of food and with their spirits broken, were forced to sing while they pulled the heavily laden cart the four kilometres to the main camp of Dachau.

On arrival at the camp, they took her to the Jourdhaus, a large white building with a red roof where the officer of the day and his staff were stationed. She caused quite a stir, as no one seemed to know what to do with her or where to take her. She met up once more with her guard from the journey, who officially handed her over to the camp commandant Obersturmbannfuhrer Weiss, with a letter from von Manstein.

"Well, it seems you are to join our camp orchestra, Frau. Apparently, you are a woman of notable talent." Weiss glanced up from the page. "We'll see how impressed Frieder is with you, eh? But where to put you?"

It wasn't to the main camp that they eventually took her, but to one of the many satellite camps a couple of kilometres away. The main camp, she learnt, was essentially for men.

The discussion had been brief. She was taken to one of the out commands, the one that housed the women, the ones used by the S.S., the Bordello. She smiled as she remembered Miriam's words. *Welcome home, Frances, you whore,* she said to herself.

Chapter 45

After Auschwitz, it was simple enough to settle into Dachau Camp. There were few roll calls concerning the bordello girls. There being only twenty-three of them, a register was taken each morning, but Frances soon learnt of the misery and deprivation that happened at the main camp.

Like the girls of the bordello, she was lucky enough to be given a room of her own, though, unlike them, she was not expected to use it for entertaining. After an initial period of distrust because she wasn't truly one of them, the other girls accepted her, even sharing some of their ill-gotten gains from time to time. Ever the gentlemen, the S.S. rewarded the girls from the bordello with little food extras—sometimes chocolate or cigarettes—if they pleasured them well.

Most of the girls were German, there were a couple of Dutch girls too. Frances noted that they all had one thing in common,—beauty.

"They promised us they would set us free if we agreed to work in this place for six months," Sybil, one of the girls, told her after she had been there for a day. "They haven't kept their promise, of course. How come you have ended up here, anyway?" she asked.

"How long have you got for me to tell you?" Frances asked, giving Sybil a tired smile.

Another girl had joined them, who introduced herself as Monika. "We don't do business until seven in the evening, so you've got until then," she said.

Frances told the girls of her past life in France and her success as a performer. She told of the exodus from Paris and how it had gone wrong and even told them how she had been rescued from the Atlantic by the

U-boat, leaving out her relationship with Mueller. Some of the other girls had joined Sybil and Monika to listen to Frances's story. She talked of her internment in Auschwitz, and it brought tears to the eyes of many. When she got to the part of her story concerning Mengele and the stories about his diabolical work in the name of science, Sybil cut in.

"You'll find it's the same here. Oh, you probably won't see anything—we're thankfully removed from it—but we all know it's going on. The torture and the torment."

"How do you know?" asked Frances.

"Sometimes the S.S. talk about it while they're here. Usually, if they are having one of their drinking parties, they joke about it. And we had a girl come here. She was from the bordello that served the main camp."

"There's a bordello at the main camp?" asked Frances, wide-eyed.

"Oh yes, there are three altogether," said Monika. "There is ours for the S.S.. There is another that is used by the soldiers, and there is one at the main camp for the inmates."

Frances was dumbfounded. "There's a bordello for the inmates?"

"Weiss set it up," said Sybil. "He reckoned that by using the bordello as a sweetener, then the men would work harder. I think it's used mainly by the camp overseers and the kapos. The other men are too tired and worn out. That was according to Katarin. And there are definitely no Jews allowed in there."

"Katarin is the girl whose room you're in. An S.S. spotted her at the main camp bordello and thought she was too pretty to be there," explained Monika. "So, he brought her here, and she told us everything. They take men and lower their temperature really low, then use women from the bordello to warm them up by, well, you know."

Frances shook her head. "How?" she asked, and the women all laughed at her.

"Copulation," said Sybil.

A picture of Mueller shot through Frances's mind. The U-boat had been sunk, and he was unconscious in the ice-cold water of the Atlantic, being kept afloat by a life jacket and two naked women wrapped around him. She shook her head to remove the bizarre image.

"So where is Katarin now?"

"Dead. As it happens, she hung herself in your room. She couldn't bear it, knowing what goes on here. She told us much more, but looking at you, I think that's enough for one day."

* * *

The next day, Frances was introduced to Frieder, who ran the all-male celebrated Dachau Orchestra. She had been taken back to the Jourdhaus and waited for him in a small room. When he entered the room, his appearance took her aback. He was white-faced and white-haired, albino almost. His eyes were pale and cold, and Frances soon found out that he had a brittle personality. Producing a Stradivarius violin, he thrust it towards her and ordered her to play, at the end of which he sniffed.

"I can use you. A woman virtuoso playing with an all-male orchestra." He looked her up and down. "Yes, it will be good. Any trouble, and I will drop you." And with that, he was gone.

* * *

Rehearsals took place at the main camp, which, though not as vast as Auschwitz, was nevertheless quite large. She was picked up at the bordello and taken to the music hut by car. The men all smiled at her when she was introduced to them, but Frieder didn't allow any talking during rehearsals. Over time, though, there were hushed conversations if Frieder left the room, and she learnt that the men also had to work in any of their spare time, though the work was less laborious than that of many others. They told her that the food ration too had improved of late.

She was told that music was of great importance in Dachau, and there were a wide range of musical activities, both forced and voluntary. Dachau inmates were afforded much more flexibility in their daily activities. Frances was happy to take part in as much as Frieder would allow her. She was often rushed to the main camp if a high-level visitor turned up. The orchestra would take up position in front of the canteen block and play cheerful music, guaranteed to deceive any visitor to Dachau into thinking that the camp was nowhere near as bad as the stories they had heard.

Sunday afternoons, the orchestra would usually play for the inmates, and she heard that there were often impromptu concerts arranged for the inmates too by some musicians without the knowledge of Frieder. Most evenings she found herself seated in a corner playing in the main room of the bordello. The S.S. had good taste, she found, and usually the music was classical. On a couple of occasions, she had had to fight off the attentions of an officer, but that was usually when they were in party spirits and things had gotten out of hand. Weiss had given instructions she was not to be touched, that she was a musician, not a brothel girl, and that there were other women to satisfy their carnal needs.

She had been in Dachau for almost seven months when she learnt the orchestra was to perform for Adolf Hitler, The Führer of the great Third Reich, in Munich at the Fuhrer Haus. Frieder had been more than a little impressed with Frances's playing. Impressed enough, in fact, to rewrite his programme for this momentous occasion to include her as the only woman amongst the all-male members of the celebrated Dachau orchestra.

Chapter 46

He, Hitler, was moving away from the orchestra now. They were all leaving the hall, mingling together, the black uniforms with the few military and naval, and the gorgeous gowns of the women. Frieder was telling them they were all to be taken to the kitchen to be rewarded with a few titbits. She bent to pick up her instrument and jumped at the unfamiliar touch of a hand on her shoulder. She turned. It was Frieder.

"There's a gentleman who wishes to speak to you."

"Where?"

"You're to go to the study. I'll take you. Come."

"My violin?"

Frieder shrugged. "Leave it there, I'll get one of the others to take it."

She followed him into a long passage and waited when he paused outside a door and knocked three times, hard.

"Enter!" a male voice instructed.

Frances did so, glancing back at Frieder. He didn't meet her gaze, but withdrew, closing the door with an ominous click.

A sense of foreboding knotting her chest, Frances looked around. The room was large, panelled in walnut. From the way it was furnished with a large, handsomely carved desk, backed by shelves of books, she presumed it was a study. A small brocade chaise sat near a marble fireplace. A fair-haired man, wearing the hated black uniform of the S.S, stood before a heavily draped window with his back to her. He didn't speak, but even so, there was something familiar about him. He turned just at her moment of recognition.

"Otto!" His name shot from her mouth. Her head went light.

"Frances, my dear." His smile lacked warmth. "Well, are you pleased to see me?"

Her mind reeled. Hatred for the man rose, burning, into her throat. When she thought of all she had suffered, the loss and degradation, the nightmare her life had become, all because of this man...

"What do you think?" she asked, and it pleased her to see the smile fade from his lips.

Still, despite her venom, he held out his hand, walking toward her as if he believed she would take it, as if he thought she could abide his touch. "Water under the bridge, my dear." He uttered the words with breezy disregard.

She backed away until she was up against the door, hating that she was trembling. Anger warred with her terror of him.

"Of course, I heard about Steven and that silly old man, Cuvier, wasn't it?"

Although Otto gave her time to answer, she didn't.

"I was sorry, but fleeing Paris was a foolish thing to do, Frances. Now, if you had been a sensible girl, and you know until then I had always thought of you as sensible, none of this need ever have happened." He paused a couple of feet from her, hand still outstretched, and giving it a little shake, he said, "Come now, Frances, you'll see things can be set right between us."

Her laugh was truncated, bitter. "Set right? Do you know all I've endured? Yes, of course, you know. You're S.S. too, after all."

"Oh, Frances, I understand you're cross with me. After I got word of the sinking of the *Etoile*, they tried to tell me you had died with the others. But I didn't believe it. We have a connection, you and me. I would have known."

Frances stared at him. Reaching behind her, she closed her fingers on the door handle. If she could wrench it open, if she could run fast enough. But she knew she would never pull it off.

"I tried to find you, but that stupid old woman, your aunt—"

Frances straightened. "Edie; you saw her. She wrote to me about it when I was in Drancy. Otto, you must tell me. Have you seen her since? Her letters stopped. She's all right, isn't she?"

Turning from her, Liechtenstein walked to the chaise and, sitting down, he patted the space next to him. "Yes, I saw her."

Frances kept his gaze, but after a long moment, her need to learn of her aunt's fate eclipsed her fear, and crossing the room, she perched on the chaise's edge as far from him as the cushion allowed. "How is she? When did you see her last?"

"A year ago, last April. I visited her on a number of occasions. She was so stubborn. Just like you."

"What do you mean, *was* stubborn? You'd better not have harmed her, Otto!"

Liechtenstein's laugh was derisive. "Oh, my dear, do you know how pathetic you sound?"

Frances half rose. "Are you going to tell me about Edie?" Liechtenstein grabbed her arm, forcing her back onto the chaise.

"Sit down, and I'll tell you. It must run in the family. That silly old woman wouldn't listen either."

"You've killed her, haven't you?" A cold knowing rose inside her, choking her. She jerked her arm, struggling to get free.

His grip hardened. "I could have you killed, do you understand?"

"Go on then." Locking his gaze, she dared him. "That's what you're good at, isn't it? Killing women!"

Liechtenstein dropped his chin as if in sorrow. "Oh, Frances, it was a mistake, believe me. One of the guards was a little overzealous, let's say. I didn't know your aunt had a weak heart."

"She was an old woman, for God's sake!" Tears burned Frances's eyes, but she refused to let them fall.

"It was unfortunate, but it's done." Shifting to face her, Liechtenstein gripped her shoulders, fixing her with his gaze. "It's our time now. Can't you see? We're meant for each other, you and I, so why fight it?"

Frances shot to her feet, blind in her fury, and before she could think, she slapped him hard across his face. "You bastard! I hate you. Do you understand? So much that I don't care if you kill me too. In fact, I wish you would."

Liechtenstein rose, hand to his cheek, mouth flat, eyes narrowed in disgust. "No, Frances, I'll not grant your wish, but I will have you, like I always said I would."

She turned from him, but he caught her, yanking her around with enough force that she lost her footing and fell to the floor. In an instant, he was on her, straddling her, one arm pinning her arms above her head, his other fumbling to open his jodhpurs.

She bucked, jerking up her hips, and he laughed.

"That's it," he urged, leering at her. "Why don't you scream?"

She worked her throat, but nothing came. It was as if it were plugged with terror.

He shoved his pants over his thighs, baring his buttocks. "Cry out if you want." He was red-faced, huffing. "No one will hear you, and if they do, they'll not bother to come."

No one will come. The truth of this penetrated the walls of her brain. He was going to rape her, and there was nothing she could do to stop him. Think of nice things, she told herself. Don't struggle, don't give him the pleasure of that. Let him use your body but shut yourself away. He can't touch your heart, your soul. Even as his hands tore her shirt open and ripped away her undergarments, she didn't react. She lay limp and compliant beneath him, her stare fixed on the books that lined the shelves behind the desk.

He forced apart her knees, and feeling him enter her, bile rose in her throat. She bit her teeth against it.

"My God," he groaned, "I've waited a long time for this."

He pounded against her, and dropping his head, mouthed her breasts. She winced, feeling his teeth on her nipples. Once, lifting himself, he went still, and looked down on her, questioningly, hard-eyed. Annoyed, perhaps, at her lack of response.

Finally, it was over, and he rolled off her and lay beside her, panting and sweaty.

Pushing herself upright, she straightened her clothing as best she could, and as she stood, the feel of his semen trickling down her legs sickened her. She fought a wave of nausea. "May I go now?" she asked quietly.

Liechtenstein scrambled to his feet, eyes filled with remorse. "I didn't want it to be like this, Frances," he said, reaching for her, voice stumbling. "You must believe me. I will make things alright; you'll see. I'll get you out. I have contacts in high places. You'll get to like it. Being with me, you'll have everything you want and more. You'll play in the top Berlin drawing rooms—that's where you belong, where you should

be, with me. I took your house in Neuilly, I've looked after it for you."
The words gushed out of him. "We can go there," he told her, smiling
now, so certain in his arrogance. "You'll see it's been well taken care of."

Frances hooted in derision. "Won't your family have something to
say about that?"

"My wife knows. She has always known there is someone else."

Otto wrapped her in his embrace. Frances didn't respond.

"I will make things all right, you'll see." His lips nuzzled the hair
at her ear.

A knock came, and a voice said, "Sir, the orchestra is about to
leave."

Liechtenstein stepped back, adjusted his clothing, and opened the
door. "Take her to join them, and mind you, treat her well. She is a very
special lady."

Frances and her escort were on the threshold when Otto pulled her
back. "You'll be out in a trice. I'll get you out, just you see. I promise."

* * *

She laughed in the back of the truck as a load of ill-fed men looked
on in amazement. She noticed all their eyes on her, taking in her state of
disarray, casting knowing looks between one another.

"What the fuck are you looking at?" she shrieked, and then the
laughter started. First, she laughed aloud, hysterically. She could hear
herself. Had they finally sent her mad? She had been raped, and she was
laughing. What had happened to the tears? There were none. Mueller
was the last one she had cried over, and she vowed she would never cry
again. Frieder slapped her hard across the face, pulling her up short.
Then she laughed inside. Oh, how she laughed. What else could they do
to her? Nothing.

Now it was her turn. She would go with Otto. Was there any choice?
And when she was done with him, he'd be begging her for mercy. He'd
regret that he'd ever been born. Or maybe if the opportunity arose and
she could get hold of a revolver, she would make it quick, and perhaps
take a few more out with him. She'd quickly follow him, of course. They'd
make sure of that, but it would be worth it, surely. Besides, what was
there in her miserable life to make it worth hanging onto? She laughed

softly now, feeling a certain sense of bitter elation, even joy. She had played that night for Adolf Hitler, the Führer, and her reward had been to be raped by one of his henchmen. Was it any surprise? None! But oh, how she wished she had made it to the kitchen for some food.

4 days later

Frances tentatively knocked on the door of an office in the Jourdhaus and waited until Frieder's voice ordered her to enter. The last time she had seen him, he had slapped her hard several times across the face to stop her hysterical laughter. She wondered if his sending for her now had something to do with that journey from the Fuhrer Haus in Munich back to the camp at Prittlbach. Was she to suffer some sort of further punishment for her behaviour, which had clearly made him angry, and had also upset several men from the orchestra, for which she was sorry? She felt the thumping of her heart in her head and the nervous trickle of sweat running down her back as she pushed open the door.

As always, she was taken aback by Frieder's appearance. The whiteness of his skin and his hair, even whiter. His reptile eyes on her, as usual, were icy cold as they stared into the amber fire of her own.

"Ah, Meyer," he said, using just her surname as if he were talking to one of the men of the orchestra. "So, it seems you are leaving us tomorrow."

Frances's stomach churned, it was worse than she had thought. They were sending her away from Dachau. Where to this time, for God's sake, not back to Auschwitz, surely?

"Well?" he asked. She stood, stupidly staring at him, unable to speak. "You're to be released. Aren't you the lucky one?"

So that was it. Otto had delivered, after all. But leaving Dachau had its price, and they would deliver her into his custody, where she would have to undergo further abuse from him. Compared to the fear, abuse, and degradation of the last fifteen months, she knew she had the strength to survive, if only to take her revenge on him when the time was right. The girls in the bordello had told her she must, and she also had to fulfil the promise she had made to the girls in Auschwitz. Ewa had been their spokeswoman. *Promise us, Frances, promise us you will make them pay. Take revenge on everything German. Revenge for all the crimes they*

have committed, revenge for the thousands they have sent to the ovens.
That was the last thing Ewa had said to her before wrapping her in a warm embrace.

Frieder was still speaking. She shook her head, struggling to concentrate on his words, her mind still full of that last sickening encounter with Otto, and how she would make him atone.

"You're to be given new clothing when you leave me, and then you will go back to the brothel for one last night. In the morning, you will be picked up and brought back here to the Jourdhaus, and then you'll be released into the custody of that idiot man who seems to be obsessed with you. That fool is going to ruin the programme for all the concerts I have planned around you." Frieder shook his head with disdain. "When you return here tomorrow, bring your instrument with you and hand it to the officer of the day."

Frances was aware that she still hadn't spoken, but what should she say? Should she thank him?

There was a sharp rap on the door, and Frieder shouted, "Come!"

The door opened, admitting a female guard. "I've come for the woman," she said.

"Wait outside," Frieder ordered. "She'll be out directly." As the door closed behind her, he crossed the room and stood before Frances. "You haven't said a word," he said, trying to meet her eyes, which she had kept throughout on the floor. "This is goodbye."

"Yes, I suppose it is. Can I go now?" she asked, lifting her head, and meeting his icy stare.

He nodded, and she moved to the door. Just as her hand took the handle, he called out, "Good luck, Frances Meyer! You have a rare talent. Keep it safe and keep yourself safe too."

She turned, briefly giving the ghost of a smile. "Thank you, Herr Frieder," she said and stepped out into the corridor, closing the door behind her.

* * *

It never occurred to her she might not want to leave the confines of Dachau, but now, as she heard the approaching footsteps, it seemed to her a momentary haven. She detested Otto, and she would steel herself and take revenge, first on him, and if she survived that, then on other things German, as the opportunities arose.

It would be a cleansing, a great purging if she could make them suffer for what they'd done to her, to her friends, to the thousands. The crimes she'd witnessed, the crimes she had done nothing to prevent. Her common sense told her there was nothing she could have done, that survival was the order of the day. Her guilt told her she could at least have tried.

She looked around her at the sparsely furnished room in the admin block of the Jourhaus, trying to find a comfortable place to stand, wondering how she would feel when she came face to face with Otto again. Would she cope and be able to carry through her plan, to bide her time and go along with him? Hate-filled as she was, it should be easy. As the door handle turned, she crossed to the barred window, taking deep breaths to calm herself. She heard the door open and the click as it closed again, and with head held high, she turned to face him.

Kristian Mueller stood taller than she remembered. Or was it just the uniform that made him appear that way? Cap in hand, dressed in blues and clean shaven, as she had never seen him before, he looked so damned good.

Milton Keynes UK
Ingram Content Group UK Ltd.
UKHW042246020823
426203UK00001B/61